COVERT AFFAIR

SEALS AND CIA SERIES BOOK 1

KENNEDY L. MITCHELL

Mattie -
Thank you
so much for
reading! ♡

klm

Kennedy

ABOUT THE AUTHOR

Kennedy L. Mitchell lives outside Dallas with her husband, son and two very large goldendoodles. She began writing in 2016 after a fight with her husband (You can read the fight almost verbatim in Falling for the Chance) and has no plans of stopping.

She would love to hear from you via any of the platforms below or her website www.kennedylmitchell.com You can also stay up to date on future releases through her newsletter or by joining her Facebook readers group - Kennedy's Book Boyfriend Support Group.

Thank you for reading.

Cover Design: Bookin It Designs

Proofreading: All Encompassing Books

❀ Created with Vellum

PREFACE

It's her fault. She shouldn't have messed in our shit. I don't care if it is her job. She says she's the best but by the shocked look on her face she sure as hell didn't see me coming.

They'll call it a betrayal, maybe even label me a traitor, but that's not how I saw it. It's survival of the fittest out here and the fittest, strongest I am not. But the smartest, hell fucking yes. I've played this information game for far too long, made too much money for this bitch to screw it up now.

So when she wakes up, if she wakes up, I'll make sure she knows this is her fault. If I had any heart left I'd feel bad for handing her over to the pieces of shit I call my business partners.

To hell with the consequences, I'm already in too deep anyway.

Come on, Agent Rizzo.

Wake up.

I don't want you to miss this.

CHAPTER ONE
LUCIA

I'm an anomaly.

A witch, if you believe some people.

It's why the CIA sought me out and laid every bargaining chip on the table to bring me on board. Little did they know the agency was where I always wanted to be. Where I'm destined to be.

People think I can read minds. I can't, well technically. What I can read are moods, body shifts, a target's presence and most importantly when they try to keep their secrets buried. Uncovering lies and secrets, finding out what those are, is my job.

Take my current subject. He's lying, that's obvious, but about what only time will tell. Which is exactly what I don't have a lot of. This conversation has already gone on too long. I need more from him before writing an official report. Need to watch him, hear what he is saying but not really saying. The two glasses of wine alone in my hotel before this dinner were a mistake, they're throwing me off my game. Or maybe it's the half a box of Parisian chocolates I ate with the wine. But I *am* in Paris, who wouldn't indulge a little?

Crap. Did he just ask a direct question?

Focus, Lucia. Turn your attention to the man across the table and not the deliciousness that's waiting back at the hotel. This agent's life is on the line after all. I'm sure he would appreciate it if I stopped daydreaming about chocolate.

I swirl the last sip of red wine around my glass as the agent keeps talking, filling me in on his current operation and what intel he's gathered so far. Dishes and glasses clink, murmuring and laughter fill the small restaurant keeping our conversation private. It was a perfect spot for this meeting, for this fake date.

Gut instinct guides ninety percent of my judgments and decisions. The other ten percent is what the agency needs, what my boss likes to call substantial evidence. Within the first ten to fifteen minutes of meeting someone I can identify a liar, but saying 'My gut told me he was a traitor' isn't an acceptable explanation to your boss when said agent is tried for treason.

Who am I kidding, like an agent would actually get a trial. A rogue agent would just disappear into thin air one day with no questions asked or explanations to loved ones. Not that any of us have real relationships, not with the lives we live. It's the lies. Most people can't handle the unknown we work in and hate being left in the dark.

"So that's about it," Agent Montford says with a sigh as he takes a sip of red wine. "I have to admit I'm confused as to why you're here. Things are going smoothly, I've given intermittent reports to the necessary people. I'm growing in the organization and people are starting to trust me. What gives?"

With a sigh of my own I lean back against the red leather of my chair. "You know how they are, even with all you're giving them it isn't enough. I'm here to get more information, in person, and I'll report back to Langley. Simple."

That's a lie. I'm here with specific orders to evaluate him as I've done with dozens and dozens of agents before him.

His eyes skirt around the restaurant, bouncing from the front door to the window, bar area and back to the door again. Maybe the agency was right to send me, maybe he has turned. But that's not the vibe I'm getting. He's hiding something, that's for sure, but a turned agent doesn't fit.

If it's not that, then what? What is he hiding?

"Can I ask you something?" He clears his throat a few times, a nervous habit that filled the first half hour of our dinner, and sits up straighter in his chair.

I do the same to lean against the table shrinking the space between us. Damn, I hope he's not about to ask me back to his place. He's a nice guy but not my type. At all. No way I can be attracted to a man who weighs less than me.

"Shoot," I say and wipe my mouth with the white linen napkin before setting it on the table. "But let's get out of here. We've been here too long plus this is a 'date' so why not take a walk around this gorgeous city. Maybe along the Seine?"

He motions for the waiter and requests our bill. "Of course, and you know it doesn't have to be a fake date, Agent Rizzo. I'm having a good time, aren't you?"

I wait to respond until the waiter leaves our table the second time. Once he's out of ear shot I say, "I don't mix work and personal, it's a rule I've always had and always will. But I'm having fun, just won't have more fun than this. Understand?"

With a sulky nod he stands and holds out his hand to help me from the table. "Shall we?"

I love Paris. Every time I'm here there's a new remote street or side cafe I fall in love with. It's the people too, they make this city spectacular. The way they love but have zero time for bullshit is fascinating. Even with the various spots of violence which have sprouted around the city it still holds onto the title 'City of Love' in my mind.

The cobblestone is difficult to manage in heels but it's worth it to see the city at night. I sigh and wrap my arms around myself. Each smell, the sounds of couples and friends at the corner café, everything I try to commit to memory. Too bad this walk has to be with Agent Montford instead of someone I *would* want to end up in my bed later.

Geez, when was the last time that even happened?

Shaking that sad thought from my head I loop my arm around his and lean against him for support. "So what's your question?"

The arm I'm gripping tenses. "Can I trust you?" he asks, his tone hesitant. "And I mean really trust you. What I want to tell you could get me killed. Hell maybe I shouldn't even say anything." He runs a hand through his sandy hair and looks over with a cringe.

The insecurity and fear radiating off him confirms what I've been sensing the entire night. He's not a traitor just unsure, too much self doubt rolling through his mind. What's messed up is the agency probably knew this and sent me here to see if the kid is an asset or a liability. They see the mentally weak as a liability, and well, the weak don't make it very long.

"Go ahead kid. Tell me anything you want. This is your one chance to have someone to talk to who you can trust. What you say stays with me unless it puts me or someone else in danger, or compromises your mission. My lips are sealed."

He huffs a laugh and wraps an arm around my shoulder to pull me closer. "Kid? Really? You can't be older than me."

But I am, just don't look like it. The Italian genes I inherited from my parents make me look younger than the thirty-four years I am. Plus I do know I'm older than him. I read everything about his life on the flight here a few days ago.

"You want to waste this opportunity of free speech discussing my age?"

Those brown eyes meet mine then drift to stare behind me. "Are you as good as everyone says you are? I mean there are legends about you and you haven't been at the agency long."

"Legend is a little overzealous, don't you think?"

"Your nickname is the wiccan. A good nickname is all you need for the foundation of becoming a legend."

Now it's my time to laugh, really laugh. We pause for me to lean against the railing and stare down to the dark water below. The cool breeze off the water brushes my dark hair across my face. I pull the strands behind my ear as I say, "Yeah well let's hope it stops there. The last thing I want is for everyone to know about me and my...abilities. Now what did you want to talk about? Clock's ticking."

He leans his back against the railing beside me and rests his elbow along the metal. "Did you ever do this? Deep cover I mean."

I angle my head so I can watch him for a few seconds. So that's what this is about. It would make the insecurity and fear from earlier make sense. To keep him talking I lie.

"I haven't but I want to."

"No you don't. Trust me. If I would have known...It's a bunch of shit. I'm scared all the time that someone will find out who I am and kill me, slowly. I have no real friends, no one can know who I am and in all this I'm losing myself. I'm forgetting who I am. No way you could want this. This life blows."

The water lapping below and the busy Parisian street above fill the long silence as we both become lost in thought.

I clear my throat to respond but he speaks up first.

"You have a hard job, I know that and I'm not saying mine is harder than yours, it's just different. Do you have any friends back home?"

"A friend, yes."

"Well I do too. Or I did at one time. I had to leave it all behind to do this op. Do you know how bad it sucks when your mom is sick or your only sister has her first baby and you have to learn about it all over a secure phone? I can't go home. And honestly I don't know if I'll ever be able to again. The group I'm infiltrating is serious shit. Like fucked up, will kill you and your whole family and maybe even your lower school teachers if you cross them, fucked up."

He's right. Based off the information in his file there's no exaggeration there. The arms dealer he's been working for is now dealing in the Middle East opium trade with various terrorist groups. We need Montford here, even if it is dangerous and he hates it. Which he clearly does and is on the path to breaking down.

Maybe that's why the boss sent me. To reassure him, keep him on the right path like only I can. When you have this ability to read people, finding what motivates them and pressing hard is an easy way to turn around any crumbling agent. I like to think I use my unique gift for good, but lately, with the different ops they have me running sometimes I wonder who I'm actually helping.

Right now I can help him. Need to help him to keep him alive. If I don't, he will end up dead at the bottom of this quiet river. That is something I'm one hundred percent certain of.

Readying to dive into a motivational speech, I turn and lean against the railing, mirroring him, but movement in the shadows to our right catches my attention.

I slide my hand into his and step closer, we are on a date after all, and have to keep up the façade if eyes are on us. "To our right, recognize him?" I whisper as I nuzzle his shoulder. His arms wrap around my shoulders, pulling me closer and putting my back to the mystery man, allowing him to get a better look.

"It's too dark to tell," he whispers into my hair. His heart hammers against my cheek.

"Well let's go find out. Shall we?"

We link arms once again and begin strolling down the walkway towards the bridge. When we're fully under, hidden from the traffic above, a man steps from the shadows, an arm extended with a small caliber gun pointed at us.

"Arrêtez," he demands in a deep voice that echoes against the stones. "Donnez-moi votre sac à main et mon porte-monnaie."

Even with the stress of the gun pointed at us I feel Agent Montford relax a fraction. Good. Whoever this idiot is isn't a threat to his mission or mine.

"We don't speak French," Agent Montford says as he holds up his hands, palms up.

"Give me wallet and purse and I won't harm," the man with the gun says and for emphasis shakes the gun a little on the last word.

Ugh. Seriously. Can't a girl just do her job and get back to her wine and chocolate? Now I'm annoyed. I cross my arms over my chest. "I'm going to go with no on that one. But thank you for asking."

The man lurches forward, his clammy hand wrapping around my forearm. "Yous stupid American bitches. I will kill you. Give me your money."

"First you say my purse and now you're saying just money. Make up your mind man, I have a box of chocolate waiting for me back at the hotel. Good chocolate too, the kind dreams are made of."

His grip tightens, my hand starts to turn red from the lack of blood flow, and his arm begins to tremor with anger. "Baise toi," he growls through gritted teeth. "Maybe I should take you instead. Good money for the big ones."

The big ones? Okay now I'm past annoyed and have moved right into being pissed off.

The look I shoot Agent Montford is one that says 'don't you dare step in, this guy's mine'. Or I think that's what my narrowed brows and eye roll convey. I hardly ever have the opportunity to use the tactical training I practice every week in real life situations. This is the perfect excuse. Take down a mugger and teach him some damn manners while I'm at it.

Like I knew he would, the idiot yanks me closer which I allow to give myself the advantage. Using the momentum I duck under his arm pulling the hand, and arm, which is still wrapped around my forearm, to his back. His grip falters. Before he can pull his arm back around I grip his wrist with my free hand and pull it up to the middle of his upper back.

A stream of French curse words flows from his mouth. The hand with the gun starts to wave wildly behind him as he searches for a target. Shit. Forgot about the gun. Definitely need more practical, out in the real world, scenarios.

With a curse of my own I grab the hand waving above his head and pull it down. He whimpers as his shoulder stretches beyond its natural limit. The gun slips from his hand and clatters to the ground.

"Please, please don't kill me," he begs. "I wouldn't hurt you."

When I glance up at Agent Montford he's still in the same spot, but now keeping an eye out for witnesses.

"Kill you? Seriously, that would be a mess and I don't want to clean it up in these heels. But listen very carefully, monsieur, tonight you tried to rob the wrong couple but you're going to live. The next time maybe the people won't be as kind." I twist his arms a little further making him cry out. "And yes you would have hurt me and my friend here. I can see it. I can feel the sick power you get from preying on the weak and defenseless. The headache you're going to wake up with will be minor compared to what I really want to do."

"Police! Police!" he starts to yell.

Before he can draw more attention I drop his arms and pick up the discarded gun, flip the barrel around to my palm and whack the heavy grip against the back of his skull. Mid yell he slumps to the cobblestone. The silence left behind is more than welcomed.

Agent Montford steps to my right. "Well that was an interesting end to our date," he says, no humor in his tone.

I nod as I use the bottom of my dress to wipe my prints off the gun. "You drag him over by that wall and I'll toss the gun into the river." By the time I return from disposing the gun he's dusting his suit off.

We link arms again and start walking.

"So, want to finish our conversation in my hotel room?" I ask not thinking of what I'm implying.

"I, um, sure that sounds great. Thought you said—"

His stumbling over words and the awkwardness in his tone makes me realize my mistake. I quickly cut him off. "To talk. You brought up some good points earlier about our...occupation and I want to help you. I can help you get through all those doubts and concerns. So let's go back to my hotel. I wasn't kidding when I said there was a box of chocolates waiting on me."

"Oh right, sure." A hint of disappointment and embarrassment laces his words. Poor guy, for a brief second he thought he was getting lucky. But we have other things to get done tonight. Somehow in the next seven hours I have to convince him to not give up and give him the confidence he needs to follow through with this operation without getting killed.

Ugh it's going to be a long night, that's for sure.

I should have bought more wine.

And snacks.

———

It's only five in the morning and the sounds of the city stirring awake drift through the windows. From my chair in the corner of the room I watch the young agent sleeping, stretched across my bed covered up with the blanket I'd pulled from the closet and draped over him after he fell asleep a couple hours ago. His breathing is deep and even, lips slightly parted. Wish I could sleep like that, feel that safe. My insomnia started in high school but worsened at West Point. Something about being surrounded, outnumbered everywhere by highly trained men, keeps you on edge. Even when I'm home I can't get the kind of deep sleep the agent on my bed is snoring through.

Wonder if I'll ever be able to sleep more than a few restless hours.

The phone tucked in the pocket of my terrycloth robe vibrates. Caller ID reads UNKNOWN.

With a quiet groan, I shuffle out of the comfortable chair and tip toe to somewhere to talk and not disturb sleeping beauty. "I haven't had coffee yet Jeremy so choose your words wisely," I whisper. Phone on my shoulder squished against my cheek I close the bathroom double doors with a quiet click.

"Why are you whispering?"

"The agent I'm here to evaluate is still here, asleep on my bed. He looks so peaceful I don't want to wake him. We were up until a couple hours ago."

"Screwing is how you read people now, interesting."

A very unladylike growl vibrates through the phone. "I told you I haven't had coffee yet so easy on the jokes. We were talking. I accomplished the objective and will be on a flight home this afternoon."

Silence fills the phone. I pull it from my ear and check to see if the connection was lost.

"Jeremy?"

"I'm here, sorry. Someone just came into my office with something urgent for you."

"Again?" I sink to the floor. My back presses against the cold porcelain tub. My knees pull up to tuck against my chest. "I've been on back to back ops for the past month and a half. Who else is there for me to evaluate? I need a break or I might break."

"I know Lu, I know." His voice so sincere it pulls at my heart. Besides Brooke, my normal handler, Jeremy knows me better than anyone. We started at the agency around the same time and have grown close since he's filled in until Brooke's return. He knows the past several weeks have taken a toll on me. "I'll put in a request for leave after this next one. Promise. Plus it looks interesting."

My attention snaps awake. "Interesting how?"

"It's stateside for one thing."

That is interesting. I pull at the threads of the bathmat I'm sitting on and process the bit of information. "How is that even possible? Won't the FBI get all bent out of shape if they hear the CIA is playing in their sand box?"

"This is different. I'll give you the basics of the op in the file for the flight home. Which, they want you back as soon as possible. Someone should be at your door…now."

A light rapping against the hotel room door makes my eyes roll to the ceiling.

"The file will be on the plane waiting for you. Hey look at the bright side, at least you get to take the agency jet home. It has a wet bar, oh and I've made sure they stocked it with your favorite vodka. I also put in a special request to be waiting for you. Hopefully it's still hot when you get there and makes your morning better."

The line disconnects. The rapping at the door now impatient and growing louder.

"Coming," I yell from the floor and push up with a groan. I rub my lower back to ease the stiffness. Maybe that chair wasn't as comfortable to doze in as I thought.

The bed is empty when I push the bathroom doors open. His blanket folded neatly at the end with a note on top. Ignoring the pounding at the door I pick up the hotel notepad.

Thank you for saving me from myself. If you ever need anything I'm here.

A small sad smile pulls at my lips. Hopefully I helped him and not just the agency. I want him to survive, so one day he might have a chance to meet that nephew of his. Not that I'll ever know. I haven't evaluated an agent twice and the agency would never go out of their way to tell me how he's doing. That's for sure.

I pull the tie on the robe tighter, making sure everything private stays that way, and start for the door.

One more mission then a break. I can do this.

Hopefully it will be different than the other ops the past several months. Something needs to be different. Each operation, dissecting these agents, has been more exhausting than I ever thought it would be. A piece of me is fading away, the part that makes me Lucia Rizzo not just Agent Rizzo, the Wiccan.

A break from the routine I've found myself in, something different, yes—all of that sounds perfect.

I just pray it's enough.

CHAPTER TWO
GABE

The boys yell back and forth from one end of the bar to the other drawing attention from the handful of other patrons in this shitty ass excuse for a bar. I shouldn't complain. Shitty as it is, they let us be as loud as we want, fight out our differences when necessary—which is often—and enjoy cold beer. Cold beer being the key to keep the fights to a minimum.

I sip my beer and look up and down the bar. Hell everyone came out. You would have thought ten days in the fucking jungle would've been enough to settle the boys and have them itching to get home to their wives or girlfriends.

A petty officer sitting on the crappy stool to my right elbows my bicep and angles his head toward my phone laid out on the bar. "Wilcox, you going to get that?"

"Wasn't planning on it," I growl and take another sip of beer.

The screen flashes showing ten missed calls.

Fuck.

The tension from the mission sits just beneath the surface making the amount of missed calls more annoying than it should be. I roll my eyes and signal for the bartender to bring another longneck.

"Seriously man, who's blowin' up your phone?"

Rolling the new cold bottle between my hands I search my memory.

Candice.

No Casey.

Candy?

Obviously not that memorable but by the number of missed calls she thought I was. My men think I'm this big swinging dick who chases tail all day and ditches them the next. Which is part true I guess, but not the chasing tail part. They all come to me which is getting fucking boring. Plus with a girl comes all the clingy, jealous shit I try to stay the hell away from.

"No one important, I can guarantee you that, man," I sigh and go back to watching the Padres game on the old-as-shit TV above the bar.

He laughs and slaps me on the back sending jolts of pain to radiate through the surrounding muscles. Not that I tell him that. Everything is still tense from sitting in one position for nearly twelve damn hours waiting for the perfect opportunity to strike and complete our mission so we could get home.

"Damn man, you're one cold hearted son of a bitch, you know that. Get them all lovesick on your dick and don't call them back. That's cold, brilliant, but cold man. Damn I miss those days. Speaking of which, I gotta run, my girl is going to kick the shit out of me when she finds out I came to the bar before coming home to her."

"You like it when she kicks your ass, don't you try to deny it."

His smile widens, taking up his entire face. "Isn't that the damn truth. See you tomorrow, Wilcox." With one last clasp on the shoulder he tosses a twenty on the bar and heads for the exit.

One by one the others slip out, leaving to be with the women they love and who love them. It's just me and two of my men left; who are too busy sticking their hands up the skirts of a couple flirty girls sitting on their laps to bother with me.

The phone rattles against the bar again. The annoyance from earlier returns ten-fold. The metal bites into my palm from my tight grip as I lift it to my ear.

"Yeah." I try to sound annoyed as possible hoping whoever is calling gets the hint now isn't the time for damn chit chat.

"G." My annoyance slips a rung at Flakes' voice on the other end instead of some broad I can't remember. "We need to talk. Tonight. Meet me at the bar."

"Already here man." There's no concealing how put out I am. The ice bath and large bed will have to wait a little longer. "Come on, I'll order you a beer." I end the call and toss the phone back onto the bar.

While I wait a young woman slides on the barstool next to me and orders a glass of white wine. I can't hold back my snort of amusement. This isn't a wine kind of place, beer and stale pretzels are their specialty. Not even the bartender knows how long that bottle of wine has been left opened. By the crinkle of the woman's tiny nose she's thinking the same damn thing.

"Um, never mind," she says and looks to my beer bottle. "I'll just have what he's having."

The bartender tosses the poured wine into the trash, pops the cap off a Bud heavy and slides it down the bar. I snag it before it can slide to the already-sticky carpet.

"Thanks for that. Nice catch. I'm Becky."

I nod and go back to watching the game hoping she takes the hint I'm in no mood to entertain visitors.

"Want to get out of here?"

The mouth of the beer bottle hovers over my lips as I turn and stare her down with narrowed eyes. "What?" I ask and press the bottle to my lips, downing what's left.

"I mean you're a SEAL right? You're here at Coronado, huge as hell, and brooding over a beer. All the signs are there."

Keeping my eyes on the fuzzy TV I shake my head. "You want to fuck me because I'm a SEAL."

"No," she says slowly to turn my attention back to her. "I want you to screw me so I have a story to tell my friends when I go back home."

Great so now I'm a fucking carnival ride. Free rides here might as well be written on my damn forehead.

"Not my type sweetheart, but you can ask one of them." I point the neck of my bottle down the bar to my two men who are still here. "I'm sure they're up for a party."

"Not your type? Seriously, like men have a type when it comes to casual sex."

I take a deep breath in attempts to calm my annoyance with the curious as hell woman. "My type is a little harder to get, difficult to keep and feisty as hell. So yeah, based on our conversation right now, you ain't it sweetheart."

With a sad huffing laugh she takes a swig of the beer and cringes. "She sounds…interesting. What else?"

I turn to the door and pray Flakes walks in to save me from this conversation. He doesn't.

"Why in the hell do you want to know, sweetheart? I already said no to screwing you tonight."

She picks at the label on the bottle between her hands. "Intrigued I guess. Tell me. Please."

In sufferance I groan and shift on my stool to somewhat face her. "Women are clingy as shit right, I don't want someone who's going to ask what I'm doing, where I'm going, where I've been every damn second. She can't get pissed when I can't talk about where I've been or when I leave at a moment's notice." I take a sip of beer before voicing another piece of my perfect woman. "And bigger than the skinny shit that's walking around these days. I hate feeling like I'm going to break a girl. That about sums it up."

The bar door opens drawing my attention. Fucking finally.

"Well my buddy is here." I raise my hand to order Flakes a beer but he bats my hand down and sits on the unoccupied stool to my left. He leans forward to get a good view of the woman beside me. My eyes roll to the ceiling. Damn Flakes.

"Who's your friend here G?" he asks and flashes a smile that usually has every woman in the room begging at his feet.

I shrug and go back to brooding over my beer. "Just met her, she wants to fuck a SEAL."

"And?" Flakes asks looking between us. "You said yes right?"

The woman speaks up before I can. "He said no, waiting on

someone more difficult or something like that." She leans forward, resting her tits on the bar, and smiles to Flakes no longer interested in me.

Not that I give a rat's ass. No way in hell could I end up with some broad who throws herself at someone like she just did. Where's the fun, where's the intrigue? Hell, the girls I've had lately have all been missing that challenge aspect.

Flakes reaches over and holds out his hand. Which I notice is already missing his wedding ring.

"Well I'm a SEAL and easy sounds pretty good right now. Give me ten minutes with this guy." He smacks me hard on the back. I stifle back a grunt. "And I'll come find you. You have a hotel room close?"

They have to be kidding.

"Yep, two blocks away. Here's my cell." My attention stays on the TV as she jots down her number and slides it across the bar. "I'll be waiting. You know if you can talk this guy"—she inclines her head to me with a smirk—"into joining, I would be down for that too."

Turning on the stool he watches her flat ass as she leaves. "Fuck dude, how can you turn down something so easy? What the hell has gotten into you?"

"Easy that's why. And what the hell man, I thought you were cleaning up your shit for your damn wife? Don't go screw it up again for an easy lay."

He reaches around, snags the full beer the easy woman left and takes a swig. "I need easy nowadays man. Life is hard shit and being married isn't all it's cracked up to be. She knew who she married, not sure why in the hell she's trying to change me now."

"It takes two people to get married you damn fool. Why did you do it if you knew you'd never give up your side tail?"

His incredulous laugh rubs my already-frayed nerves. After chugging the beer he slams the bottle against the bar and turns to face me straight on. "You and your screwed-up idealist picture of marriage. You really think one girl could make you, Gabe fucking Wilcox, God's gift to fucking women, happy for the rest of your life? When all I've ever seen from you is a revolving door of blondes and brunettes coming from your apartment. Come on stop chafing my ass and realize no one stays faithful in marriages anymore, that shit's for the Amish."

"The what?"

"There was some damn show about them last week. It was interesting. Give me a break and stop busting my balls. We have shit to talk about other than my damn love life."

With the bottle I motion for him to continue. He shakes his head and stands. "Not here, let's head out to the pier."

I toss two twenties on the bar and follow him out the door. Damn this isn't good. We've been friends since the academy, we can talk about anything, anytime, anywhere. We're over separate platoons, there isn't any confidential work for us to discuss. Our teams haven't worked together in a while.

Our boots pound the wooden planks. What the hell does he need to talk about way out here?

He pauses half way down and leans against the wooden rail. I do the same on the opposite side. The ocean at night, when the dark water and sky mold into one, scares most people but not me. Out here with the smell of salt water, cool breeze I'm free. Freedom I can't find anywhere else. The ocean is where I'm the best and there isn't any situation that could arise I can't handle. There's comfort in that. A comfort the moment I stepped foot on this pier had all the anger and annoyance from earlier slipping away. For the first time since we landed I'm able to take a full, easy breath.

Only to tense up again.

"We have a problem," Flakes says and paces between the railings. "I was called to CO's office today." A muttered curse slips. "I know, tell me about it. Seems they think I have a fucking damn rodent in my platoon."

"What?" He can't be serious. A mole. In the SEALS. Not likely.

"I'm fucking serious man. This isn't something I'd prank you on and you know it. There have been some messed up missions lately I haven't filled you in on. We've missed several objectives and it's not because of my men. CO thinks someone is leaking intel, letting the bastards know we are coming."

"Fuck."

"That's what I said."

"What are we going to do?"

"We? This is my damn problem not yours, Wilcox. Don't think you can jump in and save the day, be the fucking hero, like you always do."

I turn from the water to press my back against the wood, crossing my arms over my chest. "Careful, Flakes, you sound like a bitter bitch right now."

He runs both hands through his cropped dark hair and interlaces his fingers behind his head. "Shit, I know. Sorry. I'm just...what am I going to do?"

The roaring of the waves against the shore fills the silence as I give him a few beats to think it through before tossing out my ideas.

With a huff he says, "Doesn't matter what I would do anyway." He drops his hands and tucks them into the front pockets of his jeans. "CO says they have a solution. We will know more tomorrow. He wants to debrief both of us." I arch a brow. "I don't know why you too. Just repeating orders. Anyway sounds like they want an outsider to help us identify this son of a bitch."

I push off the rail and stand. "An outsider? Seriously."

"I know. Don't worry we'll run the fucker off and handle this on our own. If I have to deal with one NCIS jackass who thinks his dick is the biggest. Fuck. Fuck. Fuck. I just needed to vent, thanks G. We'll get it figured out."

With a nod I turn and go back to watching the water. "Text me what time tomorrow. And let me know what you need Flakes. I'm here."

"Thanks." He takes a step then hesitates. "Hey if the wife calls you—"

I shake my head and roll my eyes. He knows better than to ask that shit. "I've never lied to your wife, Flakes, and I'm never going to. Stop being a horses ass and get a divorce or stop messing around on her."

"Right, whatever. Bye man."

My bed calls but I can't resist the ocean calling stronger. Begging me to stay a while. It only takes a couple minutes to make it to the far end of the pier and I'm sitting on the ledge, feet dangling over the water.

A mole.

There's no way. How can that even happen with our small teams? Hopefully it's a mistake but that would indicate Flakes is just shitty at his job. Maybe the intel is corrupted before it even gets to us.

The guy they send to sort this shit out better be good. There's no mediocre in the SEALs and we will run their ass off our base if there's even a hint of incompetence. Hell. An outsider. This is going to suck. Maybe I'll get called out for a long stint so I miss most of the investigation.

Doubt I'm that lucky.

CHAPTER THREE
LUCIA

Exhausted, I push my apartment door closed with my back and drop my bags. After the clattering of the bags hitting the floor there's nothing. The silence which welcomes me is comforting and depressing. Not even a snotty cat or lazy goldfish here to greet me. For the first time in a long time a sense of loneliness creeps into my gut.

No. Not going to stand here and dwell. This is the life I chose. What I wanted and worked my ass off for. I'm where I need to be. Once I'm at the next level, then I can stop and think about something other than my career.

Tossing the keys and files on the coffee table I stride for the kitchen. I sniff the opened bottle of wine and cringe. It's tossed into the trash, which smells equally as bad. I start the hunt for the bottle that never goes bad.

Teetering on my tiptoes I open the cabinet above the fridge and grab the half full bottle of Kettle One. I twist the cap off, grab a high ball glass out of the cabinet, blowing into it to get the dust out, and pour some in. Somehow the ice has freezer burn, wasn't aware that was a thing, but still plop a couple cubes into the glass and take a sip.

The cold liquid hits my stomach making it churn and growl as a reminder. I need to eat.

Not even bothering to look *in* the fridge I lean a hip against the counter and stare at the side covered in take-out menus. I love to cook but the last two months of being on back to back operations have made grocery shopping pointless. As I skim over the menus my attention falls on the magnet holding up a Chinese menu. It's from Brazil. I got it about seven months ago when I was there evaluating an agent the agency thought was going rogue. He was. That was an interesting trip.

Looking over the entire fridge I scan the multiple magnets.

Sixty-three varying magnets in total. Sixty-four if you want to count the one I haven't unpacked yet.

Sixty-four cities in less than two years. No wait in a year, this tradition started within the last twelve months. The agency would kill me, literally, if they knew I kept a souvenir trail, a visible one at that, but I like it. They make me feel, real I guess. Which wouldn't make sense to most people.

I pull the Chinese menu off the fridge and take it, the vodka and my tired ass to the living room and collapse onto the couch. After ordering the right side of the menu, plus soup with extra wontons, I lay down using the armrest as a pillow.

The drink is smooth and relaxing, exactly what I needed. My gaze lands on the manila files scattered on the coffee table.

A mole in one of the SEAL teams. Wow. Jeremy wasn't kidding when he said it would be interesting. Definitely different than what I've been doing. The files were brief, just the basics of the assignment and the location were listed.

A knock at the door makes me bolt from the couch and grab a gun I have hidden between the couch cushions. No way King Wong's has gotten faster since I've been away. Gun cocked and loaded at my side I peer through the privacy hole.

What the hell?

I push my bags aside with my foot and pull the door open. My boss eyes the gun in my hand.

"Agent Rizzo."

I hold the door open for him and Jeremy to come in.

"Sir. Jeremy." They watch as I head back to the couch, grabbing the drink off the side table on my way. "To what do I owe the pleasure gents? I thought I was scheduled for debriefing tomorrow morning."

My boss smiles. "Welcome home. Yes, you were scheduled for the debriefing but the file you read on the plane is much more urgent. We can discuss Agent Montford at a later date."

I prop my boots up on the table. "Okay."

"Did you read the file?"

"Yes sir. Seems a lot of critical information was missing. I'm guessing that's why you're here."

"Yes, we wanted to discuss the specifics in person."

I nod for him to dive into it and take a cold sip.

"There is a second objective to this mission." I feel my brows raise a fraction with intrigue. "The SEALs and CIA have long ties together, sharing information, assistance when needed and of course future agent prospects. We were in talks of recruiting one of their senior officers to the agency when the suspicion of the mole came up. They gave us authority to recruit this SEAL if we send an agent down to help identify their mole."

Why would that need to be said in person? He's holding back. I eye him then Jeremy as I sip my drink, trying to figure out what's really going on. With the CIA you never really know.

"Okay," I say slowly. "I understand the importance of getting the mole and recruiting this senior officer you want. What else aren't you telling me, I feel like you're holding something back still."

With a chuckle he says, "Damn, nothing gets by you does it Agent Rizzo?"

"Not typically."

"I knew you'd be the perfect agent for this particular operation. What I haven't mentioned, we don't want to give the mole any indication we are investigating the situation. You will go in undercover. Agent Dungan will fill you in on your cover story after I leave." He clears his throat and widens his stance a fraction. Why is he preparing for a fight? "Now for the names. The man you will be recruiting is Sr. Officer Gabe Wilcox, I've instructed Agent Dungan to prepare his file for you to review on the plane. I cannot stress enough how desperate we are to have this man on our team, Agent Rizzo. His strategic ability is beyond anything we've seen. The Commanding Officer believes officer Wilcox has the potential to have his job one day."

I nod but keep my lips sealed. He's not done.

"There is only one platoon which will be under your surveillance. Over the past several months it has been this particular platoon who has been affected by the intel leak. They believe the mole is on that team since they are the only ones, outside the CO, who have the mission information."

"Okay, great one platoon. It won't be—"

"And it seems you know the senior officer of the platoon. Which is where my only concern is of sending you on this operation instead of another agent."

"What? Sir, I don't know any SEALs. I was army, remember? I don't know anyone in the navy."

"He wasn't a SEAL when you met him."

He pauses, building my anticipation. I lean forward bracing my elbows on my thighs. "Just tell me! I'm dying here. Who do I know?"

"Sr. Officer Anthony Hackenbreg. As I understand it, he goes by Tony instead of Anthony."

Tony Hackenbreg. Tony Hackenbreg. Tony Ha….oh you have to be kidding me.

"You're joking."

"I'm not, Agent Rizzo. Will this be a problem? I'm told you two had an intimate relationship at one point."

I stare wide-eyed for a few seconds before giving a harsh sarcastic laugh. Of course that idiot is a SEAL. His massive ego wouldn't let him be anything less. Little surprised he passed their psychological exam.

"Sir, no. Just no. Whatever you read about that blip of a relation-ship, which I would love to know how you even knew about, I can

COVERT AFFAIR | 25

assure you it was nothing. At least to me it was nothing. And I'm sure Tony has long forgotten about me. It's been over a decade."

His narrowed brown eyes say he's not buying it. He can think whatever he wants. It's the truth. This won't be an issue from my point of view.

"Another hurdle. Sr. Officer Hackenbreg has indicated interest in joining the CIA. Quite a bit of interest. We are not interested in him—"

"Not surprising."

He shoots an annoyed look but keeps going. "He and Sr. Officer Wilcox, whom you are tasked with recruiting, are friends. They graduated from the Naval Academy together and have been side by side through their military career. You will have to, not only, identify this mole, but maneuver between their relationship to recruit Sr. Officer Wilcox without Sr. Officer Hackenbreg knowing. Since he is the officer over the platoon in question we do not want him to know we're passing him over until the operation is finished to prevent any unfavorable actions from his part."

Hope this Wilcox guy is worth it all. He's making the next few weeks a lot more complicated.

"Do you understand everything I've said, Agent Rizzo? Do you understand the importance of you succeeding on *all* points of this operation?"

"Yes sir, I do. Crystal clear." Kind of. If he could tell me how to get all this done that would be amazing, but I guess I'll have to figure it out along the way. Reading people I've done, but recruiting someone, this is a new one.

A nod and he turns for the door when someone pounds against it. Both men draw their side arms and angle them toward the door.

I shove off the couch with a smile and grab my wallet from my purse. "Calm down you two, it's just my dinner." Shouldering past Jeremy, I pull the door and smile at a familiar face but the kid doesn't return it. Instead he shoves the food into my arms, keeping his terrified eyes locked on the two guns behind me.

"Agent Rizzo."

I nod but start pulling food from the plastic bags, organizing it on the coffee table in the order I want to devour it.

"Lucia."

That pulls all my attention. He never uses a first name. Ever.

"This is very important to the agency, if you succeed I've been told the promotion you've been working towards will happen."

The chopsticks in my hand clatter to the table.

Stunned, I don't respond. I'm still staring at the door after he's gone. The couch dips as Jeremy settles next to me.

"Jeremy," I say in a mix of wonder and disbelief. "Did he say what I think he said?"

He leans forward and grabs the chopsticks from the table and places them back in my waiting hand. "He did, you can use me as a witness if they ever try to deny it." Styrofoam crinkles as he opens the various boxes. Delicious smells grow stronger, infiltrating the entire apartment. "Did you order for me too?"

Snapping out of my daze I turn and stick my tongue out at him. I twirl the chopsticks in my hand as I pick up the first course then dig in.

"So here's the rundown of what's going to happen tomorrow—"

"Tomorrow," I groan around a mouth full of dumplings and shove another in.

Jeremy cringes in disgust. "That's so nasty, don't talk with your mouth full. Didn't anyone teach you to be a lady?"

"Shut it, go on."

"Tomorrow." He shoots an exasperated look before continuing. "You'll meet with Commanding Officer Williams, Wilcox and Hackenbreg. Now your cover story. You're a reporter writing a piece about the SEALs. Their training, life as a SEAL, hell whatever bullshit you want to spin really. I thought of a cover name you'd appreciate. 'Gracie Lu Freebush.'"

"Seriously?"

"What? You love that movie."

I set the empty dumpling box down and reach for my soup and wontons. "What if those guys have seen the movie?" Yum crunchies.

His head shakes slowly. "You're kidding, right?"

"No, I'm not. I'm sure they have girlfriends or wives who've made them watch that movie. What if they recognize the cover name?"

He leans back against the soft leather and rubs the bridge of his thin nose with his finger and thumb. "If they did it was just for a reward fuck and weren't paying enough attention to remember anything."

"A reward fuck?"

His hand falls to the cushions. "Yes. It's the only reason men watch those stupid chick flicks. The reward lay."

I furrow my brows. "A reward for…"

"For letting you pick the movie. Not pitching a damn fit when you choose, yet again, a chick flick. For not playing on our phones the entire time. For acting interested. We deserve a reward for that."

"Do you now."

"We do."

"I don't think that's a real thing."

"It's a thing." With a sigh his eyes close. "Seriously you've never given a guy a reward fuck for watching one of your stupid movies?"

Glancing away I reach for my drink and take a long sip to give me time to think of an answer. Jeremy's wanted more from our friendship since our first meeting at Langley. Him filling in for Brooke has been nice in some ways, awful in others. It's been nice having an established relationship with the person guiding me through each op but his feelings have intensified the past couple months with the almost daily communication between us. Even though I've told him, multiple times, it won't happen between us, he gets awkward, jealous even, if the topic turns toward me and another guy.

"Okay, fine Gracie Lu it is. Got it, what else?"

"Great, I'll get that information to them tomorrow morning. We've rented a house, great view too, to support your backstory of living there full time. Only the CO and I will have the address and anyone else you need to give it to, of course." He bites at his lower lip. "So, you and this Tony guy."

I set the empty plastic soup cup down and turn to him, resting the side of my head against the couch. "It was some random guy in college. A huge mistake."

He nods but keeps his eyes trained on the nonexistent spot he's trying to wipe from his suit pants. "Don't look at me that way Lu. I know it's never going to happen between us. It's fine. I'm fine."

The corners of my mouth dip. Seeing him disappointed like this kills me but he's right, we will never happen. He's a great guy and will make some woman very, very happy one day but not me. Not that I know what or who *is* for me since I haven't found a guy who sticks around for long.

"Be careful on this one, Lu."

I sigh and play with the tip of my ponytail. "I'm always careful. How long have I been doing this now and I always come home."

His brown eyes shift allowing me to feel his apprehension of what he's about to say. "I know, it's just...these guys and you. You have a way with men. I don't want you to get hurt okay. Don't let any of them get close, Lu. The last thing you need is one of them falling for you."

I don't hold back my snort. "Right, because there's an actual risk of that happening. Those guys only want to get laid and fight. Plus, to me, they're the enemy. I'm Army remember? If I were to go for a trained killer I'd have to find an Army Ranger."

He just shakes his head and runs a hand over his face. When he looks again the smile he's plastered on isn't convincing.

"So." I nudge his shoulder. "Want to watch Netflix while I unpack and pack again?" My voice chipper in hopes to turn his sulky mood around.

"Nope." He slaps his thighs and stands. "It's been a long day, I'm going home. Night, Lu. Wheels up at 0800."

"Night," I yell as the door closes behind him. My gaze shifts from the door to my unpacked suitcases still by the door needing my attention. I should unpack. Start some laundry so at least a few pairs of underwear will be clean. Instead I procrastinate grabbing my phone from the coffee table and text my best friend.

Me: You remember that one night stand I had in college? With the Naval Academy guy? I think I told you about him one night. Pretty sure I did.

I smile at the instant little thought bubble and snuggle down to wait for her reply.

Brooke: Which one?

    Me: There was only one Navy guy.

    Brooke: Tell me again. I've got the time. It's going to be a long night here.

    Me: Everything okay?

    Brooke: Besides the fact I think the child I grew in my uterus for ten months is actually the spawn of Satan? Not really.

    Brooke: Okay that's harsh but damn I need some sleep. And quiet time.

    Brooke: And of course, we're almost out of coffee. How am I going to survive the night like this?

Instead of diving into the Tony story I tap the Amazon app and search for a case of Starbucks coffee. I stare at the shopping cart for a second before adding a case of wine to the order and click purchase. Coffee and wine, her two life bloods, will be delivered to her doorstep within two hours.

Brooke: You there? I can't have sex for another couple weeks so tell me all the juicy details about this Tony guy. Was he hot?

Me: We met after a football game. In a bar. He was getting into it with a few of my buddies so I intervened.

Brooke: What you mean is you provoked him, verbally chastised him and got him to take the first swing.

Me: Maybe.

Brooke: I love you. Such a bad ass. When I get back to work I want you to teach me all your ways. I could use the workout to lose some of this baby weight.

Brooke: What happened next?

Me: Once we got into it the whole bar got into it. Somehow we ended up outside making out.

Brooke: Making out. What is this? High school? Get to the good stuff.

Me: The owner of the bar threatened to call the cops so we split and ended up in his hotel room. It was okay. The next day I didn't want to hang around so I tried to bounce but he caught me sneaking out and we ended up spending the day together. He left that night to go back to Annapolis.

Me: He got my number, tried calling dozens of times. Sometimes I'd pick up just because I felt bad straight up ignoring him but he was such an ass. I can't even start to guess how many texts he sent me over the next several months.

Me: It was all a little too much. Plus I could see through his game, no way I'd want to get involved with someone like him.

Brooke: Did you tell me why we are talking about this and I've already forgotten?

Me: Nope. Just so happens he's part of my next op.

Brooke: Shut your mouth. That will be awkward. What are you going to say when you see him?

Me: I don't know.

Brooke: Hopefully he's forgotten about it.

Me: A guy like Tony? No way. His big ego wouldn't let him.

Brooke: Have fun with that.

. . .

I toss the phone to the floor and stare at the ceiling. Brooke was right. It will be awkward on his end. He became pushy trying to see me after that weekend. To the point of being creepy.

Thinking back, I might have even told him that. Great. This is a shit show and I'm not even there yet.

CHAPTER FOUR
LUCIA

Warm, dry air fills my lungs with each deep breath. The ground crew unloads my luggage from the plane and puts it in the black Camaro waiting near the tarmac. The directions I pull up indicate the rental house is twenty minutes from the airport, another fifteen from there to Coronado.

I glance at my watch and tally the time I have before the meeting and hop in the car. If I hurry I'll have time to stop at the store for the necessities, drop off everything, freshen up and get to the base with minutes to spare.

Perfect.

———

After putting away the groceries and unpacking, plus setting up the usual safety measures, I take a second to freshen up before heading back out the door. Not wanting to show up in my travel clothes I change to my favorite black suit and a crisp white blouse. The blazer helps conceal my large chest and the pants are tailored to make me not look quite as hippy as I actually am.

Not that I don't love my curves, because I do, it's just, I've found, men take you a little more seriously when you're not throwing your sexuality at them. It's something I've dealt with since West Point, maybe even since high school. All guys see is a set of big boobs, great curves and green eyes instead of my better, less superficial, assets; two undergraduate degrees from West Point in Communication and Psychology and a Master's Degree in Human Behavior. All that plus my four years in the army are the last thing men ask about. Instead they dumb down conversations the moment I enter the room or flat out assume someone who looks like me can't understand the high-level information they're discussing.

Apparently the egotistical men I'm surrounded by believe a woman can't be beautiful, smart and kick ass. Until they get to know me that is. There's something about the mixture of fear and awe in their eyes when they realize I can read through their bullshit lies and fronts that makes my heart happy. Sometimes with the particularly arrogant agents I find enjoyment in pinpointing their insecurities and exposing them in front of their peers. It's a fun game I always win.

Shaking my head to refocus I tighten my grip on the steering wheel and try to pay attention to the directions being shouted from the phone.

Ten minutes early. Of course. I'm early to everything. Being late, or even on time isn't an option. Ever. After backing into a spot I leave the car running for the A/C to keep blowing while I wait. Wait and watch. Blue fatigued men and women storm between the various buildings. All looking like they are pressed for time or have something urgent to hand off.

These men are larger than the average agent at Langley. Hell even the army. In the army, the men I commanded were mostly enlisted kids who'd just turned eighteen. But here these men are...well men. Well built men. Men who look like they could toss me around like a ragdoll.

Which is kind of hot. Okay really hot. To be with a guy who I'm not scared will topple over if I hang on him like a koala would be a nice change.

As I'm imagining me climbing these men, a black Jeep speeds through the parking lot and whips into a spot in front of me. I watch with fascination as long blue fatigued legs exit the door and another well built man slides out of the driver's seat. The door slams behind him. Turning he makes use of the reflection on the shiny black paint to situate his hat.

My head falls an inch to the side to get an angle of his perky backside. I sigh deep at the view. My gaze moves to his strong arms, which from here look about to rip the cuffs, to his intense blue eyes staring right back.

Crap. I try to look away but can't. He has me locked in some kind of trance.

Mental note. SEALs are very observant. Or maybe just this hot one. Time will tell I guess.

I snatch my purse off the passenger seat and push open the door.

"You lost?" the man asks as I lock the door and move past him.

"Nope. You?" I respond over my shoulder rewarding me with a harsh laugh from behind me. Right behind me.

"Need help finding where you're going, miss?" he asks moving a step ahead.

I shake my head and pick up my pace to be in the lead again. When did this become a race?

When I came through the guard gate they said head towards this building, go up the stairs and CO Williams' office will be the last office on the left. Simple.

Until it isn't.

Once I'm through the building's doors my pace slows then stops completely.

The hot sailor pauses too. "Sure you don't want my help? You look lost."

I glance at my watch, five minutes until I'm officially late which makes me sweat more than I already am from the brisk walk across the hot parking lot. Frantically I visually search for a set of stairs. "I'll figure it out on my own." I mumble not looking directly at him, which I haven't been able to do since he caught me ogling from my car.

"Suit yourself." He tucks his hands into the pockets of his BDUs. At the end of the hall he takes a right and disappears.

Another glance at my watch. Four minutes. With a huff I hurry down the hall, my heels clicking along the tile, in the same direction the guy had gone. I take a right and smile. Not wasting any more time I take the stairs two by two. Thank goodness I take physical training to the extreme or I'd be struggling to breathe by now.

At the end of the hall I pause in front of a large wooden desk with another blue fatigued man sitting behind it. His smile when he looks up, eyes scrolling up and down, is wide. "Can I help you?"

Not wanting to blow the operation within the first five minutes of being on base I keep both real and cover names to myself. "I'm here to see CO Williams. He's expecting me."

Shock registers but is reeled back in. Rising from his chair he rounds the desk with his arm extended towards a dark wooden door. "Yes, they said they were expecting one more. CO Williams, Sr. Officer Wilcox, and Sr. Officer Hackenbreg are waiting."

"Thank you…"

"Travis Hershall. You can call me Travis, ma'am."

"Thank you, Travis."

Cold air whooshes through the opened door. I take a deep breath in to calm my breathing and anxiety of almost being late, and step inside.

The all dark wood spatial office is decorated throughout with random navy memorabilia and various medals and awards. A few leather chairs are tucked in the corner and there's no mistaking the symbolism of the massive wooden desk taking up a majority of the room. The man sitting behind the desk doesn't look up from his stack of papers.

"Come in and let's get started." The door clicks closed behind me. "I'm Commanding Officer Williams."

Okay I need to find out what they feed these guys and give the recipe to the army. Even their CO is large.

Freezing air blows from the left corner of the room. I begin inching that direction. Movement in my peripheral catches my eye but I keep moving.

"Sr. Officers Hackenbreg and Wilcox are here as well. I assume the agency filled you in they will be participating in this mission. Hacken-breg. Wilcox. This is Agent Rizzo."

One of the men steps forward drawing my full attention. Of course it's the man from the parking lot. Great. I slide my gaze over to the man who hung back. He hasn't changed much, bulked up a little, but still good looking if you like arrogant assholes.

I grip Wilcox's extended hand.

"Officer Wilcox. Pleasure to meet you," he says with a smirk. I roll my eyes at his sarcasm. His lips twitch on the verge of breaking the stern expression he's wearing. "And you're with the...?"

"CIA," I say and monitor his reaction. To his credit he stays stone faced and steps back and looks to Tony, waiting for him to introduce himself.

"You have to be fucking kidding me. *You're* in the CIA," Tony says under his breath. Surprise registers on Wilcox's features, clearly he doesn't know Tony and I have a past. Good.

Not wanting to back down I take a step toward Tony with my hand extended. "Agent Rizzo, nice to meet you Officer Hackenbreg. I'm excited to be here to help your platoon."

His face flushes red at my words, like I hoped it would.

When I turn back to face the CO something's mumbled behind me. Turning with a sappy sweet smile plastered on my face I say, "I'm sorry I didn't catch that, why don't you text me...a few hundred times."

The word he mumbles next comes out loud and clear this time.

"That's enough Officer Hackenbreg. Agent Rizzo is here as a favor from the agency, to help your damn platoon, so I suggest you act more damn hospitable."

"Yes sir," he says loudly before turning his angry eyes to me. "Apologies *Agent* Rizzo. Welcome to Coronado." His words come out more as a hiss.

Again my eyes roll to the ceiling, I swear Officer Wilcox chokes back a laugh, and I turn to face the CO. "Yes sir the agency did give me the rundown on the operation and my objective. Question. Why is he here?" I incline my head to Tony and quirk a brow.

"Excuse me?" Tony seethes.

"Couldn't the mole be him? After all he has all the mission information as well."

Wilcox steps forward. "It's not him."

"That's what you think."

"It's a fact."

"We will see," I say. CO Williams looks up from his desk for the first time since entering the room. In this short look I find a man I can immediately trust and respect. Something about him puts me at ease. "What I'm not privy to is the day to day details on how I'm going to gather information on each suspect. I need to talk to each of them, evaluate them on an individual basis before I dig into their lives. It could take weeks for me to do that with every man in Officer Hackenbreg's platoon individually."

He nods. "Agreed Agent Rizzo. We assessed the same thing yesterday. Officer Wilcox, whom I've assigned as your escort—"

"I don't need an escort, sir."

With a pointed glare he says, "Wasn't a question or suggestion. Officer Wilcox has the information you're looking for on the details."

On cue Wilcox moves to the center of the room standing to my right also facing their CO. "We will introduce you to Officer Hackenbreg's team and my team. You'll be allowed to watch and evaluate the men as we run through various training exercises. However, now that you're a woman—"

I look to CO Williams who's now smirking. He purposefully didn't let them know, maybe because of my previous relationship with Tony; didn't want to tip him off. Or he likes tossing out situations to see how his men react. Either way they know now. "Always have been," I say, my smirk now matching the CO's.

Gabe's blond brows rise a fraction. "We weren't aware of that vital piece of information when we made our plan."

"So no locker room visits, got it. Continue."

Again the edges of his lips twitch as he holds back a smirk. "Training and endurance exercises, after a few days we'll start interviews. You'll interview anyone you suspect along with a few of my men to keep suspicions off our real objective."

I incline my head in his direction as a thank you. "I'll need the files of every man on Ton... Officer Hackenbreg's platoon."

CO Williams stands and straightens his shirt. "Done. I'll have my HQS liaison get those to you. And have a base ID created with your cover name, should be ready by tomorrow. Your agency didn't provide me that pivotal piece of information until this morning or it would have been ready sooner. This is of the highest priority Agent Rizzo. Officer Hackenbreg's platoon has been grounded until we identify this mole. Also let me be clear, once you identify the mole we will be notified first. Understood?"

"Yes sir."

"How long?"

I mentally map everything Wilcox laid out. "Two weeks at a minimum. Maybe three. It all depends how many men are hiding something from the rest of the group."

"No one is hiding anything. I trust these men with my life Agent Rizzo. You'd do well to remember that."

My spine straightens at the vague threat. "Everyone is hiding something Officer Hackenbreg. I would think out of anyone you would know that." With a slow glance to his wedding band I look back up with a raised brow. His bright red face and twitching neck vein signal I hit a nerve. Seems nothing has changed with him.

"Is this going to be a problem?" the CO says looking between us.

"No, sir," we say in unison.

"Good. Only the three of us know your true identity and it will stay that way. The next few weeks you're our guest here and these two will make sure the other men treat you as such. But Agent Rizzo, I'm expecting good behavior from you as well. Can you do that?"

"Maybe," I say and immediately regret it. "Sorry sir. Yes. I can do that."

With a wave of his hand he sits back in his chair. "You three can figure out the logistics together. I have another meeting to get to. Dismissed."

CHAPTER FIVE
GABE

Damn.

A woman. That would have been nice to know before the meeting.

Hot fucking damn.

She has to be the hottest damn CIA agent ever in the history of that useless agency. And that quick wit. In the matter of a few minutes Agent Rizzo has climbed to the top of my 'need to do' agenda.

Flakes storms out of the office first like he's about to lose it if he doesn't get out immediately. Agent Rizzo follows, keeping her distance, leaving me to follow her. Which with this view I sure as hell don't mind.

That ass. I want to grab handfuls of that ass. I can watch the flex and move of her walking all damn day and never get bored.

"Are you done?" she asks from a couple steps ahead.

"Huh?" I respond eyes still glued on the ass I want to get my hands on.

She stops hard. I shift right to not slam into her back. "Are you done staring at my ass? If you need a few more minutes that's fine but I would prefer it if you ran ahead and calmed your water mammal buddy down enough so the three of us can talk about this operation without bloodshed."

Water what?

Oh hell.

The smirk I've been holding back since she stepped into CO's office pulls at my lips, hopefully showing off my dimples. Chicks love them.

Those green eyes stare into mine making every ounce of impatience known. Then, in a blink that impatience drops and is replaced by something I've never experienced. It's like she has a window into my thoughts, my soul, searching and exposing all that I am. I try but fail to look away. She has me locked in some kind of trance pulling me deeper and deeper allowing her to see things I've worked hard to keep hidden.

Other military personnel shift and move around us on the stairs but she just tilts her head slightly to the right not allowing my gaze to drop.

Her eyes narrow. "I know Tony's hiding something, which isn't a surprise, but you. What are you hiding?"

"Are you two coming or what?" Flakes shouts from the bottom of the stairs like a pouting toddler.

It's only when she breaks the stare am I able to do the same. Anger replaces the insecurity of what she might have found.

"What the fuck was that?" I growl. Feeling that exposed isn't something I want to go through again. Ever.

Instead of replying she shakes her head and starts down the stairs. "You can tell me whenever you're ready. You'll feel better I promise. Now go get your friend and I'll meet you two by my car."

Moving around her I jog to catch up with Flakes who's already out the doors and almost to his truck.

He turns, ready to lay into someone, sees me and stops for me to catch up. "This is a bunch of bullshit. Seriously. Her. What the fuck. Of all the damn women in the world she's in the CIA. There's no way I can work with her. We have to find a way to get her off this."

"Calm the hell down or at least wait to go ape shit until no one's around you fool." I snarl and scan the parking lot. We're lucky no one's around to question his irate behavior.

He rubs his palms against his eyes and starts towards his truck again.

This is new. Flakes worked up about a woman. Who the hell is she to him? Curiosity and jealousy mix together confusing the hell out of me. Why do I even care if she and Flakes had a thing? One thing is true if anyone is going to get a guy like Flakes worked up it's someone like her.

Wonder what her name is. Hope it's as unique as the woman it belongs to.

We stop at his truck and Flakes rests his elbows on the hood, clasping his hands behind his head.

Leaning against the car beside him I ask, "Who is she? How in the hell do you know a CIA agent and I not know?"

He groans and pushes off the truck to face me, leaning a hip against the grill. "Remember that hot army chick I couldn't get out of my head our senior year?"

Racking my brain, I come up with nothing. "Not really."

"Well it's her. That Agent Rizzo is the one and only Lucia Rizzo. I met her at West Point, one of the weekends I went to watch you play ball. We hooked up then nothin'. We talked a few times, I tried to get her to come visit but fuck me if she didn't want anything to do with me. *Me.* It drove me insane. And you want to know what else? The last thing she texted me was I was too damn needy and needed to move on. That I was fucking creepy. Can you believe that shit?"

As he talks, memories of that time flash and recognition registers. Holy hell. This woman is the one he couldn't win over and talked about all the damn time. For some reason that makes me want to smile, it's for sure a positive for her in my log.

"Okay, but hell man they sent her and that's who's going to help us find this damn mole. Stop acting like you're in damn high school and get your shit together. It's a chick that didn't call you back, get the hell over it."

A thud sounds as his fist connects with the hood of his truck.

"She's a fucking drug man and I was hooked. I couldn't get her out of my head, I swear I got the shakes. Hell just seeing her in there made me start to itch for her again. I can't...we can't work with her. We need to ask for someone else."

Like hell he can't. No way he's going to have her shipped out because he can't get over a damn crush.

"We can and you will," I command and push off the car I've been leaning against. "It's an order from our CO and we have a mole to find. If she's our best shot then you need to get your fucking panties out of your ass and come with me."

She watches, as I cross the parking lot, from her perch on the hood of her car, twirling the keys around her index finger.

"I'm assuming that conversation didn't go well," she says with a smirk as I approach.

"He'll come around, just give him a second. Sounds like you really worked him over good."

She snorts a laugh and shakes her head. "Right, sorry if I didn't feel like dating some rando after a mediocre night. Plus his issue isn't that I didn't call him back, it's that he wasn't the one to end it. His enormous ego was wounded and he can't handle it. Seriously, how did he even get into this program? Don't y'all have standards?" A red-nailed hand lifts to her face to shield the sun from her eyes to meet my not amused stare.

"Why did they send you? No offense."

"Offense taken."

"I didn't mean—"

"Sure you did. If I were a guy you wouldn't be asking that question."

"No," I say slowly trying to figure out exactly what I'm trying to ask. "I'm asking because I don't know anything about you. Who the fuck are you?"

Again that damn smirk appears. "Well then you should have said that."

I toss my hands in the air, fighting to keep them from reaching out

COVERT AFFAIR | 45

and grabbing her around the waist to pull her against me, completely irritated by the direction of the conversation.

"Holy hell, woman. Fine. Who the fuck are you?" There's something fun about the back and forth. Frustrating as it is.

Her smile drops a fraction when her gaze focuses to something behind me. "Later, sailor. Looks like your friend has come to his senses."

I glance over my shoulder and roll my eyes at Flakes dragging his damn feet like he has rocks in his boots. When he finally makes it to where we are Agent Rizzo stays silent. I do too.

"We can introduce you to the team tomorrow. 0800," Flakes finally says looking everywhere but at her.

A curt nod in Flakes' direction then that soul-searching gaze turns to me. "And you, Officer Wilcox. How do you fit in all this besides some of your men being used to throw suspicions off our true objective and my escort?"

"It's Gabe." Flakes huffs a laugh and turns to put his back to us, resting his ass on the side of her car. "I wasn't filled in as to why me and not Flakes here but those are my orders."

Her eyes divert to the hood of the car. Strange. Like she doesn't want me seeing something. "Copy," she says and clears her throat. "Tony, can you play nice and not blow this op for all of us?"

With his back still to us he gives an ambivalent shrug.

After a quick assessing glance around the parking lot she rounds the hood and stops in front of him, inches from his face. "Grow the hell up Tony. It was over a decade ago. I didn't call you back. Get over yourself. What's with you?"

The metal of the hood pops under the pressure of his hands as he pushes off. For several seconds they stare, nose to nose, in a standoff of wills.

Not backing down Flakes says, "So what's your plan here Lucia, fuck my whole platoon to get the information you need? Is that how you landed such a nice fucking gig with the CIA? You slept to the damn top. Was it your boss or his that you got on your knees—"

Enough. "Stand down Hackenbreg," I say through gritted teeth and take a step towards them to break it up before Flakes' balled fists seek action.

But I'm too late. Of course she's the first one to make a move.

She pulls back like she's going to punch him in the face, which Flakes catches with a laugh, turning them and slamming her back against the side of the car. It's her free hand that draws my attention as it withdraws something from the side pocket of her slacks.

A cocky smile forms, even though she's the one who's pinned, as she struggles beneath him.

"You've gotten rusty. Maybe you should get off your back and train more," Flakes whispers into her ear.

That cocky smirk grows with each shake of her head. "Oh Tony. Idiot Tony. You should know a trap when it has you by the balls. Now be a good boy and back off quietly so no one knows anything is wrong here or your sack will be rolling down your pant leg."

"Huh?" is his only response.

Using the car as leverage I lean to the right and look down. Sure enough she has some kind of dark knife, that looks sharp as hell, pressed against the inside of his thigh dangerously close to his favorite body part. Hell any guy's favorite body part.

It's bro code not to laugh if another guy's balls are in danger of being cut off, but there's no way I can't. "Now that's fucking funny as hell," I howl and look away because it's funny but also makes my balls jump into my stomach in fear of it happening to me.

Flakes' eyes cut to me as I belly laugh again, and again. Hell, every time I look it's funny as hell. Damn, when is the last time I'd laughed this hard? My cheeks fucking hurt.

"Damn bitch," Flakes snarls after his balls are safe a few feet away from her.

She simply smiles and starts picking at her red nails with the tip of the knife. "So, 0800 tomorrow, right?" A glance to me, Flakes, then me again.

"Correct, 0800 tomorrow. I'll come get you at 0730. I know you have IDs to get on base but before you get your bearings I can show you around. Wouldn't that've made this morning easier?"

With a smile she rolls her eyes at the jab. "Fine, but there are a few additional things we need to cover. Can you come by later? I can text you where I'm staying."

"What about me?" Flakes asks. She turns to face him looking annoyed as hell.

"Seriously, everything you've said tells me you want nothing to do with me and now you're pissed I asked Officer Wilcox over? Make up your damn mind Tony. Can you handle being around me or not?"

His eyes shift to me then back to her. "No. At least not right now. I need to go home anyway. The wife has got shit for me to do since we're stuck stateside." With a nod, directed only to me, he tucks his hands into his pockets and starts back in the direction of his truck.

We watch in silence until he's climbed into his truck and backing out.

"Well that could've gone worse," I say and reach for the knife in her hands to get a closer look. I've never seen one quite like it. She flips it to the other hand and holds it out of my reach.

"It could have gone better, he really needs someone to drop his ego a few levels. Even though I think there's more to it than that. And how about you ask first."

"What is it?"

Flipping it in her hand with the finesse of an expert, she slaps the hilt in my waiting palm. I inspect it. She explains, "It's made of carbon fiber. I had one made a while back that could fit in my pocket. I have a bigger one around my calf." Pressing against the car for support she raises her leg, lifting her pant leg for me to see. I nod and go back to checking out the one in my hand. "Most of the time I take one of the agency jets but when I do fly commercial I feel...vulnerable being unarmed. This little guy can go through a metal detector unnoticed."

I flick the serrated end back into the safety of the hilt and toss it back to her. She catches it in one hand. "So you like knives."

She gives a half shrug and sticks the knife back into her pocket, drawing my attention to her curvy thighs. "I like anything that will help keep me alive." That pulls my eyes back up to meet hers. "I'm not an idiot, I know I won't always be the biggest or strongest person in the room. But if I'm prepared I can win any fight. I just have to work twice as hard to do it."

"What do we need to talk about tonight?" Being alone with this woman is a bad idea. Just these few minutes and I'm already wanting more of her. Needing to know more about this woman who, within a couple hours, has become the most fascinating woman I've ever met.

Shouldering past she reaches for the driver side door. "You wanted to know who I am and I need to know more about you before I let you escort me around. Actually," she looks to her watch. "Why not jump in and we can go get it worked out now."

With a glimpse down at my own watch I hesitate. When I look back up those emerald green eyes search mine.

With a knowing smirk, that's sexy and scary as hell, she says, "Ah, there it is again. Fine, you do whatever you need to do. I'll text you my address, come over whenever. I'll be there."

I grasp the door frame after she slides into the driver seat so she can't shut it in my face having the final word. "How do you do that? What did you see… What are you?"

Her fingers drum along the steering wheel. With a sigh she rests her head against the head rest and closes her eyes. "It's why I'm here, Wilcox. It's why the agency sent me instead of any other agent who's equally qualified. I know Tony thinks I—"

"Flakes is a jackass. Don't listen to him."

The quiet laugh she gives makes me wonder if she believes me. "Well anyway, I'm where I am today in my career because I'm good at reading people. The best really. Listen, let's talk about it later. You go do whatever it is you need to do, which don't worry you'll tell me eventually everyone does, and then come over. But if it's past five you better come bearing food. Italian would be first choice, pizza second." I start to say that's funny coming from someone like her, all Italian, but she holds up a hand to stop me. "If you say anything about it being cliché for me to want Italian food Tony won't be the only one with a knife trained at their balls today."

Damn. "Yes ma'am." I step back and shut the door for her, popping the roof twice with my palm.

The engine roars to life and she cautiously pulls out of the parking space after looking both ways. Twice.

Two hours. It's only been two hours since I found her watching from her car and went to investigate. Now here I am standing alone in the same damn spot having no fucking clue what the hell just happened. She swooped in unexpectedly leaving me needing more. Needing to see her again, hell even if it's just to find out what she's going to say next.

My world is organized, strategic. She's chaos and her own perfect storm.

The vibrating in my pocket interrupts my unfocused stare from where she disappeared through the guard gate.

Flakes: Stay away from her. If not for your own sanity then do it for me.

Flakes: Trust me.

Great.

A line in the sand. This woman I already can't get out of my mind is off limits. Just great. Damn bro code.

CHAPTER SIX
LUCIA

The house is cozy. Way more cozy and warm than my apartment back in DC which is nice. Even if I'm not into the floral... everything. After leaving the base I grabbed lunch and brought it back here to start reviewing the file Jeremy had sent on Gabe.

Taking my burger, fries and file to the living room I settle on the floor, placing the file on top of my folded legs. I munch on a few fries and stare at the blank front. Anything and everything about Wilcox lies within. A deep breath and I flip it open to research my future coworker.

Sr. Officer Gabriel Paul Wilcox.

Age 36.

Attended Annapolis Naval Academy. Played four years of football, tight end, and national champion for sharp shooting all four years as well.

Degree in Electrical Engineering. While serving after school achieved his MBA.

I pause and take a drink. Condensation from the disposable cup dribbles onto the paper. Still I don't turn the page. The next page will be his family history, past experiences and life events. Things that aren't pure data. Reading someone's life like this is something I do before every mission. It never bothered me I wasn't giving the person I was meeting the opportunity to share the information with me first. Those missions I had to know everything, my life depended on it.

But with Officer Wilcox, it's different. I need to know this information to help identify his motives, what I can use as leverage, to lure him to the CIA but a small part of me wants him to tell me. To give him the opportunity to fill me in on his life instead of reading about each account from a third party.

How nice would it be for him to tell me something that I haven't already read? That way I'll genuinely be surprised and interested instead of acting.

The paper is nearly see-through but still I don't make a move. Not until my mind is made up. Where does all this leave me now? I need to turn the page to make recruiting him easier but I can't make myself do it. For the first time I don't want an advantage.

Frustrated, I grab the file in one hand and push off the floor with the other. Praying the saying "out of sight, out of mind" actually works, I stuff his file between the mattress and box spring.

It helps. A little.

Okay not much.

I need to clear my head. Refocus on the objective, why I'm here.

Glancing around the room the tennis shoes lined up along the back of the closet make me pause. Yes. A run. That's exactly what I need. And with the beach out the back door there's not a better place to do it.

A mile in I find my pace. The rhythmic pounding of my feet against the sand, the deep inhales and exhales help process everything that's happened since I landed this morning.

Tony's a dick, he was then and still is. How in the hell am I going to deal with his constant bitching and pouting the next few weeks? I'm all for fighting, but it could get old quick. At least the agency did me the favor in having Wilcox be the main point of contact and escort. I'm sure Tony would have escorted me right in front of a firing squad.

Wilcox seems nice, smoking hot too. Especially when he smiles or laughs showing those cute dimples. Whatever he's holding back isn't bad but it's wearing him down. It was fun going back and forth with him. There wasn't anger or annoyance in our verbal sparring simply direct exchange of words. Which is outside the norm. Most men agree with anything I say or want with the hope of getting lucky.

Which it's been a long time since *that* has happened. Which really sucks. With the back to back ops, and my personal rule against sleeping with colleagues, there hasn't been much free time to date or even find a one-night stand.

The vibration on my wrist signals I've hit the halfway point in my five-mile run.

Wilcox would be fun to play with while I'm here except for the fact he'll be my colleague soon—if I can accomplish the other part of my mission. Which means he's off limits. Plus, there's no doubt Tony has drawn a line in the sand and told him to stay away.

But...

I can't help my smile. Knowing it would enrage Tony is almost enough to damn my own rule and pounce on Wilcox.

No. Find the mole, recruit Wilcox, and get the promotion. This is my objective not screwing some hot water mammal. No way I'm going to screw up what I've worked for the past seventeen years. This is my shot at moving up into the advisory role, to be the one evaluating hundreds of operations, offering my insight, what I see, to help operations be shorter, more effective and save lives in the process.

This is my goal, not Wilcox.

Dad wanted, we wanted, me to make a difference in ways he never could. This guy, no matter how attractive those damn dimples are, isn't going to mess this up now.

There I have it. 100% positive Wilcox is off limits.

———

Steam billows out of the shower as I move the curtain aside. My hand pauses over the towel rack at the doorbell ringing through the house.

Crap. Didn't time this very well.

Ripping the towel off the bar I frantically wipe down the streams of water running down my legs and back. I wrap the towel around myself, tucking the end between my chest to keep it secure, and shuffle through the living room to end the now-impatient pounding. His hand is raised to keep knocking when I swing the door open. I incline my head to the living room for him to come in as I start back to the bedroom to finish toweling off and find clothes.

But he doesn't follow. Instead he stands there, hand still raised, staring.

"Are you coming in or what?" I ask with a quick glance down to make sure everything private stays that way. Okay, maybe answering the door in a towel, still dripping wet, isn't the best idea I've ever had. His blue eyes start at my bare toes and roam up my legs, pausing at my mostly exposed chest before locking with mine.

Crap. My heart thunders against my ribs and my stomach dips at his hooded stare.

Yep terrible idea answering the door like this if I have any chance of staying true to my earlier proclamation.

"Come in or don't," I stammer. Why does he have to be this attractive? And be nice. And have adorable dimples that make you smile when he does. "I'm going to get changed."

"Or you can stay like that," he mumbles as his gaze tracks the steady trickle of water, from my soaked hair, down my collarbone over the curve of my breast to where it disappears between them.

"Officer Wilcox?"

"I told you it's Gabe. Go change. I'll wait out here."

My throat suddenly dry, it takes a couple tries to swallow. "I trust you. You can come in."

"I don't." His voice is deep and firm.

Why did that sound sexy and seductive rather than creepy?

Turning on my heels I close the door, leaving it unlocked in case he changes his mind, and scamper back to the bedroom. Ten minutes later I'm dry and presentable in my black yoga pants and oversized eighties-style gray sweatshirt that hangs off the shoulder.

Before opening the door I whip my still-damp dark hair into a messy bun and wipe my sweaty palms. True to his word he's outside sitting on the top step, forearms resting on his thighs, staring at the street.

"Sorry about that," I say to get his attention. When he turns, a flick of disappointment flashes behind his eyes. "I went for a run when I got home from base and thought I had time, but I guess I didn't and... anyway, come in would you. I won't bite." Leaving the door wide open I turn for the kitchen.

This time he follows, a plastic bag in each hand. I eye the bags as I twist off the top of a bottle of water I snagged from the counter. When he sets them on the coffee table in the living room the Macaroni Grill label stamped on the side becomes visible.

"Looks like you went Italian. Thanks. I was starting to get hangry."

"Hangry?" he asks with an arched brow.

"You know when you get angry or pissy because you're hungry. That's hangry."

A small smile creeps up his lips as he shakes his head. "What do you want to talk about, Agent Rizzo? Why am I here?"

I hold out a hand as I walk to the living room, towards the food. "Nope. If I'm going to call you Gabe, you have to call me Lucia or Lu. All my friends call me Lu."

"So I'm a friend now?" he asks making that smile of his grow into something mischievous.

"No, right now you're just a guy pissing me off with his intense questioning before I've eaten." I side shuffle between him and the coffee table, attempting to not touch him on the way to the food, but my backside brushes against his stiff jeans. My empty stomach bottoms out suddenly not that hungry anymore.

I lift the lids of each container and lay them out in the order I want to eat them. After everything is out I look to him from my seat on the couch. "Did you not order anything?"

He moves to stand beside me, hands on his hips as he inspects the contents of what he ordered. "I did, is this not enough for both of us? I got you a salad, isn't that the shit chicks eat?"

Keeping my eyes on him I blindly reach for the container with the lasagna and pull it to my lap. "Not sure if you've noticed but I'm not the type of girl who can sustain on salad alone. I need food. Now." I grab a set of plasticware and use it to point out the food I now consider mine. "I'm taking this lasagna, and the salad and no less than three of those breadsticks in there and you're not going to say a damn word about it."

Those damn dimples make a reappearance as he says, "Yes ma'am."

As I dig into the food, he sits on the couch, on the opposite end as far away as possible, and watches.

"Don't stare, it's creepy."

He cracks his knuckles and looks around the house like he's searching for something to break the silence between us. "Want me to go over the details of the next few days while you eat?"

"Please," I say with a mouth full of food.

His head shakes as he pushes off the couch and starts pacing around the room. "Tomorrow when we introduce you to our combined teams I'll give them your cover story first then open it up to you. Expect resistance. No one wants a reporter sniffing around our lives. For the most part we keep our shit private. There isn't a lot about our lives we can share, or want to share, with a stranger."

I nod and move the fork in a circular pattern to keep him going.

"After that, Flakes—"

"Why Flakes?"

"Tony."

"Got that, but why Flakes?"

"Tony the Tiger. Frosted Flakes...Flakes."

"Clever."

"As I was saying. Flakes and I have scheduled a long beach run with weight training after. Come prepared. Now as the CO said today, Tony's platoon is grounded but mine isn't. We could be called up at any moment for a mission. If that happens, or when that happens, Flakes will be your main point of contact in my absence."

"Great," I grumble and set what's left of the breadstick I was eating on the table. "No telling what he'll have me do while you're gone."

Either the annoyance in my voice or what I just implied makes

Gabe stop his pacing and turn to me. "I know things are bad between you two, but if he crosses the line, if things get beyond what you can handle, or feel comfortable with, you come to me."

Protective but not overly done. Nicely played Gabe.

"Thanks," I say with a sigh. "I can handle whatever that idiot can toss out. But I have to admit it's nice knowing you're around."

"Why?"

I keep my focus on the napkin in my hands. The smeared remnants of garlic butter and salt suddenly captivating. "It's nice to know someone has my back. I know Tony doesn't, that leaves you as my only friend on base, heck San Diego even."

"Back to the friend word."

Smirking I dare a glance up. "Would you prefer I call you something else?"

He watches me for a second. Another. Watching and waiting. After what seems like thirty minutes he picks the pacing back up. "Fine, yes I do have your back. You're here to help us, which, let's get to what I asked earlier today. Who the hell are you?"

Wondered when he would get around to that.

Tucking my feet under my thighs I rest against the worn fabric of the couch. "I joined the CIA—"

"Before that."

"How far back do you want to go?"

"The beginning."

Unable to stop, my head tilts to the right as I try to read his angle for wanting more. I come up empty.

"I'm an army brat. My dad was enlisted and met my mom while he was stationed in Italy for a year or so. Go figure an Italian American meets a true Italian while in Italy and falls in love. Anyway they got married, moved back stateside and had me. Bounced around to different bases then ended up in Dallas finishing up high school. West Point, four years in the army, then recruited to the CIA. Not a lot to it I guess."

Man when I sum it up that way my life seems boring. Heck, it doesn't even sound like a life, more steps and checked off accomplishments.

Gabe sits on the chair opposite the couch and stares at his clasped hands hanging between his spread legs. "I don't get it. Doesn't the CIA usually go after the specialized guys like Rangers or SEALs? No offense, but why did they want you specifically?"

I don't stop my smile. I wanted the CIA, heck it's the only reason I went to West Point, but they had no idea and went to great lengths to get me to give up my command and sign their contract.

"Because I'm good at what I do, Officer Wilcox."

"And what is that exactly?"

"You already know, I read people. Earlier today you asked, "What are you?" Well the technical term for someone like me is called an empath. Other people say I'm a witch or wiccan or have some kind of mind reading power. But it's more that I can sense or feel what another person is feeling or even how a situation will play out just by being in the same room. I can read people, files and scenarios unlike anyone else. In the army I made my way into the strategy meetings, offering insight and helping guide their course of action. It got me noticed, but the CIA is where I wanted to be. It's still the only place I want to be."

Like he can feel my stare his blue eyes look up. "You like what you do?"

Now it's my turn to stand and pace. "Yes and no. What I'm doing now is exhausting but I have to pay my dues before the next step I guess. At least that's what they tell me and what I keep working toward. There's this promotion I want." I meet his eyes and quickly look away. "And it's so close but I have objectives to meet first. After that, I'll finally be in a place where I've been working half my life to be."

My feet pause in front of him. He looks up giving me a good look at what he's thinking, feeling. "Ask it, Gabe. I want you to trust me. Ask anything you want."

He clears his throat and leans back in the chair. "You mentioned your dad *was* an enlisted soldier."

"I did."

"When did he discharge out?"

"He didn't."

His features soften. "Was he deployed when it happened?"

"He was."

"I'm sorry, Lucia."

My name said in his deep, gravely voice sends a slight shiver up my spine.

"Me too. He was pretty great. I'm like him in the mind reading stuff. He would always talk about how things could be better if someone like us was at the top. It's why he wanted me at West Point. He's why I'm here today." I search his eyes and find something else lingering back there. "What else, I see other questions lurking in there."

With a laugh he leans forward. "If you can really read my thoughts, how in the hell do you feel comfortable in the same room with me after all the things I fantasized about when you opened that damn door in only a towel looking like every man's wet dream?"

I crinkle my nose in disgust. "Eww, that's not a compliment."

"Didn't mean for it to be. When you met Flakes that first time did you really know he was a piece of shit when it came to women? Is that why you told him to fuck off?"

"Kind of, it was a combination of things. Plus, I'd only known him twenty-four hours and was already bored with how much he talked about himself. He really has a crazy high opinion of himself. By the time he left I was annoyed and bored."

Gabe's loud, rumbling laugh urges me closer until I'm standing between his spread knees. "He acts like he's an egotistical son of a bitch and is a shitty husband, but he's a good SEAL. His men seem to trust him. I do. Now if I had a girl, no way in hell I'd trust him alone with her, but I trust my life with him that's for damn sure."

"How are you two even friends? You seem so...different."

He shrugs and looks around the room. "We just are. There're a lot of parts of him you'll never know that aren't that bad. I'm not telling you to give him a chance, hell if anything stay farther away from him, but don't think less of me because he's my friend."

"Okay," I sigh and sit on the coffee table in front of him, my knees touch the inside of his to make our legs fit in the small space. "He's a good SEAL and I won't judge you for being his friend. Got it. Now, want to see the toys I get to play with?"

Those blue eyes shoot to mine and widen a fraction. "Um, your what?"

Oh right.

"Not those kinds of toys you horn ball. Fun stuff from the agency I brought with me to help while I'm here. Trackers, tiny bugs even one of your guys couldn't find, and lots of other fun things."

The shock disappears with his sigh of relief. "We have all that stuff too, Lucia. We're high tech over here too, it's not just you and that damn stuffed-suit agency."

Yikes, maybe getting him interested in the agency is going to be harder than showing him some of the fun things we get to play with. I'll need to come up with a different tactic.

I'm staring at his thick thighs as I ask, "Do you like what you do?"

His answer comes without hesitation. "I'm a warrior. I love my country and I love serving this country. So yes, Lucia, I love what I do. I'll never leave this voluntarily. Either death or discharge will pull me from the brothers I fight alongside with."

Well hell.

"Gotcha. You like playing with guns in the water. Check."

Gabe leans forward putting us nose to nose. "I don't play with guns the way you play with those toys the agency makes you think you need, sweetheart."

Not knowing what to say I attempt to stand but he pulls me back to the table and closes the distance between us again. "Flakes told me to stay away from you."

I tuck my hands under my thighs to keep from reaching out and pulling his face to mine. "I know," I whisper.

"How did you…right, your witch senses."

"So now you're calling me a witch?" I arch a brow making him

COVERT AFFAIR | 61

smile. "Been called worse actually. In fact, I think your buddy Tony did earlier."

That amusement fades as he searches my face, looking for...not sure what. "He says you're a drug. That I should stay away for my sake, not his."

I swallow against a dry throat. When did it get so hot in here? He's pulling me to him without lifting a hand. Everything around us, the reason I'm here and my resolution to not act on my attraction to him, fades to a fog in the back of my mind.

"And, Officer Wilcox, what do you think?" My raspy voice is one I don't recognize.

His Adam's apple bobs. "I think you're trouble but the kind of trouble I've been looking for. Been waiting for. I think you're one hell of a woman who has no idea what she's getting into with this operation, surrounded by men, married and single, who will kill their brother to have a shot at you. I think if I'm going to be true to my friend I need to leave now because I can't get the image of you in that damn towel out of my fucking mind."

"That's a lot of thinking," I breathe.

Both hands clutch my knees. "This isn't a fucking game, Lucia."

"I don't think this is a fucking game, Gabe. I have my objectives to accomplish and screwing you or one of the other guys isn't one of them. You don't have to worry about me."

That tight grip loosens allowing his hands to slowly inch up my thighs, leaving a trail of heat in their path. Heart hammering against my chest and in my ears, I silently beg him to keep going and also to walk away while we both still can.

"But I can't," he says staring at his hands on my thighs. His thumbs begin tracing imaginary circles, brushing around and around against my inner thigh.

"You can't what?" I whisper. Why is it so hard to breathe?

"Leave. Make me leave, Lucia. Tell me to get the hell out of here before I lay you flat against that coffee table and act out every fucking detail that's running through my mind. What I've been thinking since your fine ass walked into CO's office today."

"But I can't," I choke out in a hoarse voice that gives away how his words affect me. This man, if I'm the drug, he's the dealer knowing exactly what I need. A small voice in the back of my mind reminds me of why we shouldn't happen. "This can't happen, Gabe. Too many things are on the line for us to give in. We can't and won't happen."

His hands slide back down my thighs and drop from my knee. "The next few weeks are going to be interesting, Lucia. Let's hope at least one of us is thinking straight when we're together. If we're both feeling the way I am right now at the same time, we're in deep shit."

CHAPTER SEVEN
GABE

The cool hood of the Jeep feels damn amazing pressed against my sweaty palms. What the hell was that all about? "You're the kind of trouble I've been looking for? What the hell does that even mean, fuck stick?" I grumble. I'm a damn moron. An idiot, saying shit like that even if it is the damn truth. The most truthful thing I've said to a woman ever maybe.

Damn those sexy ass curves. Damn her perfect fucking tits. Damn her funny as hell personality.

This is bad. There's no way I can be around her if Flakes really wants me to stay away from her. Maybe someone else can do the shadowing, escort her around base. Like that would happen. My hands ball into fists just thinking of someone else getting to spend time with her. Fuck no. She's my responsibility.

Yeah, responsibility, I'll go with that. It has nothing to do with wanting to be around her more.

When the boys see her tomorrow and think she's some fair game civilian piece of ass, the comments will be obnoxious. I need to get my shit under control now so I don't punch every damn one of them for saying something about her.

I turn, placing my still-hot back to the Jeep and stare at her house.

What if I walked back in there? Maybe she will have changed her mind. Will she be waiting for me or will she push me away again? Hell, wish I knew why her pushing me away, taking the damn high road, made her hotter—not sure how that's even possible.

The living room light flicks off, sending a small wave of disappointment to wash over me. Good. I should go home. There's no need to get rejected twice in one night.

As I climb into the Jeep I dig the phone out of my pocket and press Mom's cell number. She picks up on the second ring with a whispered hello.

"Hey mom. Just wanted to check in and see if you need anything tonight. I'm on my way home but can swing by if you need me."

Even her sigh sounds exhausted. I lean against the headrest and close my eyes. "No honey, we're good here. It was a long day but it's good to hear your voice."

"How's Dad?"

Her pause has me rubbing the bridge of my nose with my thumb and forefinger.

"He's okay, Gabriel. Today wasn't as bad a day as you saw when you stopped by, just a long day. For a couple hours tonight it was like nothing was wrong. It was like I had him back. Then it was ripped away, and again I was stuck talking to a man who had no idea who I was." The sniffle on the other end of the phone rips at my heart.

I grip the steering wheel as hard as I can, knuckles going white, trying to control the sweeping emotions her crying does to me. "Mom, it's getting worse. Yes, you had a couple hours but there are twenty-four in a day. Can you really keep doing this for just a couple—"

"Gabriel Wilcox, we're not getting into this again. He's my husband and I'll take care of him. No one else. Do you hear me? I'm done fighting with you about this."

I bang my head against the headrest. I know better than to start this fight over the phone. "Yes ma'am. So you're good? I don't need to stop by."

"We're good honey. Thank you for coming by today. You know I always love seeing your sweet face. Good night, Gabriel."

Tossing the phone to the passenger seat, I stare at it for a minute before picking it up again.

Me: Hey you still awake?
   Lucia: Depends.
   Me: On?
   Lucia: Are you still parked out front?

Damn. I can't help but smile at the phone. Of course she knows I'm still out here.

Me: Maybe.
   Lucia: That's a yes. So my answer is no, I'm not still awake, I'm asleep.
   Me: What the hell? I just want to talk.
   Lucia: You think I'm an idiot?
   Me: Just want to hang out.
   Lucia: Without clothes on is what you're leaving out.
   Me: Always optional.
   Lucia: Go home, Gabe. We both know this can't happen. Stop making it harder than it already is.
   Me: Oh it's hard all right.
   Lucia: OMG seriously. Go. This can't happen.
   Me: We would be fools to think it won't.
   Lucia: And fools we are not. Goodnight, Gabe. See you in the morning.

For the second time I toss the phone into the passenger seat but this time it stays there. We are fools. Two fools playing with a spark in the middle of a damn dry field. It's not a matter of *if* everything will ignite around us but *when* it will and consume us whole.

———

"Ready?" I ask over my shoulder, pausing before opening the door, officially tossing her into the lion's den. I have to hand it to her, she doesn't look as nervous as she should be. Being in a room with over twenty highly trained men doesn't seem to phase her. Which has to be the sexiest damn thing ever.

This morning she was on time, waiting on her damn porch like I was late, and was talkative the entire way here. It was difficult keeping my eyes on the road instead of the way her skirt seemed to creep up her thigh with each turn. Thankfully she didn't notice I took the longest way here, with the most possible curves to speed around. Her knuckles were white the entire drive but she didn't log a single complaint. Going fast is my style, plus taking the long way meant we had to make up time somehow.

Those bright green eyes could burn when I turn from the door, looking for a response. "Don't doubt me, Officer Wilcox. I'm always ready."

"Settle down sweetheart—"

"I'm not your sweetheart, sweetheart."

"You don't have to be nervous, Gracie Lu."

"I'm not nervous," she says, crossing her arms over her chest.

"Right." I roll my eyes to make sure she knows there's no way in hell I'm believing that shit. I might not be able to read minds but I noticed the shift in her when we walked on base. I'm no idiot. "I just wanted to make sure you're all set with the cover story. Once we're in that room there is no turning back."

"I know this," she practically hisses. "Open the damn door, I don't like being late."

"Whatever you say, Gracie Lu." I give an exaggerated wink and push the door open.

The disruptive chatter amongst the men stops dead the moment she rounds the corner. Every set of eyes are on her, taking long looks at the parts of her I admire myself. Unintentionally my pace slows to keep her close. After a minute those 'I want to fuck you' looks fade and shift to suspicion. Narrowed eyes bounce from her to me to Flakes trying to figure out what the hell is going on.

Time to start this charade.

"Listen up, boys. This is Gracie Lu Freebush. She's a reporter." And just like that the temperature in the room drops several degrees. "And is writing a piece on the SEALs. She will be around the next few weeks observing our drills and training. In addition she will conduct interviews to get what she needs for the article." Every man in the room groans. "This is a direct order from CO Williams. We will treat her with respect and give her the information she needs."

My attention swings to Lucia, but she doesn't notice. No, she's focused on the group. Those green eyes bounce from one man to another, sizing them up. I clear my throat and gesture toward the group.

"Thank you, Officer Wilcox. I want you all to know I'm not here to drag the SEAL's name through the mud or make you look bad. I'm here for the truth. I want my readers to know what you have to go through to become a SEAL, what your life is like and how difficult it is. With the Hollywoodizing of SEAL Team Six, everyone is fascinated with you but they have no idea what being a SEAL really means. I intend to fix that."

She turns back to me but Flakes speaks up before I can.

"Any questions?"

Seriously, Flakes? Questions? Don't give them the opportunity to say something that will get their asses thrown in the damn brig.

Beasley, from Flakes' team, raises his hand. Of course he fucking does. This will be interesting. Really, I figured it would take at least an hour for the first inappropriate comment, but apparently Beasley is on the accelerated plan.

He stands and faces Lucia, his eyes giving her a lazy once-over before speaking. "Is it Miss or Mrs. Freebush?"

An animalistic growl pushes past my clenched teeth. "Watch it, Beasley." He ignores my warning, keeping his attention on Lucia.

"It's Miss Freebush, and you are?" she asks, unphased by his question. In fact she looks a little bored.

"Petty Officer Barett Beasley, ma'am. Thank you for clearing that up for me. Now if you need help getting around the base or want a private showing of—"

"Knock it off Beasley, or you'll end up in the brig," Flakes yells. "No way in hell did you forget or just not fucking hear Officer Wilcox when he said we treat her with respect. Not like some damn dog in heat."

The entire room attempts to hold back a laugh. Most do while others try to cover with a cough. Lucia's eyes cut to Flakes with the promise of death.

"Thank you for the offer, petty officer, but I'm all set with escorts. Any other questions about the article?" Her tone lays emphasis on the final word.

He slouches in his chair, clearly pissed he'd been turned down and called out by his Sr. Officer. No one else raises their hand. Hell, no one even looks at her.

"Well boys, it's time for a beach run. Officer Hackenbreg and my platoon will be training together the next few weeks and I don't want to hear any shit about it. And since Beasley decided to show Miss Freebush the less civilized side of the SEALs, we'll tack on a few extra miles to the run we had planned."

Like I expected and hoped, all stares shift to Beasley. Good. Dumb, loudmouth piece of shit.

The door slams shut behind the last man. I move between Lucia and Flakes for preventive measures. No way she'll let the comment from earlier slide. But when I turn toward her, she's leaning against the wall, drumming her red nails.

"I'll meet you at the beach," Flakes grumbles as he shoulders past.

Silence settles in the room, making me shift in my stance.

"Not bad for a first day, I expected more push back. Why do you think they didn't?" she asks.

COVERT AFFAIR | 69

I slouch into an empty chair. "Oh, I'll hear about it later, that's for damn sure. My guys are going to be pissed at me for not fucking getting our team out of it all. This was so unexpected I don't think they knew what to think."

"Except Beasley."

"That dumb fuck," I respond as I stretch out my legs and arms. "Always looking for some chick to stick his dic—" I clear my throat and shift in the seat. "Sorry."

She rolls her eyes and pushes off the wall, stopping between my outstretched legs. "West Point. Army. Agency run by men who have a stock pile of rulers handy to constantly measure whose dick is the biggest. I'm not easily offended, Gabe."

How can I not smile at that? "Right, I forget you're not a normal woman."

"I like to think of myself as abnormally amazing at some things, and being able to filter out the bullshit of weak-minded men is one of them. He and Tony can go have a bitch session about me and I won't give a rat's ass."

"Are you going to make Flakes pay for what he said earlier, the dog in heat thing?"

Her sinister smile says everything.

Even though I'll catch hell for suggesting this, I have to. "I don't think you should go on the run with us."

Just like I expected, both hands go to her hips and those eyes narrow. "And why the hell not, sweetheart?"

I grin, hoping my damn dimples will ease her anger, and stand. Her head tips back slightly to hold her angry stare. "Because I have a feeling you'll be able to keep up with us and I don't know a single civilian man or woman who would be able to do that. If you run, decked out in boots and fatigues, and don't die after the first mile they'll know something's up."

She looks across the empty room. "So my options are not going or complaining the entire time and passing out on the beach so one of your sexy water mammal buddies has to give me mouth-to-mouth."

The image of someone else touching her doesn't sit well. I dare a step closer and wrap a hand behind her neck, entangling it in her dark hair. "If anyone is giving you mouth-to-mouth, sweetheart, it will be me."

Her eyes fucking sparkle, sending my pulse racing as she drags her tongue along her lower lip. Hell, this woman has to be the daughter of a devil and a saint.

"So passing out on the beach it is," she purrs.

My hand moves forward to cup her jaw. I pull at her wet lower lip with my thumb until it's caught between her teeth. When she clamps down, a bolt of heat shoots straight to my cock.

Stomping footsteps pound in the hall. Both of our eyes cut to the door at the same time, hearing the same thing. It takes every ounce of control to take a step back, then another. With each step I keep my eyes locked with hers. We're a safe distance away when the door flies open.

"What the hell is taking you so damn long, G?" The second Flakes takes in the room, what's clearly going on between us, flush spreads up his neck to his cheeks. "What the fuck is going on?"

Lucia shrugs and starts toward the door. "Your friend here thinks it's a bad call for me to work out with you boys. Says they will see right through the civilian act. So I'm sitting this one out. Besides, those files I requested yesterday should be here by now. I'll use the now free time to start my initial research."

"Everyone's?" Flakes asks, a hint of apprehension in his tone.

Lucia steps toward him hearing the same. Of course she did. Her and her witch shit. "Everyone's?" she asks.

"All the files, even mine and Gabe's here?"

Her eyes stay locked on Flakes. Time creeps by, each second dragging longer than the last, as she does whatever mind reading shit she needs to do. "Why do you care, Tony? What's in your file you're worried I'll find out?"

Breaking from her spell, he takes a step back, and another until he's a safe distance away and glances to me. "Nothing. It's fine. Whatever. You go do whatever shit you need to do and we'll meet up later."

The fire in her eyes from earlier is gone when she looks to me for confirmation. "Sounds good, but I need your Jeep since we rode together and all."

I pull the keys from my pocket and hold them in my palm a moment, deliberating, before tossing them across the room. "Be careful with her. I've never—"

"You're an idiot." Those are her last words before she walks out of the room.

Flakes' anger still radiates, the quiet strangely uncomfortable between us. "What the hell was that, man? I told you to stay away from her and I walk in to you and her still eye fucking. With me in the damn room. Damn it, G, what a friend you are."

Whoa. I lean casually against the wall keeping my rising annoyance at his shit hidden. "What do you fucking expect? She's sexy as hell and has this pull to her. How do you expect me to stay away from that? You two were over a decade ago, just let it go." The door slams against the wall. I march down the hall, without a glance back, towards the beach where my men are waiting.

I don't get halfway before he's in front of me, hand on my chest. "Don't fucking do it, man. I told you to stay away from her for reasons other than our history. She'll get under your skin and will never leave. I'm asking this for you, stay away from her. She's bad news for you and for me."

My head drops forward. I massage the bridge of my nose. He's right. What a friend I am. I can't even do what he asked less than twenty-four hours ago. I'm stronger than this. I'm stronger than sexy Lucia. Stronger than her shocking, who knows what's coming next personality. Stronger than those sexy thighs.

But, fuck me, even if I can keep my hands off her there's no way in hell I'll be able to keep her out of my thoughts.

The laughs and jarring can be heard before we see them. No doubt everything being said is about the sexy Italian American they were just introduced to.

"What took you so fucking long, Wilcox?" One of my men says as I approach the group. "Oh, I know that damn reporter was on her knees the second we were out the door for the infamous Wilcox. I saw it in her fucking eyes."

"Do we all get a ride?" says another.

"Shut the fuck up, Trigger, that woman would break you," retorts another.

"All of you shut the fuck up," I say in a tone that makes them do just that.

All except fucking Beasley.

"Watch out boys, looks like Wilcox here has a crush on the sexy as sin reporter."

Flakes strides past, sand kicking in his wake, stopping directly in Beasley's face. "Watch your mouth, you fuck stick. We're already running an extra ten miles because of your earlier lip. Don't make it ten more."

Beasley doesn't back down. His eyes flick to me then back to Flakes. A smirk forms. "Oh hell you both have a thing for her. This will be entertaining."

"Let's go," I order and start jogging, my men falling into line beside me.

As we start the now twenty-mile run, Beasley's comment runs on a loop. He has no idea how right he is. It might be entertaining to them but could be what destroys a friendship and me in the process.

CHAPTER EIGHT
LUCIA

"He stepped out for a bit," says the CO's admin from behind his small wooden desk. "Can I help you with something Miss. Freebush?" A knowing smirk pulls at the corners of his lips.

Crap, what's his name again? I purse my lips in an attempt to hold back the bitchy comments I want to shoot his way. Gabe suggesting I shouldn't go on the beach run was accurate in assessment but pissed me off just the same. Instead of taking my frustrations out on this innocent guy, I force a tight smile.

"I requested some files yesterday and was hoping they were here. Guess I'll check back this afternoon when he's in." Holding that fake smile, I turn.

"Oh those," he says making me stop my retreat and turn back to him. The way he smiles indicates he knows I'm annoyed. "They came earlier this morning. Since there were several heavy boxes I had them delivered to your house."

"Wow, thank you." It's a kind gesture but an uneasy sensation washes over me, which typically indicates something's off. "How did you get my address?"

That smile widens. A shiver has my shoulders shaking. "CO Williams. Don't worry, it's safe with me."

Pretty sure it's not. Uncomfortable with the idea of him knowing where I'm staying, I force another fake smile and nod. I look down the hall towards the exit.

"Actually, I'm glad you stopped by." Sighing, I drag my attention back to him. Again. The hopeful gleam in his eye has me holding back an eye roll. I know what's coming. "I was wondering if you'd like to go out to dinner one night."

He might be off-putting, but I'm never cruel unless I need to be, so I attempt to let him down easy. "Thank you, but I don't like to mix personal and business. Takes my focus off my work. Under different circumstances I would've loved to. Also, thank you for having the boxes delivered to my place, it was very thoughtful of you."

With a disappointed nod he looks down at the papers on his desk, giving me an opportunity to start my retreat. Again.

"Oh, I almost forgot." Damn, I was so close. I turn and take the few steps back to his desk. "Something was sent for you. Doesn't have a return label or anything. Not sure why it was sent here." Reaching under his desk he pulls up a small, brown box. Clammy fingers graze mine and linger as he hands it over.

"Thanks, bye."

Package in hand, I hurry down the hall without being too obvious I'm trying to get away in case he thinks of something else to discuss. Something about him is...different. Whatever it is triggers every caution bell even though he's the least intimidating man I've met since arriving in San Diego. Maybe his file will be among the ones he delivered today or, if not, maybe Gabe can fill me in on the guy.

———

Melted chocolate from my Snickers sticks to my fingers and lips as I contemplate my next move. Opening the boxes would be the obvious first step to diving into these men's lives but procrastinating sounds way better. I snag my phone off the counter and perch on a bar stool.

. . .

Me: Hey you.

Brooke: Hey back. How's San Diego and your rejected SEAL?

Me: San Diego is amazing. Tony is being a prick but didn't expect anything less. It's his nature, can't fault him for that.

Brooke: What aren't you telling me? Spill it lady.

Me: So there's this other guy….

Brooke: I knew it! Please say another SEAL.

Me: Yep and Tony's BFF.

Brooke: Screw Tony. Tell me about his BFF.

Me: Taller than me by a few inches. Broad shoulders. Fit.

Brooke: I need more than that, Lu.

Me: This square jaw and defined cheekbones that make him handsome but pretty. It's strange. Oh blue eyes that keep me locked in a trance. Oh and two faint dimples when he smiles.

Me: Which seems to be a lot around me which you know I love.

Brooke: Now we're getting somewhere. How about his…other qualities?

Me: I just met the guy. No idea how big his…other qualities…are. You really think I've already slept with him?"

Brooke: No, but one can hope. You need to get laid. It's been a while.

Me: Yeah I know.

Me: But as attractive and funny as he is…it can't happen.

Brooke: Why the hell not? He sounds scrumptious.

Me: He's part of my op.

Brooke: So I screwed. Married. And got preggers with a guy who was once part of an op.

Me: You're just saying that because it worked out for you. You screwed, married and got preggers with the best guy ever. If I do it, it will end up bad and you know it.

Brooke: I did marry the best guy ever.

Me: Don't rub it in.

Brooke: Like marriage is what you're even looking for. You just need to get laid and it doesn't have to end bad, Lu.

Me: It always seems to with me.

. . .

I drum my fingers along the bar and shove the last of the Snickers into my mouth.

Me: It's more complicated than that. The agency wants me to recruit this guy over to the CIA. What if in the end he thinks I only slept with him to recruit him?

Brooke: Would you be? Doesn't sound like it to me.

Me: I wouldn't. I would never do that. But what if...

Brooke: I just smacked my phone on my head several times because of you and your damn "what ifs." Stop it and just live, Lu. If it ends badly it ends badly. So the fuck what? You need to live even if that means things have to get messy. Messy is good. Especially during sex.

Me: Boss man promised me the promotion if I bring him over.

Brooke: The definition of insanity is doing the same thing over and over again expecting different results.

Brooke: They are using you Lu. I know it. You know it. And they know it. It's never going to be enough for them. Listen, just have fun while you're there. Do what you need to do but for once don't think about your career or the CIA. Think about you.

Think about me.

Just have fun.

That would be a new concept.

Damn, when was the last time I had fun? Ever since Dad died I've been nonstop trying to get where we wanted me to be. Maybe Brooke is right, but her saying it and me acting on it are two different things. Holding back has become a not-so-unique kind of torture. To keep me unhappy until I "make it" in my career.

Who says I can't have fun, identify the mole, and recruit Gabe?

Whatever, enough deep thoughts for one afternoon. Grabbing my phone and earbuds off the counter, I sit on worn carpet, put some Faith Hill on repeat, and open the first box.

———

I'm mouthing the words along to the song blaring in my ears when the hairs on my arms stand at attention. Keeping my head down like I'm still studying the file in my lap, I casually turn the music off and wait. Every muscle twitches, urging me to look over my shoulder but I keep my head down. If someone is there I don't want to tip them off that I'm aware of their presence until I'm ready. Stretching my arms above my head then down my leg, I reach under my yoga pants for the knife secured around my calf. The moment my hand secures around the hilt my head snaps back. The grip around my ponytail doesn't release.

With my free hand, I grab the person's arm and pull down with my weight behind it. The well-muscled man stumbles forward slightly. I move to the left, keeping my grip on the arm, and swing my right shin behind the man's knees. He falls hard onto all fours. Not wasting time, I slam my knees on to his back, making the intruder grunt from my weight and knees digging into his spine.

Half a second.

I have the man down for half a second before he pushes off the floor. As if I weigh nothing, I'm flung off his back. The edge of the chair breaks my fall, and all breath whooshes from my lungs. Adrenaline pumps, shoving me into self-protect mode. I look up, ready to keep fighting, only to find confused blue eyes staring back.

"What the fuck was that about, Lucia?" he demands, breathing as hard as I am.

No way this can end with him having the upper hand. The carpet burns my palms when I lunge for him. Like I predict, he rolls, shoving my spine to the floor. I fight to keep my tight grip on his shoulder.

"Do you concede to defeat?" I whisper into his ear as I angle the tip of the knife against the soft skin of his neck.

"Fuck no," he grunts.

No doubt he knows I wouldn't actually hurt him. Tony maybe. But not Gabe.

The heat pours from his palm in his tight grip on my wrist. Once. Twice he slams my wrist against the edge of the couch. The knife sails across the room.

With my right hand still in his tight grasp he shifts, putting his full weight to keep me from squirming. My left fist swings, but he catches it with ease and holds it with the other still in his grasp.

"Checkmate, sweetheart."

I buck my hips and my knees slam against his back, trying to push him off but he doesn't move a millimeter. I stop and lie panting on the floor, glaring up at him.

He pulls his hands to hold his in surrender. "I didn't start this fight, sweetheart, so don't glare at me." His blue eyes fix on my heaving chest. "Why did you start this fight?"

"You snuck up on me, asshole. And who pulls someone's pony tail, are we on the playground or something?"

The way his body vibrates and shifts against me as he laughs sends waves of heat to my belly and lower. The room grows warm. My cheeks burn and my heavy breathing shifts to more of a pant.

It must be obvious. My emotional shift. Gabe peels himself off my hips and stands. Leaning back, onto my elbows, I watch as he backs away until his back hits the wall.

"I knocked and the door wasn't locked," he says. "Guessing you didn't hear me."

Sitting up all the way, I rub my wrist. Damn, that kind of hurt. "The music was up too loud I guess, and I was focused." I survey the ransacked room. "Great, now I have to get all these folders organized. Thanks for that."

"You're the one who attacked me," Gabe says defensively. His attention shifts to the door. "We're not done talking about this," he says in a low voice as Tony walks through the door.

With his hands on his hips Tony examines the disheveled room. "How in the hell do you get any work done like this? It looks like a damn tornado went through here." He rolls his eyes and looks to

Gabe, never fully acknowledging my presence. "Seriously, how in the hell can they say she's the best?"

"Screw off, Tony," I seethe. Pushing off the floor, I fall onto the couch, dangling my feet over the arm rest. "You're just pissed you won't be able to find your file in this mess. So, boys. How did the rest of the day go? Any suspicions of me?"

Gabe shakes his head. There's something new behind his eyes, almost like apprehension, but he won't hold my gaze long enough to get a good read.

Strange.

"Suspicions, no. But every guy wants a go at you."

My eyes shift from Gabe to Tony. "Ah, well I'll make sure they know I don't mix business with pleasure." My gaze flicks back to Gabe to make sure he knows this part is for him. "Ever." He responds with an arched brow. "And what are *you* doing here, Tony?"

He huffs, almost like I hurt his feelings with such a question. "Someone had to bring G back to his Jeep. With that kind of bitchy welcome we're out of here. Come on G, let's go to the bar. Pool drills start at 0500. Be there early, Lucia."

His pounding boot steps down the wooden porch steps emphasize his tantrum.

"Have fun at the bar," I say and swing my feet back over the arm rest to pick up the mess of papers. "I can drive myself in the morning. I think it would be best."

"What was all that about, Lucia?" Large, rough hands lay on top of mine, stilling them. "Tell me."

"You wouldn't understand."

"Try me, I might."

As I glance up through my dark lashes, I find genuine concern lurking behind his eyes.

Our touching hands, his on top of mine caressing with light brush strokes of his thumb, are where I keep my gaze as I say, "Remember what I said earlier today. West Point, Army, CIA...well, let's just say you wouldn't understand because you're a guy in a guy's world here in the military. I've always been smarter, more intuitive than most of the men I'm surrounded by and it doesn't sit well with them. Weak men are scared of strong women and weak men always feel like they have more to prove."

His grip tightens.

"No one ever hurt me," I say fast to keep his thoughts from the worst. "But they would always try to one up me, catch me by surprise. Really do everything they could to make me feel weaker than them. So I guess you can say it's instinct now to immediately flip the scenario so I can be on offense. Sorry if I scared you." I nudge his shoulder with mine trying to lighten the mood. "Just don't sneak up on me again, okay."

"Copy. Or I'll send Flakes in first so he takes the brunt of it."

My fake laugh does little to ease the tension weighing in the room.

"Now the other thing."

The edge of the couch pushes into my back as I lean back to look at him, brows furrowed, not understanding. The other thing? What other thing?

"You said you don't ever mix business with pleasure. Is that why you said we can't happen?"

I give an apprehensive nod.

"That's a dumb fucking rule."

This time my laugh is genuine. "I'm starting to agree with you."

A mischievous smile pulls at his lips, making both of those damn dimples appear. "Ah, so you just need a little convincing to see how stupid your rule is. Copy that. Well Agent Rizzo, consider the challenge accepted."

I smirk and pull invisible lint off my black pants. "I don't recall challenging you to anything, Officer Wilcox."

"Sure you did. I'll pick you up at 0430."

He's almost to the door when the outrageous notion of seeing if he's even worth considering breaking my rule for forms. I call out for him to wait before he gets too far. Hands in his back pockets, he turns from the door.

My eyes on the ceiling, I mutter a quick prayer that this works because holy crap he's hot, and if he can hold me…"There's one thing

I need to know first." His brows raise, waiting for a question. But my question doesn't come in the form of words. Instead I race across the room and jump, wrapping my arms around his neck and legs around his waist.

A slight stumble from the surprise attack but he recovers quickly, regaining his balance. Both hands grip my backside, tighter than necessary, to hold me to him.

"You passed the test." Nose to nose. Chest to chest. Eye to eye. My heart pounds against my chest to his. "I'm glad."

I'm rewarded with a wide smile back. "No idea what's going on but I'm glad I passed too."

"I'm not small."

"Excuse me? I'm not following this conversation."

"I'm not a small woman and I like to be…what's the word?" Behind his head I snap my fingers as I search for the appropriate word.

"Carried?"

"No."

"Held?"

"Nope, more than that. Dang it's on the tip of my tongue."

"Manhandled?"

"Yes," I exclaim. "Exactly. Manhandled."

The door slams shut and my back presses against the wood and glass panes. The pressure and tilt of his hips against mine is his way of showing, letting me feel, how much he's enjoying me in his arms. I try to choke back the moan. I really do. But fail. In response, he flexes again, keeping the hardness of him pressed exactly where I need it.

"Well that makes us a perfect fucking pair, sweetheart. I don't like easy so this should work out just fine."

A truck horn blares from the street.

"You should go," I breathe and close my eyes, my head thudding against the glass.

Goosebumps spread along the skin on my neck in the wake of his lips. "But I don't want to. Convincing you we should happen is way more fun."

"What about Tony? He told you to stay away." I squeeze my legs tighter, digging my heels into his ass, forcing more pressure to the apex of my thighs.

Cool air replaces where his lips just were making me whimper. "Flakes is being a prick about this whole thing. Don't you worry about him. I'll handle it."

"But you two are friends."

Again a truck horn blares. And again.

Reluctantly, I'm lowered to the ground but he keeps me pulled close. "Tomorrow, Lucia. Tomorrow we can start our fun."

Soft lips press against my forehead and linger. My eyes close just to fling back open at the damn horn blaring again. With a frustrated groan, he yanks the door open and walks out without a glance back.

Unable to move, I slide down the wall until my bottom hits the floor and tuck my knees to my chest, hugging my shins. What have I done challenging a damn SEAL to win me over? No. Not win me over. Win me to bed. If we both understand it's only about sex, nothing more, it won't end terribly.

Right?

CHAPTER NINE
GABE

I'm going to kill him.

This is getting fucking ridiculous.

What the hell is his damn problem? Is he this bent out of shape for some girl who didn't call him back over a decade ago? There has to be more to it, something he's not telling me. Or her for that matter. It's almost as if he's using their past as a crutch to not get close to her, to not be in a room with her for too long. Does he know she can read people like she does?

But if he does, what does Flakes have to hide from her? Too many questions, and I'm determined to get them answered tonight. This juvenile shit ends tonight because Lucia and I start tomorrow.

The bar we stop at is trendier than our bar near base. Which I'm sure Flakes chose to have a new selection of random women to flirt with. We weave through the crowd to the bar where Flakes snags a high top towards the back.

The waitress tries to flirt with him while jotting down our drink orders, I order a beer and he does the same with a side shot of Crown Royal, but hell if he's still too busy pouting to notice. He catches my disapproval, leans back in his chair, and crosses his arms.

"We're grounded, no reason not to go in hungover tomorrow. One of the perks I guess. The only fucking perk."

"I wonder what's in those files," I muse as the waitress drops off our drinks.

Flakes downs his shot, slamming the glass on the small wooden table between us, and chases it with half of his beer. "Probably nothing. This whole thing might be a damn ghost mission. Who knows, the CIA might be trying to gather intel on us and came up with this mole theory as their cover. Stupid fucking agency. If they go after someone like her instead of someone like us, fuck them."

Nodding, I take a sip from the cold bottle. He needs this time to vent. If he gets all this shit off his chest, maybe he'll calm the hell down about her being here.

"Agent fucking Rizzo. Lucia Rizzo. Why her? Anyone but her. I can barely be in the same damn room with her man."

"I've noticed."

"Now she's the one snooping around my damn platoon. Digging up shit that doesn't need to be brought up. Supposedly saving my ass. What fucking karma."

The edge of the table presses into my forearms as I lean forward. "Give it up."

He clenches his jaw with a firm shake of his head.

"What else happened? There has to be more to all this. Why are you so fucking hung up on her?"

With a dismissive shrug he finishes off his beer and signals the waitress for another round. "It's nothing. Old shit. Let's just hope she leaves before either one of us have time to fall for her shit."

"About that," I say, rolling the bottle between my hands. "I'm not going to back down. She wants me and I want her. Simple as that."

"I know," he says with a disappointed sigh to the ceiling . "You couldn't take your eyes off her damn fine ass the first time we met her. It was a false hope, I guess, that you wouldn't end up like me."

"Bitter."

He scans the sidewalk outside the window we're beside. "She's going to make you fall for her then leave. You know that, right? You mean nothing to her, no one does. All she cares about is herself. I knew it the first time and being around her now confirms it."

The cold beer I chug does little to calm my increasing frustration with this same shit. "Nah man, I'm not going to let it get that far. Just fun. She's hot as hell and damn, that woman has a mouth on her. Not knowing what she's going to say or do next is damn fun."

"Shit man," he groans and bangs his head against the table. "You're already that far. Don't you see that? She's already got you by the balls and you're so fucking whipped you don't see it. Have you fucked her yet?"

"No."

"Man, you're in trouble. You haven't even screwed her yet and you're this wrapped up in her." His harsh, condescending laugh sends my blood boiling. "You mean nothing to her, I can promise you that."

This round it's me who signals for the waitress. Fuck, what if he's right. She could be working that mental shit and making me fall for her. But why? Other than her comment of wanting a friend here, someone who has her back. Getting me to fall for her would ensure that.

"Let's see, shall we?" he says with a smile as he digs around his front pocket.

"What are you doing," I ask, my forehead furrowed at the phone in his hand.

"Being a good damn friend. Someone around here has to be."

"Nice subtle kick to the nuts, thanks man."

His thumbs fly across the screen, taking a few drinks between responses. After a few minutes he clicks it off and slides the phone into his pocket. His face is stone when he finally looks up.

"What did you do, you idiot?" Whatever he's done has to do with Lucia, but what?

"You'll see," he says and pushes away from the table. "Hittin' the head."

Alone at the table I pull my phone out of my back pocket, hoping for something from her. A few texts from Mom talking about the day with Dad, a few sports alerts, but that's it. The wave of disappointment that rolls in response proves Flakes' point. I'm in too fucking deep.

"G." Flakes says behind me. When I glance back, my not-so-stellar mood takes a dive at the two women on his arms. "I'd like you to meet Misty and Veronica. They're pharmaceutical sales reps in town for a conference. Isn't that nice?" He grabs two extra chairs from a nearby table, ushering the two women to sit.

"What the fuck, Flakes?" He has two seconds to explain before I'm out of here. Not in the mood for this shit.

The Misty woman scoots her chair close. The thick scent of her flowery perfume has me breathing through my mouth to get a decent breath. I glare across the table to my so-called friend but he's too busy with the Veronica one to notice.

"We're just looking for a good time, soldier," the Veronica one says from Flakes' side. "Your friend here said you two were looking for some fun tonight and, well, Misty and I are a lot of fun. Wait and see."

"Gabe, right? Tell us what kind of fun you're looking for tonight," the Misty woman says leaning close, pressing her very exposed tits against my bare arm. I hold back a grimace to be polite but fuck, get me the hell out of here.

Flakes orders more beers for us and some sweet martini shit for the other two. Their high shrieking laughs are obnoxious, drawing attention from tables several feet away. Seems they've already had some fun tonight—they're nowhere close to sober. The Misty one hangs on my shoulder, gripping my bicep when she thinks something is funny or when she wants my attention. Within the last few minutes she's started grazing her long nails up and down my forearm.

My pocket vibrates. Thank the fuck. It's an awful thought but I hope it's Mom and she needs help with something. Anything I can use as an excuse to get out, I'll use. Practically peeling the giggly Misty chick off my arm, I dig into my back pocket.

Agent Rizzo: Wow. I'd be careful. You might get cat scratch fever from her. Who knows where those nails have been tonight.

· · ·

My head shoots up. I scan the bar but it's too crowded. There's no way to see through the mass of people from this angle.

Me: Where are you?

    Agent Rizzo: Now where's the fun in that?

    Me: What are you doing here? Stalk people much?

    Agent Rizzo: Spy equals stalker so yeah, I do it a lot. However, tonight I didn't put my stalking abilities to use. Tony texted me. Said I should head over this way. Something to prove?

My knuckles go white around the phone. Each move is calculated, deliberate, to not erupt. I glare up to Flakes, who's smiling like a damn fool.

"You fucker," is all I can get out. Everything else I want to say would cause a scene. What damn point is he trying to make with calling her out here? The fucking asshole. He really can't stand the idea of her and I together.

The shot glass slams onto the table. He pulls a willing Veronica to him. "We need to know if she really wants you or if she's just using your ass like I think. Isn't this the best way? If she gets all jealous then boom, you have your answer. If not, then she doesn't give a rat's ass about you and is playing you like I've been trying to warn you. Fuck, I can't wait to say I told you fucking so."

"I don't do jealous chicks. You fucking know that, you asshole." I shove the table, sending our empty bottles to teeter and clatter. The Misty one grips my thigh, pushing me back into my seat.

"Ohhh who are we making jealous? A terrible ex-girlfriend? She's a bitch and I'm not so..." Her thin fingers wrap around mine and pull my open palm to her bare upper thigh. Still in shock of the bold move, I almost miss the new text.

· · ·

Agent Rizzo: She has some balls, I'll give her that. Well for your sake hopefully not literally. Unless you're into that kind of thing, then you and I really wouldn't have worked out well.

I snatch the phone off the table and rip my hand from the chick's thigh. The wounded scoff she gives does nothing to me.

Me: Where. Are. You.

    Agent Rizzo: Somewhere I can see you but you can't see me. I'm enjoying the entertainment.

A pang of disappointment reels in my gut.

Me: Not the jealous type I take it. Or does this just not make you jealous?

    Agent Rizzo: The current situation pisses me off that Tony wants me to see it. What the hell for, I have no dang clue. Who knows what that tiny brain of his concocted.

    Agent Rizzo: But no, Gabe. I'm not jealous of the chick who looks like she's more than willing to deep throat you under the table if you give her the green light.

Enough of this confusing shit. I flip the phone over so I can't see the disappointing words on the screen. It buzzes again. And again. I can't think straight. Under the table I pop each of my knuckles to ground me. When have four beers affected me this much? Hell, not since high school but that's the only explanation for the way my mind feels like it's swimming.

    Okay, she isn't jealous. I don't like jealous anyway. But her not being

COVERT AFFAIR | 89

jealous and me wanting her to be is a new fucking scenario. Hell maybe Flakes is right. If she's not jealous, then she doesn't care as much as I do at this point which is ass backwards. I need to step back. Cut her off. Who was I kidding, thinking I wanted a difficult woman? Easy is easy.

This time when Misty grips my forearm to pull me into the conversation I don't pull away. I lean in. Nod along to their conversation and even laugh a few times at their idiotic discussion about some overrated celebrity. But as the night goes on, beer after beer to try and forget the sexy as sin woman spying on me, I can't.

By the time the bar closes, the Veronica one and the Misty one can barely stand. Flakes isn't much better off. Giggling, they pile into my Jeep. One of the girls falls face first into the seat and is laughing so hard she forgets to pull her skirt back down, giving the few people out at this hour a full view of her bare ass.

Twenty minutes. Twenty fucking long minutes to get their hotel information from them then get them there safely. I help them into the lobby and watch as they get on the elevator.

Now for Flakes' turn. The entire twenty minute car ride we're silent. When I pull along the curb he staggers out. "Told you she were no good," he slurs.

I want to defend her but how can I at this point.

"Sorry, man," The door slams shut. He falls against the Jeep and stares up to the night sky. "I really am, but I'm looking out for you. Fuck her. Be glad you know now before you're in too fucking deep."

Heading home, at a red light, I'm unable to resist a second longer. I open my missed texts to see what else she had to say.

Agent Rizzo: Ask me why, Gabe. Ask me why I'm not jealous.

Agent Rizzo: Oh, that's mature. Now you're ignoring me because you're all mad. Well guess what sweetheart?

Agent Rizzo: I'm not jealous because you haven't laughed once since she's snuggled up next to you. You're not licking your lips like you're about to eat her like you do me every damn time we're in the same room. And quite frankly she's an idiot if she can't tell you're completely bored.

Agent Rizzo: I don't play games, Officer Wilcox. Well at least this kind.

Agent Rizzo: Not sure what the objective was tonight but it only reinforced mixing work and pleasure is a bad idea.

Agent Rizzo: See you tomorrow at the pool. I'll meet you there.

A car horn blares from behind me but I don't move. I'm a dumb ass. I heave the phone across the Jeep. It slams against the passenger door and slides under the seat. I slam the clutch to the floor. Screeching echoes through the street as I peel out. Fucking moron is what I am. Believing Flakes had a foolproof way to confirm if she is into me or not. The fucker was trying to push us farther apart. The damn bastard.

"Fuck, fuck, fuck, fuck!" I yell as I speed towards home, slamming my fist into the dash until my knuckles bleed.

Idiot. I'm a damn idiot.

She needs to know what happened. Know why I did what I did and apologize. Fucking grovel if I have to. We can't end before it's even started.

I slow to make a right towards my apartment. "Fuck it." Horns blare and someone yells out their window as I cut over three lanes of traffic to make a U-turn. This gets fixed tonight.

Nothing profound or even apology-worthy comes to mind as I drive to her place. Even now staring at her front door, fist raised to knock, I've no idea what I'm going to say. After the first knock I stare, waiting, willing it open. But it doesn't.

The door rattles as I pound my fist against it. Still nothing.

I step off the porch and glance up and down the street, searching for her black Camaro. Where the hell is she? A glimpse down to my watch reads past 0200.

This time I don't knock. No, I beat my fist on the door. Worry, laced with a hint of fear, now eclipses my earlier apprehension. Still no answer.

I try the handle like earlier. It doesn't budge. Locked. Damn. Where the hell could she be? A sinking sensation settles in my gut. My heart beats faster with each second. Jogging back to the Jeep, I grope around the floorboard. When I pull the phone out from under the seat, the screen is barely legible but somehow still operational.

Me: Are you okay?

The two minutes it takes for her to respond seems like an eternity. I lose a tight breath.

Agent Rizzo: Yeah, are you?
    Me: Yeah, I want to talk. Can you let me in?
    Agent Rizzo: I'm fine, Gabe. We can talk tomorrow.
    Me: Just open the damn door so I can say this to your face tonight.
    Agent Rizzo: I'm not home.
    Me: Where are you?
    Agent Rizzo: Goodnight, Gabe.

After tossing the phone, I press my forehead against the cool metal of the door. She's okay, I repeat several times, attempting to ease my racing heart. Not in danger. But hell, now I can't stop wondering *where* she is. The images of her in danger morph into her smiling, laughing with some random fucker. It should be me. Hell, I shouldn't have let that dipshit Flakes drag me out tonight.

Tomorrow. Tomorrow I'll give her answers for tonight's shit show and up my game on convincing her we need to happen.

We will happen.

CHAPTER TEN
LUCIA

K eys. Notebook. Pen. Purse.
 I go through the mental checklist four times before gathering everything off the counter and heading out the door.

Of course he's here. What I didn't anticipate is the wave of excitement that heats my cheeks at the sight of him leaning against his Jeep, smirking, looking sexy as hell.

"I thought I said I'd meet you there, Officer Wilcox," I say over my shoulder as I secure the door.

"You did but I didn't agree to it. CO put me in charge of your well-being while you're here doing us a favor, so here I am." Uncrossing his feet, he stands and opens my door.

While he's clicking the seatbelt into place, his shattered phone in the cupholder catches my eye. I pick it up with the tips of my fingers, not wanting to start this day with glass embedded in my skin, to inspect it.

"What the heck happened to your phone?"

"Ah well, the phone and I had a little disagreement after reading your texts last night."

"Disagreement?"

"I wasn't a fan of what it said."

"Ah, are you going to get a new one?"

He turns to make sure no one is behind us as he backs out of his parking space. "At some point, I guess. It's a pain in the ass to get a new one. Either you have to wait for it to come in the mail or go to a damn store. Fucking shoot me."

I grimace at his words. "Not a good analogy in our line of work considering it can happen at any time."

His chuckle makes me smile even if it is so early the sun's not even up yet. We speed down the street and take a sharp right turn.

"I can get you one."

"One what?" he asks but keeps his focus out the windshield. Which is good by me since he drives like a speed demon.

Instead of responding, I dig around the bottom of my purse. We take another turn making me hold on to the, well anything, to keep from being flung against the door.

"Who are you calling?" Gabe asks, eyes flicking from me to the phone in my hand.

I wave him off and gesture to the road. "If you're going to drive like a maniac, pay attention, would you? Being mangled in a car wreck isn't the way I planned this day to start."

With a harmless glare he dutifully obeys.

"Well hey there, California girl," Jeremy says all perky on the other end of the line. "What are you doing up this early and why does it sound like you're in a tornado?"

Using my hand as a shield from the whipping wind I say, "In a Jeep. I'm good, the weather is great here."

"Ah so the op is going smoothly. Good to know."

"I need—"

"You do know it's illegal to talk and drive in California right. Wait, I thought I requested a Camaro for you, what are you doing in a Jeep?"

I cringe and glance to Gabe. Who of course looks over right at that moment and frowns. "I'm with Officer Wilcox. It's his Jeep. He's the reason—"

COVERT AFFAIR | 95

"Oh nice, how's the recruiting project going? Is he ready to sign his life away to the CIA?"

"No," I grumble and yank the creeping hem of my dress back down my thigh. "But I was hoping you could help me out with something. Officer Wilcox, he shattered his phone last night and needs a new one. Could you request a new one courtesy of the agency? With all the fancy things like mine?"

The pause on his end is deliberate. "Yeah sure, Lu. I think I can do that for you. I can have it to you in a couple hours, is that okay?"

"Perfect. Thanks Jeremy."

"You staying safe?"

"Always."

"Why are you with him this early?"

"Doing my job. Gotta run. Bye and thanks again."

I end the call before he can ask any more slightly inappropriate questions and toss the phone back into my purse. Only a few more weeks before Brooke is back. I'm not sure how much more of Jeremy as a handler I can take, with him questioning every move when a man is involved.

Palm trees zoom past my window. We're taking the long way to base again, not sure why but for some reason he loves this route. I pull at my dress again.

"Is this what a reporter even wears here or are they more shorts and flip-flops? All I had to go off of is what I see on the news back in DC."

At a light he turns and runs a quick assessing eye before turning back to the road. "I guess that's what they wear here. I don't watch the news, too much bullshit. But I have no doubt there's not a single reporter in this state who looks as damn gorgeous as you do in that get-up. But heels? You gotta be fucking with me. It's a pool day, remember?"

With a frown, I take in my black pumps. Okay, maybe these are a little over the top for today but I didn't pack anything else to go with this outfit. It's either these, my black boots, or tennis shoes.

Gabe clears his throat and shifts in his seat. "You know comments will be made today. It's a big pool and I can't stop them if I don't hear it. Today will be hard to keep an ear out." One by one he uses the steering wheel to pop his knuckles.

"I can take care of myself."

"That's not what I'm saying."

"Then what are you saying?"

"Where were you last night?"

"What?" The leather groans as I turn in the seat to face him, which is a terrible idea. When I'm not looking directly at him it's easier to fool myself into thinking I don't want anything to do with him. The reality is, I do. Badly. More than I've ever wanted a man. I want his handsome face pulled against mine, his kind yet fierce stares, his strong arms wrapped around me holding me to him.

"Last night," he says with a sigh, breaking my internal checklist. "It was after 0200 when I stopped by and you said you were out. Where were you?"

Right. That. No way in hell I'm going to tell him I was a little curious, not jealous—nope, definitely not jealous, to what he would do with the woman who was hanging all over him. No way am I going to tell him I waited outside that restaurant then followed them to that hotel and watched him deposit them safely. No way am I going to tell him I just drove around for the next hour trying to figure out what in the heck is wrong with me and why I was acting nuts over some guy I've just met.

Yep, no way.

Instead I turn the conversation.

"What was the purpose of last night anyway, Gabe?" I turn back to staring out the window as we hit the highest point of the bridge that takes us to Coronado.

He doesn't respond. For the next ten minutes, we ride in silence. It's not until we're through the guard gate and parked does he speak up. "I don't know what's going on with Flakes. I can't figure out why he's overreacting about you. Are you two not telling me something? Did something else happen?"

"No, I've told you everything that happened from my perspective. Not sure about his. I agree, something else is going on." I straighten all my things out on my lap into a neat line. "Even I can't figure it out. Maybe because he won't stay in the same room with me long enough for me to."

"Whatever it is, he's being an asshole and I should've known he was going to do some stupid shit to make sure I stay away from you. Or I guess last night an attempt to make sure you stay away from me."

Not trusting myself, I pull on the door handle without a glance to the sexy sailor in the driver's seat. "Maybe it's for the best." My feet have just hit the ground and he's in front of me. Large, strong hands wrap around my waist, tightening when I try, in vain, to move past him. I swallow down my rising breakfast as my insides flip and tremble. It takes me biting my lip to hold back the whimper that's desperate to escape.

"Don't say that. I fucked up, yeah. I shouldn't have listened to my best friend, I get that now."

I peer up through my lashes and freeze at the intenseness behind his blue eyes. This is a bad idea. Horrible idea. The feelings pouring through him aren't of a squandered one night-stand or fling. No, what's behind his eyes, what he's holding back—or maybe doesn't realize himself—are emotions already running deep for me.

I find my voice, able to muster a quiet whisper. "This is a bad idea, Gabe. If we do this it will be destructive for both of us."

The heat from his body flows to mine as he pushes my back against the Jeep, pressing the lower half of his body against mine. His arms come beside my head, boxing me in.

"Then we will have to make it worth it. And believe me, you and me sweetheart, we can make the good worth the bad. Give me a chance to show you it won't be good with me, it will be fucking fantastic."

Saliva pools in my mouth. "That's some speech." I remember how to swallow and say, "Okay, Officer Wilcox, let's make this so amazing that when it ends there are no regrets from either side."

"Fuck me," he mumbles into my hair and takes a deep breath in.

"That is the plan. Now let's go. We both have jobs to do this morning. And I hate being late." A light shove of his shoulder sends him back. Instantly, I miss his heat. With a quick glance down to his tight fatigues, I point and say, "You might want to take care of that before we see the guys."

A cocky male smirk forms after a glance down to his fatigues. One hand snakes under his belt and down the front of his pants. After a few adjustments he straightens his shirt and says, "There, better. Come on."

———

Three hours standing, evaluating the group in the pool and they're still going strong. Tony and Gabe bark orders and disappointed feedback at the men as they run their various drills. We told them I needed to see what a typical workout looks like and some of the pieces the men go through to get into the exclusive program.

Just like Gabe had expected, I've been on my own most of the morning. No one has said anything yet. Throughout the morning I've monitored all of Tony's platoon, noting subtle movements and stares. Most glances seem more annoyed than anything but a few of the men have monitored me. Six to be accurate. They're the ones I've paid the most attention to the last hour.

Not able to recall their names, I jot down ways to remember them in my own code like "hot hair, bad smile" or "great skin, big arms with ship tattoo" and will reference their files later to get their official names. Six out of Tony's fourteen isn't bad. Honestly, I expected more since ultimately everyone is hiding something. It's human nature. It's my job to identify who's hiding something illegal or harmful to the agency, or in this case the SEALs, then complete recon work to pinpoint what they're hiding and go from there.

Shouting draws my attention from my notes to Tony. Gabe's earlier assessment of his behavior is accurate; he *is* acting over the top about me being here and our past. He could be hiding more than him being a shitty husband. On the notepad I jot the letter T with a question mark beside it. It would make sense if the mole were someone like Tony who had all the mission information before the rest of the team was briefed. Even if the CO and Gabe don't think he's a threat.

Mission reports...

I write that in the top right-hand corner to remind myself to call the CO for those files. They could shed some light on how they went wrong and why. I underline the word call several times. No way I'm going back without someone with me or I'll get stuck in another uncomfortable conversation with the admin. Crap, I forgot to ask Gabe about him. His file wasn't among the ones sent over yesterday. Which isn't a big surprise since he has nothing to do with Tony's platoon.

I gasp and stumble back when cold water splashes from the pool and sprays down the front of my dress and notebook.

What the hell?

Fuming, I glare up from my wet notes to see Beasley pushing out of the pool.

"You looked hot," he says as he shakes the water out of his hair.

In my peripheral I see Tony and Gabe's attention turn to casually monitor our interaction.

"It's the burden I bear," I say with a smile.

"Are you getting good stuff for your article?" he asks and leans over to look at my notes. I pull them close to my chest and nod. "It's all pretty intense right?"

Again I nod, not trusting the words that might come out of my mouth if I speak.

"Yeah we go through worse when we're pups. They toss us in with our hands and feet tied. We have to figure out a way to stay alive for fifteen minutes."

My brows inch higher, portraying interest and I scribble down gibberish, acting the diligent reporter.

"The key is to not panic. That's what most of this shit is about, you know. Teaching us to stay calm under pressure, how to solve problems when you have less than ten seconds before you drown. You know, the normal nine-to-five issues I'm sure you encounter."

Peering through my lashes, I smirk. "Sounds brutal, why do you do it?" No reason his interview can't start now.

"Chicks of course." He wiggles his brows and stretches his arms above his head. Any other woman might find it distracting, but his asshole attitude and lack of respect towards women makes his tan muscles more annoying than attractive. Or it could be that my attraction and attention are all focused towards another sexy water mammal. Who, by his current body language, isn't happy Beasley is still out of the water standing so close.

"Wanna come for a swim?" he asks, inclining his head behind him toward the pool a foot away.

Turning my attention from Gabe back to Beasley I shake my head. "I don't think it would be appropriate."

"Yeah I get it, you're scared. Most broads would be. Don't worry, I'd gladly give you mouth-to-mouth if you need it. Hell I'd like to start chest compressions now just to get my hands on those fantastic tits of yours," he says to my chest instead of my face.

Feigning shock, I step back. The blood in my veins boils. Damn tool. It takes every ounce of my training to keep from lashing out and punching him in the throat.

"Come on," he continues. "You know you'd love it. Just a few minutes with me, we can sneak off. No one will notice."

I clear my throat and look to where Gabe is yelling at one of his men in the pool. Perfect, I want him distracted for this verbal chastising. "I'm willing to bet I'd need more than a few minutes."

"Not with me."

"Highly doubtful. I'm already bored with your typical male chauvinistic rhetoric."

His face flushes pink, tinting those sculpted cheek bones. "I'm anything but typical, lady. Whatever. It's not like I would've enjoyed it anyway. I don't typically go for the fat girls."

Hum. Decisions. Decisions. Blow the mission and teach this piece of crap a lesson or keep my mouth shut and ignore him. It takes less than a second to decide. Unfortunately for Tony's platoon I might get tossed in jail and the mole might go undiscovered because someone needs to teach this idiot some manners.

A quick assessment of our surroundings shows I'm vastly outnumbered and there's nothing around to help me beat the idiot. Hand to hand, he will win. Unfortunately for me, the pool is my only option.

As I prepare for the first steps of my idiotic plan, one foot slips out of my heels and then the other. I keep pressed on my tiptoes to ensure he doesn't take notice of the shift in height.

"I like to eat," I say and look away, to not meet his stare, pretending like his comment hit a nerve.

"I can tell," he huffs.

What is manslaughter these days? Or would it be an outright murder charge at this point since I'm planning it out? Eh, the agency has good legal council and let's be honest, they will ensure Beasley's body disappears before I'm even in the back of an MP's car.

In the distance someone yells my cover name over and over but it's barely audible through the blood roaring in my ears.

With a lover's touch I press a palm against his bare chest. "So that's a no to the quickie then?" His heart pounds beneath my hand, giving away the anticipation he's trying to keep hidden. Those brown eyes move from our skin-to-skin contact to mine.

"Only if you let me fuck that mouth of yours."

Bye Beasley. The world will not miss you.

With every ounce of force I can muster, I push against his chest. He stumbles back in surprise. In a seamless move I wrap a hand around his wrist and take the few steps towards the pool. Using the ledge as leverage, I pull him in the water with me.

We fall tangled together. He thrashes to peel me from his back as I hold tighter, pulling him closer against my chest. Fighting is different down here; every movement is in slow motion, taking double the effort. Not that Beasley notices. My muscles pull near to their snapping point to keep him from getting away as the air in my lungs continues to leak out my nose and mouth.

The edges of my vision darken and my hold slips. He begins to wiggle out of my hold and at the same time, a dark form spears through the water. That's the last thing I see. Even with my eyes open, everything has faded to black and the last bit of air I've been clinging to bubbles into the water.

CHAPTER ELEVEN
LUCIA

Miles away, someone yells my name. Something coarse scrapes at my back and shoulders as I launch into a coughing fit. A couple deep breaths, followed by another coughing fit, I peek through squinted lids to see what the heck is going on.

Gabe's narrowed blue eyes are an inch from mine. Hum, he looks pissed. Those eyes narrow further when he realizes I'm coherent, the rims of his blue iris barely visible but a hint of relief flashing amongst the anger.

The smack of wet feet against the deck and loud male voices draw my attention to the right. It takes a couple blinks to dislodge the water from my eyes and focus my vision. Even when everything comes into view I'm not sure what I'm seeing. A furious Tony is restrained by four men and to his right a bloodied Beasley on his hands and knees, glaring back at me.

Tony yells at Gabe, at me, at Beasley, and the pulling against his restrained arms starts back up.

"Enough, you two," Gabe shouts but doesn't look their way. "Beasley, get your fucking shit together. Do you have any idea how much damn trouble you'd be in if you'd actually drowned her? A fucking civilian on a damn military base."

The hand he offers to help me up is considerate but firm. I rock to the side as the room sways, still a tad off balanced. A hand settles on my shoulder, steadying me.

Beasley pops up from the floor and wipes his bloody nose, glaring at Gabe. "Fuck that shit. She was the one who tried to drown me!"

Gabe's harsh laugh is nothing less than mocking. "Seriously, you fool. You want us to believe a damn civilian woman tried to drown you. Here. In front of everyone."

The pool area goes silent as Beasley weighs his options. Either admit he was almost taken out by a woman, on his home turf, or take the blame for this shit show to save face in front of the boys.

I monitor his body language and watch for a shift when he makes his decision. It takes less than ten seconds. His shoulders relax, slumping to a casual stance, and a cocky smirk spreads across his golden cheeks. "What can I say, I wanted to see that pussy wet." Everyone within earshot laughs.

For the second time in half an hour, red infiltrates my vision. With a hard shove off the floor, to scratch his jugular open, I lunge at him but a strong arm wraps around my waist, hauling me back. Gabe flips me to face him, those blue eyes telling me this isn't the time to push back, and tosses me over his shoulder with ease.

"Hackenbreg, deal with that fuckstick. I'll make sure Miss Free-bush is okay," he barks as he strides through the group of men. They part like the red sea and turn to stare as he carries me away. I can't help but find a sliver of humor in the whole incident I created. The men on Gabe's platoon laugh at the little wave and smile I give before we round a corner, putting us out of sight.

Gabe's shoulder jabs into my stomach and ribs with each pounding footstep across the pavement. It's a relief when my feet are eventually lowered to the pavement, a safe distance from anyone who could overhear our conversation.

"What the hell happened?"

I give a vague shrug and divert my attention to straightening my soaked dress. "Do you think dry cleaning will get the chlorine out or is this dress done? It's a favorite so if it's a lost cause I'm going to expense this just so you know—"

"I don't give a damn about your dress, Lucia. Answer my damn question. What the hell happened back there? From where I was standing it looked like..." he trails off like he can't even voice what he thinks I did.

Which I did do.

The warm brick of the building I'm leaning against feels amazing against my wet, chilled skin. I close my eyes and angle my face to the sun to get as much heat as possible. "Beasley got a little mouthy so I decided to teach him a lesson in manners."

Gabe's head drops forward in obvious disappointment but when he looks up again the corners of his lips are upturned, suppressing a smile. "And what did that fuckstick get mouthy about, sweetheart?"

"Well, he called me fat. He said he wanted to paw at my boobs. Oh yeah and something about fucking my mouth. Rude, rude things to be saying to a lady."

The hint of amusement from seconds ago drains from his features. "He said what?" One by one he begins cracking his knuckles.

"Unbelievable considering your warning yesterday. I said this the first day and now I'm wondering it again...don't the SEALs have standards?" I squint and shield my eyes from the bright sun to see if he finds my joke to lighten the mood funny. He doesn't. "Anyway, I figured if you and Tony aren't teaching your kids lessons on how to talk to the ladies then maybe I should. I think I proved my point, don't you?"

His blue eyes wide, he shakes his head. "You really attempted to drown a Navy fucking SEAL. I'm not sure if that's stupid or ballsy."

Twirling a wet lock of hair, I smirk. "Let's go with ballsy. And I wasn't going to really drown him. Just make him pass out for a little while. I knew one of you water mammals would come in and save the day. A little near death experience courtesy of the woman he offended sounded like a valid consequence to me."

"A little brain damage for saying what all those guys are thinking."

"It—"

Tony storms around the corner, cutting me off. He shoves Gabe back and thrusts my shoulders against the brick. The force pops my head back, slamming it against the wall. Not that Tony notices, or cares. His eyes are wild, cheeks flushed, his breathing coming in short pants. "What the fucking shit balls was that, Agent Rizzo?"

I ball his wet fatigues into my fist to brace for the next push I know is coming.

"I was just telling Officer Wilcox here—"

The shove I predicted comes but this time I'm prepared. "Do you not give a shit about your cover or what you're here to do? Hell Lucia. You just gave that piece of shit Beasley the upper hand. He knows you're not some hot piece of civilian ass now. Did you even think—"

Using the wall as leverage I shove against it to move Tony back a step. "I know what I'm doing, damnit."

"Do you?" he yells and recovers the step I'd made him retreat. I see Gabe grip Tony's shoulder in an attempt to hold him back. "You're a piece of work, Agent Rizzo. So fucking selfish back then and even more so now."

The humor from earlier fades. "Me. Selfish," I say, trying to keep my voice even. No way can I let him know how deeply his words wound.

"Yes, you. Oh, I know you think you're all perfect but guess what? You're not." He turns to face Gabe, who's still pulling on his shoulder to keep us separated. "I asked a buddy in the agency what they knew about some bitch Lucia Rizzo. You want to know what he said?" He turns back to me, his face red, lips pulled into a snarl. "He said he's heard she's smart as hell, can fucking read minds even, but only cares about one thing. Herself. That she's a selfish bitch who everyone knows will do whatever it takes to climb the damn ladder and doesn't care about anyone who gets in her way."

The wet material slips through my fingers and my arms fall to the side as all the fight, the anger that was building, disappears, leaving behind a vulnerable void in its place.

"So yes, you're fucking selfish, Lucia. Of course, all you thought about was yourself and whatever the hell point you were trying to prove by pushing Beasley into the pool. Never considering how your actions would affect me. Affect my team. I don't give a shit about our past Lucia. We fucked, whatever. But now, today, you're putting my men in danger."

The stinging of unshed tears causes my throat to burn. I keep my eyes focused on the pavement so he can't see how his words affect me.

The sound of Gabe's boots crunch against the loose pavement. "That's enough, Flakes."

But Tony doesn't seem to think so. All the anger he's held back the past couple days has unleashed and appears to have no plans of stopping until he has his say.

"This mission is screwed because of you. Only you. When one of my men die because more information is sold it's on you. You fucking cun—"

"Enough," Gabe says in a menacing, firm tone. "Stand down. Now." Wisely, Tony listens. "Walk away. Walk the fuck away now."

Still staring at the black pavement, I see the toe of Tony's boots take a step away and pause. "She will fuck you over man. They don't come more selfish than her."

Even after the stamping of his boots has faded I still can't muster up enough courage to look up. Tony's accusations of being selfish aren't anything I haven't heard before but it still hurts when someone hits an insecurity as hard as he did.

A warm, heavy arm drapes over my shoulders and pulls me close. He doesn't say a word, just holds me snug against his side. I look up, tilting my head back to meet Gabe's blue eyes.

"Let's get you home," he says softly as he brushes a wet piece of hair from my face and tucks it behind an ear.

"No." Clearing my throat I move out of his hold. "CO Williams will want an update and if anyone's going to get their ass chewed for this mess I want it to be me."

A knowing smile spreads across his face. "How selfless of you. Trying to prove a point, sweetheart?"

"No," I say too quickly.

He shakes his head and looks towards the building where the CO's office is located. "Well, I'll talk to him about what happened. Flakes doesn't know the full story and depending on his mood CO might agree with your near drowning sentence for Beasley's comments. Besides, you in a wet dress," his eyes roam down my damp body, lingering at a few key spots where the dress is suctioned to my skin. "We need to get you home before anyone has a chance to make more inappropriate comments."

"Who says I want to fuck your mouth anyway?" I muse as we move across the parking lot towards his Jeep. "Besides BDSM-loving billionaires, that is."

He stumbles. I turn to see what he tripped over on the flat surface of the parking lot but find nothing.

"Do you know a lot of BDSM-loving billionaires?"

"One," I say with a smirk, which is a small miracle after the reaming Tony just laid into me. Gabe's hand hovers over the Jeep's door handle and raises his brows. The warm metal of the Jeep from sitting in the morning sun is amazing against my back. "One *fictional* BDSM-loving billionaire."

Those dimples appear as his smile widens. "I don't even want to know what tips you picked up reading that shit. Wait, on second thought maybe I do. Climb in, I'll drop you off at your place then come back to update the CO."

CHAPTER TWELVE
GABE

"That was fucking brutal," I mumble to myself as the door to the CO's office clicks closed behind me.

Travis stands from behind his desk and smiles. "Sounded like it. I could hear almost every word from out here."

I pause at his desk, knowing the conversation isn't going to end there. Been here too many times to think I can get away with just a few words from him.

"How's Miss Freebush's article going?" he asks as he looks down at his desk, shuffling a few papers around. "Is she getting all the information she needs?"

I glance up then down the hall to see if anyone is close by to save me. Fuck, no one. I lean a hip against his desk and run a hand down my face. "Yeah, she's getting what she needs. Just hard on the guys. They aren't used to having a female around. Difficult for them to turn off their bullshit. Hopefully she gets what she needs soon and we can be done with her lingering around."

No idea why I said that because the complete opposite is true. I want this to take as long as possible to keep her around.

"Not me," Travis says, looking back up with another big smile. "I don't mind seeing her walking around here. Hell I wish she were the CO."

Heavy, squeaking footsteps sound through the hall, pulling my attention to a still furious Flakes. He stops in front of Travis' desk but doesn't acknowledge he's there.

"How'd it go?" he demands.

A quick goodbye nod to Travis and I grab Flakes' arm to get him to follow me. We're almost to the stairs when I say, "How the fuck do you think it went?" I start down the stairs only to have Flakes pull on my shoulder. I shrug him off and jog the rest of the way down. Usually I'd be happy to hang around and shoot the shit with him, but not now.

Right now there's this pull to get back to her, to see her. Hell, what am I saying. This is just about sex. I'm craving to get back to her for sex. Yep, fucking her, that's the only reason I need to see her right now. Not because when she climbed out of the Jeep earlier there was no fire in her goodbye, no happiness in her small smile.

Nope, nothing to do with comforting her. Just sex.

That's the only reason I'll punch fucking Flakes in the face if he tries to stop me from getting to her.

Sex.

Only sex.

I'm climbing into my Jeep when Flakes catches up to me.

"You're going to see her right now aren't you."

"Yeah, so what?"

He just shakes his head and takes a step away. "When she screws you over because she sees this as nothing and you don't, don't come crying to me. I've warned you enough. She's a damn drug man. Watch yourself."

Waiting for the security gate to lift, I glance back in the review mirror. Flakes is still standing where I left him, hands in his pockets, staring right back.

———

The purring of the engine dies when I cut it in front of her place but don't move to get out. Today was complete shit. I should go home and forget about the gorgeous brunette inside. But I can't. Even after having my ass handed to me by the CO and the argument with Mom on the way over, all I want is to be here. She can't make any of that better, and I can't take away what that dumb ass said to her today, but maybe if I see her, sit by her, the day won't seem as shitty.

I'm lying to myself if I think this is only about sex. Hell was it ever just about sex? From the moment we met, yes, I wanted to have her but the more I'm around her that's not enough. I want all of her and fuck if I know why, but I want her to want all of me too.

I'm hooked. Like the fucking junkie Flakes said I would become.

My whole life has been planned out. Nothing has been a surprise until her. From the moment we spoke, every priority that has dictated my life was demoted, my life has been flipped on its head. And hell if I know why but I want more of it. Need more of her uprooting the only structured life I know.

Sitting out here staring at her house is creepy. I should go in and see how she's doing but these few minutes of quiet are needed to get my shit together. If not she'll do that witch shit and read through each thought like an open book.

I lean back against the headrest and shut my eyes. Something about today I can't put my finger on felt off. Like an itch I can't scratch, it's gnawed at me since stepping out of the CO's office. Yes, Lucia messed up, that damn Italian temper, but that's not it. It worsened when Flakes demanded to know how the debriefing went.

Maybe that's it. The way he reacted seemed over the top, even for a fucking drama queen like he is. Could his resentment for Lucia be clouding his otherwise already cloudy judgment? If it is, he needs to get his damn priorities straight.

With a deep exhale I push the driver side door open and step out onto the street. My pulse inches up, growing faster and faster with each step, something I can normally moderate by focusing on it. But right now I can't. The anticipation of seeing her only makes it increase.

Damn traitorous body.

Shit if I'm reacting this way *now*, before I even get her in bed, how in the hell will I be able to survive after? I need to get my damn shit together, that's what. Yes she's beautiful, smart, crazy as hell...wait, where was I going with this?

A desolate thought floats to the forefront of my mind. This beautiful woman won't be here forever. This beautiful woman will soon identify the mole and go back to her home in DC. Her life. Away from me.

Damn, why couldn't this just be about fucking sex?

The old wooden door rattles beneath the pounding of my fist.

Silence from the other side. Again, I thump on the door and peer through the window pane, searching for any movement. The lights are on and I noticed her Camaro parked a ways down the street. Lucia has to be home. Trying the knob, it turns freely.

"Lucia?" I call out to attempt to honor yesterday's request of not sneaking up on her.

The scent of peppermint and something else hangs in the air. She's been here recently. But where is she *now*? A quick but thorough inspection of the living room and kitchen shows nothing amiss. The bedroom is spotless too.

Fists on my hips, I visually scour the small home again. With this second pass my gaze keeps returning to the back door. It's closed tight but somehow, the pull from earlier as a guide, I know I'll find her on the other side.

The urgency to see her, to make sure she's safe has increased the last few minutes. So when her silhouette comes into view, a relieved breath pushes between my clenched teeth. The setting sun makes her dark hair shimmer in the fading light. Even without seeing her face, the way she's sitting all alone in the sand staring out onto the water, I know she's still upset.

Sand shifts beneath my boots as I approach and stop two feet behind her. She doesn't turn or give any indication I'm here. But I'm sure she's known since I opened the back door.

"If you want me to go..." There's no finishing the thought. I don't want her to want me to leave. Fuck I don't think I *could* leave if she does ask. Every arm muscle twitches to wrap around her slumped shoulders and pull her against me. To hold her close. Anger toils deep in my gut. I'm going to punch that asshole the next time I see him for making her feel this way.

A red-nailed hand stretches from her side and pats the sand to her left. Her right hand also reaches but only to retrieve what looks like a decent bottle of vodka from the sand. Not giving her the opportunity to change her mind, I plop my ass down on to the sand beside her and lean back on to my elbows to watch the fading sun. Except for noise from the few beach goers and the waves crashing along the beach, we sit in silence.

I take a deep breath in and let it out slowly. Only when the last bit of sunlight has dipped behind the horizon and the pinks and blues of the sunset have faded does she speak.

"How did it go with CO Williams?" she asks, keeping her gaze straight ahead, and takes a swig from the bottle.

The mint and herb smell from the house floats by with a flip of her partially wet hair over her shoulder. Fuck, did she just get out of the shower? A mental image forms of her under the streaming hot water, steam filling the bathroom, her soapy hands massaging her tits. Women do that in the shower right? If I had cans I for sure would.

I clear my throat and pull my lust-filled stare away from her to the now dark ocean, hoping it will help clear my hungry thoughts enough to answer her question. "He was pissed, I'm not going to repeat what he said. I don't want to end up almost drowned." With my shoulder, I nudge hers hoping to get a smile. Hell, even getting her to look my way would be a damn win. But she simply nods and takes another swig from the glass bottle. "But it's all good. When I explained what happened, that you were not the one to start the altercation just end it, he seemed satisfied."

Those red-painted toes of hers dig in and out of the sand. "So the operation is still a go?" she asks, a hint of desperation in her voice.

"Yes, now Flakes on the other hand—"

"Thank you for taking care of that for me," she cuts in.

Okay, note taken. Not ready to talk about his comments yet.

"Why are you here?"

I shrug to play off how cruel her words sound in my ears. "I can't seem to stay away," I murmur and reach across the sand for a tiny shell.

"That will fade."

"I'm not sure you're right about that one, sweetheart."

She gives a humorless laugh into the bottle at her lips. After wiping her mouth with the sleeve of her sweatshirt, those green eyes finally cut to me. "Sure you will. You'll get tired of dealing with my temper. Me leaving on a moment's notice then not being able to tell you where I went or what happened. The secrets, the secrets will eat at you, then you'll start picking fights and we will end."

After tossing the shell as hard as I can into the ocean I say, "Sounds like a speech I'm used to giving more than receiving."

Finally. Finally. She turns in the sand to face me which should bring relief. But it doesn't. Because now I can see her pointy nipples poking through the damn sweatshirt. Fuck she's not wearing a bra. My dick twitches against the coarse material of my BDUs.

She's talking, I should listen. But hell if those damn tits don't have me in a trance.

"...Sure that's okay for you. Don't you see?"

Shit.

What did she say?

I shake my head, hoping that's the correct response. Thank the fuck she keeps going.

"Women are supposed to be okay with that kind of life from a guy. But when the tables are flipped everything goes to shit."

Oh that. Okay now I'm tracking.

"I don't think so," I say. "I think it would be pretty damn amazing to have a partner who understands what I go through. What I do. How it's just as hard on me to keep those secrets."

Something flares behind those green eyes, making me wonder if I'd said something wrong. "I'm not looking for a partner. Hell I'm not even looking for a sidekick. I just…" Her words trail off as if she's holding back.

"What?" I ask. And mean it. How is she the most fascinating person alive? With great tits. And ass.

"I want more than this. I want people to look at me and expect greatness rather than the inaccurate stereotypical woman bullshit. I'm more than that."

"I know you are, Luce." Oh hell, what did I just call her? Out loud. Fuck.

Thank the fuck she smiles. My apprehension drops a level. "Luce, huh?"

"It fits," I say, staring out to the ocean.

"Anyway, you're just saying all that to get in my pants."

"Or top. I'd take either."

A smile and now a laugh from her. Damn, I feel like I've won something.

She's still laughing when I say, "Seriously though, I'm not saying that to get into your pants. Look at me. I know you can tell when I'm lying or holding back the truth. I might be an ass with my men and have been plenty of times with women in the past but not now. Not with you."

Her eyes search my face looking for the truth. "We could use someone like you at the agency, Officer Wilcox."

"Well maybe I can come do a seminar on expectation equality or something."

The humor fades from her face and she starts to draw in the sand with her index finger. "Do you think I'm selfish? I mean what you know of me."

I bite back my response until she looks up, I need her to see I'm telling her the honest fucking truth. "I don't know a lot about you, Luce," she smiles at the nickname, "But from what I've seen, no you're not selfish. You're passionate but that's very different than selfish."

"You know what's messed up about this whole thing?"

"What?"

"If I had a dick you know what the guys at the agency would say about me? That I was driven. Not a selfish bitch climbing to the top."

Huh. I frown as her words sink in. "Never thought about it that way I guess."

She shoves my shoulder and takes another swig from her bottle. "Yeah, well you were born with the right reproductive organs so you haven't had to. Now lay down."

What the...

With a groan of impatience she shoves my shoulders back to force me to lie down in the sand. She snuggles up next to me laying her head on my chest and those big, soft tits cuddled against my ribs.

Fucking hell.

As we lay in silence my fingers drift to her hair, the scent of mint grows stronger each time I thread them through.

"Whatever happens, Gabe, I want you to know I'm not that selfish person Tony spewed about today. When this goes bad, know that I'd never use you."

Funny, I was about to say the same thing to her. To let her know she's not some random lay or side tail until she leaves. But why would she think I would ever think that about her?

Luce shifts in the sand, turning so she's more on top of me than lying on the sand. "Promise me," she whispers against my neck, her warm breath a stark contrast to the cool night air. With each exhale that heat absorbs into my veins and flows straight to my cock.

"I know you wouldn't use me," I breathe.

At the first press of her soft lips against my skin I flip us over to put her back on the sand. "I've been fucking dying, the worst case of blue balls, waiting to kiss you. You're not going to take that from me," I groan.

Both her hands reach up to my face, and urge me down. No way in hell is she going to run this. Gripping both of her hands in mine I hold them above her head, causing her back to arch. Those green eyes flash as she pulls against my grip but it only reinforces it. There are about five different moves she knows that would get her out of my grip with ease, but she's not using them, she wants this as much as I do.

"Gabe," she whines as her hips shift under me.

"Patience sweetheart. Let me enjoy the view first." Gathering both her wrists into one hand I cup her jaw with the other. "You're so damn gorgeous, you know that right? You have to know every damn man on this planet wants to be me right now."

My lips skim up her neck and she shudders beneath me. Serving my country and teasing Luce are now tied for the things I want to do for the rest of my life or die trying. Her naturally tan skin is soft against my tongue and lips as I work down her neck to her collar bone and back up again.

I pull back to get the full gorgeous view again only to find her eyes closed and a lazy smile stretched across her face. I kiss one corner of her lips then the other before pulling back again. "Luce, how much vodka have you had?"

Please don't say much. Please don't be fucking tipsy right now.

"Hum?"

Fuck.

I reach for the bottle she's been sipping. Shit, it's light.

"Luce," I say. "Answer me."

"Not too much. Please don't stop, Gabe. I need you to not stop."

Damn.

Her hands wriggle free from my grip to pull on my shirt, trying to get me closer. Okay, two options. Be the good man Mom taught me to be or be the guy I want to be right now and not give a shit she's been drinking. Any other girl this willing and a little tipsy, whatever. But this isn't some other girl, it's Luce. And somehow in this split second I know I'll regret it more if I *don't* stop than if I do.

"Sorry sweetheart, not going to happen tonight."

"What?" Her eyes stay closed but her bottom lip sticks out. Fucking hell. Maybe just a little taste of the lips which have been teasing the hell out of me the past few days.

The second that lower lip is sucked between mine I rip back like it burns. Hell. Should have known there are no small taste tests when it comes to this beauty. Groaning out of frustration and the effort it takes to stand up, I push off the sand and pull her up too. Luce stumbles to the side from the quick movement. I wrap an arm around her waist and pull her tight. Exactly where she's meant to be.

"Gabe?"

"Luce."

Eyes still closed she smiles and says, "Will you carry me?"

"Sure, sweetheart," I whisper into her hair and inhale deep. Fuck, why am I stopping this again? After swiping the vodka bottle from the sand, she waits. "What, no running and jumping on me tonight?"

That genuine smile grows wider. "Is that what you want, Officer Wilcox?"

I almost say yes just for a good laugh at seeing her try to run in this state, hell she can barely stand. But instead I lift her into my arms. As I dredge through the sand she wraps her arms around my neck and nuzzles her nose against my skin.

This soft, vulnerable side is a shock. But then again almost everything she does is.

Once inside I lay her on the bed and take a step back. Her hand reaches out and catches mine. "Don't go. Please stay. I'm not that drunk," she says softly while those green eyes search mine and her fingers start trailing up my arm.

The vibrations in my pocket stop me from responding with "there's no way in hell I can stay here a second longer without ripping your damn clothes off." Through the cracked screen I read we're being called out.

"I got to—"

"Be safe and there's a new phone for you on the kitchen counter. You can wipe your old phone or leave it and I'll get someone to wipe it for you." She burrows under the blankets and pulls them up to her chin.

"What?"

Her eyes flutter open. "You needed a new phone, so I got you a new phone. I can guarantee you it's amazing too. Perks of the agency. Told you we get all the cool toys. Grab it on your way out."

The phone in my hand buzzes again. Shit, I need to go.

"I don't know when I'll be back," I say hesitantly, giving her another once over committing it to memory.

"Go. I'll see you when you get back."

"The interviews—"

"Go," she shouts and points to the door.

The bed shifts under my weight, causing her eyes to pop open in surprise. "I'm not leaving until I know what's waiting for me." My lips mold against hers as I weave a hand into her hair, holding her lips tighter against my own. When her mouth parts, opening for me, it's like a fucking gift from heaven. Her tongue tangles with mine, flicking and teasing. The heat from her mouth, the movement of her tongue has me groaning for her mouth on other parts of me.

This simple kiss is everything. She's damn perfect.

Damn, was that a moan?

Still fully clothed, only a kiss—a hell of a kiss—and my cock is ready to bust out of my pants. How will I last two seconds once I'm actually inside her? Hell, just seeing her perfect body naked might do me in.

My pants vibrate, from the phone not my cock, pulling us from the fantasy world our kiss pulled us into.

"Go," she whispers against my lips. "I'll be okay."

After one more taste of her lips I pull back and storm out the door. Whatever the hell this mission is it better be good. As in saving the fucking world good or someone is going to pay.

CHAPTER THIRTEEN
LUCIA

The screeching of tires against asphalt fades into the distance as I lay clutching the blanket to my chest.

Wow. My lips still burn from his. From the heat of a simple kiss.

So much, just wow.

I trace my lips, gliding my fingertips along the edges, remembering how his lips felt against mine. Crap, and now I have to wait how long? It was stupid to drink tonight. But it did help numb the wound left by Tony's words so at least there's that.

But seriously. What guy stops when a girl is a little drunk and overly willing, anyway? What kind of willpower does that man have? And why does it make him so much sexier? With a groan I roll over and pound my face into the pillow.

This better be a short assignment. A small part of me wants to finish what he started on my own but then again the build up, the wait to see him again, could make our first time together that much more amazing.

Rolling back over I stare at the ceiling—which isn't spinning, so that's a good sign—and blindly search for my phone on the night stand.

. . .

Me: Hey new little mama, how's it going over there?

Nothing. Dang.

Me: Hey Jeremy, what are you up to?

Again nothing. Double dang.

It is super late back in DC so no surprise they aren't texting back, but disappointment simmers all the same. I search around the room to find anything to keep my still turned on mind off Gabe. Watching TV doesn't sound fun, neither does reading. The stacks of boxes in the corner of the room snag my attention.

"Ugh." I give an annoyed shove on the covers and swing my legs out of bed. After grabbing several files from the top and changing into pajamas, I crawl back into bed.

———

Hair on the back of my neck and down my arms prickles, pulling me awake. But I force my eyes to stay closed for five seconds to assess what woke me.

Deafening silence fills the room and the rest of the house. Against my will my breath quickens.

One breath in.

Long, shaky, breath out.

Not a sound.

I give my eyes a moment to adjust to the darkness in the room before moving. Mimicking a sleepy stretch I tuck a hand under the spare pillow. Reassurance flows through my veins, spurring a relieved breath, as my hand wraps around the hilt of the knife I had hidden there the first day.

Eyes adjusted, knife gripped, I'm ready for action. In a swift, easy move both feet plant on the cool carpet. I take in everything but nothing is amiss. Still the sensation of something being off turns in my gut.

With silent, bare feet I tiptoe to the living room.

Nothing but quiet.

Same in the kitchen.

After securing the locks and checking the standard hiding places for monsters, I allow myself to relax with each cleared room. But the moment I walk back into the bedroom it comes roaring back. Light fills the room, I blink against the bright assault and begin to inspect the room with scrutiny.

Hands resting on my hips, I scan every square inch. It looks like it did before I fell asleep. Glancing at the clock, I realize I've only been out for an hour or so. Not finding anything out of place, I check under the bed one more time and crawl back under the covers.

Wide-eyed, I stare at the ceiling. There's no chance of going back to sleep now. Might as well make the most if it with more work like I always do. Picking up where I left off, I grab the top file, flip it open and...

What the heck?

The last file. I swear, the last file I was reading was on Brandon Lovall. I left it on top, opened, now that I'm thinking about it, but that's not the file in my hand. No, the one on top of all the others—on my bed beside where I was sleeping—is Tony's, not Brandon's. Either I was sleep-working or...

Glancing at the rest of the files, I see they're neatly stacked. Which is something I'd normally do but I was tired and didn't give a crap about how neat the files were and just fell asleep. Which, I rub my tongue along my dirty teeth, I need to brush my teeth.

Was I drunker than I realized?

A shiver rakes down my spine, shaking my shoulders. I wrap my arms around my shoulders and rub my hands up and down for warmth. I wasn't that drunk. An unsettling thought enters. Someone was in my house while I was asleep. They stood over my bed and sifted through the files, maybe even watched me sleep.

And since Tony's file was the one on top, could it have been him, sneaking in to get a peek at the file he's obviously worried about. Or was it the mole, rifling through it all trying to find out what information I have so far, and Tony's just happened to land on top?

Or are the mole *and* Tony—one in the same?

———

Tony leans against the wall, arms crossed over his lean chest, waiting outside the interview room when I pull open the heavy metal door to building two. Half of his platoon today and the other half tomorrow, plus a couple of Gabe's men, who weren't selected to go on the recent mission, scattered in. Nine interviews—covert interrogations, really— is a lot for one day but I'm ready to get this part over with. The sooner these interviews are done the sooner I can solidify the potential mole pool.

The other day, before the incident with Beasley, I'd jotted down six names. Now's my opportunity to verify if those six names stay or, if after hard questioning, the number can dwindle to a more manageable amount.

My feet slow the closer I get to Tony. There's no denying my reluctance to see him, for many reasons. We haven't talked since the pool incident and because I still suspect he might have been the one who broke in two nights ago.

But with Gabe still away, Tony's my point man until he returns. I still have a job to do. Annoying, petty, old one-night stand or not, these interviews have to happen. The one-on-one time with him might prove beneficial too. I can get a better read on him without Gabe's damn cute dimples around as a distraction.

The file on Tony is spare at best. He's an average SEAL and a less-than-average leader. His men on a couple of occasions have voiced concerns regarding his leadership under pressure. This could be the reason he got so worked up when he found out I had requested all the files.

"Good morning. You look like shit," Tony says, assessing me.

"What happened to you?" With a push off the wall, he's striding to meet me halfway.

Getting pissed at his comment would take more energy than I have. Plus I saw myself in the mirror this morning, and he's only telling the truth. I do look like shit. The couple hours of tipsy sleep were all I've gotten the past forty-eight hours.

"Thanks for pointing out the obvious, asshole."

His laugh has no amusement behind it. "Seriously, you sick or something? I can show you where the sick bay—"

"Why are you being so damn nice when you've been nothing but a prick since I stepped on base? What gives?" He tucks his hands in his pockets and looks across the hall to some random painting he now finds interesting.

Seriously, sleep deprived or not, there's no missing this shift in him. He's relaxed, less like he has something to prove. He could be trying to throw me off tilt. Thinking if he is pleasant I won't suspect him of being the mole or the one who broke in. Only way to find out is to be direct and see how he reacts.

"Anyway, I look like crap because I've been sleeping less than usual. Normally if I get 2-4 hours of good sleep I'm okay but the other night..."

I pause to gauge his reaction, which is genuine in the way his focus swings back in anticipation of what I'm going to say.

"The other night...what? Just spit it out."

"I think someone snuck into my house while I was sleeping."

It happens so fast. One second he's over there, and the next he's so close I'm stumbling backwards. His firm grip on my shoulders keeps me upright. "Tell me. Now. What happened, Lucia?"

Oh geez, here comes the typical overprotective bullshit. "Nothing happened. I woke up and something felt off." His sigh of relief moves through my hair and he loosens his grip to take a step back. Eyeing him, I monitor every move and feeling. The relief he showed was genuine but is it because I wasn't hurt, or because I have no proof someone had in fact broken in, leaving him in the clear?

"Do you want me to find you somewhere else to stay?" he asks and digs a can of tobacco out of his back pocket. He pops a lump into his lip and leans against the wall. "I'd offer my place but the wife and I... hell, I don't even want to be around for our fights. No doubt you wouldn't want to be either."

"No, I'm fine," is what I say instead of "I can't." No way I'm going to give the agency any hint this operation is more than I can handle. So someone snuck into my house, watched me sleep, and read some files. I've upped the security around the house. No way I'm running away from this guy.

"Of course you are," Tony replies looking to the ceiling like he doesn't know what to do with me.

"What does that mean?"

"Nothing. You ready? Blinker is in there waiting."

"Are we going to talk about the 'incident'?" I ask with an arched brow.

He wipes some spit off his chin with his sleeve and goes back to staring at the painting. "I'm sorry for what I said, Lucia. This whole shit of why you need to be here and *you* being our fucking CIA contact. Anyone else in the world and the one woman I...hell. I guess we both have tempers we need to work on."

"Guess so. Sorry I almost drowned your guy."

His curt laugh cuts the tension between us. "He deserved it. Damn tool. Great SEAL but a dickhead and a pain in my ass most days. Listen, I don't know how I feel about you being in that place alone with you thinking someone broke in. I can get someone to come stay over. My guy Matt has mentioned several times he'd cut off his damn leg for more time with you."

"Thank you but no. I have to say, this nice side of you—I'm not sure I like it." I pat his cheek, a little harder than necessary and start toward the interview room. "Kind of prefer the prick side. Way more entertaining."

Tony's smile widens, the bulge in his lips grows larger. "Well sweet cheeks, I'm more than happy to oblige. Now hurry the fuck up and let's get this boring ass day started."

With a sappy smile plastered on my face I reach for the door pull but he beats me to it. As the door opens I flash back to the first day when I'd met the teams, which of course makes my heart ache for Gabe.

Damn I wish he was here.

———

"Well that went a hell of a lot better than I expected it to," Tony says as we walk out of CO William's office.

The CO's admin stands as we walk by and asks how it went. Tony ignores him completely. I wave as we rush by.

"That was rude," I say and jab the end of my pen into his bicep.

He huffs. "Like I care."

"Ah, back to being the ass I know and barely tolerate, I see." He smiles and nods as we descend the stairs. "And I think five is a great number. Plus I think explaining why I have so many men on the list helped. They aren't all hiding something bad but they are hiding something. I'll find out what it is and one by one we will sort through the crap and find our mole. Simple as that."

"It would be simpler to beat the shit out of all them and make them tell us what they're hiding."

I shake my head. "Simple in the moment, yes, but then you've a mess to clean up with all the men who aren't the mole. Plus we are all hoping I can find this guy without him knowing anything's amiss and identify who he's funneling information to."

"My way's more fun," he grumbles. The heat from the parking lot, compared to the near freezing temperatures of the CO's office, smacks me in the face when Tony opens the door. "Hey, now that the boring-ass interviews are over, let's celebrate. It's been a long two days, we deserve a drink. I can even invite the boys so you can have more time with them."

Not a terrible idea. I don't have anything else to do. "Under one condition."

A touch of flush tints his cheeks. "Not sure if you heard me or not but I was doing this for you, so you can go fuck off with your conditions."

Such a damn toddler.

I cross my arms across my chest and wait, knowing he's going to change his mind.

"Fine," he yells across the parking lot. "What's your damn condition?"

"We meet at six but you tell the boys seven," I yell back.

Even from here his cocky smirk is clear. "I'm glad you remember I can last a full hour."

I flip him the bird and his laugh rumbles through the parking lot. "Fine, six at the fancy bar I lured you to the other night to meet me and G."

Prick.

He waves and climbs into his truck.

I glance down at my watch. Only four in the afternoon, perfect. Plenty of downtime. Hopefully tonight, with a little probing, he'll open up to why he's been acting like a jackass over a simple one-night stand years ago. There has to be more to it. And tonight, I'm going to find out.

CHAPTER FOURTEEN
GABE

The hum of the plane engines have lulled everyone in this tin can to sleep. Everyone but me. Sleep would be amazing after being up the past few days, no idea how I'm not passed out like the rest of them. Fuck, that's a lie. It's the damn woman who popped to the forefront of my mind the second our mission was complete and haven't been able to kick out since.

Four days. A lot can happen in four damn days.

"Fuck," I grumble and look at my watch. Two more hours until expected touchdown. Two more fucking hours in this dumbass tin can before I can see her. If she still wants to see me, that is.

The entire row of chairs bounce with the bobbing of my foot against the belly of the plane.

"Damn it to hell man," Brad yawns as he sits up and adjusts in his chair. "Get some sleep and stop thinking about that stupid reporter broad."

The glare I shoot makes him laugh instead of keeping him quiet like I intended.

"We might not be as smart as you, man, but we can see when some guy is pussy whipped. And you are whipped. Bad. Real fucking bad."

The laugh I give in return doesn't carry any weight in making him think I'm not whipped. Giving up pretending, I rub a calloused hand down my face. "What if she's moved on? It's driving me fucking insane not knowing."

"Listen," he sits up straighter, stretches his arms out in front of him, and turns in his seat. "If she has, then to hell with her anyway. If she hasn't but gives you hell for being gone so long then fuck her, literally, and leave. But if she hasn't moved on and is cool when she sees you...hell, marry the chick, man. I've never seen you this worked up."

I smack him on the shoulder and hold it in a tight grip. "Great advice except for the last part."

"Hell man, you're a damn moron. Sir. I've been in the same room with that chick. She's the hottest woman I've ever seen, ever, and my wife is damn gorgeous. Plus there's something edgy about her. The first time we met her it was like she was assessing the room for threats. Hell if I know why that made her hotter, but it fucking did."

"Your point," I growl and tighten my grip on his shoulder.

"Don't break my damn shoulder, man, for speaking the truth. Any one of these guys would kill for a shot at her. If I were you I'd kidnap her, take her to Vegas and get her so drunk she wants to marry you."

"How in the hell did you land someone as amazing as your wife with shit like that running through your head?"

"She likes my kind of crazy, man. We just fucking work. Now get some damn sleep because if that Miss Freebush is waiting for you then you'll want your energy. If you know what I mean."

"I know what—"

"Sex. I'm talking about fucking. Now let me get back to sleep because I know where I want to use my damn energy when we land."

He smacks me on the back then leans his head back and closes his eyes. With a sigh I do the same. Brad's right. About everything. What happens when we land is out of my control, which pisses me off, but what I can control is being rested for when I see her.

Sleep.

I'll sleep. Land. Then find out if the woman who hasn't left my mind is still thinking about me too.

Me: Back.

    Luce: Well hey there sailor. Welcome home.

    Me: Where are you? I want to see you.

Damn fool. Lay it all out there like an idiot.

Luce: Same.

    Luce: I'm at that bar where you and Tony went that night and he had me stalk you—for reasons still unknown.

    Luce: Crazy stuff has happened in the past 4 days. Tell you all about it when you get here.

    Me: Are you okay?

    Luce: PS—Tony is here and a few of his guys too.

    Luce: PSS—I'm glad your back.

Shit. Crazy stuff. What kind of crazy stuff. What the hell does that even mean? And what is she doing at a bar with Flakes when just a few days ago they couldn't be in the same room together?

    Fuck, what did I miss?

CHAPTER FIFTEEN
LUCIA

There's no hiding my wide, stupid happy grin as I swirl the last bits of vodka around the melting ice cubes in my highball glass. He's home and safe, plus he wants to see me. The hint of insecurity that has been growing stronger with each day he was away is pushed aside with his texts.

My hopes of what the night will entail makes my smile grow wider. How is it he's not even in the same room and I'm already turned on? The way we left things with so much anticipation, it's only grown since he stormed out the door.

"What are you happy about?" Tony asks from the barstool to my right.

I down the last of my drink and push the highball glass toward the bartender. The hour before the other guys arrived was what he needed. There were things that happened that night long ago between us he needed to hash out but hasn't been able to since Gabe or someone else has always been around. No way Mr. Ego would let anyone else know he fell in love with me those few hours we had been together—if you take his word for it. Or that I shattered his heart—again if you're believing him—when I wouldn't give him the time of day after such a fun night together. Seems I was the first woman, and last, really he has to be exaggerating, to break through his cocky exterior and get to the man he really is.

The man he really is, isn't bad. Yes, he's a shitty husband and can be a complete ass when he wants to be, but deep down he's a decent human being. Which is why he went into protective mode when he thought I was sick that day.

While he vented I listened, but one thing continued to be clear as he spoke that I can't tell him; no, our relationship needs to mend a little more before I start throwing out the hard stuff. Which is, underneath the ego and bravado, Tony's a very insecure guy. He's looking for the next achievement to make him worthwhile. Which is what the CIA would have offered him after the SEALs. He didn't mention it specifically but I know he holds it against me that I'm in the agency he's been vying for. He thinks I did some kind of favors to be where I am today instead of being good at what I do. Chauvinistic prick.

"Gabe just texted," I say, still grinning ear to ear. "They're back. Safe." The bartender holds up my empty glass in a silent question if I want another. I wave him off. No one has noticed it was still my first drink while everyone else is on their third or fourth round. Not only do I have to drive home but there's also a strong possibility I'll fall asleep sitting up if there's too much alcohol flowing in my veins.

The corners of Tony's lips dip and he leans back on the stool to dig his phone out of his pocket. "Fucker didn't text me," he complains as he scrolls through his texts. I flinch when he slams the phone down on the bar.

I give him a comforting pat on his shoulder and use him as leverage to swivel on my stool around to face the growing bar scene. Only two of the men on the potential mole list had shown up. The other three men are no threat. Matt, the one Tony already made me aware had the hots for me, stayed by my side at the bar, trying to strike up small talk, until he had to leave about thirty minutes ago. Franks, the other suspect, is still here, leaning against a high-top table texting on his phone and milking his light draft beer, ignoring the long stares from the table of women to his left.

"What's his story?" I ask Tony, who shifts on his stool to see who

I'm referring to.

"Oscar Meyer? Boring as shit. Married, happily if you believe that bullshit. Has three kids. The guy even coaches their soccer teams and spends every spare second with them. Great SEAL but no interest in being an officer, will probably tap out when his contract comes up."

"What do you think he's hiding?"

"Honestly I bet he's hiding that he hates his life and his big ass smile he wears all the time is a damn lie, too."

Turning the stool to face him, I lean my ribs against the bar, a deep crease between my brows, and say, "You really don't believe in marriage do you? That there is one person out there only for you and you only for them who can make you both forever happy."

"Fuck. You and that dumb ass G. You both have this naive fucking picture of what marriage is. Do you want to know what it really is?"

"Enlighten me."

He chugs the last of his beer, slams the bottle on the bar and motions to the bartender for another. "It's waking up to the same damn face every day. It's fighting about the same thing over and over and fucking over again. Nothing is ever good enough for the other person. And it's the constant questions and the talking and the damn interrogations every time I come home."

"Well you are cheating on her so...."

"It's not what I expected."

"What did you expect?"

"You."

Mouth gaping, I take a second to recover. What do you say back to that? "Tony, I'm not that great. I would still be the same damn face every day. And if I thought you were cheating on me I would skip the interrogations and go straight to waterboarding. Don't think I'm spec—"

"I know, Lucia. I do want things to be better, it's just a lot of hard fucking work and maybe marriage isn't something I'm cut out for. I like the easy lay, no commitment."

"Then why did you even get married in the first place?"

He shrugs and drinks a swig of beer, keeping his eyes on the game playing on the TVs above the bar. "Thought it would be nice having someone to come home to." His brown eyes flick to me but focus on something going on behind me instead. "Looks like our time's up, sweet cheeks."

The word "huh" is on my tongue but when I look over my shoulder his comment makes sense. Gabe's intense stare is focused on me, only me. But I can see what he can't; every woman he passes blatantly stares at his firm ass as he moves through the crowd. Can't blame them, I'm staring too. He looks edible in his dark jeans, black boots and black t-shirt which hugs his strong arms and chest.

I'm at a loss for words when he stops in front of my stool, smirking.

"Miss Freebush," he says and reaches over to grasp Tony's shoulders. "Hey fucker." He gives Tony's shoulders a good shake and turns back to me.

That smirk falls as he takes me in.

Damn. Thought I did a decent enough job on the makeup tonight to make my sleep-deprived self look somewhat presentable. Apparently nothing gets past this guy. We would make a hell of a team.

"Let's go," he says. His commanding tone sends a shiver of excitement down my spine. I like this domineering side, hopefully it comes out again later tonight. With his hand pressed against my lower back we maneuver through the crowd until we're standing outside the bar.

He intertwines our fingers on one hand and pulls me against his chest.

"What happened?" he asks, searching my face with his eyes and caressing my cheek. "Are you sick?"

"We have a lot to talk about, Gabe. Now how are you, everything go okay? Something's up with you, what aren't you telling me?"

"Don't start with that witch shit right now, we're talking about you. What the hell happened, you look…"

"Like shit."

"I wasn't—"

"It's okay, I know I do. I haven't been sleeping. That night you left for your mission, I think someone snuck into my house."

"What?" he growls and clasps his fingers around mine so hard I have to bite back a tiny whimper.

"It...I know someone was in the house but I don't know who. I have an idea but nothing solid yet." Unwelcome tears build but I force them back before they can spill over. Must be from the sleep exhaustion. Unable to hold myself back a second longer I shake my hand free to wrap my arms around his neck. Those strong arms of his wrap around my back and hold me tight against him. It does me in, there's no holding back my exhausted tears from spilling down my cheeks. "It's a hell of a lot better now," I murmur against his skin as I bury my head into the crook of his neck.

"Ditto, sweetheart. A hell of a lot better."

My lids grow heavy in the safety of his arms and I start to sway, nearly falling asleep standing.

"Gabe?"

"Luce."

Even half asleep my nickname, said in his deep voice, is everything. "I need to go."

"Wherever you're going I'm going," he whispers into my ear. My cheeks burn from holding this wide smile for too long. "One thing, sweetheart." I pull back to see his face and find him smiling too. "You have no fucking idea how badly I want to strip these clothes off you the second we get where we're going, then take my time memorizing every inch of your beautiful body, but..."

Who needs sleep? His plan sounds way better than going home and begging him to stay so I can get a few hours of good sleep.

"But what? Your plan sounds amazing to me."

With a deep chuckle he pulls me back against his chest and rests his head on the crown of mine. "But, I'm so damn tired. I didn't sleep the last four days either."

"Didn't you sleep on the way back?"

"Couldn't...had stuff on my mind."

"I feel like you're doing this for me because you know how tired I am. Which is fine because I am but you're getting the raw end of the deal."

"Fuck no," he says and takes a step back. He finds my hand and pulls me down the sidewalk. "Sleeping by you all night sounds amazing. Then tomorrow, when we're both not zombies, the real fun can start. And how convenient we'll already be in a bed."

I wait, rubbing my arms to keep the night chill at bay as he opens the door. "Good thing I went to the store earlier, then." He arches a brow and leans against the opened passenger door waiting for me to explain. "I have plenty of food for breakfast, lunch, and dinner. No need for us to leave the house at all."

"Fuck me." His forehead falls to mine. "I don't think I've ever been this damn excited to wake up before."

"Here's the thing, sweetheart," I say, taking his face into my hands so he can't retreat. "You keep saying the phrase 'fuck me' but pretty sure I've tried twice now and it's either you saying I'm too drunk or now you're too tired. Calling your bluff, Officer Wilcox."

Those blue eyes widen a fraction before narrowing with determination. "Get in the fucking Jeep, Agent Rizzo, and I'll show you how fucking wrong you are. You and me, this starts tonight."

A shiver of thrill courses through my veins at his command. I hop into the Jeep, tuck my legs in and watch him, with anticipation doubling each second, round the hood. We peel out of the parking spot, speeding through the packed street of the Gas Lamp District. I watch him as he drives. Confident, commanding—dominant. Have I ever been with a man like this, where I can let everything go and he will take control? Take care of me.

Most of the men I've dated were meek, afraid they would hurt me or just too dang weak to push back when I pushed. But not Gabe, no, not this man. I can ask for what I want or maybe he will already know. No games, just us.

The down shifting of the Jeep, taking us to a slower speed to park, amps up the thrill. Heart pounding at the unknown, I watch him walk, casually—slowly—around the Jeep, and stop outside my door.

My breaths come in shallow pants as I watch him watch me. Damn, he hasn't even touched me. What's going to happen when he does?

The passenger door swings open but he stands blocking my way out. Grasping above my knees he turns me in the seat to stand between my spread legs.

Every nerve ending tingles at his touch as his hands slide up my thighs. Higher and higher until his thumbs meet the apex of my thighs. Torture. Pure torture as he brushes a thumb along the seam. My eyes flutter shut. My core heats and trembles as more and more pressure is applied.

"Gabe, no games," I plead. I try to close my legs around his hand but his legs between mine stop me. Reaching up I grasp his shoulders and tug, to pull his lips against mine but he holds firm with a stupid cocky grin on his face.

"Listen up, sweetheart." His voice is deep and powerful, pulling all my attention. "When we get inside I'm not going to fuck you." He chuckles at my frown. "I meant it when I said I want to take my time, but since you're an eager little vixen, just because we're not fucking doesn't mean I can't have a little fun. Go inside. Take off your clothes while I watch from the bed. I'll tell you what to do next."

Well, hell.

I try to swallow the saliva building but I've forgotten how.

That's so damn hot.

With an arm extended towards the house he steps to the side allowing me the room to shuffle past. Each step is difficult this turned on. Once inside he walks straight to the bedroom. I follow.

He kicks off his boots and climbs onto the bed, resting his back against the headboard, tucking his arms behind his head. "I'm waiting, Agent Rizzo. Start with the shoes and work your way up."

The hungry look in his eyes, the anticipation radiating off him builds my confidence. With a smirk of my own I bend over to tug off one wedge bootie, then the other, working my way through my socks and wiggle out of my jeans. When my thumbs hook around my lace underwear to pull those down too, he stops me.

"I want to do that. Skip to your top. Now," he demands through clenched teeth. The cocky smirk has faded, a predator like focus now in its place.

I pull off my light sweater and reach behind my back, unhooking my bra and sliding the straps down my arms. His blue eyes shutter and close for a brief second like he's trying to reign himself in. When they open, the blue in his irises has darkened as has his overall expression. "Come here," he commands.

His tone and hunger for me has my thighs clenching as I tiptoe over. As soon as I'm within arm's reach, his hands wrap around my waist and guide me to straddle his lap. The firmness beneath me has me pressing against him trying to find any relief for the ache building there.

Coarse hands brush around the bare skin of my waist, down my spread thighs and back up to my breast. He mumbles a verse of curses as he cups his hands around me, massaging. My head falls back, sending my hair cascading down my back as his fingers tease and pull my peaked nipples.

Panting, needing more, I reach out to bring his face to my chest.

"You're so fucking gorgeous. Perfect," he mumbles to himself. "Your body." I cry out when he flicks both nipples for emphasis. "Your smart ass mouth." His thumb brushes my lower lip before pushing through. His focus stays on my mouth as I suck and nibble, possibly turning me on more than him. "Your mind, you're so damn brilliant."

His eyes search mine and in this moment I'm bare to him. Stripping off my clothes was nothing compared to letting him see me, the real me.

Vulnerable. Tired. Strong. Proud.

And scared shitless.

Sex is the plan. Not this. Not sweet words I need to hear, not the adoring way he's looking into my soul as I sit naked on top of him.

Enough.

Gripping what short hair I can, I pull his lips to meet mine. There's no holding back my groan when he gives in. One hand weaves into my hair, fisting and pulling my head all the way back, exposing the length of my neck. He sucks and bites down my neck making the build between my legs almost painful.

Widening my legs, I press firmly against him and rock forward.

The pressure is barely enough to keep from screaming in frustration. He kisses down to my chest, between my breasts and pauses. "Fuck, I love your tits." As he pulls back his eyes lock with mine. I watch with pure lust and fascination as he leans forward with a smile to graze a nipple between his teeth.

"Gabe," I gasp and arch my back trying to get more.

I need more. I'm so close. He's too much. We're too much.

"Damn I love hearing my name on your lips. All fucking breathless from me. Sweetheart, you gotta stop rubbing against me like that, and sounding like you do, or I might fucking go in my pants."

Taking his words as a challenge, I grasp his shoulders and press down harder against him.

One second I'm on top of him, the next I'm staring at the ceiling with him between my legs.

"Why are you still dressed, damn it."

The rough scruff on chin and cheeks scrape down my stomach as he trails down, kissing my bellybutton along the way. Up on my elbows I watch him slide my underwear down my thighs and toss them to the side, never looking away.

A hand on each knee, he spreads my legs farther apart exposing me completely to him. Heart about to hammer out of my chest, I see him slowly lick his lips. Those eyes flick up to mine and a mischievous grin spreads across his face.

Gabe kisses up one thigh then the other, dragging his tongue and blowing cool air against my heated skin. My hands fist the sheets at the first touch of his lips against my tiny bundle of nerves, flicking it with his tongue making my back arch off the bed.

In a slow rhythm he sucks me between his lips and releases. Each time I beg for more which he gives, increasing the pace. A single finger slides inside. Every nerve focuses on his finger and lips moving, teasing me. My pulse thunders in my ears.

When the second finger plunges in, filling me more while flicking his tongue right above, all concept of reality fades to black.

CHAPTER SIXTEEN
GABE

Everything about her is fantastic, even the way she tastes. Hell, who knew her squirming beneath me and hearing my name breathless on her lips would be hypnotic. I don't give a fuck about me, even if my dick is throbbing in my jeans aching for its turn. Making this last as long as possible with my face between her legs is my only goal.

I suck her between my lips, my teeth gently clamping. She curses and moans in the same breath. More of her, more of her sounds, more of her body. All of her is what I need. The only thing I'll ever need.

What the hell was I thinking that sleep would be better than this? I've no idea how I'm even conscious right now but there're some things in life you have to power through for, and Luce is one of those things.

The world goes silent, cutting off the deep rattling of her labored breaths, and sweat drips down my temples as her thighs squeeze tighter and tighter around my head. She's close, this fucking beautiful woman is about to fall apart because of me. Vibrations from my deep, primal growl shove her over the edge.

Okay. Her breathless saying my name is one thing, but that fucking whispered, broken scream is beyond amazing.

Continuing to stroke her through the tide of her orgasm I watch with fascination. Damn, she's beautiful. Perfect. Relaxed against the bed, the shudders that had racked her body gone, my lips trail up her naturally tan belly to her collarbone and lie beside her on the bed.

Those green eyes don't greet me, only her deep, even breaths.

"Luce?"

"Hum," she responds softly.

With a content sigh I kiss her cheek, push off the bed and start to strip down. Still staring at her, my fingers hover at the top button of my jeans as I take her in. For the first time she looks peaceful, relaxed. Happy even. How often does she get this kind of reprieve from her work, from the life she's been building?

I grip my still-hard cock as I step out of my jeans, kick them aside, and try to think of anything other than the beautiful brunette in front of me so I can at least try to hit the bowl when I go in there to piss. A shower would be amazing, maybe take care of the situation in my hand so tomorrow I can last longer than two seconds, but with what she said about someone breaking in, there's no way in hell I'll leave her out here alone.

Careful not to wake her, I scoot her to the top of the bed and pull the covers around her before crawling in beside her. That sexy bare ass of hers scoots up against me.

"You're big spoon," she grumbles into her pillow.

Never been one to cuddle but she really didn't ask. Which makes a smile break out across my face. Rolling on my side, I pull her against my chest and wrap an arm around her, which she grabs and tucks between her soft breasts.

I choke back my groan as my dick nestles against her ass. My balls grow bluer than they already were.

Deep, low breaths signal she's already back asleep. Something she hasn't been able to do in four days. Reflexively I pull her tighter against my chest to keep her safe, for her to feel protected while she sleeps. I hope that fucker does come back. With me here. I'll take care of him for her, make sure he never gets close to her again.

For four days she couldn't sleep but two seconds in my arms and she's out. Any woman can get me off but this, knowing she trusts me to protect her, does things to my pride and ego like nothing ever has before.

My eyes grow heavy with the heat of her pouring into me and her even breaths slowing my own. Somewhere between awake and asleep the moment from earlier flips to the forefront of my mind. When she was sitting on top of me there was something behind her eyes that didn't make sense. I felt the vulnerability she had but there was fear there too. But why would she be afraid of me?

Before I can think it through, the last several days catch up to me and I'm out.

CHAPTER SEVENTEEN
LUCIA

And he thinks I'm beautiful, perfect even. He has to see the same in himself. Propped up on my elbow I watch him sleep, maybe even pull the covers down a little to get a full view of his naked chest and abs. He's the real life version of a hot action figure. Strong, lean muscles cover every inch of what I can see. Interested to see if those muscles go all the way down I lift the covers to take a little peek.

Yep. Everything looks strong…

To keep from squeaking in excitement I bite my lip and lay the blanket back down. Maybe I should wake him. I glance at the clock on the nightstand.

Ten in the morning.

How is that even possible? I haven't had more than a couple hours of sleep at a time in years much less sleep in. Even if I try to deny it there's no logical way to. I slept because he was here and I felt safe in his arms. This morning not only do I feel rested but there's no tension in my shoulders, nothing running through my mind of what I need to do next. Like somehow him being here has taken the weight of the world off my shoulders, or maybe half of it because he's shouldering the other.

A groan of pain. His muscles twitch, a snarl pulls at his lips as he

tosses and turns, mumbling things through gritted teeth I can't deci-
pher. But I don't need to know what he's saying to understand what
kind of dream he's having.

I have them myself. Not as often now but those first few years out
of the army they plagued me like they seem to be plaguing him.

Enough waiting. I brush the tips of my fingers down his sculpted
chest, through a scatter of blond chest hair, to the waistband of his
boxer briefs. As I trail along the band he stills recognizing, even in his
sleep, I'm no threat.

My hand barely dips beneath the fabric and his hips buck trying to
guide my fingers to where he wants them. But what he gave me last
night, the blissful sleep, I want to return and no way will my hand do
that for him. Tossing a leg over his thighs I climb on top and begin to
kiss down his chest, following the same path my fingers had forged.

I tug his boxer briefs down. He groans but doesn't fully wake.

Good.

Gripping him with both hands I begin to stroke up and down as I
lean over to kiss the corners of his mouth. Tempting. Waiting. Blue
eyes flicker open, blink a couple times and focus on me. It takes half a
second for him to catch onto my intentions. When he does, a lazy
smile spreads across his cheeks making those dimples appear.

"Good morning to you, too," he says in a sexy deep morning voice
I hope sticks around all day.

"Sorry for falling asleep last night. I was hoping to make it up to
you this morning."

"You don't have to make up anything, but if you want to. Fuck
yeah."

I press my lips hard against his, taking his lower lip between my
teeth and pulling. His cock twitches in my hands. Scooting back I lean
down and take the first inch of him into my mouth and swirl my
tongue. His hips shift to the side like he's trying to keep from
thrusting into my mouth.

Gabe's whispered curses and groans fuel me to keep going, taking
him deeper and deeper. Doing this has never been a turn on until
now. Until this sexy sailor beneath me, totally at my will, letting me

take control. I'm doing this to him. No one else. Heat builds in my core begging for a repeat of last night.

Hands snake into my hair holding me as he lifts and pushes into my mouth. Those grunts come faster, his grip on my hair tightens.

"Fucking hell Luce," he growls. "I'm going to…if you want to—"

Looking up to meet his pained, questioning stare I shake my head. No way in hell I'm going to quit now.

Three more deep thrusts and he's pulsing in my mouth, cursing and praising my name. When his grip on my scalp loosens I look through my dark lashes. Bright and clear eyes stare back.

"Well that's one hell of a way to wake up," he says with a grin then yawns. "What time is it?"

"After ten. I'm about to start making breakfast or I guess brunch at this point."

Gripping me under my arms, he hauls me up beside him and turns on his side to face me. "Breakfast?" he asks and plants a tender kiss on my lips. "Want some help?"

I shake my head and try to bite back a smile. "No, I have it handled but if you want to come be my eye candy, I wouldn't mind."

"What the—"

"Just don't put a shirt on, okay? I kind of like you better without clothes."

"Well now I feel like a damn party favor," his eyes flip to the ceiling like he's thinking it over. "But I fucking love it. I'll be your eye candy any day of the week, Agent Rizzo."

We roll out of bed simultaneously and tug on clothes. To make sure he doesn't cover up the amazing chest I'm excited to stare at while I cook, I slip his discarded t-shirt on and saunter into the kitchen. Two seconds later he emerges wearing only his jeans. A quick look down shows no elastic band of his boxer briefs beneath those dark jeans. Heat flushes my face and settles between my legs.

"Is this acceptable madam?"

"The court approves. You may sit," I say with a smile and start gathering all the things I'll need. I sense his stare as I cut the potatoes. "What?"

"Nothing."

"No, what?"

I toss the potatoes into the skillet and start on scrambling the eggs I'd set aside.

"You look damn good in my shirt is all. What are you making?"

After grabbing the tortillas out of the small pantry I lean against the counter and shift the now sizzling potatoes around the pan. "Breakfast tacos."

"That doesn't seem very Italian. Who taught you to cook?"

"My mom and other ladies at the different bases we were stationed. We were stationed at this base just south of Dallas for the longest time so Tex-Mex is ironically one of the better things I cook. Plus breakfast tacos aren't exactly that difficult."

Switching to the other pan, I fold the eggs over to keep them cooking evenly and go back to the potatoes. "I like to cook when I have time. Or when I'm home, which isn't that often."

"Why not?" he asks and grabs a hot potato out of the pan to pop into his mouth.

"Work obviously. The past couple of years have been hard, working towards this promotion, and the last several months I've been on back-to-back ops."

"So what do you do for fun?"

"Fun?"

"Yeah, on your days off. When you take leave. What do you do for fun?"

I laugh and put my back to him to start warming the tortillas in the oven. "A day off. I haven't had one of those in…crap I can't even remember."

The silence makes me turn to gauge what he's thinking. When our eyes meet he smiles. "Well, we're solving that today. You're taking the day off."

I start to object, the spatula in my hand raised in the air to accentuate my point, but he cuts me off.

"Seriously, you deserve it. No reading files or coming up with ways to spy on these guys, which is going to be difficult as hell but we're not going to talk about that right now. Let's do something fun like go surfing or something. Something you can't do in DC."

Against my will, my eyes widen at the surfing suggestion which he notices.

"What?"

"Nothing."

"Listen if you don't know how to surf I can teach you. Come on it will be—"

I stop him with a raised hand. "It's a little more complicated than that, sweetheart."

"How? It's a board and waves."

"Ah, so the ocean part...funny thing is," I flick off all the burners and keep my eyes on the food. "Learning to swim was never a necessity so, I never actually did learn...to swim."

I dare a glance up. Complete and utter shock registers on his face before he collects himself. A flash of recognition comes next. His eyes narrow and lips purse together. "You pushed a fucking SEAL into a damn pool and you don't know how to fucking swim?" He kind of yells, kind of doesn't. At least I can tell he's trying not to yell.

With a shrug I grab plates from the cabinet. "Yeah didn't think that one through at the time. Damn temper, gets me into more trouble." I turn and grab the four tortillas out of the oven and slide them on to our plates. After loading them up with eggs, potatoes, and cheese I place his plate in front of him and round the counter with my own to sit on the adjoining stool.

He hasn't said a word, or dropped the accusatory stare.

Finally after taking a bite of delicious taco I say, "What? I get it. Not my smartest move, you live and learn right?"

With a shake of his head he bites into his taco. "This is amazing. Thanks for breakfast. Wasn't expecting this."

"What were you expecting?"

Now it's his turn to look away and shrug. "No point of reference, Luce. I'm usually not around the next day to know what to expect."

"Ah, so no girlfriends in the past?"

Again he shrugs and starts to dig into his second taco. Dang, maybe I should have made him more.

"Nothing serious just a couple months here and a couple months there. Most women don't like me leaving on a moment's notice for who knows how long. I've come back from a few missions to them being gone, which is fine."

"That's harsh. At least I give the guy the whole 'it's me not you' speech and end it to their face. Leaving is kind of asshole."

"Never really mattered because the girl never did." His phone dings in the other room. We both freeze. He pops off his stool to check it. Crap. I've just had the best night of sleep in my adult life and now he's going away again? The smile I plaster on, as he walks back into the kitchen with the phone to his ear, is one I've practiced a million times. "Yeah I'm good. Sorry I didn't..." The person on the other end cuts him off. I watch those blue eyes roll to the ceiling. I try to hold in a laugh. "I know mom. I'll try to stop by later, but I'm not sure if...Okay, love you too."

He slides the phone on to the counter and plops on to the stool. "Sorry, my mom. Forgot to call her and tell her I made it back safe."

"That's kind of dickish."

He huffs and stands to grab two bottles of water from the other side of the sink. "That's what she just said, verbatim. Listen, I have an idea."

I shove what's left of my second taco into my mouth and nod for him to continue.

"I'm going to teach you to swim today."

Egg and potato shoot down my throat, making me choke and start coughing uncontrollably. Gabe pops the top off my bottle of water and hands it over with a concerned look on his face.

"What?" I manage between coughing fits.

He takes my plate and his own to the other side of the counter and places them in the sink. "I'll teach you to swim. It'll be fun. Get dressed and we can buy you a swimsuit before heading over to my apartment."

Not really feeling his plan, I look over my shoulder towards the front windows to check the weather.

"It's heated even though it's plenty warm outside."

Water splashes along the counter and over his bare chest as he starts on the dishes. His broad smile is infectious. How can anyone say no to that grin?

"Wait," I say but he keeps his eyes on the water. "Is this the SEAL version of 'let me help you with your golf swing'?"

He gives a reluctant "no," making his dimpled smile somehow grow bigger.

CHAPTER EIGHTEEN
LUCIA

I'm drowning.

And the hateful bastard is letting me. This I expect from Tony but not Gabe.

A strong arm snakes around my bare middle and hauls me to the surface.

"What the hell, Luce?" Gabe snarls with little bite to it. Or it could be the way his hands carefully search my face to make sure I'm not hurt, which takes away the anger in his tone.

"Why are you trying to drown me?" I yell as I shove his hands aside to wipe the water from my eyes.

A deep laugh rumbles across the pool. I peek up.

"I'm not trying to drown you. I told you to kick with your legs, not sink to the bottom like a damn rock. Besides, you're in four feet of water, sweetheart."

Right, I knew that.

I secure my feet to the bottom of the pool and stand on shaky legs but immediately drop back into the water for its warmth. For a summer day in San Diego the air swirling around Gabe's rooftop pool is cool.

"And this is the woman who jumped into a pool attempting to drown a Navy SEAL."

I start to respond but he cuts me off.

"Sorry, I guess I thought—" He runs a wet hand down his face and looks up to the mid-afternoon sky. "Okay, so basics. We will start with the basics."

"It's where we should have started in the first place like I suggested," I grumble under my breath.

"What was that?" he says trying, and failing, to sound annoyed.

"Nothing, sweetheart. Let's get started on these basics."

"How in the hell did you survive the army? You must have been a damn handful for your superiors," he says, sounding a little put out. "On your back, let's teach you how to float on your back first."

Okay, not too scary. At least my face won't be in the water. He grips my shoulders and tries to lean me back. I don't budge.

"Good grief, Luce. Relax a bit, this is your day of fun, remember?"

"Yes, this is my day off but I think you're having all the fun. Eyes up here, sweetheart, I don't want to drown because you're too busy staring at my boobs to notice I need help." His gaze shoots up from my chest. Of course there is only a cocky smirk instead of any remorse for being caught ogling.

"It's hard not to stare with that tiny ass bathing suit you have on. And I know what's underneath so it's even more fucking distracting, okay?"

"Every bathing suit is tiny when you have boobs like mine."

"I wasn't complaining," he says as his eyes drop down to my chest.

"Focus." With two fingers placed under his chin I tip his face up.

"Lean back into my arms, I won't let you drown. Promise."

Faking confidence in his words I give in and lean back. The second my back touches the water I tense and try to stand.

"Calm down. You're fine, I'm here. Just relax or you will sink. You have to relax to float."

He continues talking, walking me through what he's doing, how well I'm doing and it helps.

"There you go, Luce. Look," I open my eyes and find nothing but pride shining on his face for this tiny little accomplishment I've done. "You're doing it on your own."

I can't help but smile.

"Now," that smile fades at the dread of what's coming next. "We're going to roll you over. So," He grabs my shoulders, flips me over in one smooth motion and grasps my arms. "Start kicking."

Trying to find traction in the water my legs go every which way. When I look up to him for guidance he's shaking his head.

"What. The. Hell. Was that?" he asks as he helps me stand.

"You told me to kick."

"Not like you're in fucking martial arts class. Damn Luce, have you ever watched someone swim?"

With pursed lips I look to the sky and think for a second. "That would be a negative, sailor."

Amusement floods his features. Which again makes me smile. It seems I do a lot of that when he's around. In fact, unless I'm talking to Brooke, I don't smile at all anymore. The next several minutes he demonstrates with his hands, then with his own legs and feet on the proper way to kick in the water.

Simple enough.

Take two goes smoother. I kick around the pool for several laps before my swim coach has me add in arm movements. With each kick and push of my arms he's by my side encouraging. The sun is starting to dip by the time he's satisfied with what I've learned for the day and we step out of the pool. As we're drying off a loud grumble comes from my stomach, reminding us it's time for dinner.

"Your place or mine for dinner?"

"My place, I have plenty of food and wine," I say, drying off quickly to slide on my warm, dry coverup I'd purchased along with the skimpy bathing suit.

"Luce?"

"Gabe."

When he doesn't say anything back I look up from my phone. He grabs it out of my hand, sets it down on the wooden table beside us, and pulls me against him. "Did you have fun on your day off?"

With no hesitation I nod with a big smile and lean in to brush my lips against his. "It was exactly what I needed." Who knew a day away from my phone, away from those files and the reason I'm here in San Diego was exactly what I needed. Or maybe because my day off was with him made it extra special. Either way I feel free. I'm not not free, per se, but with the agency pretty much owning me until my contract is up and their constant demands for more, sometimes it doesn't feel that way.

This day is more proof I need to start living my life instead of working my way through it.

"Want to know my favorite part?" I ask as I wrap my arms around his back and hold him close. "You in a bathing suit. You're one smoking hot water mammal, you know that? I'm glad we were alone in the pool this afternoon, kept me from having to fight bitches off you."

Those blue eyes go wide and a confident smile pulls at his lips. "Funny, I was thinking the same about you."

Biting my lip and looking to the side, I act like I'm thinking about his comment and respond with, "Surprisingly I'm not that attractive to women so you shouldn't have to fight bitches off me."

"Come on smartass, let's get you back so you can cook me dinner. I need to change first, though."

Hand in his I follow him down the hall, into the elevator and down to the fourth floor. When we'd stopped into his apartment for him to change before the pool I didn't get a chance to snoop but now that he's taking a quick shower...

The white, no pictures at all, walled living room is scarce. A TV, decent-sized couch and a lamp are the only things in here. His bedroom isn't much better. Nice bed, of course another TV—no surprise there, and a simple nightstand with a couple stacks of paper-back books of varying thickness on top.

With a quick ear to the bathroom, listening for the shower to make sure it's still on, I plop on the bed and pull off the top book to inspect the title. Rotating it in my hand to look at the back, it looks to be some kind of military strategy book. I toss it to the bed and pick up another.

Same thing. The next one is similar but a documentary from soldiers in World War II. Each book I inspect has something to do with military, strategy, or history.

I stack them all neatly on the nightstand once again, in the same order so he doesn't know I was snooping, and groan into my hands. How in the heck am I going to get him to consider the CIA? If there was any question of where his loyalties lay, the books validate it. He's military through and through. Me, I used the army, it was never where I wanted to stay.

"I can't leave you alone for a minute," Gabe's deep voice says behind me.

With every intention to tell him he didn't tell me I couldn't look around, I turn but stop short. All words, and anything not involving getting him out of that towel, slip my mind and I'm left staring, lips parted, at this hot-as-hell sailor standing in front of me. He rubs another towel against his hair, making his abs and arm muscles flex and stretch with the movement.

"See something you like?" he says in a mocking tone but when I'm finally able to tear my eyes away from the dang towel draped around his hips, his gaze holds intensity instead of humor. Still I say nothing. For the first time in my life there are no quick comebacks. "Come here," he demands.

I pop off the bed eager to obey his command.

Deft fingers untie the sash around my cover up and slip it off my shoulders, allowing it to puddle on the floor. He stops, those blue eyes searching mine asking a silent question. Instead of answering with words I wrap my arms around his neck and kiss him hard as I scratch my nails through his short hair and down the back of his neck.

Having his answer he pulls me close, crushing me against his bare chest. The bathing suit top falls to the floor and he starts working on the bottoms, his fingers leaving traces of fire along the bare skin he grazes. Ready to see all of him I grip the towel around his waist and pull.

The discarded towel acts like his green light to push us faster. He rips my bathing suit bottoms off with as much ferocity as I did his towel and grips my backside firmly with each hand, massaging and urging me harder against him. There's no way to silence my groan as I feel him hard against my stomach.

Pulling back to catch my breath I whisper, "bed." In one swoop my legs are wrapped around his waist and his hands are beneath my ass carrying me the few feet to his bed. After tossing me on the bed he stands over me, watching the rise and fall of my heaving chest and allowing his gaze to wander lower to my already-spread legs.

One hand strokes himself as the other reaches for the bedside drawer and pulls out a condom.

Every nerve ending tingles. Desperation I've never experienced before builds in my belly and between my legs. I squirm beneath him as he climbs over me, raising my hips to find any type of friction but he pulls away with a throaty laugh and begins kissing down my neck.

With each kiss he mumbles something against my skin.

"Do you have any fucking idea what you do to me?"

"I've wanted you like this since you brushed me off that first day."

"Your tits, damn I love your fucking gorgeous tits."

"Where have you been my entire life?"

"I look forward to doing this to you every fucking day."

"Forever Luce. Fucking you forever might not be long enough."

The last one stays with me, running a loop in my mind as he kisses down to my chest, but the words evaporate the second his teeth graze my hard nipple. I hiss as he uses his teeth to tease me to the brink while a hand explores up my thigh.

His growl of approval at the wetness he finds vibrates against my skin and sends another shock of pleasure to shoot down my spine and fuels my thundering heart. He thumbs and presses my center as one finger, then another, slide in. With a very unladylike groan I spread my legs further to give him more room to move. My hips start moving with the swirl of his thumb pushing me closer and closer to the edge I've been building towards since he came because of my mouth this morning.

"Fuck, Luce," he groans as he lightly clamps down on my breast, like he's doing everything he can from pushing over the edge himself. I shatter. Fall apart around his still moving fingers, breathing his name over and over.

Gabe moves to kneel between my legs, grips my thighs and raises my hips to reach his. Blood pounds in my ears as he slides in inch by inch giving me time to acclimate to his large size. I'm no virgin but I've never been with someone built like him. Shots of pain morph to pleasure as he stills.

"You okay," he hisses between clinched teeth. "Fuck, you're like a damn vice on my dick."

Eyes wide, I nod.

"I need words, Luce. Use your damn words."

I start to respond, but not fast enough for him apparently. Before I can voice a word his open palm smacks against my backside with a loud smack.

Panting, I stare, not understanding what the heck is going on.

"Words. Now."

"Yes," I whimper, loving whatever he's doing to me. The stinging from his palm starts to fade, making me want him to do it again. "Do it again," I say and fist the comforter beneath me.

His hand connects with my ass again, harder this time, causing garbled curses to explode past my lips.

He pulls out, leaving a void that my body is now begging to be filled again. This time when he thrusts back in there's no softness to his touch. Again and again he pushes inside. The faster he moves the build up between my thighs starts to grow again.

How is this even possible for this to happen twice in one night?

Gabe's rough hands knead my backside and hold me steady as he takes control. Those blue eyes staring, locked with mine with each push. Sweat drips from his forehead on to my skin leaving wet trails down my stomach and thighs.

I whisper his name as I come close to falling apart again for him.

Instead of responding with words he moves a hand to where our bodies connect and applies the smallest amount of pressure with his fingers. "Gabe!" I scream and clench around him. Everything except for the pulsing between my legs and him yelling my name disappears.

When I recover I open my eyes to find his head hanging, that sculpted chest of his heaving, and sweat now gleaming on the tan skin of his shoulders and arms.

Finger by finger he loosens his grip to set me gently on the bed and pulls out with a groan. I'm still in the same spot, staring at the ceiling, when he returns from the bathroom and wraps me into his arms.

Those soft lips of his press against my shoulder, kissing me as he says, "That was fucking amazing."

I smile and nod but with my back tucked against him he can't see my happy, flushed post-orgasm face.

"You okay?" The hint of worry in his voice has me rolling over to face him.

"I'm great. It's been a while but I sure as heck don't remember it ever being this good with anyone else. Do they teach you special skills during your SEAL training or something?"

The breath from his laugh brushes past the sweat on my temples. "I thought I was going to hurt you. How long is a while?"

"A while."

"You said that."

"Just hasn't been on my priority list I guess."

"Why the fuck not?"

"Most days I'm surrounded by co-workers, which I don't cross that line, and when I'm home I'm too tired to go out and find anyone I guess."

Fingertips trace up and down my arms sending goosebumps flaring in the wake. "Lucky me."

After a minute of lying in silence I peek up to find his eyes closed, but those fingers keep brushing against my skin, signaling he's still awake.

"Gabe?"

"Luce."

"Can I tell you something?"

His eyes slowly open and meet mine. Searching, a hint of uncertainty building that wasn't there before. "Anything."

A smile creeps up my lips as I say, "I've never been with a guy who takes that kind of control before." I pause giving him a second to ponder what I'm going to say next. "And I love it."

A dimpled smile appears. "Well then, Luce, I guess we're a good fit because as much as I let you boss my ass around everywhere else I'm not giving up control here."

A loud ringing cuts through our moment. We tense. He rolls off the bed with an annoyed huff. Not wanting to miss the show I roll to my side and watch his perky naked ass flex and move as he stalks to the living room. His phone is at his ear as he walks back in and plops on the bed.

I reach for a blanket, slightly uncomfortable lying here naked while he talks on the phone, but his hand smacks mine, stopping me.

"Yeah I know, but...yeah I get..." He rubs the bridge of his nose with a thumb and finger, showing his growing tension. The way he's talking, the annoyance mixed with love, there's only one person who can be on the other end of the line. His mom. "Something came up and I don't think I'll make it tonight but I promise, unless we get called out, I'll come tomorrow. What?" He glances to me then to the ceiling before replying. "Yeah Mom, I can do that for you, I've told you all you have to do is ask..."

The conversation, or should I say his mom talking, continues for a few more minutes before he tosses the phone to the side and runs a hand down his face.

"If you need me to go I can—"

"No. It's fine. I'm going over there tomorrow to help."

Silence fills the room as I wait, hoping he's ready tell me what's eating away at him, what he's been hiding from me and his friends.

"Okay, so dinner at my place still?" There's no way he can miss the hope dripping off each of those words.

"Yep, but now I need another shower."

With a nod, I start to roll off the bed to gather my clothes but instead he pulls me to him. "So do you," he says, nipping at the back of my neck.

With me in his arms he stands and starts for the bathroom.

Yes, this I can get used to. I cringe as the thought floats into my mind. I can't get used to this. This is not long term. Heck, it shouldn't have even been short term. I have a job to do and getting wrapped up in him, a man who someday—hopefully—will be a coworker, isn't a part of that job.

And what sucks the most is that our relationship has an expiration date on it and Gabe doesn't have a damn clue.

CHAPTER NINETEEN
GABE

Holy hell, this woman.

The wind whips her dark hair as we race back to her place. I had her two more times, in the shower and once more before we could get out the door, and even still all I can focus on is getting her naked again. Screw her making dinner, I'll order whatever the hell she wants just for fewer distractions.

For the second time in the last minute I catch her staring.

"What?" I ask as I slam the clutch and gearshift to make it through the yellow light.

"Can I ask you something?"

"I told you before, ask anything."

"Why do you have all those strategy and war books by your bed?"

"I like reading them?"

"But why, do you see them helping you long term in your career in the Navy, are they just light reads, or what?"

My fingers tighten on the wheel and rotate against the soft leather. How many women have been in that apartment? Too many. And how many have asked about my books? None. What the hell is she getting at with her witch shit questions?

"I guess I hope they make me better yeah, but I do enjoy reading them too. It's chess in real life. Moving people around, reinforcing certain areas. If I read about what's happened, hopefully I won't make the same mistakes as the ones before me. And if every thought I have is about who is best played where, and how long and why then hopefully I give my team better odds to come home whole. That's what it all comes down to, isn't it? Making sure I'm at my best to lead the best our military has to offer."

Something about the damn Rangers is mumbled from the passenger seat but it's lost in the roaring wind.

"But you can't be a SEAL forever."

My teeth grind against each other. Damn this woman and her questions. The semi that was building in my pants vanishes.

"No, I can't, at some point I'll have to move up or out."

"So which is it?"

"Is what?"

"Up or out for you?"

"Fuck, I don't know. What's with the million damn questions, Lucia?"

In my peripheral she shifts in her seat to face the windshield.

Shit. Smooth move, you idiot. All she's doing is asking a fucking question and I snap her head off. There's no way in hell she knows that question is the same damn question I've been asking myself the past couple months. With my contract up within the year everyone's wondering and asking what I'm going to do.

Stay and fight for the country I love and fight with the best damn team ever, hell yeah, but can I? I'm already old for this gig and each mission my body reminds me with the aches and pains. The recovery is getting longer, the missions more intense. When will it be my time to bug out?

And when I do, what will I do?

Fuck, who the hell knows? But one thing is for certain, I shouldn't be taking it out on her.

A large SUV pulls from the curb right in front of her rental as we approach, leaving the perfect opening. As I parallel park her green eyes never flick to me, staying trained on the rental house.

"Luce, listen, I—"

"Something's off," she says, still not looking to me.

"I know, I know, I didn't expect that question. I'm sorry I snap—"

"Not you, you idiot. The house, something's off." She doesn't point towards the house but doesn't take her eyes off it either.

Eying the place, nothing seems out of place to me, but before I can say so she's out and sneaking up to the front porch.

Oh hell no.

"Lucia." The door slams shut behind me as I race to catch up with her.

She's crouched beside the wooden front steps when I catch up, feeling underneath them like she is searching for something. "What the hell are you doing?"

Relief washes over her face and she stands, now holding a 9 millimeter and clip. She rips the silver tape off, pushes the clip in, and pulls the slide.

Holy fuck.

My dick twitches in my pants ready to see her do it again, naked. When she makes a move for the house I grab her elbow, which rewards me with a "what the fucking hell" look from her.

"I'll go first," I say.

Her lips purse and she looks to the dark night sky like she's gathering all the patience she can before responding. "I'm the one with the gun, you idiot."

"Then give it to me and I'll still go first."

"No," she hisses. "It's my gun. You should have brought your own."

"I didn't know I would need it, sweetheart, I was just coming over for dinner, remember?"

"Well then maybe you should have been a better SEAL, sweetheart, and learned to always be prepared."

As we banter our voices rise a level with each pass until we are almost yelling.

"So what, every time I'm around you I need to be prepared for a fucking gun battle?" I yell and toss my hands in the air. This woman is exhausting.

She wiggles the gun in her hand taunting me and smirks. "I am, sweetheart."

Enough.

I lunge for the gun half a second too late. She anticipated my move and not only moved out of my path but is now up the stairs, pushing the front door open, gun extended.

Fuck. I can see the news report now.

Navy SEAL is tossed out of the Navy because he let the hottest fucking woman on this planet go into a building, armed when he wasn't, because she was better prepared than him, first.

A loud "what the hell?" sends me taking all three stairs at once to the top of the porch and slamming the door open wide.

Huh?

Flakes?

Luce still has her gun pointed at him when she says. "What the heck are you doing in my house when I'm not here, Tony?" she demands.

The cocky prick he is shows no sign of fear as he lounges on the couch eating something from a red plastic bowl.

"You're going to need more grapes, sweet cheeks," is all he replies.

A shrill, no other way to describe the sound, pours out of Luce before she sets the loaded gun on the counter and drops to a crouch. It's only then that I see her trembling hands. Whether from adrenaline or rage, who knows.

As I unload the gun I say over my shoulder, "What the fuck are you doing here, Flakes? Do you have a key or something?" For the first time in a long time jealousy seeps into my veins, clouding my thoughts. But Luce replies before I can go apeshit.

"No, he doesn't have a damn key, Gabe. I didn't invite him over either," she says from the floor.

"Ah but you did," Flakes swivels on the couch to face us. "Last night before you got the text from G saying he was back you mentioned coming over to talk about the mole shit and what's next."

I squat down beside her. "You okay?"

"Yeah just need a second, a lot going through my mind right now."

The comment from earlier still needs to be apologized for but right now isn't the time. Grabbing two bottles of water from the counter I set one down in front of her. It's freaky seeing her like this. There's no emotion, like she's locked in her own mind searching for answers when I don't even know the damn question.

"You have to be kidding me," Flakes mumbles as I sit in the chair opposite him. "You fucked her, didn't you? Now you're all nice and shit. I warned you, a fucking drug that one, and now my friend you're a damn addict. I bet all you're thinking about right now is getting—"

"Shut the fuck up, Flakes," I say. His mouth opens to keep going but the look I shoot him promising death and dismemberment, probably not in that order, makes him hesitate.

Finally Luce pushes off the floor. "Where's your truck?"

Huh. Yeah, where is his truck?

Not flinching at the accusatory tone he says, "Had to park halfway down the street to find a spot."

"How did you get in?" I ask as I track Luce crossing the living room. She leans against the wall, stiff and unwelcoming. Which is strange since it seemed they were fine yesterday. Her defensive stance, the furrowed brow stare she's giving him, says something's wrong.

"Old house, old locks."

Flush spreads up her neck to her cheeks. "You broke into my house?"

He shrugs and looks to me. "She wasn't answering the door, her car was out front and need I remind both of you she thinks someone broke into her house a few nights ago so I was worried. I broke in to make sure she wasn't hurt or dead."

"Then decided to rummage through my fridge," Luce says, still not breaking from her stiff posture.

What is she seeing that I'm not?

"I'm an opportunist, what can I say?" Flakes smirks and stretches his arms along the back of the couch.

Something's grumbled from her direction.

Eyes locked with mine in a stand off of sorts, Flakes asks, "Ready to get started?" The fucking cocksucker knows exactly what he's doing. He'll probably post up here all damn night just so I can't be alone with her as soon as I want. Which was ten damn minutes ago.

Not dropping his asshole gaze I say, "She needs to eat."

"Women get so angry when they're hungry." He shakes his head. The tension he's been holding onto since we walked in slips a rung. Hopefully his dickhead attitude goes with it.

I lean forward, placing my elbows on my thighs. "She calls it hangry."

"Hangry?"

"Yeah angry because you're hungry. Hangry."

Flakes digs around his back pocket while he says, "Clever. Think she came up with it?" He pulls out his can of snuff, pops one in and extends the opened can to me with a raised brow.

"I'm standing right here you know. And no, I didn't come up with the saying but I'm absolutely getting hangrier by the second so let's do something about that." She shoves off the wall so hard the walls groan and stalks to the kitchen.

Even as she starts banging around, pulling out pots and pans, we don't make a move. He leans forward and whispers. "I'm scared to go in there. Too many weapons."

I cover my laugh with a fake cough. "Fuck, I know. I'd rather take on a truck full of armed men buck-fucking-naked than go in there."

"At least she likes you, she'd probably cut off my balls for shits and giggles then use them for shooting practice."

There's no covering my rumbling laugh this time. "No way man, I'm in the same damn boat. I pissed her off right as we pulled up."

"Why'd you do that you dumb ass? Great, now neither of us are getting out of this alive. I bet she even knows how to bury our bodies so no one will ever find us."

"Lye."

We shoot up from our seats and reflexively cover our balls. She's leaning a shoulder against the door frame of the kitchen twirling a knife in her hand.

A smirk pulls at her lips as she says, "Lye will help decompose a body so less chance of being found and almost eliminates the possibility of identification if they are." Our shoulders slouch in unison when she turns back towards the kitchen but snap back up to our ears when she turns to us again. "But I have people to do that for me. If I wanted you gone you would be. Not a single trace you ever existed. Think about that as you both sit on your butts not offering to help me make dinner."

"How is that hot?" Flakes whispers once she's out of sight.

I clasp him on the shoulder and move by to see what Luce needs help with. "I don't know man, maybe we are both fucking twisted because I agree."

This woman might be the death of me in more ways than one.

But ask me if I fucking care.

———

Damnit to hell that idiot was right. I need to marry this woman.

I fist my hands at my side to hold back from grabbing the plate and licking off what's left of the homemade sauce. Glancing over, Flakes isn't shy about using the garlic bread to soak up every drop.

"There is more, Tony," Luce says between bites. She's eaten as much as we have, maybe more if you count all that garlic bread.

The fact she eats and isn't ashamed of it notches up her attractiveness.

Glancing from his plate to the pot on the stove, Flakes hesitates then says, "Screw it, yeah I want more. A lot more."

He slides his plate to her and nods to the pot. Arching a brow at his plate she says, "Um, I'm not your maid. Get it yourself you lazy ass."

Not ready to be done either I do the same, but as I pass by her sitting on the stool at the counter I wrap an arm around her waist and pull her against my chest. "I'm going to eat you for dessert," I whisper into her dark hair.

"I fucking heard that you tool," Flakes complains.

"You cook, you know your way around a firearm, you read fucking minds, is there anything you don't do, Luce?" I ask as I load more noodles on to my plate expecting it to be a rhetorical question but should have known better when it comes to her.

"Yeah, anal."

All the noodles I'd just loaded on to the plate slip off and plop to the floor when I wheel around to face her, in the same second half chewed spaghetti is spewed across the kitchen by Flakes. We look to each other then to her only to find her doubled over, no sound, only her shoulders shaking uncontrollably.

When her hands pull away from her face tears are dripping down her cheeks and her smile is so big it looks like it hurts. Quick shallow breaths are all she can manage as she continues to silently laugh so hard. Seeing her like this, carefree, happy, I smile too.

"Don't knock it until you've tried it," Flakes says as he wipes the remnants of spaghetti off his face and shirt.

That only makes Luce laugh harder.

"Your…." She says in between laughs. "Faces…" Again she starts silent laughing.

"Damn woman, you made me waste food," I say with little bite mostly because of the stupid grin on my face.

After we've cleaned up our mess, had more to eat, and Luce is able to have a normal conversation again, everyone is in relatively good spirts. It's close to ten by the time we're making our way back into the living room. Flakes and I fall on to the couch, so full it's uncomfortable, as Luce sits in the chair opposite us and tucks her feet under her.

"I'm starting tomorrow," she announces while examining one of her red nails.

"What?" Flakes and I say in unison.

Her hand falls to her lap as she pins us with a determined stare. "I'm starting the recon part of all this tomorrow night. And I'm going to start with Franks."

I can't see Flakes but no doubt he's staring dumbfounded like me.

"Who's going with you?" Flakes asks hesitantly.

Those green eyes narrow at him. Even though they aren't narrowed at me my hand itches to cover my crotch for precaution.

"I think what he's trying to say is these aren't your normal marks,

Luce. They are SEALs. If they make you, shit is going to hit the fan. And more than likely, they will make you."

That narrowed stare slides to me. This time I can't stop my hand which of course she notices.

"That is quickly becoming my favorite part of you, Officer Wilcox, don't worry I won't injure it," she says, almost hissing. "Now listen here boys. I'm good at what I do because of the way I read people, yes, but I can also blend in. I'll go unnoticed. It will be fine. And side note, if this is going to work at all, me telling you my plans, you both can't go ape alpha protective male on me every time I mention doing something dangerous. It's my damn job."

We nod in unison.

Lucia fucking Rizzo just handed two SEALs their balls in one breath. I'm an idiot if I don't kidnap her and make her marry me.

Flakes clears his throat and says, "What's your plan with Oscar Meyer?"

A jolt of adrenaline shoots into my veins as a wicked smile spreads across her face.

CHAPTER TWENTY
LUCIA

Rattling on the nightstand pulls me from a deep sleep. But I don't move. Gabe's strong arm is wrapped around my middle, tucking me against his chest, and a leg tossed over my hip. I'm too snuggled in this protective cocoon to care who's calling so early.

It stops. My eyes drift shut. Only to have the rattle start up again seconds later.

Who the heck needs me this urgently at five in the morning?

I try peel out of Gabe's grasp but he pulls me back to keep me against him. I rock forward, and this time he allows a little movement, enough to stretch across the bed. It stops vibrating the second my fingertips graze the rubber case.

Of course it does.

But I pull it into the bed and keep it close. It will start up again soon. Whoever is calling is persistent.

I swipe the phone when the screen lights up.

"Hello," I grumble letting whoever this 'unknown caller' know I'm not happy they've woken me up so early.

"Agent Rizzo. We need to talk."

Shit, the boss.

I jolt upright, sending the warm blankets to pool around my bare waist. Even though he can't see me, I think, my need for coverage has me reaching for the blanket and pulling it up to my shoulders. "I need a recap on your current operation."

Recap. Right. Heck when was the last time I even talked to Jeremy? This lack of communication isn't like me. A quick glance to the sexy, naked man in my bed reminds me of where my priorities have been lately. How could they not?

"Yes sir, I've identified six men whom I believe are viable suspects. Tonight I'm starting exploratory missions to see what each are hiding and who is our mole." The five I told the CO plus Tony.

"Time frame."

"Two weeks, maybe less." My heart falls heavy. Only two more weeks of him. Of us.

"Excellent Agent Rizzo. I want the names of those six men. Get them to Agent Dungan as soon as possible."

"But—" I start but he cuts me off.

"And what about your other mission? How are things going with Officer Wilcox?"

Thankfully Gabe doesn't try to hold me back this time. The sheets are cool against my skin as I slide out of bed. The early morning air causes goosebumps to prickle my arms and legs. I retrieve a hand-made throw on the back of the living room chair and wrap it around my shoulders.

"I'm not sure exactly. He's not giving me much. Honestly I'm not sure he even knows what he wants to do. I've thought about outright asking him about coming over but..." But I don't want to ruin what we have.

His deep voice is impatient. "Agent Rizzo."

"Sir."

"It's your job to make sure the CIA is what he wants to do. Do you understand?"

Of course I understand, but that's not going to change the outcome is what I want to say, but instead I say yes.

"One more thing, Agent Rizzo."

The phone bites into my hand. Of course one more thing. It's always one more thing with them. What else can I give? What do they want from me now?

"Sir."

"We've decided this is an excellent opportunity for us to find new players in the intelligence trade. When you identify the mole, not only do we want you to let us know who, but we also want you find a way to identify his partners, who he's been selling information to."

The yarn of the throw goes taut around my bare shoulders. "I don't understand, you want me to interrogate the—"

"No, Lucia. We don't want you to interrogate anyone."

My stomach churns and dips at what he's wanting but not asking.

"We'll be in touch once you identify the mole, if you can get all the major players in this. I don't need to explain how positive it will be on your record when you interview for the promotion."

Interview…I thought it was mine if I did all this. Of course. Brooke was right, I'll never get it. They're using me and I've been too driven to notice it.

"I'll be in touch."

Cool air brushes against my warm ear as I stare at the blank screen.

Shadows shift behind me. I turn. "What's wrong?" he asks, searching my face with his beautiful blue eyes. He's leaning against the doorframe still gloriously naked. Staring.

"Nothing," I mumble and pull the throw tighter.

"Don't lie to me, Luce. Tell me you don't want to talk about it or it's none of my business, but don't ever lie to me. That's my line in the sand."

Keeping my eyes to the floor, so he doesn't see my guilt, I nod and start towards the bedroom ready to be snuggled in the warm bed with him. He lets me pass without another word. Falling on his back, he stares at the ceiling instead of pulling me to him.

I do the same.

"I've never been on this side," he says in the dark a few minutes later. "I guess I've never thought how the other person feels when they want to know what's going on in my life and I can't or won't say a damn word. This fucking sucks."

Rolling on my side I face him and curl my knees to my chest. "I'm sorry, Gabe, I really am, but it's my job. There are so many pieces to this operation you can't know them all."

"I know, it will take some time getting used to it is all. I'll make it work." The bed shifts and dips as he rolls over, putting us nose to nose. "Just tell me this. Are you okay?"

"You want the truth?"

"Always."

"Then I don't know. I'm not really sure what that call was about. It's always like that. I have to decrypt what he was saying but not saying at the same time. It was my boss on the phone."

His hand takes up my entire cheek as he cups it and brushes gentle strokes along my cheekbone with his thumb. "You're too good for them, you know that."

"Most days I'm inclined to disagree with you. But right now I feel like it's never going to be enough. That no matter what I do I'm never going to be enough."

His hand slides back and tangles into my hair. "Fuck that shit," he spits. My eyes fling open at his ferocity. "Who's your damn boss? I'll call him back right now. What exactly did he say?"

My teeth sink into my bottom lip to hold back a small smile. "Thanks, but I can handle it."

His soft, full lips tease mine. The remaining tension disappears with each of his warm breaths. "But that's just it, Luce. You don't have to handle it on your own. I'm here, let me help. I want to help."

"Not sure I can do that. I'm so used to doing it all on my own. Not depending on anyone is second nature now. Is that so bad?"

He pulls back a fraction but keeps his hand wrapped in my hair. "For us, the SEALs, yeah. We work as a team in everything. If we don't, then we don't all come home. It's about teamwork, trusting each other, knowing if you falter there's someone there to cover your ass. I know I can't do this all on my own."

It's too much. The call. Him. His words that shouldn't sting but do for some unknown reason. I try to roll on my back, attempting to avoid his intense stare, but he holds me in place. "Yeah, well that's not the way we are programmed at Langley. We have to operate alone in the field so I guess we never adapt back when we're stateside."

The corners of his mouth dip. "So you don't have any friends."

"A friend."

"A?"

"Brooke. She's my best friend. I tell her everything."

"Oh really," he says with a smirk. "And what have you told this Brooke person about me?"

"I haven't gotten to talk to her much since I've been here but I did tell her I met this hot water mammal."

"That's something. And what did she say?"

"She told me to have fun, that I can work and have a good time while I'm here. She's the reason I jumped you that night, why I was okay with breaking my rule with you."

Both dimples appear. "I like this Brooke chick already."

I drum my fingers along the blanket. "The conversation with my boss keeps running in a loop. I need to think. Wanna go for a run?"

"Or." His smile turns mischievous. My heart races and I inch back along the bed. "I can take your mind off it completely here."

My protest evaporates the second he rolls on top of me, pinning my hips with his. The first touch of his lips against my neck has my eyes softly closing, shutting off everything but us.

This.

Him.

Right now he's exactly what I need.

———

"Seriously?" Jeremy says, clearly frustrated.

"It's just six guys. Come on, it will take someone like you two seconds to get all the dirt on them through cyberspace. I'll do the people watching and you do the data watching."

He groans into the phone. But I know it's only a show to make me feel bad for asking all this last minute.

"Fine."

"Thank you, Jeremy," I squeal.

"How's everything else going?" he asks a little too nonchalantly. I hear what he's asking but not asking.

"It's good. Trying to get all this wrapped up so I can get home. There was something I was going to ask you," my fingers drum against the fabric of the couch. "But for the life of me I can't remember."

"No surprise there. I swear you have the memory of a...what animal has zero memory?"

"Dolphins."

"How in the hell do you remember random facts like that but not stuff that matters?"

"You got me. It's strange, I know."

"Anyway, what about this Officer Wilcox? Sounds like you two are spending a lot of time together."

The jealous undertone makes my eyes roll to the ceiling. "Yeah, well he is part of my op and if I want the promotion I have to do what I have to do, right? I'll make sure he comes around."

Silence on the other end says everything. "Right, well do what you need to do, I guess. I just don't want to see your reputation go to shit, you know."

Flipping to my back I lay on the cushions, my feet dangling over the armrest. "And how would that happen?"

He clears his throat once. Twice. "That you're willing to take it to the physical step to get this op done."

"And what physical step would that be, Jeremy? I hit, I kick, isn't that physical? Does me kicking someone's ass mean I'm 'taking it down to the physical side?'"

"Don't be a bitch. You know what I mean."

"I hope I don't."

"What the hell is wrong with you?"

"Maybe I'm tired of things being a one way street with the bias between men and women agents."

"Wow, didn't realize this was going to turn into a full-fledged gender thing. All I'm saying is watch how you bring him over. If you take it too far, it won't look good, Lu. I'm saying this as a friend. You might accomplish your mission but that stigma sticks around."

His biased way of thinking makes Gabe's response the other night even more special. He understood what I was saying, why can't Jeremy?

"So the traces and stuff?"

"I'll have it to you later today. And Lu."

I let awkward silence settle, not responding. Acknowledging him is too much at this point.

"You know I'm only looking out for you. I don't want to see your career hurt, the one you've given so much to. I know it's not fair, but it is what it is. You're not going to change that."

It is what it is. Invisible weight settles on my chest, making every breath a struggle. "Talk to you later." Not waiting to hear another word, I toss the phone on the table and bring my hand up to cover my face.

Good thing I waited to make that call until Gabe was gone, doing whatever he's still keeping hidden, or he would have lost his shit.

Every time Jeremy's words loop I get angrier. Heavier. Male agents get smiles and pats on the back when they score, but women apparently have a stigma attached to them if they do the same.

I grab the phone again to text Brooke but an incoming text from Gabe pops up instead.

Gabe: What time do we start tonight?

Me: You don't have to have a reason to text me you know. You can just say hi and that you were thinking about me.

Gabe: Hi. I was thinking about you. What are you doing?

Me: Sitting here kind of mad, kind of sad.

Gabe: I feel sorry for the dumbass who made you mad. You'll kick their ass, then I'll kill them for making you sad.

Gabe: What's up, Luce?

Me: Same old stuff, I guess. My handler just said something that irked me.

Me: It's just hard playing by certain rules sometimes, different expectations than the rest.

Gabe: I have no idea what you're talking about.

Me: Pretty much he told me not to sleep with anyone for the op because it would look bad for my reputation. But I know for a fact he would've never said that to a male agent.

Me: See, sad and mad.

Gabe: I'm torn.

Me: Why?

Gabe: Because I agree, I don't want you sleeping with someone for the op. I only want you sleeping with me. But I get what you're saying about the bias bullshit.

Me: Yes, bullshit.

Gabe: Want me to beat them up?

Me: By them you mean the CIA?

Gabe: I have friends, we could take them.

Me: Careful what you say, they might take that cool new phone away.

Gabe: I don't give a shit about the phone. If they pissed you off they pissed me off.

Me: Six tonight.

Gabe: Diversion. Well played Agent Rizzo. What's the plan?

Me: Tony's going to call Franks up to get him out of the house, then act like he's leaving with some strange. We will see where Franks goes from there.

Gabe: Where?

Me: Not sure yet.

Gabe: I'm not sure I can be there right at six but I'll try to be there as soon as I can.

Me: So covert, Officer Wilcox.

Gabe: I have to keep something intriguing.

Me: If it's a girlfriend or some side tail like Tony, just know I will make you disappear.

Gabe: What the fuck?

Me: Just saying.

Gabe: It's family stuff, no side tail. And honestly it fucking hurts you think I'd be anything like Flakes.

Me: Sorry?

Gabe: The question mark on the end of that loses all effect of the apology.

Me: Sorry!

Gabe: Nope, the word has lost all meaning now.

Me: Guess I'll just have to show you the next time I see you.

Gabe: Now you're talking.

Gabe: Gotta run. See you tonight. Text me the details.

Me: Okay.

Gabe: I'm serious. Text me the details. I want to go with you.

Me: Okay, officer bossy pants.

Gabe: You like me bossy.

Me: You have no idea.

Gabe: I actually do. Last night you told me multiple times how much you "fucking love my bossy ass."

Me: Well there you have it. Who knew I'd like to be ordered around in bed but absolutely nowhere else?

Gabe: Not sure what I'm supposed to say here.

Me: Hey, thanks.

Gabe: For?

Me: Cheering me up.

Gabe: Anytime, sweetheart.

Gabe: Now about that apology…

Me: Men. One track mind.

Gabe: See you tonight.

Me: Bye.

. . .

Even a minute after his last text my cheeks burn from my wide smile. Somehow in the matter of a few minutes he managed to turn my sad heart into completely forgetting about the conversation with Jeremy. Phone still in hand, I flick to Brooke's text string.

Me: You were right.

    Brooke: I knew it! I'm always right. Boom, best friend of the year.

    Brooke: Question. What was I right about?

Me: Gabe. Officer Wilcox. The hot water mammal.

    Brooke: Did you two…..

Me: We did. And I'm going to continue until I head back. It's so much fun, Brooke. I don't know if it's just me letting go that is so fun or if it's because of him.

    Brooke: Are you smiling right now thinking of him?

Me: Maybe.

    Brooke: It's him. And just so you know I'm smiling right now knowing you're smiling about him.

    Brooke: Seriously, my heart is so damn happy.

Me: How are you?

    Brooke: Good. Really good. We found a nanny today so that's a huge weight off my mind. So ready to get back to work.

    Me: Me too. I like having Jeremy as your stand-in but I miss you.

    Brooke: Just a few more weeks. But I'm ready to be back now. Can I say that?

    Me: I think you can say whatever the heck you feel like saying. Why wouldn't you?

    Brooke: I don't know, mom guilt I guess. Some of the moms at Gymboree have made me feel bad for wanting to get back to work. Like I'm a bad mom for wanting that piece of my life back where I'm me again. Not just a mom.

    Me: Give me their names and they are dead. I know people.

    Brooke: By people you mean you.

    Me: Well, I didn't want to incriminate myself over text. Thanks for that. But yeah, I'd off them. Those bitches.

Brooke: Didn't realize it would be this hard.

Me: I say that about ten times a day. Nothing is as easy as we think it will be. But at least you have me and that hottie of a husband of yours.

Brooke: When are you coming home? I need a girls' night.

Me: A week or two, not sure yet. But yes, girls' night is priority when I get back. I'll even write it down so I remember.

Brooke: I love you. And thanks.

Me: I love you too. And you're welcome. I'm here when you need me. Tell me anything. Tell me everything. Even if its just to vent. You're my lobster.

Brooke: Something tells me I won't be your lobster for long.

Me: Whatever. You'll always be my one and only.

Brooke: Okay lobster. Calm down. I'm your lobster forever.

My fingers still on the screen at the pounding against the front door.

What the heck? Flicking back to my other texts, there's nothing from Tony or Gabe about coming over. With an exhausted groan I flip my legs back over and shuffle to the front door.

Ignoring all training, I pull open the door before looking to see who it is.

Big mistake.

"What the hell? What are you doing here Petty Officer Beasley?" I ask and tighten my grip on the door. Of course I didn't grab a gun, or knife, or heck a lamp would work at this point. Damn that Gabe for making me so comfortable and protected when he's around that I'm dropping my guard even when he's not.

"Miss Freebush." His hand connects with the rickety door, pushing it wider for him to maneuver through. "Take a seat, we have a lot to discuss."

Well hell.

CHAPTER TWENTY-ONE
GABE

W here the hell is she?

A glance at the phone in my grip. Still nothing.

It's well past six, okay two minutes after, but still I expected to hear from her an hour ago with the plans. Fuck I want to text her. But I'm not going to. She said she would let me know the details when she knew. I can wait. I can be fucking patient.

Tick. Tick. Tick. My watch is on a damn speaker, amping my tension with every second that passes.

Fuck it.

Me: Where the hell are you?

Subtle. Nice, jackass.

Luce: Running late. Tony and Franks are at some bar near the base. I'll be there in ten.

. . .

Late? She doesn't do late.

Me: Everything okay?
  Luce: Interesting afternoon. Stop texting. I'm driving.

What the hell does interesting afternoon mean?

"Guess I'll find out soon enough," I mumble and grab my keys off the entry table.

———

It's a clear night, the full moon gives enough light to find the Camaro without being obvious. I park several spots down and jog to where Luce is waiting with a clear view to the sports bar.

"Hey," she says as I maneuver into the passenger seat. Damn sports car, so damn small.

"What—"

"Tony just texted. He put the tracker on Franks and will be heading out in about twenty. We have a few minutes to kill."

She talks to the windshield instead of me. Her mood is hard to read plus her damn hat means I can't see her face. Tension grows. What the hell happened in the past couple hours to make her go from happy texting to this weirdness?

"Something wrong?" I ask and immediately want to kick myself in the nuts. I sound like a clingy chick.

"Nope, all good."

The pop and crack of my knuckles echo in the small interior. Maybe it has to do with her wanting to know where I went earlier. At this point there's no reason to keep it hidden, especially if its going to make her act like this. I'll offer anything to have normal Luce back.

"It's my dad," I say and turn to the window. "He has dementia and it's just not something I want anyone to know about."

"Gabe, I—"

"He was diagnosed a year ago and it's gotten progressively worse since then. The past couple of months have been hard." I stare ahead, keeping my eyes locked with the moon even as her hand clasps mine. "My parents have been together since high school and she can't let go. It's about to kill her, trying to take care of him on her own, but she won't fucking listen. I suggested putting him somewhere. Somewhere he will be safe and taken care of. Then she can go back to having a normal life."

Condensation lines the window from my heavy breaths. As difficult as this is to talk about, with each word the weight of the burden lessens.

"This is the first time I've talked to anyone about this. Flakes knows something's up but he doesn't ask. I don't know what to do. It's my responsibility to know what to do in this situation. I can lead fourteen men to near hell and bring them all home but I can't help my own family? When I'm stateside I try to help as much as possible. But it doesn't feel like enough. Fucking hell, why am I saying this?"

I run my free hand down my face before turning to her. Sometime during my rant she'd turned in her seat but her face is still hidden in the shadows of the hat.

"Can I ask you something?" she says finally.

"Sure, sweetheart."

"What does your mom want to do?"

"She wants to keep him at home, which is fucking ridiculous."

"Why?"

"Because he needs to be in a home. She can't do this on her own. She's not happy."

"Did she say that?"

I narrow my eyes at the dumb fucking hat since I can't see anything else. "No, but how—"

"So what you're really wanting her to do is what you would do."

Well fuck.

"Here's what I think. I think it's hard on her, yes, but it would be harder for her not to be with her best friend. To know someone else is taking care of the person you've spent a majority of your life taking care of…would be a smack in the face for me. You say you want her to have a normal life but it seems, for her, there is no life without him. For better or worse and all that. But I'm sorry you're having to go through all this alone. I can tell it's wearing on you. Wish there was something I could do to help."

By simply listening she already has.

"Take that damn thing off," I growl and yank the hat off her head.

The world stops.

I rip my hand from hers to grip her chin, reining in my anger to not hurt her, and angle her face towards the dim light of a streetlamp a few feet away.

"What. The. Fuck. Happened. To. You."

My fist slams into the overhead light. She mumbles a curse and slams her fist against it to turn it off.

"Surveillance, you idiot. Remember why we're here." She moves, trying to jerk from my firm grasp. "It was an accident."

"Tell me. Now, Luce."

With a huff she lets go of the fight and leans into my hand. Damn, it feels good. Her cheek in my palm is everything I never knew I needed. "Interesting afternoon. Beasley showed up at my front door and honestly I was prepared for the worst considering he's a cocky prick that has an ego the size of a…SEAL." She smirks. "But he's really not that bad. He's all bravado, no bite."

My hand slides to her hair making the faint scent of peppermint waft through the car. "Then how the hell did you end up looking like this?"

"Yeah well, once I figured out he just wanted to talk I offered him a drink. He showed up to make sure I wasn't going to write anything bad about him or the SEALs in my article because of the pool incident. Said he was told to come apologize. Anyway he took the drink I offered. Then another. Then another. The guy was swaying by the time he left. Which is why I was late, took me forever to get him into the car and home."

"How did you—"

"Files, remember. I have everyone's information."

"Still doesn't explain your face."

"Well as I was lugging his drunk ass out to the car he stumbled, and he's a big guy, so I went with him. We slammed into the door frame and my face took the brunt of it. He flipped out when he saw my lip bleeding knowing you or Tony would kill him for it. Which of course I reassured him neither of you would."

"Fuck that. He's a dumbass for going over there alone anyway. I'm surprised the CO gave him your address."

"I know."

"Are you making all this up so I don't go kill that shithead now?"

"Are you asking if I'm lying?"

I suck in a breath and hold it. That tone sounds menacing. Backtracking would be wise.

"I know you're not lying, Luce. Just give me a minute okay."

"Fine." Her phone vibrates in the cup holder. After a quick glance at the screen she tosses it to my lap and turns on the car. "You'll have to fester on this another time, sweetheart, because our boy Franks is on the move."

My attention shifts to the front door of the bar.

"I love this part," she whispers. "The anticipation of what's going to happen next, finding out what he's hiding. I love it."

The excitement in her voice is contagious. As I look over she's smiling out the window like it's fucking Christmas morning. There's something about her energy right now, that smile and her focus. My cock eagerly twitches against my jeans.

Starting at her knee I slide up, lightly grazing her inner thigh as I go. Her focus never leaves the bar but doesn't stop me. The instant I reach my ultimate destination those green eyes flick over.

"And just what do you think you're doing?"

"You're so fucking sexy right now," I practically purr as I keep my hand between her legs wishing it was my cock instead. Even through her jeans I can feel the heat pouring from her, growing hotter as I stroke.

"You do realize I'm working. Trying to find out who's leaking mission information. And this guy, the guy now walking out of the bar, just might be the asshole endangering his fellow SEALs. Endangering your best friend."

Well, there goes the mood.

Kind of. My dick's still hard as a rock.

I pull my hand back and stick it down the front of my pants to adjust.

She's laughing as she backs out. "Later, sweetheart. I promise."

CHAPTER TWENTY-TWO
LUCIA

"Where the hell is he going?" I mumble as we weave in and out of traffic. We've been driving for half an hour. Hopefully this night isn't a bust.

The yellow turn signal on his truck blinks up ahead and he slows to pull into a sparse parking lot meant for the public beach nearby. Not wanting to be too obvious I stay straight and park along the sidewalk a ways down.

From where we sit the only thing visible is the entrance and exit, nothing more, not ideal.

"We can't see anything from here," I say and grab my hat off the floorboard. "I'm going to get..." The click of the passenger door opening sounds before I can finish. "A closer look," I mumble and slide out of the car.

Ducking and weaving between the few parked cars, sticking to the shadows, we pause behind an older model SUV where we have a clear view of Franks' truck. The dome light is on, illuminating him sitting alone in the cab.

I crouch beside Gabe and bounce on the balls of my feet. "What do you think he's doing out there?"

"No clue," he mumbles. He's confused too. "This would be a good place for a drug deal but we test for that shit all the damn time. No way he's here for drugs. Right?"

I nod. Whatever Franks is hiding I didn't get a drug vibe from him during the interview. After a minute of waiting I stop bouncing and move to shifting my weight from one foot to the other. Gabe, on the other hand, hasn't moved a millimeter since we crouched here several minutes ago. Heck, he hasn't even blinked. His focus is intense, intimidating even but seriously hot.

Tired of the burning in my toes, I lean forward to rest my knees on the hard pavement. "Were you and your dad close?" I whisper and scoot closer to the heat radiating off him.

His shoulders rise and fall. "I guess."

"That's a no." In the dim light I see blue eyes cut over. "Or was he too involved, pushing you in sports and stuff?"

"You have my file, right?"

"Yeah."

"Then you know everything about me already."

"Well…" I say, trailing off.

His knee nudges my thigh. "Well, what?"

"I didn't read yours."

"Interesting. Why not?"

"Wanted to hear it from you."

"Well, what you missed in all my personal shit is that yes, he was… driven with me. Wanted me to be the youngest Admiral the Navy has ever had. Once I graduated from Annapolis, I stopped being as driven to that goal. I switched my aspirations to the SEALs. We weren't that close after I told him this was the route I wanted to go. Not that we were before that."

"Was he military?"

"Navy, was working his way through the ranks when he was wounded and discharged on medical."

I start to ask more but a generic black sports car whips into the parking lot. The headlight beams sweep across the parking lot where we are crouched. We press against the side of the SUV to stay hidden. The car parks in the spot beside Franks' truck and cuts its engine.

With the car parked on the other side of the truck we can't see shit. A car door slams shut, footsteps shuffle across pavement, then another door shuts.

Interesting.

I start around the SUV but a hand grips my bicep.

"I'll go," he says and moves towards Franks' truck.

This time I grab his wrist to hold him back. "Um, no. You stay here and if something happens you're the distraction."

"No, I'm going. You're not."

"Why is that, Officer Wilcox?" I try not to hiss, but damn this man.

"Because I'm better trained."

Oh hell no.

"Oh so those years at West Point, the army, CIA training, none of that can compare to the invaluable, near godly ways of SEAL training?"

"I don't want you hurt, damnit. Stop fucking fighting me on this. I go first."

"No."

"Fucking hell, Lucia—"

"Pretty sure I didn't ask. This is my op not yours. You're just around for some eye candy, sweetheart."

"What the—"

"So stay here and *I'm* going to take a closer look."

I'm halfway across the parking lot, inching closer to the black sports car, before he's processed everything I'd said.

Keeping low, I attempt to peer over the hood. A disapproving grunt comes from across the lot. I squat back down. Idiot, overprotective water mammal.

Again I peek over the hood towards Franks' truck. The windows are already fogged and the sounds coming from the cab are unmistakable.

An affair, not drugs. That's it? That's what he was desperately trying to keep hidden?

Yes, he's married but the way he was acting during his interview, the questions he was dodging and how angry, defiant he became when

I started getting close to what he was hiding, made it seem like more. Why keep this from me or the team, especially when he knows Tony's view on marriage? Unless Tony was right and Franks doesn't want to admit his happy life is a sham.

Even that doesn't fit, though. There's more to it. I know it. Feel it. But what?

I need to know who this mystery woman is. It could help piece everything together. Hopefully. And all I need is her license plate and everything I could ever want will be at my fingertips.

Well, Jeremy's fingertips. If this is her car. Could be a friend's. Shit, I need something else.

As I start to duck back to cover, something on the dash makes me pause midair. Some kind of ID tag. One that looks familiar because I have one just like it. Voices carry from the truck. I need to get whatever I need. Now.

Daring a few more seconds I stand a little higher for a different angle on the windshield. "Shit," I breathe as the glare from the nearby street light shifts and I'm able to read whose badge is on the dash.

That's a twist I didn't see coming.

Karma's a funny chick.

Standing. Staring. Processing. This is need-to-know information. Who exactly needs to know Tony's wife is banging one of his men? Distracted by my own thoughts on the next steps, I fail to hear the truck door open until it's too late.

Fuck. I drop down, hoping she didn't spot me. "Hey," says a shocked, angry female voice. "What are you doing to my car?"

I'm halfway across the parking lot, sprinting, before Franks has exited his truck but that doesn't stop him from pursuing. A loud crash makes a car alarm blare. Thank you Gabe. I take a second to look over my shoulder. Franks paused at the distraction giving me a few additional seconds to increase my lead. Good thing I'm fast.

I don't turn a second time. The pounding of boots says he's too close and closing my minimal lead. A right, then left, sprinting between houses and businesses but his steps grow closer and closer.

Out running him isn't an option.

I make a hard right down an alley and lengthen my stride, desperate to put more distance between us.

Shit. I skid to a stop. Metal bites into my shoulder and cheek as I slam into a chain link fence. The gap between the joined tall fences might, might, be wide enough for me. But Franks...no way.

Now or never. Sharp metal pulls at my long sleeve t-shirt, scraping the skin beneath. I wince but squeeze through another inch. Trickles of blood drip down my back as I push the rest of the way through and around the corner. Pushing flat against a shop window, I silence my heavy breathing and wait.

Metal rattles and groans as the fence is shook with so much force I'm scared it might come down. A loud barked curse breaks through the night with a final push on the fence.

Air burns down my throat and in my lungs as I lean over and grip my knees, gobbling up as much air as possible with each deep inhale. That didn't go exactly as planned but I did get what I needed so there's a positive. He's not our mole.

"Need a lift?"

I jolt up. It takes a second to see the Camaro on the other side of the street with its lights off. I nod and jog towards the Camaro. The second I slide into the passenger seat he takes off.

"So *that* went according to plan." Each word laced with a bit of sarcasm and anger.

Instead of going off on his snarky ass I keep my mouth shut and lift my shirt to inspect the damage.

"The fuck you doing, Luce?" Gabe asks trying to keep one eye on the road as I pull my shirt over my head. His confusion shifts to concern. He slams the overhead light, takes one look at my bleeding chest and stomach, and whips into a parking lot. I hiss in pain when the seatbelt catches and bites into my raw skin. "Seriously, how in the hell did you manage that?"

I give an unconvincing shrug and blot the blood with my shredded t-shirt. "I was out of options." I raise a hand to his face. "I know what you're thinking but she caught me staring into her car—"

"That much I saw."

I narrow my eyes but keep going. "There was an ID badge on the dash. A base ID and when I saw whose it was, I was stunned. Karma's a bitch is all I have to say. Can you get the scrapes on my back and tell me if they're deep? I really, really don't want stitches tonight."

Tossing him the t-shirt, I move my hair and angle in the seat for him to have a better view of my back.

Tender fingertips skim between cuts. "Shit, sweetheart, your back is worse than your chest." I don't hold back a whimper of pain as he pushes harder in certain areas. "None are too deep but you need to get these treated as soon as you get home. Hope you have a tetanus shot."

With a nod I face the dash and tentatively lean back against the cool leather.

"What is it, Luce? You're killing me here."

"I don't know if I should tell you," I say honestly.

He thinks about it as he shifts the car back into drive and speeds back onto the street. "Do you not trust me?"

Not with this I want to say, but not because I don't think he can keep it from Tony but because I don't want him to have to.

"Because he's not our mole. I know what he's keeping from us now and me spilling the secrets of Tony's men isn't what I'm here for. Can we leave it at that?"

We speed through a few yellow lights before he responds. "Yeah, I get it. I don't like it but you're right. I only need to know what's being hidden if it affects the safety of the team or the man himself." Even though his words say he's okay with my decision, his pouty tone doesn't.

Awkward silence fills the car the next twenty minutes and grows tense as we sit in the idling car. Too exhausted for this, I lean back against the headrest and wait for the frustration or questioning to come. It always happens. I can't talk and the guy gets mad or won't let it drop, thinking I'll give in and tell him.

"Let's go back to your place, patch up your cuts, then I have to head out."

That response is not expected. I roll my head to him.

"I promised my mom I'd help her tonight with Dad so I'll be

staying the night there." The leather groans as he turns in the seat, and those blue eyes lock with mine. "I don't like you sleeping alone at your place with all that has happened." He focuses out the window behind me. "Fuck it, and I want to sleep with you tonight so you're coming to my parents' house with me."

Parents' house?

I clear my throat uncomfortably and try to swallow against a dry throat. "Gabe, listen, thanks but I don't—"

"It will be fine, it's late already so my mom will be in bed if that's what you're worried about."

Part of it, yeah. But the sincerity in his offer is genuine. It's not like I want to sleep alone. I've grown used to his warm body next to mine.

"Okay, but if it looks like your mom is still awake, I'll just sneak in through a window or something. I'm not ready for a meet the parents moment."

A wide grin spreads across his face, making both dimples pop. "Deal. Do you have another shirt or something in the back seat?"

Drumming my fingers against my thigh, I mentally go over what's back there. Candy, snacks, water...no change of clothes.

With a dramatic exasperated sigh at the shaking of my head, he's removing his black shirt. The scent of the ocean and spices fills the car when it lands in my lap. "Put that on, and meet me at your place."

CHAPTER TWENTY-THREE
GABE

There's something easy—comfortable—about her being here with me. The last ten years of my childhood were spent in this house so it's home. Thank the fuck mom was asleep when we arrived, there's no way in hell I was going to sneak a woman in here at my age.

I open the door to my old bedroom and gesture for her to go in. Just like at my apartment she starts looking around the room, assessing every detail and analyzing it unlike anyone I've ever known. It's damn sexy watching her mind work, the way she sees things and pieces them together is fucking brilliant. No wonder the CIA has her running nonstop. If I were them, I'd want her opinion on everything too.

She stops in front of the George Strait poster, a souvenir from a high school era concert, and smirks.

"You a fan?" I ask as I cross the room to stand beside her.

She nods. "More a fan of the female artists during the same time. Reba, Martina, Wynona, Pam, Faith...there is a long list of artists who molded me with their songs and powerful voices. Not like the stupid bro country crap that every radio station plays on repeat."

With a huffed laugh I pull her to my chest. "I fucking hate it. When you grew up appreciating George Strait, Garth Brooks, and Tim

McGraw, it makes all the shit they play on the radio seem like...well, shit." Her arms wrap around my waist but I don't move my hands from her shoulders. "How's your back?"

"Stings but good. Thanks for helping me take care of it."

"We'll want to check them in the morning and put more antibiotic on it."

As she starts cataloging the room again, looking at the different awards and knickknacks, an unsettled twisting sets in my gut. This room is a piece of me only Flakes has seen. The way she's analyzing my past leaves me vulnerable.

"Let's get in bed," I say, cracking my knuckles one at a time. Not waiting for her I strip down to my boxers and lay on the faded blankets.

The squeaking of the bed makes her turn. "What are you afraid I'm going to see, Gabe?"

Shit. Of course she read every thought and insecurity I'd just had.

"Not afraid, per se."

"Ah," she says with a wink and turns back around to the bookshelf stuffed with various awards. "Well don't worry, Officer Wilcox, I won't let this second place ribbon in field day from the ninth grade make me think less of you."

Eventually she makes her way around the entire room and settles on the bed.

"This room makes me sad, I think," she whispers. She rolls over to her side and tucks her freezing ass toes under my thigh.

Ignoring the shot of cold I search her big green eyes. "Why is that, sweetheart?"

With a shrug she looks over my shoulder like she's searching for the answer herself. "You had a life in high school. You played sports, have pictures of friends, concert tickets still hanging on the wall. I didn't. It was my own doing I guess."

Reaching over to where she's curled on her side, I brush a few dark locks from her face and tuck them behind her ear.

"I was too focused, you know," she continues. "I wanted West Point so bad and I wanted them to want me so everything I did was for that goal. And then once I was at West Point, I was focused on being the top of my class, being the best in everything we did so I would get noticed by the CIA." Keeping those toes tucked under me she rolls to her back and stares at the ceiling. "I'm not sure I've ever *not* had a goal in mind that I'm working towards."

Staring at her staring at the ceiling, I'm at a loss of what to say next. I've gotten here by working hard, yes, but I've had a fucking hell of a good time getting here too. Still am.

"So you never went to parties in high school or snuck booze onto campus at West Point?"

Her shaking head moves the bed. The way she bites her lower lip distracts from the conversation for a second. I know how that lip feels between my teeth, between my lips. Fuck, I even know what it feels like wrapped around me. Remembering the warmth of her mouth, the smoothness of her tongue makes my dick respond to the memories.

Fuck. Not the time.

"The one wild night I had at West Point has apparently followed me into my adult life."

My genuine laugh shakes the bed. A smile comes back to her gorgeous face.

"So you never snuck into some friend's house, drank all night, then passed out and stumbled out the window all hungover the next day so you didn't get caught by their parents?"

"That is extremely detailed. And no, I never did. I got straight A's and followed all the rules. Couldn't afford to have anything on my record unlike you it seems, Mr. Athletic, who could have done anything and still gotten into the Naval Academy."

Damn if she's not right. A nostalgic smile pulls at my lips as I remember all the fun memories from high school, from this room. It is sad she never had anything fun, never felt free to let loose or toe the line.

An idea churns and forms.

"Luce."

"Gabe."

"Tonight."

"Tonight?"

"We're going to fix that."

"What's broken?"

I laugh and lean over the bed. "It has to be here…ah," I pull up a half a bottle of Jim Bean from under the bed. "I started storing an emergency bottle for nights when I stay over to help mom." I pull the top off and take a swig.

Her eyes narrow at the bottle I'm trying to make her grab. When her fingers wrap around the glass she lifts the bottle to her lips and pauses. "What are we doing again?" Her head tips back taking a longer swig than I dared.

"Well you've already snuck into a guy's house whose parents are downstairs asleep and now we're drinking and going to fool around. It's pretty much like any high school party I went to. We're just a little older now."

A brow raises in response.

"Okay, a lot older but it can still be fun. I have no doubt you don't want my mom walking in on us." Her eyes widen and she takes another swig. "See just like high school. Drinking and scared of parents."

Everything fades to black at her megawatt smile. Damnit if that's not the fucking proudest thing I've done, putting that face-splitting grin on her face. I did that.

"Damn, you're beautiful." Pulling the bottle from her grasp, I take a swig, hoping it will keep my heart from pounding out of my chest.

"You're getting laid tonight, sweetheart, you don't have to say that you know." She yanks the bottle from me and takes a sip. "But thanks, it's nice to hear it from someone who actually knows me instead of saying it about this." With her free hand she gestures to her chest then down to her legs and back up again.

"Your huge-ass tits help a lot."

A pillow comes flying at my head but I catch it before it can connect with my face.

"Wrong type of party, sweetheart. No pillow fights here, just drinking, stripping and screwing."

Luce's responding giggles fill the room. "Sounds like a good party except one thing."

"What's that."

"Snacks. I'm kind of hungry."

"Hangry or hungry?"

"Hungry for now."

"On it," I roll off the bed on a food mission.

The cool air of the hall cools my hot skin. Fuck, how does she turn me on so damn fast and fully clothed, no less? I avoid the few stairs that creak with any kind of weight as I creep down to the kitchen.

I catch myself smiling at the packages of food as I rummage through the pantry. Damn, Flakes was right. She's a damn drug and I'm an addict. What's going to happen when I can't get a Luce fix? The food labels blur as I stare unfocused. What the hell am I going to do when she leaves?

Giving up, I fall onto a wooden kitchen chair.

We're having fun but what are we, past that? Hell, what do I want past that? My stomach drops at the thought of never seeing her again after all this is done. That can't happen. I won't let it happen unless… fuck, what if she doesn't want to see me? She did it to Flakes. What if this is it for her? Fuck. Fuck. Fuck.

The calluses on my hand scrape down my face as I drag both hands down it and lean forward, resting my elbows on my thighs, clasping my hands behind my drooped head.

"Girl trouble?"

I shoot up from the chair. "Mom, what the hell. What are you doing up?" A quick glance to the clock on the microwave says it's just past midnight. "Do you need something? Where's Dad?"

"Everything's fine, Gabriel. How did your work stuff go tonight?" The chair scrapes along the linoleum as she sits down and tucks her long robe around her legs, warding off the cool air.

"Fine. Not ideal but we got done what we needed to accomplish."

"Tell me about her."

"Who?"

"Gabriel Wilcox, I'm old, not a damn idiot."

With a pursed smile I shake my head. "Luce is pretty great. She's smart as hell, beautiful, and no nonsense. You know what you're getting with her. Perfect actually, well perfect for me. That's shit for me to say, though, I've only known her all of a handful of days. Fu... I'm just being an idiot."

The growing silence says she agrees with my idiot assessment.

"I knew on my first date with your father that he was the perfect one for me. Nowhere near perfect but no one is. There are a handful of people who are meant for you, meant for your life, Gabriel. Some are friends, some are more than that, but only a few out of all the people in this world. So if you think this woman is one of them you better not be a fucking idiot and let her go just because you don't think it's been long enough to know what you clearly already suspect."

I start to respond but she throws up a hand.

"Now I'm going back to bed. There's some candy in the top of the pantry, I have to keep it hidden from your dad or the bastard eats it all, and a bag of popcorn on the shelf below it. She'll love that."

There's no way to conceal my dumbfounded look. "How did—"

She simply smiles and shakes her head. "I'm a mom, Gabriel. We know everything."

Minutes tick by but I'm stuck in the chair, thinking over everything she'd said. Could she be right. Do I already know she's perfect for me? There have been girlfriends but no one who made my heart near bursting with so many emotions when they are around like Lucia does. And she's strong. Damn, she's strong, but vulnerable when she knows she can be which only seems to be around me. I fucking love it.

And I can't even go to my damn best friend for advice. The bastard will figure out a way to make me question it even more or hell, who knows, do something to make her leave for good.

I need a plan. I need to figure out how to let her know what I feel without laying it all out there. One option is to not say anything and let this ride out. The other option is to tell her and either know now she doesn't feel the same way or if she does then figure out what the fuck we're going to do when this assignment is over. Laying it all out is easier said than done considering I've never done it before.

Where do you even start?

Hey Luce, I really like you and want to know if you like me too or if you're just using me for mindblowing sex.

Sounds like a damn high school note you pass between classes.

Groaning out of frustration, I push from the table and start rummaging through the pantry for the candy and popcorn.

As soon as I'm through the door, food in hand, Luce's head pops up from her phone.

"Guess what," she says, bouncing on the bed.

"What?" I dump all the food on to the bed but her green eyes stay on me instead of digging through it, which I've found is a normal reaction for her.

"Jeremy just texted." Physically biting my tongue to keep my mouth shut, about some dumb fucker texting her this late, hurts like hell but works. "And we are now down to two mole suspects."

"That's great," I try. I really fucking try to be as excited as she is but I can't be. All I heard was our time together was just cut shorter with no fucking warning.

"Yeah he ran their phone records, credit cards, and other digital stuff and knocked off two of the guys. He went over everything he found and it's not mole related from my opinion but things I'll bring up to the CO at the end of the investigation. How are you not excited? I'm getting close."

It is selfish wanting this to drag out. Hell, Flakes and his team's lives are at stake. I'm an ass.

Needing to numb every undecipherable emotion coursing through me, I say, "Where's the bourbon?" A drink will help put some distance between me and whatever feeling this is. Which fucking sucks, whatever it is. It's like being sad, but jealous, and angry all mixed into one, but happy too because she's happy. What the hell is wrong with me?

"What's wrong?" she asks, narrowing her eyes at me, doing her witch shit. "I thought..."

Between the talk with Mom and now this, everything's happening too fast. I snag the bottle from the bed and take three fast pulls in a row. Wiping some dribble from my chin, I glance back to her expecting tears or anger at my sudden mood shift but instead she's shifting through the food.

"Luce," I start, but take another drink for liquid courage instead.

"Thanks for the food, Gabe. This is perfect. M&M's and popcorn. Yum." The bags are ripped apart seconds later and she starts mixing them together on the comforter. "Here, try it." She scoops a little of both into her hand and walks on her knees across the bed. "Open up."

Obeying, she places the combination on my tongue and shuts my mouth with two fingers under my chin.

It could be the most amazing combination ever invented but I can't taste it. As it melts along my tongue my eyes stay locked with hers, trying to give her access to my thoughts so I don't have to voice my fears out loud.

Instead of asking me what I'm thinking about, her hands slip behind my neck and start tracing tiny circles along my skin with her long red nails. A mischievous smile grows, pulling at her lips as she shifts to drag her nails down my chest, over my abs, stopping at the band of my boxers.

If I didn't know her so well at this point, know what to look for, I would have missed the small falter in her smile as she says, "I know, Gabe. I know what you're thinking and I don't know, either. All I know is this moment, you giving me the best make up high school party ever, and I don't want to ruin it. We can figure the rest out later, right?"

Unable to respond verbally, I move my head up and down giving my reluctant answer. I like answers. I like things figured out. I like fucking plans. But when it comes to her, when it comes to us, I'll just have to wait. If I open my mouth now, I'd destroy this night with my insistent questions. Clearly, by the way she's toying with the band of my boxers, figuring it all out now isn't what she wants. And with a woman like Luce I can't push, or force the issue. She will come around when she's ready, and when she is, I'll be here.

From this point I'll always be waiting for her. Waiting for her to be ready for us.

As terrifying as it is, not having control, somehow there's no tension in the decision as long as we're both on the same page that she will be a part of the end game.

Soft, wet lips slide down my chest pulling me to the present as her hands dip beneath my boxers to grab my ass and shove them down my thighs.

How in the hell did I get so damn lucky?

My hands weave into her thick hair and hold on. She dips lower and lower to my straining cock. The warmth of her mouth, her soft tongue on my stomach is too much. My knees buckle on the bed. Fucking hell.

I bite back a hiss when her cold hands wrap around me.

"No hands, sweetheart," I somehow get out through gritted teeth as I move deeper into her mouth. With her hands gone I'm in control. Pushing farther and harder. Her humming, loving every damn inch, I'm done faster than ever, cursing and mumbling some garbled shit as I cum.

Her eyes shine bright as they peer up from her kneeling spot on the bed in front of me. She's licking her lips at the taste of me which has to be the hottest damn thing ever.

Grabbing the bottle from the bed I press it to her lips and angle her head back with two fingers under her chin. Her head tilts back, eyes staying on mine, as I pour the last few drops into her mouth and watch her throat move as she swallows the bourbon just like she swallowed me.

"No idea why that's fucking sexy as it is, but hell."

"I think it's just me," she says and sits back on the bed and grabs two handfuls of the snacks.

"That's for damn sure." Needing more room to move for what I have planned next, I step out of my boxers and kneel back on the bed. My fingers grip the hem of her shirt just as hers slam down, keeping me from ripping it off her.

"I think maybe you should leave my shirt on tonight."

"The fuck?"

"My scrapes and cuts. I don't think you'll be able to look past them and every time you look at them you go crazy mad."

"I'm getting you naked, Luce. I don't give a damn about the cuts right now. I'll be careful. I can promise you I'll just be staring at your gorgeous tits."

This time when I tug on her black t-shirt she allows it to slip over her head. The one positive to her injuries, the only positive—the fact she even has them still pisses me off—is it hurt too much for her to put a bra on earlier.

They really are perfect. Helps I'm a tits guy too.

What am I saying? She has a great ass too, so maybe I'm a tits and ass guy.

Or maybe I'm just a Lucia Rizzo guy.

Her lying back on the pillows, half naked, my dick twitches and hardens again. Out of habit I wrap a hand around and grip tightly as I memorize the unbelieve scene.

"Gabe," she moans beneath me. "You can't get me drunk and horny and not touch me. So do it."

Losing all humor at her bossy ass tone, I say, "I'm the one giving the orders tonight, Agent Rizzo."

CHAPTER TWENTY-FOUR
LUCIA

What in the hell have I been doing my whole life, wasting time with men who *are not* officer Gabriel Wilcox?

Holy hell.

The weight of his hips presses against mine as he sucks and teases down my neck. My skin flushes and goosebumps pop in the wake of his full lips against my skin. His weight makes it difficult to breathe, but who gives a damn right now. Or the lack of air supply could be from the hammering of my heart.

His first nip at my nipple as he rolls the other between his fingers extracts an unladylike groan from my core. My fingers slide through his cropped blond hair and pull him harder against me. "Don't stop, Gabe," I whisper between gasps. "Don't ever stop."

Cool air replaces where his lips had been. With the sudden contrast, I peel open my eyes only to find him looking up from my chest. Those blue eyes hold an emotion I don't want to admit I see. And recognize.

"Don't worry, sweetheart, I won't stop until you make me."

My eyes shutter closed again when his lips wrap around my hardened nipple and suck hard. All focus goes to his teeth and fingers, blocking out anything else going on but us.

The soft cloth of my yoga pants brushes down my thighs. In what seems like a different world I hear them fall to the floor.

The agonizing throbbing between my legs begs for his attention immediately but he has a different plan. Up my calf and inner thigh he kisses and nips his way up, getting so close to the apex I can feel the warmth of his breath when he moves over to start up the other leg. By the time he's back where I need him most my mouth is dry from the shaky, shallow pants I can't stop.

"Roll over," he commands.

I don't make a move. I can't move.

His weight shifts, jostling the bed. With a whimper of annoyance and utter sexual frustration I roll on to my stomach. An arm wraps around my waist. Keeping my knees pressed on the bed, he pulls me back to his chest. The fabric of the comforter slides beneath my knees as he pushes them wider and wider apart with his own.

He slams into me and at the same time he bites the sensitive skin of my neck, holding me in place.

"Oh fuck," I breathe once I'm fully lowered against him and he begins to thrust again and again. I'm helpless, there's nothing I can do but take what he's giving me in this position.

The world evaporates. There's just him and I, molding into one as he holds me so tight against him it's almost painful.

"Every damn day," he growls into my ear as he bites at my lobe. "I want to do this to you every damn day. Forever, Luce."

He picks up the pace, sending the word forever to the back of my mind to focus only on him. Every move takes me closer to the edge. A hand brushes up my inner thigh to my tiny bundle of nerves.

Fuck. Yes, forever sounds damn good. This. Him. Us. Forever might not be long enough.

"Gabe," I nearly scream as I fall apart around him. Blood pounds in my ears as he continues to move, dragging out each second of the mind-blowing orgasm he pulled from me. "That," I breathe, "was amazing." Gathering my hair off my damp skin and forming a makeshift ponytail, I turn with a happy, lazy smile.

His dimpled face can only be described as triumphant.

Cocky bastard.

Who am I kidding? I love it.

"I'm not through with you yet, Luce," he mumbles against my shoulder before pushing me forward so I'm on all fours. "Nowhere near done with you."

Again, he pushes inside, slowly this time, building the low ache between my legs again.

Yes. Forever. I can do this forever with him.

———

Darkness is all I see when some distant sound pulls me from my exhausted sleep. I give myself time to figure out what's going on. My fingers skirt along the sheets, reaching for Gabe but only finding empty space. Beneath my palm the sheets are still warm. A phone chirps from the floor.

Trying to reach the phone without getting out of the bed's warmth, I nearly topple to the floor.

Jeremy: I don't have anything new for you on that Tony guy you told me to look into. Besides living way beyond his paycheck, there's nothing here to make me think anything is up.

Jeremy: But I also know to trust your gut so keep digging if you think there is something there.

Jeremy: Boss man wants another update soon. He mentioned you're going to try and get the mole's partners too. That's amazing but beyond anything you've been doing. Think you're up for it?

Jeremy: Don't get mad. I'm not saying you can't, just saying those guys…it's not your typical gather intel, assess, and leave op. Be careful. I really think Brooke would skin me alive if I let anything happen to you while she's out.

. . .

I tuck the phone beneath my pillow and turn to look at the empty bed. Okay, so keep pursuing the Tony angle, somehow, and look into these other two agents. And still try to recruit Gabe. So far Tony hasn't mentioned his interest in the agency. Maybe he decided it wasn't for him when he found out it's where I am. Wouldn't be surprising.

So, one of those three men has to be the mole or I'm up a shit creek with no answers to give the CO or boss man. And unfortunately for Tony my gut is pulling me towards him but until I know for certain I'll keep that information to myself. If the other two guys check out then I'll tell Gabe I think his best friend is a traitor. Simple.

Or not.

Something since the first day has kept me weary of Tony. I can't push that aside. He could have too many dang walls built with egotism that I can't see to the real him. Or he could be the mole and evading me every time I get close. Frustrated, I groan and bury my face into the warm pillow. A familiar smell of the ocean and spices fill my nose.

Gabe.

What are we going to do? If I recruit him, we will be in the same state, well based out of the same state, but not together. But if I don't recruit him not only will I not get the shot at the promotion, but I'll also lose him because he won't move to DC and I won't move here.

So there's a stalemate on what happens next.

Grabbing beneath the pillow, I pull the phone back out.

Me: Tell me I don't need a decision now.

Several minutes pass of staring at the screen before her response comes through.

Brooke: Are you safe?
Me: Yes.
Brooke: Are you happy?

Me: Yes.

Brooke: Are you having fun?

Me: You have no idea.

Brooke: Then no, you don't need a decision now. That will come later. Plus you don't have to have a plan, Lu. Just be. Please. For me.

Brooke: Just enjoy life for two seconds damn it.

Me: Oh I just enjoyed a lot of life for a lot longer than that. Who knew I could have so much fun…multiple times in a row.

Brooke: That comment makes me sad and want to punch the past douchebags you've dated.

Brooke: I want you home but take your time down there. There's no rush. Well, besides finding the bad guy.

Me: Bad guy?

Brooke: I haven't read up on the op. I assume there's a bad guy and that is why you are there, and once you find him you will tell the clean up crew and he will be gone. You know. The average op.

Me: Slightly different ending but yeah. Sums it up.

Brooke: Why are you texting so early? What is your boy toy doing? Is he passed out from giving you multiple happy endings?

Yeah, where is Gabe?

Realizing how much time has passed since I woke finding him gone sends my heart racing as all the worst case scenarios start running through my head.

Tossing back the covers I climb out of bed and start yanking on wrinkled clothes from the floor. My pants are halfway up when I pull the door open an inch and angle an ear to the gap.

Soft male voices float up the stairs along with some background noise like a TV. Careful to step lightly on each stair, I descend in near silence. I crane my neck around the door frame to see into the next room.

An older James Bond film plays on TV while Gabe watches from a couch, directly across the room from where I stand, and an older man, I'm assuming his father, watches from a dark leather recliner. For a minute I simply watch. Few words are exchanged and those that are are about the movie.

Starting to feel like a creeper, I turn to head back up the stairs, but not before one more glance at him. When I do, those blue eyes are shining bright, locked with mine. He doesn't smile. Heck, he doesn't even blink as I stand waiting for him to drop the intense, questioning stare.

Instead he inclines his head towards the couch—a silent gesture inviting me to sit with him.

I shake mine.

Again he nods to the couch, this time with more impatience to it.

Again I shake my head, my impatience matching his.

"Dad, want to meet my girlfriend Lucia?" he says without looking away. Wow, he went there. Now there's no way to sneak back up the stairs. A grunt comes from the man in the recliner as I cross the room but he pays no attention to me.

"Girlfriend, huh? Interesting, didn't know we were at the label stage yet. Good to know." I maneuver around the recliner, his dad grumbling something when I pass in front of the TV, and sit beside Gabe. A shiver rakes through my body, shaking my shoulders from being close to him. My body ready for round...ten. Not missing anything, he reaches behind the couch, pulls up a worn blanket and drapes it over my legs, then tucks me against his chest with one arm draped over my shoulders.

"So that's my dad. Not very social if you can't tell."

In response his dad grunts like us talking is interrupting his movie.

"What are you doing down here?" I whisper and snuggle closer against him to steal his body heat.

His gaze shifts to his dad. "He doesn't sleep in long stints. My mom is usually the one who gets up with him just to make sure he doesn't hurt himself. A couple months ago she woke up and he wasn't there. When she went looking for him she found him in the kitchen. All the burners on the gas stove were on but not lit, gas was filling the kitchen and he was standing there staring at the stove with a box of matches in his hand." My eyes widen in shock at how lucky they were she found him. "Since then if he wakes up she wakes up. But it wears on her." As he talks I nod, rubbing against his chest letting him know I'm listening, that I'm here. "So sometimes when she's at her limit she'll ask me or my sister—"

I jolt, the blanket falls to the floor. "Sister?"

"Damn, you really should have read that report."

I jam an elbow into his ribs and pull the blanket back around me. He whimpers and holds his side, like I actually broke through those walls of muscles and hurt him.

"Yes, my sister. She's four years older. Lives in LA. Anyway, sometimes my mom needs a break, which is where I come in, or my sister. This way mom can sleep all through the night knowing someone else is here keeping watch."

"Your mom is lucky to have you two to help out." His eyes shift from mine to the TV. He doesn't believe me. "I'm serious, Gabe."

"I don't do enough."

"You do plenty. I've seen it, I know how much you help out when you can."

"I should do more."

"Stop. You're being an idiot."

His unamused gaze shifts back to me. "Am I?"

"Yeah, you are. Yes, there is more you could be doing." His face crumbles a little. "But you're doing what you can. Between your job…" I start to say me but I don't want to admit out loud I'm the reason he's been more absent lately.

"Stop."

Playing with a loose thread on the blanket, I keep my eyes on my hands until he grips my chin to make me look at him. Still I'm too ashamed of what I'm doing to his family to look him straight in the eye.

"This is about me, Lucia. It has nothing to do with you."

"But you've been spending so much time—"

"Sweetheart, I wouldn't change anything since the time you declined my help the first day on base." He maneuvers his head lower to look me in the eyes. "My guilt has nothing to do with you. It's about me and not being in control of all this shit. Don't you fucking dare think I'd miss one second with you, I know there aren't many left."

Ending the discussion, he kisses my forehead and turns me to face the TV, pulling me against his chest once again. The tips of two fingers brush up and down my arm lulling me, soothing me. We watch the movie for several minutes before curiosity gets the best of me.

"Gabe?" I whisper wondering if he's asleep behind me.

"Luce," he grumbles, his voice deep and raw as if I did wake him.

"Have you had a lot of girls over to this house? I mean you know, who met your parents and all that."

"A few, but more in high school. No one since I left—" A loud, annoyed grunt comes from the recliner and the sound on the TV inches up another couple levels. "For Annapolis," he finishes with a roll of his eyes.

"Why?"

"Why what?"

"Why no one since then? Has your sister or mom met anyone you've dated recently?"

He groans and pulls his arm from my shoulders to lean against the arm rest, facing me full on. "This seems like a bad idea."

"What?"

"This conversation."

"You're the one who called me your girlfriend. As said girlfriend I feel like I should know who has come before me."

His smile is one of awe even as he shakes his head. With a sigh he tucks his hands behind his head. I can't help but stare at his thick muscles, pulling at the sleeves of his black t-shirt and the way it hugs his broad chest distracts me.

"Fair enough, but know this question will be turned on you if I answer." The arched brow he gives makes me nod in return, urging him to continue. "I told you before I don't really do the girlfriend thing. Lots of one night stuff here and there but there's been a couple girls who stuck around long enough to at least be mentioned to my sister. That's as far as it's ever gotten."

"Why?"

"I told you, they get tired of the life we live. The secrets, the leaving at a moment's notice." He laughs hard and looks to the ceiling. "One time I was with this girl, we'd been out a few times when I got a call to leave. And I just pulled out, pulled up my pants and left without looking back. She didn't return my calls after that." He's still chuckling when it hits me.

"But that night with me." I stop as I think back. "You got the call and didn't immediately leave. You even stuck around longer than you should have to make sure I was okay. For that one great kiss." The memory sends goosebumps down my arms and legs. "You acted like I was hard to leave."

He shrugs and looks to the TV avoiding my stare. "I guess from the start you've been different."

"How?" I slide closer, tucking between him and the back of the couch. He huffs as he readjusts to not fall off the edge. With his arm tucked around me, my chest resting against his as he lays back, there's no way for us to get closer.

"How? Hell if I know. Just are. You're just you. And that's everything." Silence settles between us as I try to process his words. The perfect thing he'd just said. "Now your turn, Luce," he says with a shake of my shoulders.

"Not much to tell. I've dated but like you they never last because of what I do. Most end bad."

His arm tightens "Bad?" His tone flat, menacing even.

"Yeah kind of like Tony I guess. They just don't let go easily even though they know it wouldn't work if they stayed. I don't know why but it always just seems messy. But none have been like you, that's for sure."

"Explain."

Looking up, I rest my chin on his sternum. "You treat me like an equal I guess so that's new. You're not scared to push back, which is very new. And I've never had someone make me feel so..."

His brows furrow.

"Desired."

"I find that very hard to believe."

"Ah, that's the thing, Gabe, anyone can make me feel desired because of what they see, but you're the only one who's wanted all of me, naked or not. I can tell you just want to be with me, and when you're with me there's nowhere else you'd rather be."

Daring a look up to see what he thinks of my confession, a new, happy—genuinely happy—smile is stretched across his face so wide his dimples are nonexistent.

"Want to know when I knew you were mine?"

The motion of my nod digs my chin harder onto his sternum, drawing a hiss from him.

"Tonight. You tucked your cold-ass toes under me to get them warm. That's a girlfriend move. And hell if it didn't feel right."

There's no give of muscle as I burrow my face against his chest. Strands of hair pull and shift as he weaves his fingers in and out. It's a perfect moment, the perfect moment I might never have again in this lifetime, but it's the thoughts of the future that ruin it. "But Gabe, we—"

"Not tonight, sweetheart. Not now. Later. I'm not going to let it ruin right now."

Across the room movement makes him tense. Raising up, I watch his dad stand from the recliner and start toward another room.

"Dad," Gabe calls out, but his dad pays him no attention. With a quick worried glance down, he pushes off the couch to follow.

I wait tucked under the blanket until their voices elevate. If they get any louder, it might wake his mom, which will defeat the purpose of Gabe being here. Wrapping the soft blanket around my shoulders, I shuffle in the direction they disappeared.

"How about eggs or something like that? I can cook you anything," Gabe says staring at his dad, not acknowledging me as I enter the room.

His dad shakes his head and starts for the fridge. Gabe cuts him off. "Get out of my way kid, I told you I want my damn dinner. I want my leftover steak from dinner last night."

The furrowed brow and deep frown say everything. The agony

shows in Gabe's face. Not sure what memory his dad is reliving but it's not in the reality Gabe and I are in.

Normally the words I'd use to describe Gabe are confident, driven, and commanding, but the Gabe standing across the kitchen from me is tired, sad, crushed even. Crushed I'm having to witness this exchange, crushed because he can't give his dad what he wants, crushed because this shell of a man is who he's left with for a father figure. Whatever the reason it shreds my heart into slivers.

"You know what," I say and step deeper into the kitchen. His dad turns. "I accidentally ate it. Yep. I ate it. Sorry, I like to eat." I shrug and pull the blanket tighter hoping I'm reading the situation correctly and making it better instead of worse.

"Nothing wrong with a girl who likes to eat. Was it good?" he asks, those empty crystal blue eyes staring into mine. Before I can answer the topic turns to something else. "Where's the candy?"

"I ate that too." Now at least I'm not lying to him about that. "Since I'm the one who ate all your food how about I make you more? You go lay back down and I'll come get you when it's ready."

"Steak and eggs?"

"Sure."

"Alright then, soldier."

My eyes widen and shift to Gabe. How in the hell did he…

"Wake me when it's ready." He turns and shuffles down the hall, Gabe close on his heels.

The weight on Gabe's shoulders as he left made him appear more agonized than anyone should ever feel. For the first time ever, I'm thankful I lost my dad at an early age. It was painful then, but watching a parent deteriorate like this has to be worse.

I dig through the fridge for eggs and by some miracle a thawed steak I promised my boyfriend's dad. With my head in the fridge his heavy footsteps signal he's back. At a click of the fridge door, I turn. Tears well and burn in my eyes. He sits in a small wooden chair, head in his hands. The weight of the world on his shoulders.

Reading this much emotion pouring off him is easy. I just wish I knew how to stop his agony. Bumping his arms with my backside, he sits up and I crawl on to his lap. My arms wrap around his neck and pull him as tight as possible. Gabe relaxes in my arms, surrendering— letting me be the strong one, stealing from my strength. And I let him. Let him take it all.

Seconds turn to minutes as the clock on the wall ticks on. But I hold him in silence as he holds me like his life depends on it.

"Thank you," he says against my skin, his voice hoarse.

"Anytime, sailor," I whisper back and pull him tighter.

CHAPTER TWENTY-FIVE
LUCIA

Sand shifts and flies under my pounding feet as I race down the beach, trying to evade my own thoughts. Faster and faster, pushing myself. The salty air burning my lungs and throat but it's not helping. He's still there. The only damn thing on my mind when I need him not to be.

I need to focus. Get my head back into this op but every time I start, something reminds me of him, of us, and the floodgate of memories opens, bombarding me.

It's happening too soon, too quickly to be real. Even though that's how it feels. Maybe I'm out here running to chase away the worry and pain of him being gone instead. The ache in my stomach. My heart still trembling since he got a call to head out again.

It's been two days. Two days since I woke in his parents house with him wrapped around me like he was afraid someone might snatch me in the night. Two days of silence.

Last time I worried if he would still want me when he came back. There wasn't anything real there. Then. But now there is. And I'm left worrying if he will come back to me. Of course I didn't say anything, I simply gave him a quick pat on the ass, a great goodbye kiss and went back to the files I was studying like he was leaving for a normal day's work. Neither of our jobs are normal but we have to act as if they are to keep any sense of sanity.

Between worrying about Gabe and missing him I somehow found time to get some work done, studying Tony's file and the other two mole suspects. And a whole lot of thinking. Too much thinking. I needed to get out of my own head.

We are both torn. Wondering what's going to happen next, but neither able to hold back. We are too drawn to each other to try, addicted maybe.

My pace slows as my rental house comes into view, and slows further when a man standing on the back steps comes into focus.

"What are you doing here?" I ask through labored breaths.

"Checking in on you and the progress. What update can I give the CO?"

"I gave him one this morning." I grip the railing in one hand and my foot in the other, pulling my leg behind me to stretch my tight muscles.

Tony's face falls but recovers quickly. "Right, anything new you can tell me?" he tries to pry. Something is going on with him. The way he avoids my stare says he's trying to keep whatever it is from me. Which reminds me...

"By the way, thanks for warning me about Beasley. Could have used a heads up on that one."

"I was told the CO wanted him to apologize to you face to face. Who am I to argue with orders?"

That's a lie.

I asked the CO about it earlier this morning and he said he didn't give the order. That it must have been Tony's, a not well thought-out plan to smooth the water between me and Beasley. But I keep coming back to why. Why would Tony tell Beasley that unless he was trying to scare me off? When the break in didn't send me packing, maybe Tony thought Beasley would do the trick.

Sweat trickling down my neck, I pull the hem of my dry fit t-shirt up to wipe it away.

Eyes wide, staring at my stomach he says, "What the hell?" Tony's grip on my wrist is tighter than necessary. "What kind of kinky ass shit is that fool into? Your face too," he says louder and grips my face between his fingers to angle it towards the setting sun. "Is that a bruise and your lip...I'm going to kill him."

I pull from his tight grasp. As I fix my shirt I say, "long story, but not Gabe." When I look, it's obvious he doesn't believe me. "Come on, you know I wouldn't put up with that crap. Unless I liked it." My fist slams against his shoulder hoping to lighten the mood.

"You lying to me, Rizzo?"

I narrow my eyes. Wisely he takes a step back, palms up. "Okay, you're not lying. No need to go all Kill Bill on me."

Not responding, I brush past him into the house. Things turn awkward once we're in the living room. Not like I'm nervous awkward, just awkward. He's standing, hands in the pockets of his BDUs looking around the room like he's trying to find something to talk about. I don't have time for this. A shower is needed so I can finish getting things ready for tonight.

"So I need—"

"Who do you think it is?" he asks, cutting me off.

With a shrug I grab a bottle of water off the counter to buy time to drum up a decent, vague response. "We've cleared a few of the guys but there are still some I need to do more digging on. Actually I'm glad you asked, you can help me with something."

"What's it worth to ya?"

My eyes roll to the ceiling. "Those missions that went wrong, what happened to make you think intel was being leaked? I've requested those files but they are so redacted it's mostly blacked out."

In a dramatic fashion he falls to the couch and props his feet up on the coffee table. Digging into his back pocket, he pulls out a can of tobacco and pops a pinch into his lip. "Hard to pin it on one certain thing." He motions for me to toss him the empty water bottle I've been attempting to juggle. "Thanks. Our missions are detailed down to when we can fucking piss, which isn't often mind you, so they go smoothly. Usually. But a few of the ones we were on, everything went according to plan like they knew we were coming and gave us what we wanted to get us out quick." He shrugs and spits into the bottle before continuing. "One mission though, it was like they were waiting for us. Shit got real, fast, and I…" His head shakes, eyes going distant. "Anyway, nothing that will help you, sweet cheeks."

I rub my back against the wooden door frame and watch him. He's telling the truth and the blip he won't say seems more condemning to his leadership skills than exposing him as the mole.

Not getting what I need from that question, I try a different angle. "I don't get how someone could do it, you know."

"What?"

"Betray their country, put their friends at risk. All for what?"

"Money," he says, but is quick to follow up with, "I guess."

"Still don't get it." I flop onto the chair across from him but he doesn't notice. His eyes are fixed on the bottle half filled with his dark spit.

"That's because you wouldn't."

"What does that mean?" I say defensively.

The condescending look he shoots has my nails digging into the arm of the chair to keep from attacking him. "It means, you seem to be driven by other things."

Ah, so his accusation after the pool incident had some truth behind it.

"I want a career, I want to move up. That's not bad."

"No, but don't go saying you don't understand how someone could do this when I'm sure there is a lot you'd do to keep moving up the chain of command."

Dang. He's more insightful than I give him credit for.

Maybe the CIA is wrong in not pursuing him. If he's not the mole, that is.

"What's that?" he asks, pointing toward the black device I have tucked between magazines on the coffee table. He leans over and pulls it free, lifting it close to inspect it.

"Not sure really, it was sent to me by the agency. I'm guessing some kind of jammer or detection device. I keep forgetting to ask Jeremy, my handler, what it's for. Until then I figured I'd leave it out."

With a nod he tosses it back on the table and reaches into his back pocket for his cell. He frowns at whatever he finds on the screen. "Not a jammer. I have full service. Are you filling me with shit and recording all our conversations?"

"What? No. I wouldn't do that."

"The fuck you wouldn't. Hell, Lucia. What do you think you're going to get from me? Huh?"

His anger inches higher and higher with each word. My temper responds, matching flare for flare.

"Do you have something to hide, Tony? Scared I'm going to find out—"

"Fuck, you already know I'm a shit ass husband. What else do you think you're going to find out? Damnit to hell, Lucia, you're making it sound like..." His eyes narrow then widen slightly. "You think it's me."

Silent deep breaths reign in my temper. I cannot lay all my cards on the table with him tonight.

"I—"

"Go fuck yourself, Agent Rizzo." He shoves off the couch sending it rocking on its back legs, almost toppling over from the force and storms for the door. Pausing at the threshold to the porch he says to the door, "Does G think it's me?"

The hurt and betrayal in his voice makes me hate I'm the one who put it there. "No, just me. And I haven't—"

He's out the door and down the steps before I can finish.

Shit. That couldn't have gone worse.

Showing my hand about my suspicions was not in the plan. The front door clicks into place and I turn for the bathroom to get ready for the night ahead. Hopefully a hot shower will clear my head and help me figure a way out of this one.

One positive that came from Tony stopping by is Gabe's no longer the only thing consuming my thoughts.

———

The mini Twix wrapper I toss on the floorboard lands on the mountain of other candy wrappers which have accumulated the past few hours. Brandon Lovall hasn't left his apartment since I followed him here from the gym thirty minutes ago. A glance down at the dash reads seven o'clock. Reclining back and cracking the window, to let the cool breeze into the stuffy car, I twist in the seat to watch the garage gate and be more comfortable. Even if I do miss him leaving it won't be a big deal. The tracker I put on his truck last night will lead me anywhere he goes.

It's Friday night, surely he has something to do. *Has* to. I'm not sure how much longer I can sit here stuffing my face. Last night his truck stayed in the garage, per my tracker, never leaving his apartment. Hopefully tonight will be more eventful but I'm not getting my hopes up at this point.

Brandon is definitely one of the more attractive men on Tony's platoon. His dark hair and chocolate eyes blend well with his smooth, tan skin, plus there is an intensity about him, which makes him even more alluring.

Not that I've noticed.

I glance down at the phone in my cup holder for the tenth time in the past minute. Still no word from Gabe. The last mission lasted four days; if that is the norm, then I only have one more day of waiting. Hopefully.

The grinding of metal against metal pulls my attention to the gate. Brandon's brand new Silverado truck inches out, making sure the road is clear of traffic, before easing out on to the street.

The engine of my Camaro roars to life and I adjust the seat back to its normal position.

"Finally," I mumble as I pull out of my parking spot. Maybe tonight won't be a complete waste after all. The phone vibrates in the cup holder. Heart racing in the hopes it's Gabe, I intentionally slow at a yellow light. Disappointment sinks in at the name on the screen.

· · ·

Tony: It's not me. I'll stop by later. We need to talk about it.

I flick my eyes up to make sure the light's still red.

Me: Can't. Out.
   Tony: Out where?
   Me: Doing my job.
   Tony: Oh hell. Who are you looking into?
   Tony: Are you alone?
   Tony: Shit balls Lucia. G will kill me if you get hurt.
   Tony: Where are you?

The console on the Camaro illuminates. I toss the phone back into the cup holder, not that I would have responded anyway. The overprotective bull annoys me to no end. There's no way I'll let him think he can swoop in and take charge. I don't give a shit if he is a water mammal officer.

Brandon's truck slows and pulls into a shady gravel parking lot. Coasting past, I turn into a parking lot just past his and cut the engine. Through the rearview I watch him emerge from the truck, grab a duffle bag out of the back, and start towards the back door of the building I'm parked directly in front of.

This is looking good for me. Not so good for Brandon.

My neck cranes as I search out the windshield and windows to find a sign of some kind. Nothing.

What was in the duffle?

Could it be for carrying out cash after the information is passed on? Him being paid in cash would be why Jeremy couldn't find any type of large deposits. Cash can easily be stored until needed.

Jeremy also mentioned Brandon's digital finger print was spotless. Doesn't mean he is, though. Something set off my gut instincts initially and during the interviews, I have to follow that. Plus after looking over his testing, he's smart enough to know how to avoid detections from us and the Navy.

A dark-paneled van rips into the parking lot and skids to a stop in the spot beside me. The leather groans as I sink down to stay hidden and watch. A scream rattles through the night. I reach for the loaded hand gun in the door panel. More shrieks and yelling pour out of the van.

What the hell is this guy into?

Human trafficking too? Hell, how many women are in that van?

By the way it's rocking and the voices growing louder and more frantic, there have to be at least ten to twelve packed in.

Careful to not draw attention, I engage the slide and rest the gun on my thigh. I have to wait. As much as this sucks I have to wait to see how many armed men are in the van with the victims.

My sweaty grip tightens at the click of the lock disengaging.

Hand on the door handle, I take a ragged breath and...

Women. Laughing. Screeching.

My hand drops from the door. Dumbfounded at the turn of events I can only stare at the scene. Women dressed like they're ready for a night on the town. Happy. Laughing, screaming at each other as they pour out of the van. The last one literally falls out of the van and would've landed face first, but a few giggling women catch her and set her upright. After adjusting her "bride" sash, the gaggle links arms and stumbles up to the building.

I can't stop staring. They approach the building and push open a somewhat concealed door and disappear inside. My eyes still on the door, another car pulls into the parking lot. Then another. Every car filled with women dressed for a night out and already very drunk.

My brows pull together as I compare my outfit to theirs. Black jeans, short sleeve black t-shirt and black leather coat in the back seat. Definitely won't fit in if I go in, but there's no way I can't.

Plus, it could be fun.

The heel of my boot connects with my opposite calf, searching for the reassuring firmness of my knife strapped around, just in case things go bad. "Let's do this," I say into the rearview and push the car door open.

CHAPTER TWENTY-SIX
LUCIA

Deafening bass rattles in my chest the second I'm over the threshold, confirming my suspicions. Following the other women down a long, dimly lit hallway I try to blend in, not making it too obvious I'm the only one here alone. Because who in their right mind comes to a strip club *alone*.

Looking to the ceiling, collecting myself for what I'm going to find inside, I take a deep breath and immediately regret it. Gagging amounts of air freshener and perfumes that have infiltrated the hall singe my nose and burn in my lungs.

The man at the end of the hall doesn't pay my coughing fit any attention as he takes my twenty bucks for the entrance and opens another door.

I stumble forward a step when the door smacks my backside from where I stopped cold. So many things to take in.

A small smile pulls at my lips as I take another step into the large room filled with other women. For the first time in my life I'm in a male strip club. Better late than never, I guess, and might as well be on the agency dime.

Disco balls bounce the pulsing light around the room as the music blares from speakers above. A few men dance on stage dressed in firemen pants, no shirts, as women flank the stage screaming and shove money down their fire suits.

"What can I get you?"

Turning to say vodka on the rocks, I stop. It's rude to stare, and I hate it when guys do this to me, but I can't stop from checking him out from head to toe. Those tuxedo pants and bow tie look... clearing my throat I meet his eyes. "Vodka on the rocks. Make it a double." I toss a twenty on his tray and maneuver through the crowd to find a seat of some kind. Surely there are seats.

The men on stage rip off their fire suits. The screaming inches an octave to near glass shattering.

Finding a lone booth on the right side of the stage I slide in and sit where I can see most of the room. The other men around the room dressed like the server earlier aren't Brandon. It's a sauna in here. I pull my jacket off and use the movement to make it less obvious as I look behind me. Two bouncers stand guard outside a door. Neither are Brandon.

Where the heck did he go?

The waiter reappears and sets my drink on the table in front of me. "I dance at eleven. You should stay for the show and after." And he disappears into the crowd.

To ease the shock of it all, I down half the drink in a single swallow and turn my attention back to the stage. Bad idea. The firemen are now down to...well, just their God given hoses. No wonder this place is unmarked.

The women down front paw at the stage, trying to get up to the men but security keeps them back. One of the dancers points to a woman, the one who almost face planted outside wearing the bride sash, and crooks his finger.

The high pitch screams from her and her clan have me covering my ears to keep my hearing intact. There's no concealing my fascination as I sip my drink and watch her get pulled on stage and sat in a chair. The three men take turns dry humping her, which she clearly is loving, as she shoves more dollar bills between their teeth because that's the only place for it to go at this point.

Not that I want to be up there having some guy's random dick rubbing up and down my thigh but watching it is kind of a turn on, entertaining for sure.

Damn it, where's Gabe when I need him. After all this I need him for…boyfriend benefits.

Their song starts to fade and the men take a bow before exiting the stage. The future bride's clan have to pull her near limp body from the stage and back to the safety of their table.

"Another," asks a male voice I recognize.

Sliding my gaze from the stage I find Brandon standing beside my table. Not knowing what cover I'm going to give, didn't plan this through well—guess the possibility of seeing hot naked men had me forgetting that when I walked in—I nod. Thankfully he smiles and walks away to retrieve my drink.

Hell.

There's little time to come up with a cover as to why I'm here, alone, dressed like I'm…on a recon mission, before he comes back with drink in hand.

He slides into the booth and sets the drink on the table, pulling my empty glass to him. The glass rolls between his hands as he says, "A guy came backstage saying the hottest damn woman he's ever seen in here was at one of his tables. As soon as he gave the description of Italian, smoking hot and fantastic cans I knew it had to be you. He's already called dibs on you by the way."

The ice I was chewing on catches in my throat. "What?"

"What are you doing here?" His gaze searches the area around us before coming back to me. New suspicion behind it. "Where are your friends?"

With a shrug I take a gulp of vodka.

Damn, what can make him go away? The idea hits and I think of the saddest things that have happened in my life or I've seen in movies.

Tears well in the corner of my eyes and I look down to my drink.

"I uh, my boyfriend and I…" I stop like I can't finish the sentence. Fake tears now spill down my cheeks as I look up. "He's such an asshole. He cheated on me while I'm doing this assignment saying I wasn't home enough to take care of him." I duck my head but keep an angle to see his reaction, and shake my shoulders like I'm sobbing.

Fear flashes across his face.

Nothing like a crying woman to scare even a trained warrior away.

"Listen, I—"

"I just wanted a drink and distraction," I sob and scoot closer to him. "My friend said I should come here." I sniff and take another drink. "What are you doing here?"

Those dark eyes search my face then look to the door the two bouncers are guarding. "Sorry about your boyfriend. Strange, I thought you had something going on with Wilcox. At least that's what that idiot Sherman's been complaining about non-fucking-stop." He pauses like he's waiting for validation. With a shake of my head he slips from the booth. "Well anyway, stay and drink. But…" The change in his demeanor, the intensity behind it and I already know what he's going to say. "This. You seeing me here. You knowing about this does not go in the article. Do you understand? No one can know about this."

His shoulders relax at my nod.

"Then stay. Drinks are on me, have fun and forget about the bastard. How the hell anyone could cheat on a woman like you?" His gaze falls to my chest then back up. "Have fun. I'll come check on you after the show."

I shouldn't be as excited as I am at his closing remark. But with his chaps and dueling pistols at his hips how could I not.

While the new act finishes up on stage I sip my drink and pull out my phone to see if there's anything from Gabe.

Tony: I'm giving you a direct order. Tell me where you are.

Oh hell no.

Me: I'm not in your platoon. Nor am I in the Navy. I don't give a rat's ass about your direct order.

Tony: You're an idiot, woman. You know that.

Me: Been called worse. By you actually.

Me: Plus I prefer stubborn.

Tony: I want to help.

Me: No, you want to protect and control.

Tony: Is this because you think I'm the guy?

Tony: You don't trust me.

Me: Maybe a little but mostly because I'm good. I don't need you or Gabe to get this job done. Safely.

Plus, no need for backup. Brandon isn't our mole, he's the nice guy I thought he is. He's just keeping the little piece of him being a male stripper from his water mammal buddies. Even tonight offering to buy my drinks instead of jumping on the opportunity I'm lonely and hurt shows his character. There is nothing manipulative or dangerous about Brandon. This I can feel in my gut.

"Ride a Horse" blares through the speakers and I tuck the phone back into my pocket to give Brandon my full attention.

He saunters on stage, every eye now zeroed in on him. He's attractive, yes, but there's something else there too, he's dynamic—the SEAL part of him seeps out somehow, letting every woman in the room know he can handle whatever she throws at him. Plus by the moves he's making on stage he's hot and a good dancer. Dangerous combination.

The bulge in his banana hammock helps the whole scene too.

From one side of the stage to the other he works the crowd. I swear a woman faints when he unbuckles the chaps and pulls them off. He's halfway through when the fascination of this place wears off. I pull my phone back out.

Nothing.

Nothing from Gabe. Nothing from Tony. From Brooke. From Jeremy.

That blank screen shifts my fun mood, and suddenly feeling out of place without friends, a sad, lonely feeling creeps in.

I want Gabe. Okay maybe not here, who knows what he would do in a place like this. But I want him. Somehow in the short time we've known each other he's had me looking forward to talking to him, getting his random texts and of course seeing him.

He's my guy so it shouldn't surprise me but it still does. Similar to what he said the other night about me being different, he's different. The relationship isn't a chore, it's fun.

Taking the last sip of my drink, I go to set it down but a waiter steps up and takes the glass from my hand. "Brandon said you're having a pretty shitty day and we should take care of you. This one's on the house." He sets a new drink on the table and walks away.

Well, I wasn't really having a bad day until seconds ago. And really it's not a bad day, hell it's a great day. I just cleared another mole suspect I should be celebrating. But I can't.

Real tears this time build in the corners of my eyes threatening to fall.

Damnit, I miss him.

How does my heart physically ache just by thinking of him?

I'm still dwelling in my pity party when Brandon slides into the booth.

"I'm going to try and not take offense even my dancing can't distract you from your shit ass boyfriend," he says and takes a sip of water from the bottle he'd brought with him. He's changed out of his chaps and is back in the jeans and t-shirt he'd arrived in. "Come on. I'm taking you home."

"What?" I ask confused to what his angle is.

"Yep. You're better than sitting in this place drinking alone. I'm taking you home and don't say no or I'll carry you out of here."

My mouth snaps shut to hold back my smart ass reply. There's no need to be bitchy with him, he's right. I don't belong here. After downing my drink I scoot out of the booth.

"Okay, sailor. Let's go."

Instead of leading me toward the door I came in through he guides me to the back door I've been eyeing.

"Do you have that many women trying to break in backstage that you need two huge ass guys at the door?" I ask as we pass the men who shoot me the evil eye, which of course I return with a sappy smile and wave.

"That's what I mean you don't belong out there. The women who come here are desperate, they can't get a guy naked if they begged them." He looks down to me as we walk past a few opened doors. I arch a brow in return, making him laugh. "Yes, okay, not all the guys have my training and some of the women can get...aggressive, so we have the security at the door."

A high pitched shriek comes from the room we just passed, making me pause. Brandon stops when I do but doesn't move to help the woman still shrieking.

"That's Harbor. He probably just doesn't like his hair tonight. Come on." His grip on my elbow is firm as he tugs me down the hall and out the back door.

"I don't like leaving my car here. I'm okay to drive home. Really. I have a high tolerance."

He shakes his head and leads me to his truck. He opens the passenger side door and he says, "I'm not going to let you get booked for a DUI and make your shitty day worse. I'll drop you off then come back before my next show."

Once I'm tucked safely in the passenger seat of his truck, he shuts the door and rounds the hood. I list off directions to the rental house as we pull out of the parking lot.

"How's the article coming?" he asks, keeping his eyes on the road.

With a heavy sigh, hating I'm having to lie to him again, I say, "It's good. I think everyone will be happy with it once it's done. Can I ask you something?"

"I think I know the question but go ahead."

"Why do you do it? The dancing I mean."

He shrugs and switches hands on the wheel to lean against the door armrest. "The money. And it's fun. I paid cash for this truck. No way in hell could I've done that on my military salary. I'm good at it too, so that helps."

"Yeah." I leave out that the image of him in those chaps will forever be ingrained in my mind.

"I love being a SEAL. I love the danger, the strategy, the brother-hood it comes with. I love saving the lives of people and the lives of future people because we take out the major players. There's that thrill. But this, me dancing, is mindless. It's a distraction. We are all wound so tight all the time, one mistake and people die. On stage I make a mistake and I can play it off. I need this as a balance."

Never thought of it that way. Maybe I need a balance.

"None of the guys know. They pay me under the table so there's no paycheck and obviously all the tips are cash so I just keep it at home until I'm ready to buy something."

Out of the corner of my eye I watch him as he drives. The squeaking of his windshield wipers against the glass makes the silence unbearable.

"Aren't you afraid some of the other guys will tell your SEAL buddies?"

"Brothers," he says and shoots a look my way. "And no. There are other guys like me who dance, who simply need a break from their high-stress lives. We all have a lot to lose if anyone finds out, which, I meant what I said tonight about the article."

"I won't say or write anything about it. Promise. Dredging up your secrets isn't why I'm here." Damn, three lies in one night, I need to get to confession soon.

His fingers drum along the steering wheel. "Do you think less of me as a SEAL or as a person because of it?"

I smile and shake my head. "I actually think it's pretty brilliant. I might need to try and find something to balance me too."

"What do you need a balance from? The journalism gig doesn't seem too high stress."

I purse my lips in annoyance. Damn observant water mammal.

"Right, it's no saving lives but it is stressful."

He pulls along the curb in front of my rental and stops. "What are you going to do about your boyfriend?"

I shrug and unbuckle my seatbelt. "Not sure. I'll figure it out tomorrow I guess."

His warm hand grips mine before I slide fully out of the truck's cab. "You deserve better than some piece of shit who cheats on you. All women do, but especially you."

"You don't even know me," I breathe before I can stop myself.

He smiles and lets go of my hand. "I know enough. Good night and next time...bring ones."

I giggle and step out on to the wet sidewalk. The truck stays waiting as I climb the porch and even though I wave him off, he stays parked until I'm safely in and the door is closed.

The loneliness from earlier creeps back in the moment I step into the empty house. Still no texts from anyone and I'm left kind of tipsy, standing in my dark rental house wishing for the first time I had someone to come home to.

No. Not just someone.

Him.

CHAPTER TWENTY-SEVEN
GABE

The waves pound against our Zodiac, mist making it hard to see as we bounce along the water. It's impossible to hear anything between the water and the wind not that any of us are talking. The tension between the men is almost at a snapping point. The past seventy-two hours have been one surprise after another which was not in the plan. Fuck the plan was blown to shit the moment we stepped into the jungle.

What the fuck happened?

CHAPTER TWENTY-EIGHT
LUCIA

My jaw protests as I jam another stick of gum into my mouth trying to stay awake. The final mole suspect, not counting Tony who is still on the possibility list, is quite an active guy. When Petty Officer Matt Sherman isn't on base he's working out or hanging out with friends who are not water mammals. Seems he knows everyone in this town. Tailing him the past couple of days has been brutal, constantly shifting from one location to another.

Other than the information in his file—from San Diego, single child, both parents gone, and the information Jeremy sent over with his digital footprint—I'm still at a loss of who this guy is. The biggest thing Jeremy found was the fluctuating bank accounts. He will drain them, get behind on bills then pay everything off and stash thousands back into the account.

Strange.

My question is, where is all the money he takes out going? His car is paid off, rent is lower on his side of town and he's single, so no family draining his funds.

Even Jeremy couldn't find where all the money was going.

So far in all my tailing nothing shady has popped up. Which is why

246 | KENNEDY L. MITCHELL

I'm giving myself TMJ by chewing all this stupid gum to stay awake and find something on him. There has to be something.

The phone chirps from the cup holder.

Tony: What are you doing?
Me: Working.
Tony: G's back

Unblinking I stare at the phone. Breathing becomes difficult. My heart races as all the awful possibilities fly through my mind.

Me: Why are you telling me this not him?
Tony: He's fine.

I exhale a deep shaky breath in relief.

Me: Next time, lead with that.
Tony: Well he's back and alive. Not sure about fine.
Me: Stop with the cryptic shit. I get enough of that with the CIA.
Tony: The mission went sideways. Everyone came home. But if I know G he's dwelling on it.
Tony: And since he didn't tell you he's back, that confirms what I'm thinking.
Tony: They landed twelve hours ago.

There is no way to stop the sting of finding out he's been back for so long, that I wasn't his first call when he landed like last time.

. . .

Tony: Go talk to him. I think he needs you more than me right now.

Me: Wow, this is a shock. You're pushing me towards him? Look at how grown up you've become.

Tony: I don't give a shit about all that right now. I know how G is taking this. I've seen it before. Hopefully you can get him to come out of it sooner than later.

Me: How long does it normally take?

Tony: Days. He gets wrapped up in his head.

Me: Where is he?

———

The cold breeze off the ocean brushes against my cheeks, whipping my dark hair as I walk down the dock searching for Gabe. This is my second stop, one of the four places Tony said Gabe normally went when he needed to step away from life. The heels of my black motorcycle boots click against the wooden planks echoing down the pier.

About halfway down a man sitting on the railing, legs dangling over the dark water, comes into view. Pulling my black leather jacket tighter I pick up the pace. The silhouette only confirms what I felt the second I stepped out of the car, I knew he was here. There's a pull inside me guiding me towards him and it grows stronger each step I draw closer to the end of the dock where he is.

My fingers play with the lining of my pockets as question after question runs through my mind. The worry in my gut builds and intensifies at the sight of his slumped shoulders.

There's also a hint of trepidation. What if he pushes me away?

My feet pause behind him. He doesn't turn, doesn't acknowledge me at all.

What do I even say.

Then I remember my bad day on the beach and what he said to me.

"If you want me to go…" I say tentatively.

And exactly like I did he doesn't say a word but pats the railing beside him.

Careful not to push him over, I lean against the railing and stare down into the dark water. Even with me knowing the basics of swimming thanks to him, the vastness of the ocean, the things that lurk beneath the waves are terrifying. No way in hell I'm sitting up on that ledge. I don't care what he says.

"Sit with me," he breathes and turns to me.

And just like that, the agony behind his eyes—my urge to take it away—I forget my fears and climb up. Careful not to fall to my watery death I flip my legs over the rail, mirroring his. He glances down at my white-knuckled grip on the wood then up to me with a small smile.

"You know I won't let you fall."

"Well gravity is a bitch and you have no control over it, sailor." I say through clenched teeth and tighten my grip as all the bad outcomes of me falling float across my mind. "Want to talk about it?"

His head shakes and he goes back to staring out across the water.

"Okay well, I have some news to share." Pausing, I wait to see if he takes the bait. He doesn't. "Brandon isn't our mole. That leaves us with Matt who I've been following the past couple days, and nothing has turned up yet."

He doesn't say a word, just pulls my fingers from the wooden railing and interlaces our fingers.

The warmth seeping from his hand to mine, the closeness of him, has me whispering against my better judgement, "I missed you."

His grip tightens.

"Tell me what happened," I plead, pulling our hands to rest on my thigh instead of his.

With a sigh his head drops forward, officially breaking my heart into a million pieces. "It went to shit the second we landed and it only got worse. We all made it out, we met our objective but..." He brings my hand to his lips to brush kisses against my palm. "We handled it."

"I'm not letting you off that easy."

"I can't give you details, you know that Lu—"

"Did I say anything about details?"

Huffing a laugh he drops our hands to his thigh. "No you didn't, sweetheart."

"Do you think the mole had anything to do with it?"

His flinch says more than his words. "We are still going through post-op debriefs to figure out what went wrong. It could have been bad intel."

"That's not what you really think, is it?" I question, staring at him and hoping my gut is wrong.

Like his flinch, his silence speaks volumes.

"Fuck!" I yell and start to swing my legs back over the edge but he grips my waist, keeping me seated. "Let me go, Gabe. If I would have done my damn job by now you wouldn't have been—"

"That's shit, Lucia. You're working on it, we all are," he says calmly into my ear. "Now stop moving around or you're going over and I don't feel like getting wet tonight."

I immediately stop pushing against him, remembering my surroundings.

"I'm so sorry, Gabe. I—"

"Do you know why I'm out here?"

"Reflecting on how I fucked up and haven't been able to do my damn job and stop all this from happening? I know I would be." My eyes close in attempt to slow my racing thoughts.

"Not even close. We handled it, it wasn't ideal but that's what we train for. It's why we go over every possible scenario before we even get on the plane. We did our job. But that's not what has me out here trying to figure out what's going on in my head."

He nudges my shoulder but I don't look up.

"Look at me, Luce." Warm fingers grip my chin to angle my face to him. "You. You're the reason I'm out here."

"Yeah, because I couldn't—"

"Stop it with that shit. For the first time, Luce, I was in battle and all I could think about was making sure I came home. Came home to see you one more time. To kiss you one last time. To hear you fucking laugh or put me in my place one last time. With each bullet I fired, every man I took out I knew I was one step closer to coming home."

Oh.

"I've always known not coming home was a possibility, but now..." He rubs the heels of his palms against his eyes like he's trying to figure out what to say next. "I'm not scared of death," he says finally and looks to me. "But I'm fucking terrified of not making it home to you."

As much as I want to respond I can't. No words come out when I open my mouth. What do I even say back to that?

A strong arm drapes across my shoulders and pulls me to him. "Just tell me we can make it work," he whispers into my hair. "That I don't have to be dreading these next few days because they are our last."

Deep breath in. I can do this.

"Yeah, Gabe. We'll figure it out," I say sounding so convincing I almost believe it. Now would be a good time to lay it all on the table, tell him everything about the CIA wanting him and we could be a possibility but something holds me back. This moment, what he shared, is too deep, too personal to bring it all up now.

Later.

Another day I'll explain everything. Tell him how we might have a chance if he wants to move to DC.

Even as I think it my stomach turns, knowing what he will say.

This is his life even if he thinks he doesn't want to live it without me.

Which would be worse, knowing he didn't choose to come to DC with me—knowing what was on the line—or him never knowing and me making the decision for him? The latter seems less heartbreaking but both leave me without him.

———

"Thank you." Taking the cup of coffee from the guy behind the counter, I head to a table by the window. Men and women move about the sidewalk on the other side of the glass going about their day but not me. Oh no, not me. I'm sitting here for the second morning in a row, waiting.

So. Much. Waiting.

A few nights this week Matt went into the building across the street and stayed all night. Last night was one of those nights. All the businesses in the surrounding area and in the building itself are legitimate, leaving me with nothing to go on when trying to understand where he disappears to.

But this morning that is going to change.

I'm tired of waiting.

A glance down at my watch shows it's a little after seven. Matt should be coming out any time now if he stays consistent. My phone chirps on the table.

Gabe: I hate waking up alone, damn it.

    Gabe: Back watching Matt?

    Me: I tried to wake you up.

    Gabe: Negative.

    Me: Okay, fine. You looked so cozy plus I'm just watching from the coffee house again. Nothing new.

    Me: See you later.

    Gabe: Running by the house to see my mom and check on Dad. Then hell yes. Just tell me your place or mine.

    Me: I know we've been playing us on the DL because of my cover but...

    Gabe: Why am I nervous.

    Me: You could take me out on a legit date. I hear girls like that.

    Gabe: Done. Tonight. Pick you up at six.

My cheeks ache from the wide smile I can't drop. We haven't been out of the house together, this could be fun or terrible. Guess we will see.

The coffee cup in my hand pauses at my lips as my target walks out the front doors of the building in question and down the brick steps. His clothes look slightly wrinkled but not like they've been on the floor all night.

Everyone turns to look my way when the legs of my chair screech across the floor as I push away from the table. Yesterday morning was a simple walk by the building to see if anything was visible through the glass doors from the sidewalk but today I'll venture in. Tossing my near empty cup into the trash, I push out the door and jog across the street.

The building is older, the tile beneath my feet cracked in a few places, and the dark wood paneling makes the entire hall feel smaller than it is. Per Jeremy there are four businesses on the bottom level and two upstairs.

Strolling down the hall, I take my time reading the business name plates on each door. Nothing triggers the feeling of things being off. Now for the upstairs. With each step up the easygoing feeling from downstairs fades and completely vanishes, replaced with apprehension, when my sneakered feet hit the top step.

My gold New Balance tennis shoes help me inch down the hall without a sound. Just as I turn a corner I bolt back around it and seal my back against the wall.

In the quick glance before ducking for cover, two well-dressed, armed men stand in front of a nondescript door. I'm about to take another look when their voices carry down the hall.

My ears strain to hear what they are saying but it's in a language I can't immediately place. Easy solution to that problem. Pulling my phone from my pocket I hit the record button and angle it towards the men. After a minute of recording I tuck it back into my pocket and inch back down the hall and down the stairs.

Outside I take a deep breath in of the fresh San Diego air and shake the tension from my shoulders. At least now we know there are six legitimate businesses in the building and one not so much.

And it's *that one* that has me smiling.

CHAPTER TWENTY-NINE
GABE

How in the hell we made it out the door tonight is a fucking mystery. The second she opened the door, wearing that black dress, showing off her amazing legs, and enough of her tits to be a tease, I wanted to rip it off her. Tried actually, but she laughed and walked out the door, leaving me staring at her fine ass.

Even sitting here, all I can think about is getting her naked and under me. Hell, I'd take just getting my hands up her skirt at this point. My dick twitches in my dark jeans just thinking about skirting up the smooth skin of her inner thigh and teasing while everyone in here is fucking oblivious.

What would she do if my hand starts to wander from her knee?

Not wanting to wonder all night, my hand skims up her inner thigh, pushing the hem of her dress farther up with each inch I climb. I can feel the heat radiating off her, can feel the dampness of her underwear when her hand dives under the table and grips my wrist, pulling my hand back down to where it started.

When she looks up from her menu her lips are pursed, trying not to smile. "Listen, sweetheart. I need food, then we can play. But food first."

Hell yeah.

Adjusting my jeans to stop them from crushing my now fully hard cock, my gaze lands on her chest. Damn. Maybe we can get the food to go. Cannot fucking wait to make her moan my name tonight. I love her breathy cries. Hell, I love her everything...

What. The. Fuck. Did I just think?

Did I admit to myself that I love her? That's not possible. This is our first damn date, no way I can start mentally tossing around that shit.

Great. Rolling my shoulders and neck to clear my mind, I try to focus on the menu in my hands instead of my internal declaration of fucking loving her.

"What?"

As I glance up she's pinning me with a questioning look. "What?"

"What made you all tense just now? What's going on in that head of yours?"

"Damn, sweetheart, you don't miss a beat, do you? Ever think of coming to work on our side?"

"We're all on the same side."

Instead of telling her that's a bunch of bullshit, I shrug and go back to looking at the menu. The waiter arrives with my beer and her vodka and starts to talk about tonight's specials. Which of course she orders along with other food she thinks looks good. Fuck, I love that about her.

Damn. There's that word again.

Get your shit together, man.

"Seriously. What's up with you?" she asks and takes a sip of her drink. The way her tongue drags along her lower lip, catching some of the escaped liquid, causes my pulse to tick higher and higher.

"Just ready to get you naked." And I might fucking love you.

Her smile turns mischievous as she pushes away from the table. "I'll be right back."

A table with five guys doesn't even try to hide their gawking as she walks by.

Not okay, but no need to make a scene, I'd probably be doing the same thing if she were to walk by, plus she'll have my balls on a chopping block if I do.

But then their gawking turns to talking about all the things they would do to her. One fucker goes as far as saying he would bend her over and give it to her in the ass, completely mortifying the old couple beside them.

Time to step in. If anyone's going to talk about nailing her ass it's me. Not that I'd dare. Again I like my balls attached to my body. Plus if she hears them there will be no way to explain how a civilian reporter maimed five men.

Their chatter stops the second I approach the table. Smart on their part. Gripping two fuckers by the shoulders I squeeze as I say, "That's my girlfriend you're talking about. Shut your damn mouths you pieces of shit." The guy in my right hand starts to tremble.

Not going to lie, it feels fucking good.

"Gabe?"

Ah, hell.

When I turn, her arms are crossed and all the amusement from earlier is gone.

"Yeah?"

"What are you doing?"

"Teaching them some manners." She'll pick up on the hint. She almost drowned a man trying to teach him some manners.

With a nod she walks back to our table and sits.

"I just saved your pathetic lives. She would have fucked you up worse than me. She likes good vodka if you pieces of shit would like to send her an apology bottle." One of the guys across the table goes wide-eyed with true terror behind them. With one more squeeze, making the guy on my left hiss in pain, I drop my hands and walk back to our table.

"Sorry," I say as I snatch my napkin out of my chair and sit.

Damn, it's fucking hot in here. Undoing the cuff buttons I roll them up as I continue. "Those dumb asses were running their mouths."

After looking between the right arm and left sleeve, making sure they are even, I glance up to see if she's pissed. But she's not. Instead those green eyes are bright and she's biting her lower lip to keep from smiling.

"Just when I didn't think you could get any hotter, Officer Wilcox." Her head shakes as she breaks our stare to take a drink.

"What?" Damn, this woman is confusing. I would've laid bets on her hating being defended like that. Not that it matters, had to be done.

"Oh, did I tell you what I discovered today?" Those lusty eyes from earlier are now filled with excitement. "I have a lead on what Mr. Sherman is hiding."

"You think he's our guy?" It has to be a solid lead to make her this excited. Hell, she's practically bouncing out of her seat.

"I do. I really do. This morning after he left the building I've been monitoring, I went in to see what's inside. And—"

"You what?"

"I went inside," she says slowly like I'm hard of hearing.

"I heard what you said but you told me this morning you were only watching. I can pull up the damn text you sent me if you want."

"Plans change."

"I doubt that."

"What the hell does that mean?" she hisses and takes a gulp of her drink.

"It means you knew what you were going to do this morning, which is why you didn't wake me up. It's fine, just don't fucking lie about it, Luce. Tell me the truth. I only ever want the truth."

With a sigh she plays with her glass and looks up. "You're right."

"Next time, just give me a heads up, okay? I just want to know as much as I can. I know there are some things I have to be in the dark on but the things I can know about, tell me."

She nods and starts but the waiter delivering a large bottle of Kettle One vodka to our table makes her stop. With a raised brow she accepts it and looks to me.

"From the table of gentlemen." Gentlemen my ass. "Who just left with their apologies," says the waiter then turns and walks towards the kitchen.

"Gabe?"

"Just smile, sweetheart."

"Fine," she says with a smile. "What was I saying…? Crap, I can't remember what I was telling you before you called me out on my sneaking."

"What you found today when you went into the building."

"Oh yeah," she exclaims and leans closer to me. "There is one business in there that needs two armed bouncers outside the door. Looked suspicious for sure. Ah shit, I forgot to email Jeremy the voice recording I took." Her eyes flick to the ceiling like she's frustrated with herself.

It's odd. The woman is fucking brilliant, smart as hell, but when it comes to remembering shit like this she's done for.

I'm smiling at the thought when what she said clicks. "Why did you take a voice recording?"

"They were talking in a different language." Reaching into her purse she pulls out her phone and swipes it open. "After listening to it a few times today I'm thinking Eastern European."

The phone slides across the white table cloth. Holding it up to my ear, since the restaurant is too damn loud to hear anything, I play it back a few times and hand it back to her.

Fuck, what has this guy gotten himself into?

"Russian." I lean back in the chair and balance it on its two back legs. "You say he's there all night and has lots of random banking habits?" She nods but holds out a hand for me to stop when I start to go on. Seconds later our food arrives. Once everything is on the table and the servers have moved on she motions for me to continue and dives into her food.

For a second I just watch. There's something about being with a person at your level that makes it sexy as hell. Of course she was monitoring the restaurant to make sure our conversation was kept private. I'm a fucking idiot if I don't ask her to marry me, to move to San Diego for good before all this is over.

Which will be soon if this guy is the mole.

"Gabe? Were you going to finish your thought?" she says between bites, pulling me out of my internal haze.

"Sorry, yeah. I've heard of a place around town that's run by the Russian mob. It has everything illegal someone could want. Girls, drugs, but mostly people go for the gambling."

The murmur of the people fills the silence between us as her mind works overtime processing everything. Not wanting my food to get cold, I start on my steak as she stares ahead, thinking.

When she speaks up several minutes later it catches me by surprise.

"We need to know," she says and takes the last sip of her drink. Before she continues, I motion to the server for another round. "Thanks. What I'm thinking is we need to know exactly what this guy has gotten himself into, how deep, and who he's selling information to. I...we need to know who his partners are."

I nod but keep eating. Her plate is already clean and if I don't hurry she'll start to take bites of mine. Which is not okay. Hell, she's already eyeing the potatoes I've been saving for last.

The hopeful look on her face when she looks between my plate and me is unfair. I don't have a damn chance against it. With a mock-annoyed huff I slide my scalloped potatoes over and am rewarded with a happy smile as she picks up her fork and digs in.

"What are you thinking?" I ask and shove another slice of steak into my mouth.

"I need to get inside."

To delay saying "hell fucking no that's too dangerous" then having her tell me to screw off, I slow my jaw to chew at a snail's pace. But the plan backfires. Instead of continuing she waits for me to finish, staring me down the entire time.

"What?" I finally say into the beer bottle at my lips.

"You heard me."

"I'm not sure about that, sweetheart. Explain it again."

Her eyes narrow then roll like a teenager having to repeat herself to her parents. "I need to get inside."

"And how are you going to do that, sweetheart? You have to be invited into those types of places. And that's not your only hurdle. If you do get inside you will be alone, no backup. It would turn into an international incident if I went in with you."

A mischievous smile widens on her beautiful face, making those green eyes of hers sparkle with anticipation. "I think I know how to get an invite. But you're not going to like it."

Oh, fucking hell.

———

"Luce!" I yell after her as she storms up the porch to her rental. "Lucia, just hear me out, would you?"

Fuck, she's pissed.

"Unless you're changing your stance of 'no way in hell are you going on a fake date with that douchebag' then no, I'm not going to hear you out, Gabe. And guess what," she whirls around causing me to stumble to a stop, almost slamming into her. "I don't need your permission."

The calluses on my hand do nothing to soothe me as I run it down my face. "But you do need CO's."

Wrong fucking thing to say.

Her face flushes a shade of red that reminds me of Christmas and her hands ball into fists.

"In reality, no, I don't. I just need my boss's approval to go in. We are doing you dumb water mammals a favor remember, not the other way around. So you can go fuck yourself with this whole permission bullshit. Now get the hell off my porch."

Nope.

"Luce, I—"

"I said go away, Gabe." Her hands fumble with the keys in the lock, clearly flustered. When the lock pops she pushes inside and tries to slam the door in my face but I stop it before it can close. "And here I thought you were so different. Thinking you knew I could do this on my own. I thought you were helping because you wanted to be around, not because you didn't think I could do it on my own."

Okay now this is funny. I can't help but smile at how wrong she is. As soon as she sees me smiling the look on her face makes me wish I was carrying.

"You fucking asshole thinking this is so damn funny—"

"Enough, Luce."

"No. I'll tell you when I'm done, damn it. I—"

"Enough."

In a few quick steps her back is against the wall. I catch one of her punches mid swing and hold her hand above her head, the other follows close behind. Damn, I love her fight.

Her tits bounce as her chest heaves, begging for my attention. When I look, licking my lips, she fights harder and starts yelling another chorus of curse words.

Rage and hurt linger behind her eyes when I'm finally able to pull my gaze up.

"I like you pinned," I say and drag my free hand down her waist and thigh.

"Not in the damn mood, Gabe," she hisses but there's more hurt than anger in her tone.

"Let's get one thing straight, sweetheart. I said what I said tonight not because I don't think you can do it. Hell, I'm not sure there's anything you can't do once you've got that stubborn ass mind of yours set on something."

"But you—"

I cover her mouth with my palm.

"I said what I said because I don't want another guy taking you out. Fuck, all I was doing during dinner was imagining you naked beneath me. Why in the would I be okay with you being out on a date knowing some other dipshit would be doing the exact same thing? Thinking about my girl naked, and thinking he has a damn shot." I take a deep breath in to settle the growing fury just at the thought of some guy looking at her that way. "It's not about your ability, sweetheart, there's no questioning that. It's about mine."

Something's mumbled beneath my palm. I shift my hand to cup her jaw.

"It's our best option."

"I know it is. Believe me, the entire time you were ignoring me on the ride here, I was trying to come up with a better option. But there isn't one that will work in the time frame we are dealing with."

The way her eyes scan my face, analyzing and calculating, tells me she's doing her witch shit. Trying to see if I'm filling her with bullshit to get her naked or if I'm telling the truth.

She can look all she wants, all she'll find is the truth.

A relieved look washes over her face, making all the tension and anger from earlier disappear. "Kiss me."

Not giving her a second to rethink her demand, I press my lips to her and suck her bottom lip between mine. She pulls and fights against the hold on her wrists but instead of letting go my grip tightens keeping her hands pinned against the wall above her head.

My free hand brushes fingertips down her neck and along her collarbone in long lazy strokes. Beneath my fingers her chest rises and falls faster and faster. A small tug on the little strip of material holding her dress together and it falls open.

Releasing our lips, I pull back to take in her almost naked body pinned beneath me and almost cum in my pants.

Fucking hell.

Her whimpering my name, begging me to hurry nearly pushes me over the edge again.

A deep, gravely moan pushes past her lips the moment I wrap a hand around her huge tit and tug at her hard nipple, making my dick grow harder than I've ever thought possible. Holy hell, this woman will be my undoing.

With each pull on her nipple and flick of my tongue against hers she flexes her hips against mine trying to find any friction she can. The soft, sexy as hell whimper returns when I head south and tuck between her thighs. This I'll take my time with; watching her squirm, trying to get my fingers and hand exactly where she wants them, is sexy as hell.

Our lips still against the others as my finger dips beneath her thong and slide inside her.

"Holy fucking..." I mumble against her lips but can't finish. I'm too busy trying to get my damn belt off with one hand.

This time when she yanks against my grip I allow her to break free. Immediately her hands go to work helping me rip the belt around my waist free and start undoing my pants while I search my pockets for a condom.

Scratch marks will surely be on me tomorrow the way she rips my jeans down my thighs and grips my cheeks urging me to her. The desperation in her need makes getting the damn condom out of the wrapper a fucking impossible task.

"Forget it," she cries. Her legs wrap around my waist and she reaches down between us and wraps a warm hand around me. "Just fuck me."

The pictures on the wall rattle as her back slams against it when I push into her in one hard thrust. Barely audible pleas fall from her lips, urging me harder and faster.

"Yes," she breathes. "More, Gabe." Luce leans back, resting her head against the wall, eyes shuttering closed as she gives herself over to me. Giving me all control of her fucking gorgeous body.

Digging into her ass cheeks, holding tighter and tighter as I slam into her over and over. Sweat drips down my heaving chest and my muscles start to tremble as I hold back from making this moment end.

But that thought is lost when she erupts, clenching my dick like a vice.

"Fuck," I hiss against the skin of her neck and bite down slightly.

With her forehead on my shoulder, dark hair sticking to my sweat-slicked skin she says, almost breathless, "Gabe?"

"Yeah sweetheart," I respond, kissing along the shallow teeth indentions on her skin.

"We should fight more."

I know she's smiling by the slide of her cheeks against me making my own spread across my face. Fighting. Fucking. Smiling. Who would have thought this would be the perfect moment for both of us?

CHAPTER THIRTY
LUCIA

The clicking of my heels echoes in the hall on the way to CO Williams' office to explain our plan. Well my plan, really. Everything has been set in motion. Yesterday Tony texted Matt with some encouragement for him to ask me out. It took less than three minutes for Matt to call. And three minutes is a long time when it's a pivotal piece to jump start your plan.

I was a mess waiting. So much so Tony decided, without my approval, to send a follow-up text saying he heard I got off on giving head.

Fucking bastard.

But it did help, I guess, because it's all set. Tomorrow night. Much to Gabe's chagrin. He's been pouting since Matt's number showed up on my screen.

"Hey stranger," says the CO's admin as he stands to round the desk when I approach. "How's the information hunt going?"

I furrow my brows at him. How in the heck does he have that kind of information? "I'm sorry?"

He gives a little laugh like he's in on some inside joke which I'm oblivious to. "Your article. The information you're here to get from the boys."

The flipping of my stomach signals something's off. This guy is the extreme of confusing, I can't get a read on him. His eyes roam up and down, no doubt imagining what's underneath my pantsuit.

A shiver rakes down my spine as he takes another step closer, closing the gap between us, but I hold my ground. Thankfully before he can come any closer the door to CO Williams' office opens.

"Come on in," CO Williams says and turns to walk back into his office.

"See you around, Miss Freebush." The mocking tone irks me further.

I have to maneuver around him and don't turn back but can sense his stare with each step.

Damn, how do I keep forgetting to ask Gabe about this guy?

A sense of nostalgia envelops the moment I step through the door. So many things have changed since the first time I stepped into his office weeks ago. Who would have thought the hot guy in fatigues I was admiring that first day would be the guy I'm falling for? Or have already fallen for. More than likely the latter if I'm being honest with myself. But really who wouldn't fall for his dimpled smile, honest eyes and soul as genuine as a George Strait song.

There's no missing the shift in CO Williams' presence today from our prior meetings. Before, he was always behind the desk, all business, but today he's relaxed in one of the leather chairs in the corner of the room with a full highball glass in his hand, and another on the side table beside him.

His nod towards the chair across from him isn't a suggestion. I sink down into the leather and angle my head towards the drink. "Mine?"

His smile is my answer as he takes a drink out of his crystal glass.

There is no hesitation in grabbing the drink and taking a sip. This man I'd immediately trusted the first day and it still stands now. There's not a single fleeting thought of him putting something in here or him trying to ply me with alcohol to take advantage. I've been around enough of those types of men to identify them quickly.

"I'm not going to like this, am I," he says as a statement, not a question.

"What I'm wanting to do could go one of two ways," I say and take a sip of the delicious bourbon. "Either I obtain valid proof Sherman is our guy or I start an international incident, which the CIA will not take responsibility for, leaving me to figure a way out on my own."

The disapproving look he shoots hurts more than angers me for some reason. "And these are the people you want to work for. The people you want to take my best damn SEAL to work for."

The too large sip of bourbon I take to keep from responding burns down my throat. He's right.

"Seems to me your agency has a way of using their assets until they're no longer needed, then leaving them without a glance back. That is not the Navy, Agent Rizzo, and I guaran-damn-tee you it's not the SEAL's mentality. We work as a team, train as a team, and come home as a team."

Again I sip the drink instead of responding. Everything he's saying is accurate and has become clearer since the day I landed. Still with nothing to say back to his statement I shift the focus back to my reason for calling this meeting.

"Here's the plan, sir." The crystal thumps against the table when I set it down and steel my spine, readying to give him the same talk I gave to the boss a few hours ago. He was fine with it, no concern, which now is concerning to me. This isn't going to be easy and can go wrong quickly. "Sherman seems to have connections with the Russian mob but we don't know how deep yet, which is what I need to find out. Tomorrow night he's taking me out then through the night I'll convince him to take me to the place he disappears to a few nights a week. I'll gather the info we need, find out who the players are, then leave. Simple."

"And the CIA is okay with this. You going in alone."

"Yes, sir."

"How in the hell your boss will allow you—"

"Hey, sir, I mean, I can handle myself—"

"I wasn't done talking soldier, you keep your trap shut until I'm done." My lips instantly seal shut at the pure command. "It's not about you being a damn woman so don't go spewing that shit. It's about working together. The fact they gave you the green light to go without any backup, without even a basic damn plan is ignorant."

"I have a plan," I grumble like a pouting teenager.

"What was that?" He leans forward in his chair, balancing his elbows on his massive thighs.

Playing innocent, I shake my head and try to keep silent until he's finished. Yes, I trust him and respect this man, and now there's a bit of fear mixed in with it too. He didn't get to this position by being a pushover.

"If your damn agency isn't going to make a few demands then I will. First, you will give me details down to the damn second on how the mission is going to go and what we're going to do if shit hits. Second, you are not going in alone, but since you can't take someone with you I want Wilcox in your ear. And above all I need your word, Agent Rizzo, if shit hits you get out. No sticking around and being stupid. If things go bad, you get out."

Rolling the crystal glass between my hands I keep my eyes on the moving liquid inside. "I have other orders."

When I peer up through my lashes his scowl says everything. "I know what your orders are and quite frankly they're bullshit. What they want you to do, who they want you meddling with is putting personnel in danger when it's not needed—"

"But if it could help us get more information—"

"We will get the information, Agent Rizzo. Don't you see that, or have they brainwashed you to only seeing things their way? They want the information first, they are willing to risk your life to get it. Hell, I bet they've already told you to let them know who the mole is first instead of me."

Not wanting to comment I look over his shoulder to the massive bookshelf. My hands are shaking when I set the glass down on the table with a loud thunk.

"I still have a job to do."

"So do I, but we have different objectives, Agent Rizzo, and that is what you need to see."

Gathering enough courage to look back to him, only sympathy fills his eyes. Hell, what am I missing. "I don't understand what you're saying, sir. And please stop looking at me like I'm a kicked kitten."

Immediately the softness evaporates and the hardcore CO is back. "Your objective is to come here and find the mole so you can get whatever they've promised you if you do, plus recruiting Wilcox." I nod to keep him going, still not understanding where he's going with this. "My objective, Lucia," oh no, using the first name, this must be bad,"Is to do whatever I can to protect my men. This bastard is leaking information which is risking their lives and national security. Finding this mole means I increase their odds of coming home and that's what's driving me." He smiles a bit and tips back the rest of his drink before continuing. "And I'm going to make the bastard wish he was never born once I get my hands on him."

It might be sadistic but his words make a happy smile pull at my lips.

He wants to protect his men and the agency wants to throw me into the fire drenched in lighter fluid. Either they have incredible trust in me, assuming I can do anything, or they don't value me at all and I'm replaceable in their eyes.

"I want that too. When I first joined the CIA I was excited about saving the lives of people who had no idea they were even in danger. Cutting off the threats before anything could be acted out. Gathering the intelligence to stop it." I drum the tips of my fingers along the leather armrest. "What are they turning me into?"

"That's for you to figure out, Agent Rizzo. Now back to your mission. Do you agree if anything happens you'll get out, no stupid hero shit?"

The look he shoots says now's not the time for jokes or backtalk. "Yes, sir."

"Good." He rounds his desk and sits in his chair and leans back. "Get me the details and let Wilcox know what you need for listening devices."

"I brought my own."

He smirks and leans forward, resting his elbows on the wooden desk. "I'm sure you did. Your agency and your toys. Dismissed, Agent Rizzo."

Hand on the handle I remember something. "Oh, Sir, did the team ever figure out if Officer Wilcox's mission the other day went south because of bad intel or from leaked information?"

The smirk falls, his face turns hard as granite. "We are still going through debriefings to figure out what went wrong, we aren't sure if it's mole-related or not."

I nod and turn back to the door. Dread makes my stomach drop as I push it open knowing his admin will be out there waiting. But instead of him greeting me at the door it's Tony, who's in my face the second the door closes behind me.

"How'd it go? Are we good for tomorrow night? Did he approve of it all?"

Pushing against his shoulder I try to maneuver past but he side steps, blocking my path and grabbing my shoulders to keep me in front of him.

"What the heck are you even doing here, Tony? Do you have some damn tracker on me?"

"Wilcox. Now tell me, are we good?"

"Yes, damn it. We are good."

The anxiety and tension drains from his face and his hands drop to his side. "Good."

"Miss Freebush, is he bothering you?" The CO's admin says, already rounding the edge of his desk.

Instead of looking to him I turn to face Tony, hiding my face from the admin and whisper, "Get me out of here."

With his brows furrowed he gives a slight nod and grabs my arm. "She's fine, fuck stick. Not like you could do anything about it if I was. Hell, from what I remember it only took you a few hours to ring that damn bell." The last part is said over Tony's shoulder as we walk away.

Once we reach the stairs he drops my arm and turns. "Want to tell me what that was about?"

With a shrug I start down the stairs.

"Tell me," he demands, keeping a step behind me.

When we hit the bottom floor I pause and turn. "I don't know, something's just off with him. He's not creepy, it's more like arrogant. Something's just off and he's already asked me out once—"

Tony's bellowing laugh roars through the hall, making everyone look.

"He's got bigger balls than I give him credit for if he thought he had a shot with you."

"That's the thing, Tony, arrogance is what drove him to ask me out, not the size of his damn balls. It was like it never crossed his mind I would say no."

He raises his brows and rests his hands on his hips. "Which you did, right?"

"Of course I did, you stupid water mammal."

"Just making sure. I'm betting Gabe would explode if you went on not one but two dates with other guys. Hell, he's on the verge now and he knows what's on the line. Which..." He looks around the hall monitoring the people watching us. "Let's talk outside." With his hand on the small of my back we stride down the hall and out the doors, not speaking a word until we're in front of my Camaro.

"What?" I ask and sit on the warm hood. The heat from the sun on the black paint seeps through my pants, warming my backside after CO Williams' near freezing office.

He shifts back and forth, keeping his eyes anywhere but on me for a few seconds, then straightens, pulling his hands behind his back and widens his stance.

"Thank you."

My loud laugh at the buildup for the basic statement of gratitude has him narrowing his eyes and pursing his lips. Clearing my throat of my giggles, I sit up straight and motion for him to continue.

"I know you're suspicious of me and with our lack of evidence on these other guys, fuck, who knows, I probably would suspect me too. But it's not me, Lucia, you have to believe me. I've got my demons but being a traitor ain't one of them. Do you really think Matt's our guy?"

Staring at my drumming nails for a second, debating if I should tell him the truth or not, I glance up and shrug. "He has to be, right? If you're not the guy," I try to kick him but he dodges it with a scowl. "Then it has to be him. Everyone else checks out. So yes, it has to be Matt. If not, I'm fucked."

"You're fucked? Hell if Matt's not the guy how in the hell am I going to trust anyone in my platoon? Ever? And believe me, that shit will get me killed or one of them. We need trust to survive. Trust and each other."

Dang, what is it with these guys knowing all the reasons why the agency is a lying piece of shit? And I'm the idiot for going along with their mind games as long as I have. For what even? A hope of doing more? To grow in the agency? Hell, I can't even remember why I wanted the promotion anymore. It's just been the goal for so long I guess the meaning has faded.

"What's your problem?" Tony asks and leans against the truck parked beside me. "You just went all sad."

With a shake of my head to clear the thoughts, or at least tuck them away for another time, I stand. "Nothing. Listen, I gotta go. Want to come over tomorrow morning to hash out all the details of tomorrow night?"

"Sure." He opens my door but blocks me from getting in. "I mean it Lucia. I know the way I acted at first was—"

"Juvenile. Idiotic. Pathetic."

"Whatever, just let me fucking finish," he huffs. "It means a lot that you haven't given up. That you are going to find this guy no matter what. Just thanks. It's not enough, I know."

Without a second thought I pull him in for a hug, his arms tentatively wrapping around me. "It's plenty, Tony," I say into his shoulder. "And being here has given something back to me."

He pushes me away and takes a step back. "Shit, you have to bring up G now?"

"Not Gabe, even though that has its perks," his gagging motion makes me smile. "Being here has given me clarity."

"I don't get it."

"But I do. Now."

With a nod he shuts the car door and I carefully back out of my spot. The whole drive back to the rental the lies and games the CIA have been playing since day one become clear and I'm finally able to see everything for what it is.

Who knew a bunch of water mammals would end up being my damn Oprah?

CHAPTER THIRTY-ONE
LUCIA

"One more time," Gabe says from where he sits on the bed while I finish getting ready for the date with Matt. Setting the flat iron on the sink, I peek out the door into the bedroom. His head hangs between his shoulders, fingers laced behind his head as his right knee bobs with the bouncing of his foot.

"Gabe," I say and cross the room to sit in his lap. When those blue eyes look up to mine there's too many emotions to make out what exactly he's feeling. He's apprehensive of the plan, that much is clear, since he's asking a third time to go over the details, but there's something else in there too. Almost like fear. "It will be fine. We've gone over this twice tonight and a ton more this morning with Tony. If things get bad, I get out. Simple as that."

His soft lips brush along the tender skin of my neck, causing goosebumps to appear down my arms. "That's what scares me. It's too simple. Luce, I..." His forehead presses against my shoulder. "I've just found you—"

"And you're not going to lose me. You and Tony will be with me every second. Now stop it with all the questions or I'll start to think you don't believe I can do this."

I should tell him. Now would be a good time. But where do I even start with everything I've realized over the past twenty-four hours? It still confuses me. I would be a jumbled mess if I tried to say it out loud. The one thing I know for certain is there's no way in hell I'd try to convince him to join the backwards, manipulative agency I've sold my soul to. I'd rather fall on my own knife than bring him into this twisted world where up is down and everyone is your ally until they're not. He has a family here, one I'm starting to envy. No way will I take him from this.

Not when I now see what they've turned me into. What they've turned my dreams into.

"Luce?" Warm hands grip my face. "Are you having second thoughts? What are you thinking?"

I plaster on a fake smile and shake my head. After a chaste kiss I push off his chest and head back into the bathroom to finish getting ready. "Just thinking."

"About?"

"You."

"What about me? You can't say that and walk away."

For a half second I debate telling him, but decide against it and ignore him. Later. After we get the evidence tonight on Matt I'll tell him. After tonight we'll have plenty of time to figure us out. Figure me out.

After tonight.

———

As soon as we are in the car and Matt says where we are headed for dinner a full array of banter begins in my ear between the two boys.

"Fuck stick, trying to show off," Gabe said.

"It's because of that last text, he's showing off to get head."

"Fuck you, Flakes! Say something like that again and your ass is on the fucking concrete."

"Shit man, she's been with him for seven minutes. Your ass is going to be on the concrete if you can't calm the fuck down."

The. Whole. Way. Here. They bantered. Which sucked, since most of the crap they were saying was hilarious making it hard to pay attention to the million questions Matt pelted nonstop.

The restaurant is spectacular, it seems Matt went all out with the reservations. Like a gentleman, Matt pulls out my chair and scoots it in before taking his own seat. A waiter decked out in a black tie takes our drink orders, tells us the specials, and leaves us so we can look over the menu.

"So Gracie Lu, I was surprised to get the text from T you were interested in me. I didn't get that vibe during the long-ass interview and after at the bar."

"Yeah, well, I guess I was trying to keep things professional until all my stuff was done. Now I just get to have fun, you know? All the interviews are over and I have everything I need for my article. Sorry if I was rude."

"Or it could be because you're a fucking tool. Sweetheart, if he touches you, use that knife by your right hand, I know you left yours at home tonight. Looks plenty sharp from here to slice his femoral artery."

"No you dumbass. We need her to get Matt talking. Give him a handjob under the table, Lucia. He'll tell you anything if you get him to the breaking point."

"Stop it, you two," I say under my breath.

"What was that?"

Peering above the menu, Matt's staring, brows furrowed.

Well, hell.

"Oh sorry, it's nothing. Just reading the menu out loud, helps me choose."

Lamest excuse ever but he buys it. With a nod he goes back to reviewing his menu.

"Well, that's good. Glad you're done with it all now and we get to be here tonight. I think everyone knew how much I wanted a chance to take you out."

"You mean get into her fucking skirt. Piece of shit trying to sound like a stand up guy. Fucking dip shit."

"You had the same thoughts."

"Fuck off Flakes."

"Well I'm glad you reached out and we're here too. So tell me about yourself, Matt, things I didn't get from the interview," I say with a smile and reach across the table to grab his hand.

A few minutes later the waiter comes back with our drinks making Matt pause his life overview, which of course is old news since everything he's saying is in his file. After the waiter leaves I grab my drink and raise it to his.

"Here's to getting to know each other," I say and clink his glass.

"I'd like it to go a lot farther than that, Gracie Lu," Matt says after taking a sip of his red wine.

With a shy smile I take a long drink, keeping my eyes locked with his. "And whatever do you mean by that, Matt?"

His smile says everything his words aren't. "You know getting past the first date shit, the just getting to know you crap. It gets fucking old, don't you think?"

I nod and take another long sip of my vodka soda.

"Slow the hell down on that drink sweetheart."

"So what do you have in mind?" Dang, this could be easier than we thought.

"Nothing in particular."

"Yeah right!" say the two men in my ear in unison.

"Okay, well let's start with some of the basics then. What do you do for fun? The most fun I've had recently was at this strip club on the other side of town." They didn't need to know it was filled with screaming women and sexy naked men.

Crickets from the men in my ear and the man across the table. At least with Matt I can see his reaction. It's nothing short of priceless.

The shock morphs into an excited smile. "Well if that's what you want to do after dinner I'm down."

"Did you take her to a strip club? Nice, G."

"Fuck that, who took her to a damn strip club?"

"What if she went by herself. How hot is that? Fuck, I didn't think she could get any hotter."

"Stop talking about my girlfriend like that."

"Fuck, girlfriend? You're so pussy whipped. Might as well go buy a damn minivan."

It's almost impossible to think with these two bickering.

"Already did that this week, what else can we do? I'm so tired of the typical date too. I mean can't we just have fun? I want to do something I've never done before, something I could never do on my own. I can go see boobs anytime."

Matt chokes on his wine nearly spewing it across the table. He uses his white napkin to cover his mouth as he tries to recover. While he does, the boys are having a field day.

"She's perfect."

"If you don't marry her, I'm going to."

"Fuck that, you're already married and she's turned you down once already."

"Low blow man. Fucking punch to the balls."

"Suck it up, pussy."

"Can you say that with her listening? She might cut off your balls."

"What do you have in mind?" Matt says and takes a sip of water. He's nervous. I'm calling him on his earlier bluff. No way did he expect me to be okay with moving this date along quicker than normal. Hopefully if I keep pressing he'll show his hand.

"You tell me. Know of anywhere I haven't been before that I'd like. Somewhere we can have fun, just you and me?"

"Tell me what you like."

With the tip of my index finger I trace my collar bone, dipping down my chest as I stare off to the side. "Well Matt, here's my secret." His eyes follow the sweep of my finger, keeping him in a slight trance. "I like everything. The more dangerous, taking me to the edge is what I like. So what do you say, Matt, how close to the edge are you willing to go with me? Tonight."

"Fuck."

"She's good."

"Sexy as hell man."

"She's working him over and he has no idea."

"The fucker won't be able to stand up for a while after that show. Fuck, I can't stand up right now."

"Shut your damn mouth, Flakes!"

The waiter returns, shaking Matt from his lusty trance. After ordering he looks back to me, a hint of lust still lingering in his brown eyes. "You've taken strip clubs off the table. What else is there?"

"Know any places around here where we can...play?" Angling my head down I peer up through my lashes giving a hint of insecurity.

"Play?" he asks his voice noticeably deeper.

"Yeah, play. No rules, just have a good time and see where the night goes."

The intensity between us is palpable, but it's not enough. The way he's looking past me says he needs more convincing. Which is fine, it would have been boring if he gave up all his secrets without any pushback.

Upping the ante, I lean over enough for him to have a straight shot down my dress and grab his hand. "I hope you don't think I'm too forward, it's just..."

"What?" he rasps as he stares down my dress.

"What I liked about you was you seemed to be a risk taker. That you lived your life on the edge more than the other guys. You're like me and it was..." With a deep sigh pushing my breasts against the fabric of the dress I breathe, "Sexy."

"The edge?"

"You said you wanted to do more than just get to know me, Matt. Well, this is your chance. I'm up for anything new tonight."

"New."

"Yes."

"The edge."

"Yes," I say with an excited tone, which isn't fake.

"How about we sneak you on base and I fuck you on the beach?"

Disappointed, I sit back in my chair and take a sip of my drink. "Not really what I was thinking, Matt."

"Well that's what I was thinking," he says and sits back in his chair with his glass of wine in hand. "Or..."

"Or?" I sit up and lean forward.

"You like to gamble, Gracie Lu?"

"She did it."

"I knew she could."

"Can he stop looking at her tits now? Fuck, sit back in your chair, Luce."

"They are great cans."

"Get the fuck out, Flakes."

"But I—"

"Now."

"No."

"I need to talk to her, just me. Give me five minutes, you fucker. Five damn minutes."

"Fuck you. I'll be back with coffee."

"I don't think Vegas is a good idea tonight," I say, playing dumb.

"Not Vegas. Here in San Diego. There's this place I know where there're no limits. If you want it, you get it. Simple as that."

I stroke down his index finger with my own. "Sounds like my kind of fun. Have I been there before?"

"Doubtful."

Our food arrives, breaking us apart, but his brown eyes never leave mine as he says, "If we go, it doesn't end up in the article. You don't speak of it to anyone, ever. Do you understand?"

"Yes," I respond with a huge smile.

"Listen here, Luce. I know what you're doing. You're using what you have to get the objective met, simple as that. But just know I hate how he's looking at you, fuck, I hate it. Staring at those tits I've kissed and sucked on, making you fucking squirm beneath me. He wants to get under that sexy as hell dress you're wearing, wants to pull it up and fuck you senseless but he can't because I will. I'm the one who makes you scream. My name is the one you moan when my face is between your thighs."

Staring at my plate, I set my fork down and tuck my shaking hand under my thigh so Matt doesn't notice.

"If it were you and me right now, I'd scoot your chair over to mine so I could touch you. I'd start at your knee and work my fingers up your thigh but this time you wouldn't stop me. Would you?"

My head shakes as I stare at my plate looking like a damn lunatic to anyone watching.

"With each inch I move up your skirt bunches in your lap, making you nervous, but I'm watching, don't worry sweetheart no one will see me as I move aside that black thong I've already pulled off you once tonight and stroke up and down, giving you a little tease of what's to come tonight—"

"Gracie Lu? Are you okay?"

No, I'm not okay. Holy hell.

"Uh, um, yeah," I stutter and push away from the table. "Excuse me for a minute."

By the time I'm in the women's restroom, with Gabe chuckling in my ear, I'm barely able to see straight. Not even caring if there is anyone else in here. I wrap my hands around the cool porcelain sink and I stare into the large mirror. "Listen here, sweetheart, stop it with that shit." This makes the chuckling stop. No doubt he can hear the tremble in my voice from restrained anger. "I'm trying to work here, and I cannot do it with you saying all that in my ear and while we're on this topic, you and your little friend need to cut the damn banter."

A flush sounds behind me and just as a stall door opens a woman steps out. Not once does she make eye contact as she washes her hands and bolts out the door.

"Luce, I can't stand it. The way he's looking at you. Thinking he has a fucking shot with my girl."

"I don't care Gabe. Did you forget why I'm here? Why I'm doing this? Because I sure haven't forgotten how you almost didn't come home because I haven't done my damn job. I'm doing this for you and all you're doing is distracting the hell out of me. Stop."

"What did I miss?"

I roll my eyes at my reflection. "Hey, I was just telling your friend here to cut all the unnecessary chitchat. This is your only warning. If either of you can't do that I'm pulling this out of my ear and doing the rest of the mission truly on my own. Do you understand?"

Silence fills my ear instead of their acknowledgements.

"Do you understand, gentlemen?"

"Yes."

COVERT AFFAIR | 281

"Fine."

"No more banter, Luce, no more distractions. I'm sorry I didn't think it through, you're right. We're here if you need us but you won't hear from us again."

"What the hell did you say-"

The audio cuts Tony off, which is a good thing. I'm so done with both of them tonight.

Staring at my reflection I try to refocus on tonight's objective. But the lingering heat between my thighs from Gabe's random seduction act makes it hard to concentrate. But I have to. For Tony. For Gabe. For all of them. I will focus and get what needs to be done, done.

Focus, Lucia, I mouth to my reflection.

Gather evidence on Matt.

Get his business partners.

Get out.

I can do this.

CHAPTER THIRTY-TWO
GABE

Hearing her laugh at his lame ass jokes, watching him look at her like she's already a done deal makes me want to punch something. That fucker in the face actually. Flakes has already held me back a few times from going in when he's said something inappropriate, but like a damn pro, Lucia handles it on her own.

It's unreal, for hours I can sit completely still, pissing on myself to not give away my position, but with her in the mix I'm shaking and twitching like an addict who needs a damn fix.

Flakes was right all along, she's a drug. My favorite kind, one I never want to be without.

"They're on the move," Flakes says beside me and reaches for the keys hanging from his dash. "Can you handle this, man? If not I'll leave your big ass here and finish this up with Lucia alone."

"I'm fine."

"You've said that ten times already yet you're still about to come out of your skin. She's okay. Lucia is just doing her job, let her."

I run a calloused hand down my face and groan into my palm. "I know she fucking can but that's not the point. The point is...."

We stop at a red light three to four cars behind Matt and Luce. Flakes turns in his seat and motions for me to finish my thought.

"I think I love her."

"Fuck, man."

"I know."

"What'd you do that for? I warned you about this shit. You can't fall for a girl like that, believe me I know. Remember?" He shoots a glare before turning his attention back out the windshield. "You're a damn fool."

He's right but it's too late now, there's no coming back from this.

As I watch her climb the front stairs, holding his hand, and disappear into the building an uneasy quiver in my gut rolls. I should call the whole thing off.

Damn, I hate this. What if she needs me, what if something goes wrong and I'm too late and she never knows?

The phone on the dash lights up and vibrates, drawing my attention from the building doors. My stomach drops at Mom's face filling the screen. Fuck, please don't let there be something wrong. Not tonight.

Before answering I clear my throat, "Mom, everything okay?"

"Gabriel, honey, it's your dad."

And that's how the night went from shit to complete shit in three little words.

CHAPTER THIRTY-THREE
LUCIA

It takes everything I have to not tremble as large Russian hands roam over every inch of my body before allowing me into the club. For two seconds I'm alone in a red lit room before Matt is cleared.

With a hand pressed to my lower back he guides us to another heavily guarded door. "You're going to love this. Nowhere like it in San Diego," he says into my ear as one of the armed men opens the door with a "try anything inside and I'll gut you" look.

Across the threshold I'm transported to a different world. Women in revealing formal dresses stroll around the older red carpet; the ones in black carry trays with glasses on top, while the women dressed in red smile and laugh as the men at various tables grope them from head to toe. Tearing my gaze from the obvious prostitutes, I take in the room.

Everything is a shade of red from the carpet to the eighties-style wallpaper. Large crystal chandeliers hang over ten tables scattered around the room and in the back a row of slot machines line the wall.

Pressure against my back has me turning towards a hand carved dark wood bar to our right, but three men step into our path stopping us. The one in the middle is short and fat, chewing on the end of a large cigar. The two flanking him must be security of some kind based on their height and bulk.

It doesn't take someone with my skills to know the short one is the boss of the place and not someone to be left alone with. But even as his sinister smile grows and his eyes roam up and down my body, sending a wave of disgust to turn my stomach, Matt doesn't flinch, his demeanor never shifting to one of concern or alarm.

"Mr. Sherman. Welcome back. Who is your lovely guest?" the short one says in a thick Russian accent to my chest.

"My date, Victor. She's clear."

"I'll be the judge of that, come with me, Miss."

I flinch at Matt's audacious laugh. "I don't think so. She's staying with me, hence the date part. We're just here to have a little fun then we're out of here."

The man's dark eyes shift from my chest to Matt's and narrow, suggesting a battle of power in their stare. "Ah, I see you want her all to yourself tonight, Mr. Sherman. Have your fun but she's not leaving until I have mine too."

After he's gone and we've resumed our path to the bar I wrap my hand in Matt's and give it a squeeze. "Matt, I know I said I liked dangerous but..."

"He's bluffing, he wouldn't piss me off, I'm too valuable to him. He's probably just trying to get under my skin to throw me off my game."

Continuing to take in every detail of the place, I say, "What game is that?"

"Texas hold 'em. What do you want to drink, Gracie Lu?"

"Vodka on the rocks."

He smirks and gives my order and his to the bartender. "Vodka in a Russian club, smart."

While we wait for the drinks I turn and look around the club. "How did you even find this kind of place?"

"I know people," he says with a sad smile. "Unfortunately."

The bartender delivers our drinks and he begins to guide me through the club once again. "Why do you say unfortunately?"

"Want to play?" he asks, avoiding my question and sits down at one of the tables. He tells the dealer to add a few hundred on to his account and turns to me expectantly.

With an easy smile I drape an arm over his shoulder and say, "How about I just watch? Maybe I'll be your lucky charm tonight."

"Fuck, Gracie Lu, I'm out on a date with you, something I thought would never happen, I'm already lucky." With all the confidence in the world he turns to the dealer. "Watch and learn, Gracie Lu. You know, that name, every time I say it, it doesn't seem to fit you. It seems…" He looks at his cards, keeping a straight face, and places them back on the table. "Made up."

Without my consent, sweat builds on my palms and the food from earlier churns.

"What's the saying, 'you can take the southern girl out of the south but you can't take it out of her name'…something like that."

He chuckles but keeps his attention on the cards. "So where are you from?"

"Everywhere, so teach me the game. I don't really understand it." His skin prickles under my nails as I drag them up and down the back of his neck in hope of distracting him from my vague answer.

"Sure thing doll, watch and learn."

For over an hour I casually sip my drink and observe him and the entire room. Two things are apparent, Matt is a terrible poker player, and there's no way to keep count of how many armed men are in here. Their shifts and positions constantly change and I haven't figured out the pattern of their rotation. Seeing their massive guns has me longing for the security of my knife strapped to my calf or at least somewhere within reach but I left them at home knowing, if Matt did invite me here, a thorough pat down would be done before being allowed in, and this dress has zero places to conceal any type of weapon from searching hands.

Everything was left at home, even my phone. With the boys in my ear and having insight into every move I make, there was no reason to bring it and have it potentially taken and hacked by these meatheads.

After another thirty minutes or so of watching I start shifting on my feet and yawning, hoping Matt will pick up the signs I'm bored and will show me around the rest of the place. So far, I haven't witnessed anything, other than his affiliation with this place, that points to Matt as our guy. I need more.

Without looking away from the table he reaches into his wallet and pulls out a hundred-dollar bill. "Here, go play the slots until I'm done with this hand. Shouldn't be much longer."

The second the cash is in my hand and I've taken a step away from the table, the sense of vulnerability has me swallowing against a dry throat. All eyes are on me, watching each step I take towards the back of the room with predator gazes. With the Victor guy's comment at the door and now every male in here staring like I'm a piece of meat to be shared, I need my friends back in my ear, something to reassure me I'm not alone. Something to calm my nerves and to get me out of my own head.

"You guys there?" I whisper and take a seat at the machine in the middle of the row. "You've been quiet since the restaurant." The machine beeps and rings as I push a few buttons not having a clue if I'm doing it right.

But it's only the beeps and rings I hear, no response from the boys.

"Guys?"

Nothing.

"Listen, I'm sorry if I was pissed earlier but I need to know you're both there."

Again nothing except now with the sounds of the machine the loud thundering of my increasing pulse fills my ears.

"Gabe? Tony?"

Shit. We didn't plan on them having some kind of signal blocker in place for the frequency we're using with this two-way communication device, it was designed by the CIA to still work under any type of blocker.

Closing my eyes I take a deep breath in and hold it. Most of my operations I'm alone, I can do this. Nothing has changed; I still have to meet my objective with or without backup.

"Looks like you could use some help."

My eyes fling open to find Victor and his goons, two on my left and one on my right effectively blocking me in.

"I think I can figure it out, but actually," I stand on shaking knees and turn toward Matt who's still at the poker table. "I should go find Matt."

The way the tip of his tongue rubs along his top teeth as he takes me in again from head to toe sends my blood boiling. The fear from earlier is now gone, only to be replaced by anger, which is good and bad. Fear has the potential to get me killed but the anger, my temper, will for sure get me killed. The odds of me leaving this place without an international incident are better if fear sticks around.

"Come with me."

"No."

"Come."

Sausage-like fingers wrap around my bicep and squeeze. I hold back my hiss of pain and frustration and turn my angry stare to the goon holding onto me. The other guard grabs my other arm, making me follow behind Victor across the floor towards a concealed hall I hadn't noticed.

Before we can disappear down the hall, Matt steps into our path making the four of us pause. His dark eyes narrow at Victor. "Just where in the hell do you think you're going with my date?"

"Go back to your game, Sherman, she is of no concern to you right now." Without looking back, he inclines his head towards the hall. "Come."

This time Matt stops him from advancing with a hand on his shoulder.

Fear or anger smolders behind Matt's eyes, hopefully a healthy mix of both like me.

"No, she stays with me."

"You do not make the rules here. I do. She comes with me. She will be payment for your playing tonight."

A hateful smirk pulls at Matt's lips. "I've given you what you wanted, several times now, to cover my fucking debts. You are not taking her. You touch her and our deal is off old man."

With a scoff Victor tries to brush past Matt but the hand now wrapped around his throat stops him.

"I wasn't done talking to you," Matt hisses between gritted teeth. "You and me are done. This is the final straw you piece of shit. I've given you what you wanted because it's been fun coming here but not her. So tell that fucker to drop my girl or I break your damn windpipe."

"You'll regret this before you even step out the door," he breathes. It's so quiet I wouldn't have heard it except the whole club has gone quiet.

"Our deal is fucking over, Victor. We are walking out of here, unharmed, and you'll never hear from me again. Deal."

Victor says nothing. Matt's knuckles whiten as his fingers tighten around Victor's throat. He gives him a little jostle, making Victor's body shake like a rag doll.

"Deal," Matt says again as a statement, not a question.

Victor can't respond, heck he can barely get enough oxygen to stay conscious. Instead I see his head bob up and down in a nod.

No way in hell Matt trusts Victor enough to let him go. I for sure don't. At this point if we make it out of here unscathed it will be a miracle. But the odds *are* swayed considering the two people the odds are against are a navy SEAL and army sergeant turned CIA agent. If I were a betting girl I'd bet on us walking out of here with the whole damn building ablaze.

Now to decide to break cover to help us get out of here alive or stick with the reporter act. Based on the conversation Matt and Victor just had, Matt's our guy. Not sure *how* but Matt's our mole. I have to hand it to Matt though, he's willing to lose everything—including his life—to keep me out of the hands of this piece of shit.

The second the goon's meaty fingers loosen, I yank the rest of the way free and step behind Matt.

"Please tell me you have something besides your damn hands to get us out of here."

"His office, the hall behind us, second door on the right—" Matt lurches back just as the bang of a gun being fired echoes in the room. Another shot fires and the wall to the right of my head splinters.

Matt grips my wrist and yanks me to cover down the hall as bullets spray around us. On the floor he protects me with his body, the blood from his shoulder oozing into my hair and down my face.

"Is there another exit?" I shout over the deafening rapid fire.

"His office, maybe. Go."

He flings me into the office and starts maneuvering furniture around the room to block the door. "Search the office for anything we can use against these fuckers. Fuck," he says through gritted teeth as he slams his back against a bookshelf again and again to knock it over.

The drawers of the desk rip easily from their hinges as I frantically search for any kind of fire power, the bigger the better. "Two .40 cal glocks and one revolver." Checking both clips and the barrel of the revolver, I say, "All three fully loaded. Must be our lucky day." There's no way he can miss my sarcasm.

"How in the hell?" He looks from me and the guns on the desk.

"If you just hand over the beautiful Italian I'll forget the earlier incident, Mr. Sherman," says a muffled voice on the other side of the wall. We pause to listen. "Or we can just wait until you bleed out and we will take her then. Your choice."

Looking up from the guns to Matt I know Victor is right. Matt is losing more and more blood by the second. The skin on his face is paler and he's now leaning against a flipped couch to stay upright.

"Come here and let me patch your arm," I whisper and start to open closet doors in search of anything to plug his bullet wound.

The second closet creaks as I pull it open. My hand slips from the door knob as I take in what's stacked inside.

CHAPTER THIRTY-FOUR
LUCIA

"What have you done, Matt?" I mumble and take a step closer toward the stacks of military-grade ammo cans and other military lockers, each stamped with US NAVY on the side in white.

Shouting, someone yelling at us to come out snaps me back to the rathole mess we're in.

"We need some kind of distraction, we're sitting ducks back here. As soon as we try to come out they'll take us out." Matt muses to himself, as he takes a seat on the desk waiting for me, not expecting me to have an opinion. To his defense he does still think I'm just a reporter, a reporter who really knows her guns.

"You didn't happen to sell him any grenades along with the ammo in this closet, did you?" I sneer and slam the closet shut. There's nothing in this damn office to use as a sling or tourniquet except for… I look down at my dress and sigh. This operation is proving to be a hazard for my wardrobe. Once I rip this one to shreds, the navy will now be responsible for replacing two of my favorite dresses.

I begin to rummage around the disheveled mess on the floor for the pair of scissors I saw and discarded during my gun search. Pulling them from the pile I start slicing along the seam of my sleeves.

"What are you-"

"Answer my damn question. What all did you sell these assholes?"

With a pull on the sleeve the seam rips the rest of the way and the material falls down my arm. "Here." I toss it to him and start working on the other. "Make a sling out of it if you can."

"Who the hell are you?"

"Doesn't matter right now. We don't have time—"

"Like hell it doesn't," he growls. "You're no damn reporter. Any other woman would be in a ball in the corner by now. Who sent you?" His angry gaze shifts from me to the closet and back to me, realization now in his stare. "You knew."

"I knew about the information, not the shit in that closet." The second sleeve rips and falls down my arm. "I think you're a piece of shit for putting your brothers in danger, for selling these bastards US weapons, but I don't want you to fucking bleed to death on my watch so move your damn shirt so I can see the wound."

When he doesn't move I reach up and tear his shirt open and inspect where to put pressure.

"I'm not a damn traitor you fucking cu—"

Victor's bored voice cuts Matt off. "Give it up, Sherman, either die or open the door. My patience is growing thin."

"We don't have time for this right now. We need a game plan," I hiss and shove the sleeve in my hand against his oozing bullet wound.

"How many boxes were in there," he says through gritted teeth, trying to choke down the pain.

"Twenty, thirty maybe."

As I tend to his arm, making a sling to relieve some of the tension in the muscle, he starts rambling. "Everything in there was decommissioned. We were going to destroy it all, but I'd gotten in deep and needed the money. Fuck if they didn't get me in here and know what I had access to. When I couldn't pay they suggested." He hangs his head and watches my hands work. "I know I fucked up and I'll tell the damn truth about what's in that closet but I have no damn idea what information you're talking about. I'm. No. Traitor." The last words are bitten out, taking what little energy he has left to file his anger.

When I'm done securing the sling he stands swaying as I reach out and steady him. With my help we shuffle to the closet. Not caring about the noise or the mess he digs and tosses boxes, searching for something in particular. About halfway to the bottom of the stack he stops.

Curious, I peer over his shoulder and look at the tube he has gripped in his left hand.

When he looks up his smile is weak. "MK3A2's. Grenades."

"Well that will work," I say and snatch them out of his hand.

"Shit, easy with those things. Do you even know—"

The look I shoot back as I pull the grenades out of the tube makes him stop.

"Of course you do." Not able to stand on his own any longer, his back slams against the wall and he slides down it until he's on the floor.

We're running out of time. Turning to face the room, I assess our options and start to form a plan. A plan where I'm the only player, there's no way Matt can help at this point.

"He needs help," I yell to the men outside the door. "I'll come out but you have to get him help. Do not let him die."

"Of course. You have my word."

"A lot of good that is," I mutter under my breath and start for the door, but not to open it. This plan will either blow us to bits or be the brightest idea I've ever had. Hell if I know which way it will go, but it's our only chance. Matt needs a doctor now and there's no way I can take out all these men on my own.

Looking between the toppled furniture in front of the door, I search for the perfect place for the grenade then move back to Matt.

"Matt, you gotta get up. I can't carry you." But he doesn't move. Pressing three fingers to his throat I hold my breath and pray he's still alive. I release a breath at the faint pulse.

Mustering up every ounce of strength I've been honing and building the past several years, I drag his limp body inch by inch across the room toward another closet, one that's not filled with bullets that could explode when the grenade goes off. Rolling him into the closet I wipe my sweaty brow and turn toward the heavy desk and sigh.

I grab the three guns from the desk and put them beside the unconscious Matt. My muscles burn and quiver as I shove the desk toward the closet, where I've planned for us to hunker down, angling it to provide the best protection. I say another silent prayer and go back to the office door.

"Okay, I'm coming out," I try to yell but it comes out as a cracked whisper. With a deep, shaky breath I pull the fuse and run like hell to the closet as I count in my head.

One one thousand.

Two one thousand.

Three one thousand.

The carpet burns my knees and hands as I dive into the closet and slam the door shut. Covering Matt, I squeeze my eyes shut, press my palms against his ears, and try to use a raised shoulder to cover one of mine and his shoulder to cover the other.

Five one thousand.

The room erupts shaking the building. My jaw aches from gritting my teeth as the blast rockets us even with my makeshift shield. When the ground stops shaking, I pry open my eyes but it's too dark to see anything, the blast must have cut the electricity. Feeling around the ground, my hand lands on one of the guns I'd set aside.

Gun at the ready, I open the door an inch and crawl out of the closet. Smoke fills the room, a small fire crawls up the wall but it's the only movement. By the flashing of the emergency lights and the downpour from the sprinklers I know the fire alarm must be ringing, but it's not. Nothing is making a sound. Heck, there isn't even ringing in my ears.

Fucking great, if this mess couldn't get any worse. I'm drenched, can't hear, and alone.

Wood and debris crack and shift beneath my heels as I inch across the room, gun raised to take out anyone who steps in my way.

Damn, hearing would be amazing right now.

It takes a little maneuvering around what's left of the furniture and the massive hole in the floor from the blast, and I don't acknowledge the four dead bodies surrounding the door.

Something shifts in my peripheral at the end of the hall. With no hesitation I swing around and pull the trigger. Through the strobing light I watch a body fall through the air and hit the ground with a little bounce.

Smoke burns my throat and lungs making me cough and wheeze as I stalk down the hall towards the open room.

Where in the hell are Tony and Gabe? There's no way they didn't hear the blast with or without our signal blocked.

With a trembling, wheezing breath in to steady my nerves I round the corner exposing myself to anyone hunkered down.

Something hard cracks against my wrist knocking the gun, sending the gun skittering across the floor. Falling into my training, my right elbow sails up but it's blocked before it can make contact. Whoever it is, the flashing light disorienting their face, doesn't stop my knee from connecting with his groin. There's a slight shake beneath my feet when his knees connect with the floor. This time, my elbow meets its mark at the base of his head. He falls limp on the floor.

Leaping across the unconscious man, I dive for my gun and grip it just as shadows move across the room. The chandeliers flicker as the electricity tries to restore light, the strobe lights flaring and damn it to hell, the silence in my ears has now been replaced with a high pitched ringing, all distracting me from the threats lurking around the room.

Not aiming, I fire off a few rounds for cover as I crawl behind a poker table. Crouched under the table, I pull out the clip and count how many rounds are left.

Ten.

Water drips from my hair, down my forehead and into my eyes. I try to convince myself, unsuccessfully, it's only water from the sprinklers cascading down my cheeks.

I can't stay here forever, I have to move. I have to get Matt help. Hopefully it's not already too late.

With a steadying breath I raise on my toes to peek over the table.

Through the water I watch as someone near the front door fires off rounds into the club. Holding my breath, I wipe my eyes, praying that what I think is happening is actually happening.

Gun extended in front of him, Tony steps closer to where I'm hidden, his eyes frantically shifting around the room as his mouth moves like he's yelling.

"I'm here," I yell and push off the floor to stand, but my knees buckle, sending me falling to the floor. "We have to get Matt," I yell again, still not able to hear my own voice, as I push off the table to try and stand again.

Tony's lips move fast with zero sound.

"In the office. Closet on the right. He's hurt and lost blood. Get him," I wheeze and stare at the front door expecting Gabe to come barging through any second.

But he doesn't.

Tony emerges with Matt slung over his shoulder but I'm still staring at the door. His voice is faint but a few words I understand. "....fuck....go."

Inching backwards and keeping my gun drawn to provide cover for Tony, I don't let it drop until I'm in the main building's hallway and halfway down the stairs.

Following where Tony had taken Matt is easy, I just follow the steady trail of blood. By the time I make it out, Tony's loading Matt into the cab of his truck.

"Go," I tell Tony when he turns to me. "Get him help. I'll be fine."

"Wait...Gabe...back." With a furious inspection of my current state he turns and digs through his truck, pulling out an old duffle bag and tossing it to me. "Police...clothes...safe."

He doesn't look back as he rounds the hood of his truck, climbs in and peels out down the street.

Either the ringing in my ears is growing louder or sirens screech in the distance.

Or both.

Probably both.

With a groan I toss Tony's duffle over my shoulder, my muscles screaming in protest, and limp towards the alley beside the building that would give enough shadowy cover to slip a few blocks over, change clothes, and wait.

CHAPTER THIRTY-FIVE
GABE

That's three—fuck—now four red lights I've sped through to get back to Luce and Flakes. I bolted out of the emergency room, leaving mom confused to what the hell was going on, after the text came through from Flakes that things had gone sideways and they needed me. Now.

The thought of her needing me and not being there has me pressing the gas pedal down to the floor board pushing the Jeep to over ninety. Weaving in and out of cars, blaring my horn and swerving into oncoming traffic, I finally turn down the street I need.

Both feet slam on to the brake, sending the tires skidding along the road.

"Fucking hell."

Cops.

Everywhere. Even a damn SWAT van.

And what's the damn fire department doing here?

No way she and Flakes stuck around for this. I drive the next block over and park. The need to hold her, make sure she's safe after seeing all this commotion and billowing smoke, is as important as the need to breathe. Before climbing out, I lean over and grab my sidearm from the glovebox, just in case.

As I tuck the gun into the small of my back, I call Flakes to see where the hell they are. Before the first ring ends he picks up.

"Did you get her?" he yells over the shouting of other men in the background.

"You left her?" I growl back. "The fuck is she, damnit."

"I told her to wait for you. Matt's shot, brought him to base they are-"

I end the call to not waste any time and start jogging down the street. Keeping the gun hidden but ready, I search up and down the surrounding area. What the hell was Flakes doing leaving her out here alone?

A pulse of fear weaves into my thoughts.

Hell, if Matt's hurt....

My pace quickens with each alley I clear. My gut rolls at the image of her being out here alone, hurt and scared.

Too distracted by my own worry-laced thoughts, I almost miss movement halfway down an alley as I passed. Pulling to a quiet stop, I drop to a crouch and start towards the figures, ducking between dumpsters to stay hidden.

The light shifts, bringing one beautiful, angry face into focus.

Everything stops.

The world and sounds go silent.

Hell, it's only years of training that keep my breath from stopping too.

Two men. One Lucia.

One is behind her, holding her arms at her back, while the other takes free punches to her abdomen.

The gun in my grip provides balance, reminding me that even in my crouched position, I have the upper hand. As I begin standing to get a better angle on the group, Luce starts talking.

"Is that all you got, Victor?!" she yells louder than necessary before spitting on the ground, only missing the guy's feet because he jerks away. "You have to hold me back so you can get your shots in? Man, mother Russia will be disappointed when they hear how soft you've gone."

Oh, hell Luce. But even as her taunting scares the shit out of me I can't help but be proud too. Of course, my girl isn't cowering or breaking under the beatings, she's a fucking badass.

My badass.

The guy pulls back his arm, his aim higher than her stomach this time. No fucking way, not while I'm watching.

The guy holding her is the first one I take out. His head explodes onto the building behind them, spraying the yellow stucco red. She doesn't make a sound as she ducks to cover.

Good girl.

The second guy, the one I want to bleed out slowly for inflicting pain on my girl, is now running down the alley like the chicken shit he is.

"Nice try," I whisper, and I fire off two rounds, one for each shoulder.

The crunching of trash and crumbling asphalt are the only sounds in the alley as I stalk the man who's now trying to crawl away. Luce appears at my side as I hold him to the pavement with the heel of my boot pressed into one of his wounds.

"What did he give you?" she shouts, again way louder than necessary, and a little concerning since the cops are only a few blocks away and I just fired off three rounds. She kicks the shithead in the ribs making him groan in pain. "Besides that damn ammo what did he give you?" When he doesn't answer, she crouches down, flips him over, and presses an elbow into his bullet wound, making him shriek. "Tell me the damn truth. Is it him?"

Between the gun shots, her yelling, and now this chicken shit crying like a baby, there's no way the cops aren't on their way.

"Luce," I say and pull at her shoulder, only to have her shrug me off.

The man screams again as she digs into his wound. "What has he told you?"

We don't have time for this, which she would know, too, if she wasn't so focused on the spur of the moment interrogation. The intensity in her, the focus—there's no way she'll listen to reason.

Damn, she's going to be pissed about this one.

Wrapping an arm around her waist I toss her over my shoulder and start running back the way we came.

"Put me down, you asshole. I need him to talk. He has to tell me," she tries to scream, but it's mostly a crackled whisper. "Fine. Grab Tony's bag. There."

Retracing a few steps to where she's pointing, I grab the duffle and haul it and Luce down the alley.

It only takes a few minutes to cover enough distance between us and the burning building to feel somewhat safe, and to be far enough that she wouldn't risk running back. The moment her feet hit the pavement, I take a step back, ready to block whatever punches she has planned.

Shocking as hell, instead of being pissed, she drops to a crouch in front of the duffle and pulls back the zipper.

"What are you doing?" I ask and pull my gun again. Even though we're far enough away, farther from the shit storm they created would be better.

"My feet are killing me. I've been in heels long enough tonight. Hopefully, Tony has some damn shoes or boots in this...ah." Through the dirt and soot, a relieved smile appears on her face as she pulls out a pair of old sneakers. "If I catch some kind of foot fungus," she says with a grimace, as the shoe slides on to her bare foot, "I'm going to make him pay."

I keep watch as she tucks her heels into the duffle bag and stands.

"Start talking," I say and sling the bag back over my shoulder. Since she's giving no indication she'll run back, I don't toss her over my shoulder, too.

I need answers. Now. Fuck, I just blew the damn head off a guy on US soil, that's going to be a hard one to explain.

"What?" she asks, brows furrowed as she stares at my lips.

"What's wrong with your damn hearing?" I ask.

"What? Sorry. I can't really hear." She presses the palms of her hands against her ears and starts rubbing circles. "Maybe this will help." After a minute her hands fall to her side and she looks up expectantly.

"What the hell happened, Lucia?" I try to demand, but there's no force behind it. Not when she looks like this. Drenched, dirty, and I'm praying the red covering her is from the dipshit I shot back there—not her own blood.

"Nope that didn't work. It was that damn grenade—"

"Grenade?" What the hell?

"Covered Matt's ears instead of my own since he was passed out from blood loss. Where the hell were you, by the way? Damn Russians—it was a cheap shot when they shot him."

"Luce," Trying to rein in my frustration from lack of details, I drag a hand down my face. Hell, she's practically deaf, but answers are needed. "Lucia!" I yell finally, to get her attention. "What happened?!" I yell again, hoping she can hear me but no one else.

"Oh, did you not talk to Tony?"

I shake my head instead of replying verbally. Each second that passes with her not in my arms seems like an eternity. I clench and unclench my hands to keep from reaching out and pulling her against me. Grenades, Matt being shot, Russians—hell, it's amazing she's standing here right now.

She's safe. She's here.

Get her talking. Get her home. Then never let her go.

This is the mantra I run on a loop to keep my focus and not slip into the thoughts of what could have happened to her.

"Oh, well, sorry. Thought he had explained everything. Long story short, that old guy, Victor, the one you pulled me off of..." The glare I shoot her is noticed but not acknowledged. "Anyway, he made it clear to Matt what he wanted from me, which Matt wouldn't allow. Everything went downhill from there." With each word her voice grows more pained, the last words barely a whisper. As the silence between us grows I know she's holding something back.

"What?" I yell.

"What?" she asks but doesn't look up.

I stop and wait for her to turn before I speak up again. "What are you not telling me?"

She throws her hands in the air and turns to start pacing. "I don't know. Something is off, and I don't think Matt is the mole, and if it's not him then I'm fucked. It's what I was trying to confirm..." Her mouth slams shut to keep herself from continuing.

But she doesn't need to. There's no doubt in my mind in what she was going to say. No way in hell was she not able to get out of that fuckers hold earlier, she wasn't fighting back. Not only that, I'm willing to bet she knew those asses were following her, and she allowed herself to get caught.

"You were trying to get more information," I say in a normal tone.

"I think I have brain bits in my hair because of you."

Right, can't hear unless I yell, which is the worst possible thing for us to do right now. Maybe....

Pulling my phone from the front pocket of my jeans, I start to type:

Tell me the fucking truth. That's all I've asked for this whole damn time is the truth. Now tell me. Were you trying to get more information, were you allowing them to detain you?

When I'm done, I hold it up to her face and give her a second to read it.

Those green eyes scroll across the screen then up to me. "Fine. Yes. I might have allowed them to keep me there to hopefully get answers from them. Then you came along and ruined it. I now have many questions that will go unanswered."

Yanking the phone back to me I slam my fingers onto the screen as I type. When I hold it up to her again, she knows I'm pissed:

. . .

I watched him shove his fist into your stomach over and over again. Then aim for your damn face. I only wish I'd had time to let him fucking suffer.

Her lips purse together as her eyes shift to meet mine. "I'll agree with you on that one. He wasn't that great of a guy. He pretty much just wanted to rape me, and he was willing to let Matt bleed out in his office to get me. Damn Russians."

That word. Any decent man hears that word as a call to arms and when it's coming from the lips of the woman you love—everything I once thought was important fades; everything except killing that motherfucker slowly.

Bile rises in my throat but I choke it down and speak as calmly as my fury will allow, but it comes out more like a growl. "What?"

Not hearing me, she moves onto another topic. "Matt's selling ammo and other gear to them, but…" She drops down to her thinking pose, her way to shut out the world and process everything running through that witchy brain of hers.

After a few minutes I crouch beside her and stare. Soot, or maybe what's left of her eye makeup, is smeared down her cheeks, her damp hair does in fact have bits of brain in it and her normally-tan skin is clammy and pale from being drenched and out in the cool night air.

Reaching up, I cup her cheek and wipe away streaks of black with my thumb. I lean in and whisper into her ear, hoping she can hear this close. "Let's get you home and cleaned up, okay? Come on, Luce. Let me take care of you tonight. Please."

Her shoulders rise and fall as she exhales and leans into me. "Where were you? Why did you leave me?"

If she knew how bad those words feel to hear, what they do to me coming from her lips, there's no way she'd ever say it again.

"I got a call, sweetheart. My dad, he's fine, but…" I drop my forehead to hers. "I'm so sorry, Luce."

"He's okay though?"

I can't help but laugh at the audacity of her asking if someone else is okay after everything she's been through tonight. "Yeah, he's okay. A concussion, they are keeping him overnight. Now, come on. You know CO will want answers after this shit show, let's get you cleaned up before all hell breaks loose. Let's get you home."

"Gabe."

"Luce."

"Will you stay?"

"Of course, sweetheart."

"I don't want you to go, I need you tonight. Just you. Just me. Okay."

"I'll kill anyone who tries to stop me."

Right here, in some dark ass alley in San Diego, is the most honest moment of my life. It's not perfect but neither are we. She needs me, she wants me with her. Vulnerable, scared, exhausted, and she wants me with her. This strong woman will allow me the opportunity to take care of her for a night.

Fuck, there's no coming back from her.

I'm ruined by this woman, addicted, with no hope of rehabilitation.

Scared shitless and happy as hell somehow.

Even if loving her kills me, what a way to die.

CHAPTER THIRTY-SIX
LUCIA

The scalding hot water of the shower I jump into—the moment we enter the rental house—is glorious as I attempt to wash away tonight's evidence from my body. It takes ten minutes of lather and repeat on my hair before I even dare to take my eyes from the ceiling. I've seen enough blood tonight, no need to see it wash down the drain, too.

Pins and needles prick my skin, starting at my toes and fingers as the water warms them to a normal body temperature. After a half an hour under the hot water, it cools, signaling that it's time to get out and face the reality of tonight's shit show.

As I wipe away the water trickling down my chest and legs, I open and stretch my jaw several times, trying to get my stupid ears to clear. Some of the hearing is back in the ear that had my communication piece, but for the other ear everything still sounds hollow—distant even.

Like now, the sound of the TV in the living room is muffled, but I can tell there's something coming from that direction.

Flipping my hair forward, I have to grip the sink to keep from falling over. Shock must be setting in, throwing me off balance or maybe the blast to my ears set off my equilibrium. Either way I'm a mess. A mostly deaf, off balanced, exhausted—mentally and physically —mess.

The only thing keeping me together at this point is Gabe. Knowing he's out there waiting. We need to talk, about a lot of things, but mostly about what I discovered tonight with Matt. Everything he said in the office, delirious from blood loss, tells me he's not our mole. But if he's not, where does that leave me in the search? Everyone else is cleared.

Everyone but Tony, that is.

But do I really think it's Tony? A week ago I would've said yes, but now—hell, I don't know. Everyone will want answers after tonight's incident but I don't have them. This is a first and I'm not quite sure how to handle it.

It would be easy to blame my lack of results on Gabe, telling myself he's taking attention away from the objective of being here, but it's not true. It would be a sorry excuse for my inability to identify this mole. Through this whole mess something else has been going on in the background, but I can't pinpoint it. Whatever it is, it has kept me from uncovering the truth. As soon as I start circling the answer, something pulls me back.

If I think about it that way, Tony does sound like a suspect again.

I groan into the towel at the thought of having to tell Gabe I suspect his best friend of being a traitor. And not only that, I have suspected it this whole time but have kept it from him.

The towel in my hands freezes. Muffled, loud sounds pull my eyes to the closed bathroom door.

What the heck?

After securing the towel around me, covering what needs to be covered—barely—I crack the door open and listen. The bedroom door is closed, blocking me from seeing out, and Gabe isn't on the bed waiting.

Tiptoeing across the room, I lean my good ear against the door.

"No," I hear, and feel, Gabe say. It's like he's pressed against the door, his voice sending vibrations through the wood.

Another man says something, but with the door, and my lack of hearing, there's no way to make out anything. I assess the towel clutched to my chest and debate tossing on real clothes, but it would mean a delay in finding out who's in my living room pissing off Gabe.

Screw it.

The door pulls open, but Gabe's back blocks the view into the living room.

"Please tell me you're in more than a towel, sweetheart," Gabe says, not turning to face me.

Yeah well…ducking under his arm I step into the living room.

Oops.

The boss and Jeremy stand, staring, from the middle of the living room arms crossed and looking royally pissed off.

"We will wait, Agent Rizzo. Go put some clothes on," the boss says with disgust in his eyes and tone.

"I'm fine like this," I say with a shrug, but not too high, so everything stays covered below. "What are you doing here?"

"We've been trying to call you all evening to see how the op went. But like the rest of this operation, your lack of communication has forced our hand. Agent Dungan and I landed moments ago to gain answers."

"Answers to what?" Hell, I'm not ready for this. I take a step backwards, then another until my back is against his chest, hoping to steal some of his strength. He knows I'm hanging on by a thread at this point.

"Get out. She'll come debrief you when she's fucking ready," Gabe growls. His warm hands rest on my shoulders and pull me closer to him.

"Stay out of this, Wilcox. This is a CIA matter. It has nothing to do with you."

"If it has anything to do with her, it has everything to do with me you fuck stick. I don't give a damn which fancy ass agency you're with. You can go fuck—"

"Gabe," I say as I turn to face him, placing a hand on his chest. The anger and fury behind his eyes is enough to push me back a step.

When his eyes shift from the two men to me his features soften a fraction. "What's going on?"

Instead of answering, he grabs my hand, leads me into the bedroom, and closes the door behind us. "I don't know, Luce. They showed up while you were in the shower. But you don't have to talk to them until you're ready. How's your hearing?"

Shit, didn't think about that. There's no way they can know about this current weakness. No doubt they would exploit it somehow.

"It's okay. One ear is better than the other. Shit, I'm not ready for this." I sit on the edge of the bed and bury my face into my hands.

The bed dips and a strong arm wraps around my shoulders, pulling me against him.

"Yes, you are. You're ready for anything, Luce. It's just who you are. It might not feel like it right now, but you can do this."

Angling my head to look up, those blue eyes stare back full of an emotion, neither one of us have the courage to share.

"I'll get dressed."

When I try to stand, he pulls me back against him. "I don't know, it's a nice distraction from me wanting to rip their heads off."

With a huffed laugh, I push off his thigh and rummage through drawers, pulling out black leggings, a black long sleeve t-shirt, and sports bra. The moment my towel drops to the floor he's behind me, griping my waist and pulling me against his chest.

"They can wait," he whispers into the ear I indicated was somewhat working, as his hands roam along my body like he's worshiping every inch of my curves. His voice is ragged, "You scared the shit out of me tonight. When I couldn't find you...Don't do it again. I can't take it."

Leaning back, I interlace our fingers and wrap his arms around my chest. "I know, nothing went as planned tonight."

"Nothing we can do about it now except move on. Get dressed, tell these guys whatever they want to hear, then as soon as they're gone..." The room rotates as he swivels me around, pressing my chest against his and grabbing my ass with both hands. "I'm going to make you forget this night for a few hours. I need to be between your thighs, feeling you around me, hearing you breathe my name. Fuck, I need it. And you need it too."

His hand slides from my backside to between my thighs, making me groan and press my forehead against his muscled chest.

"Forget about them," I breathe and spread my legs to give his fingers room to explore. "I need this now."

"Work first then we can play," he chokes out as he slides a finger inside me. "Fuck."

"I need this now, Gabe," I plead and dig my nails into the back of his neck.

I feel rather than see him look to the bedroom door, contemplating his options. With a curse he lifts me on top of the dresser and steps between my spread legs.

"I think you could convince me of anything, sweetheart." His lips press against mine and his hand finds its way between my thighs once again. A deep groan mimics my own as he teases with his fingers. "I could play with you all night, Luce, and never get bored. Fuck, I love you."

His hand and lips still.

Eyes open, I try to remember how to breathe normally.

"Gabe," I start but he silences me by sliding a second finger inside. "Not now. Later."

The movement of his thumb, tracing lazy circles against my tiny bundle of nerves, along with the deep strokes of his fingers, pulls me to the edge faster than ever before. His lips dominate our kiss while his other hand teases a nipple between two fingers, like he's done before when he sees I'm on the verge of shattering. Increasing the flick of his thumb and the drive of his fingers, I come apart with his mouth devouring mine, muffling my soft moan and curses. Deep, ragged breaths in and out, I try to regain some kind of composure but it's hard with his fingers still stroking.

When he withdraws, the loss leaves me empty, ready to beg for more.

"Hey," he says tipping my chin up from his chest. "This is just the beginning Luce. You and me, we're just getting started. I love you, and

I'm not going to let anyone take you away from me. Whatever they throw at you out there, we are in it together. I have your back, always, never doubt that. Now," his hands grip my waist, lift me off the dresser and stay until I can stand on my own, "Get dressed and let's get this shitshow over with. Then we'll really have some fun."

The open palm slap he lands on my backside makes me yelp and jump to the side to avoid another unprotected attack. Before he opens the door he turns to gain one more good look. As those blue eyes visually devour every naked inch, a mischievous grin spreads across his face.

"Damn woman," he mumbles as he closes the door, leaving me to get dressed alone.

I hop from one foot to the other, tugging on my clothes in double-time. The faster we get through this debrief the faster Gabe's hands can be back on my bare skin. A quick once-over in the mirror makes me pause.

Ah, hell. Cheeks flushed, eyes glassy and lips cherry red like someone's been sucking on them.

There's no way those two out there will miss my post-orgasm glow.

A few splashes of cold water are all I have time for, it's not much, but will have to do. This time when I pull open the bedroom door, there isn't a Gabe wall blocking my view. Instead he's leaning against the door frame of the kitchen, glaring at the two men still standing in the middle of the living room.

I give a small smile to Gabe, tucking a wet lock of hair behind my ear, and walk to confront the men who've flown across the country to see me. This isn't my first debrief but it is the first one after a disaster of a mission like tonight. But Gabe behind me, knowing he has my back like he said earlier, strengthens me.

"What do you want to know?" I ask when I'm directly in front of them both. "Ask what you want, I have nothing to hide about what happened tonight or since I started the op."

"Start by updating us on your operation, Agent Rizzo."

So I do. All of it. Well, all of it minus my still-confused thoughts on

Tony. No way I'm going to throw that out there right now, not without preparing Gabe, and not until I know for sure. Right now it's only the lack of other suspects that has me questioning Tony's involvement further. When I'm done, boss's face is bright red. You don't need my abilities to know he's about to lose it.

"Let me get this straight, you let our only suspect get shot and bleed out before you could get the information we need?"

I start but he starts up again, his voice raising with each word.

"And you failed to get any information on the Russians, you couldn't even get them to tell you their involvement with Sherman and what he was selling before you ran away? What a fucking waste of resources you are, Rizzo." He turns to face the wall, putting his back to me. "Did you at least accomplish one part of this operation? Is he ready to come over?"

No. Not now.

All words, the ability to speak, leave me. I open my mouth to respond but nothing comes out.

Jeremy picks up on my hesitation, reading me like an open book and loving it.

"He doesn't know, does he?"

"Who's he?" Gabe says behind me.

Still I can't speak. What is there to say now, there's no time to explain.

An evil smile spreads across Jeremy's face. "You, Officer Wilcox. She was sent here to find the mole and recruit you to the CIA. To convince you, with any means necessary to come back with us to DC."

"Luce?"

"Stop," I whisper. My heart hammers against my chest, making it even harder to hear.

"Did she also leave out that the promotion she's wanted, that she's been working towards for over a year, is contingent on you signing with us?" His huffed laugh, at what I assume is a pissed off Gabe, makes the blood in my veins boil. Fuck him, enjoying this. Turning to face Gabe, to explain, Jeremy chimes in saying, "I knew she was

316 | KENNEDY L. MITCHELL

willing to do whatever it took to get the promotion, should have knowing fucking someone to get it could happen."

"Gabe, I didn't—"

Jeremy steps to my side but I keep my eyes on Gabe, who's looking like he hates me. Too many emotions roll through him to get a read on how he's feeling about this, but one emotion is clear. Fury.

"Did you also tell Officer Wilcox you suspect his best friend of being the true mole? That all these other men have been decoys as you try to gather more information on officer Hackenbreg?"

Gabe's confused, hurt glare burns through my soul, making my heart race and stomach sink. He can't believe them. Part of what they're saying is true, but the rest is lies. Just like they've done since joining the agency. Lies, truth, and more lies all mixed together until you don't know up from down.

Like now.

"I didn't....Gabe you know I wouldn't—"

"You let one of his SEAL brothers bleed to death tonight, Agent Rizzo." My wet hair smacks my face when I whip around to face my boss. "That's right, while you were busy letting the Russians get away, the SEAL you were with tonight bled out. How can Officer Wilcox believe anything you say now? You are the reason he died tonight."

Their words, coupled with exhaustion, make my knees buckle. I catch the corner of the chair before falling to the floor. "No." My voice shakes like the rest of me.

"Stop," Gabe says in a commanding tone I've only heard when he addressed his men.

Boss smiles, taking in my crumbling state, then to Gabe. "You have no say in this room, Officer Wilcox. In fact, if you're not one of us, then you need to leave this debriefing. Now."

"You're fucking breaking her." I don't turn to him, there's no way I can watch him leave. Because he will, with everything they just revealed, how could he not? No matter what he said before, all he's ever wanted was the truth, and now he knows that's exactly what I've been holding back. "Luce," he says as the floor creaks under his weight. "You don't have to stay here and listen to their bullshit. You can come with me. Leave with me, sweetheart."

The arrogant smile on my boss' face grows. "Wrong, Officer Wilcox. That's where you're wrong and she knows it. She can't leave. This is her operation to see through until the end and it's not over until we know exactly who the mole is. Her contract is with us, her life belongs to us. You're a fool if you think she'd ever choose you over the agency. I know where her priorities lay, and it's not with you. No matter what she told you in attempts to recruit you over. We are her life, we're giving her the opportunity to grow, to be great in the agency who chose her, and that is what she will choose, every damn day."

The silence in the room has me hoping it's just my hearing going out again. But I know that's not true. The longer the silence goes the harder it is to breathe.

"Good choice, Officer Wilcox. We'll be in touch."

I turn just in time to see Gabe halfway out the front door. My hand smacks over my mouth to keep from throwing up on the carpet.

"Go fuck yourselves," he says over his shoulder and slams the door closed behind him.

The door blurs in my vision as tears well.

"Gabe?" I whisper into my hand. "Gabe," I yell a little louder and start for the door to chase after him but a hand gripping my shoulder stops me. "Get the hell off me," I growl and try to pull out of Jeremy's grip but there's no energy behind it.

"Now that he's gone, tell me the real story, Lucia," says my boss beside me. "Do you think we'll be able to get anything out of Sherman once he comes to?"

What the hell?

Slowly I turn to face him. "What did you just say?"

Jeremy shrugs. "He didn't exactly bleed out, he's in ICU but expected to pull through."

"You...earlier...Why?"

"We needed to see where Officer Wilcox's loyalties lie, with you or with the SEALs." I narrow my eyes at Jeremy's smug ass smile. "And, well, as you can see, it worked. Wouldn't you rather know now he'll choose his career, his so-called brothers, over you? Now tell us what you really obtained from the Russians."

I stumble away from them, my back smacking the wall. No, this can't be happening. They planned all this. Every damn word they've said tonight was planned to get Gabe and I separated.

But for what purpose?

At this point, who gives a fuck.

I should be done with this debrief and in Gabe's arms right now. He should be on top of me, his calloused hands scraping across my skin as he says over and over how much he loves me.

Loves me.

His words from earlier strengthen my spine and give power to my voice. "Get out."

Both men look to each other then back to me.

"Get the fuck out of my place, now."

"Lu," Jeremy says and takes a step closer with his hands raised like he's approaching a wild animal. "Stop. I know you're upset about Wilcox but we need to find this mole. It's for his own good, don't you see that? If we find the mole and find his partners we can help save them. Now tell us. Is it Matt?"

I shake my head and lean against the wall for support.

"Is it Tony?"

This time my head shake lacks confidence.

"Then who is it, Lu?"

"I don't know!" I scream. "I don't know who it is, okay. It's no one, it's everyone. I don't know." Each breath is harder and harder to take in. The weight of the night is finally catching up to me. I'm strong, but this, tonight and these two assholes, it's too much even for me. "Get out. Both of you."

Not looking up from the floor, I watch their shadows move and shift across the room towards the front door.

"Lu?" Mustering up the last of my strength I glance up to Jeremy, who's standing at the opened door. "Did you really fuck him?"

"It's none of your damn business, Jeremy, if I did or didn't."

"I can't believe you'd sleep with him for that damn promotion. Good to know that's why you never gave me a shot. There wasn't enough in it for you."

The door slams shut behind him, rattling the pictures on the adjoining wall.

The quiet of the house is comforting and terrifying.

Unable to hold on any longer, my knees give out and I fall to the floor.

CHAPTER THIRTY-SEVEN
LUCIA

My hip and shoulder ache from lying here so long. I need to get up, but I can't. I physically and mentally can't muster up enough energy to pull myself off this floor.

Instead minutes tick by as I wallow in guilt and failure.

I've no concept of how much time has gone by when the need to find Gabe, to talk to him and explain everything—to see if he still wants me as bad as I need him, pulls me off the floor.

Well, kind of off the floor.

Not having the energy to stand, I crawl to the living room and pull my phone off the coffee table. Rolling on my back I hold the phone above me.

Ten missed calls, plus a few missed texts from Brooke.

Large tears well and spill down my temples. Seeing her 'miss you' text has me calling her instead of Gabe like I'd planned.

"You're calling me. What's wrong? You never call me," Brooke says after the second ring.

But I can't talk, all I can do is sob into the phone. Deep, soul crushing sobs. My whole world has fallen apart around me. There are no words to explain that, only my heartbroken tears.

I never call, and I never cry.

"Lu? What's wrong?" Her tone turning to panic. "You're scaring the shit out of me, Lu!" she yells. "Are you hurt?"

"No," I choke out, but the thought of explaining what just happened, what happened tonight with the op, makes the sobbing start anew.

"Are you safe?" The tension in her voice eased, but there's still a bit of panic in there.

I wipe my nose with the sleeve of my t-shirt. "Yes. Brooke, it's bad."

"You're not hurt and you're safe. Whatever it is, love, we can figure it out, those are the non-negotiables. Now tell me what's going on."

So I do.

All of it.

It takes over an hour to tell her everything from the past several weeks, from tonight at the Russian club to what went down with Jeremy and the boss right here in my living room. By the time I'm done my head throbs and I'm utterly spent from all the crying.

"Wow, I mean...."

"I know Brooke. I know. And now I'm laying here on the floor unable to do anything but be sad and so damn frustrated with myself. What the guys said tonight was true, I've failed this op and in a way I've failed Gabe. I have no idea who this mole is. How can I go back to the agency—"

"Hold up, you're going back to work for those dip shits after all they said to you tonight? They let you believe a man died on your watch, Lu. They blamed you. Died! And he didn't. That's all kinds of fucked up. I don't know if I even want to work for them anymore."

"What else would I do? This is my life, I have nothing else."

"You have Gabe, it sounds like."

"I don't think so, not anymore."

"I think you're reading into him leaving. He said you two were in this together right before all that, and he doesn't seem to be the type of guy who would toss that out there for anyone. Plus, he loves you. He said he loves you."

"He loves me."

"Yes, he does, Lu. So hold on to that, you're not alone, you have me and him. And the three of us together will figure it out."

"Okay," I sniffle and smile against the phone pressed against my cheek but it falls. "I still have to find this guy, Brooke."

"I doubt you don't know who this guy is."

"I don't," I say exasperated "I really don't."

She sighs and the sounds of her adjusting on her leather couch come through the phone. "Lu, you know I wouldn't feed you bull, so I'll give it to you straight. You're the best at finding the truth, at digging out the lies, but you also have this gut instinct no one else has. You know who this guy is, I know it. So think about it. Who have you talked to in their platoon who seemed off?"

In my head I roll through the roster checking off each man as I go. "No one I can think of, Brooke. Maybe my gut is broken. Maybe I'm broken."

"Oh hell, don't go pity party on me now, Lucia. Do you think Jeremy missed anything with the guys you gave him to look into?"

My fingers drum against the carpet as I think it over. "No, he's a jackass, that's for sure, but he's good at his job."

A baby crying in the background has Brooke sighing. "Sorry, love, I gotta go. But call me later, okay, and we will figure it out. All of it. Promise me you won't do anything stupid until we talk again."

"I won't do anything career-ending until we talk again," I say with an eye roll.

The crying turns into an all-out wail. "Ugh, babies. Love you, Lu. Bye."

The call disconnects before I can say anything back.

Pushing to lean back on my elbows, I look around the living room. I'm going to miss this place. It's not what I would choose in decor but it was homey and even though it's only been a short time, a lot of fun memories have been made here.

As I survey the room the gadget Tony was playing with the other day catches my eye on the coffee table. Grabbing it, I flip it over a few times.

As the metal flips in my hands a gnawing starts in my belly making me pull it closer. Tony was right, if this is a jammer, it doesn't work. It doesn't look like anything from previous ops. Wonder why the agency sent it? Actually the bigger question is why hasn't anyone asked about it? With other new gadgets Jeremy's asked how new equipment is working out in the field to report it back to our engineers.

"What the hell is this?" I ask out loud. "What are you and where did you come from?"

I blame talking to a small black box on being exhausted and having little mental stability left.

Pushing off the carpet, I take the gadget to the kitchen and grab a knife from one of the drawers to pry it open. It takes another couple minutes to find a flashlight to help me see inside.

But what I see doesn't make sense.

A few cords and chips lay perfectly organized inside the hard plastic covering. It looks similar to the simple inner workings of...

"What the fuck," I whisper and dash to the living room.

After I press the call button I pace the living room waiting for Jeremy to answer.

"Agent Rizzo?" My eyes roll at the annoyance in his tone.

"What the hell are you doing listening in to all my conversations here at the house?" I seethe. "You should have warned me."

"Lu, I—"

"And if you knew what was going on here, why did you ask if I was sleeping with Gabe? You knew I was. Why did you want me to admit it?"

"Lucia—"

My grip tightens on the phone as I think of Jeremy and other agents listening to Gabe and me the few times we never made it to the bedroom. "You fucking asshole." Tears start cascading down my cheeks in frustration. "Did you and the other guys get a kick out of listening to us? Did you—"

"Agent Rizzo," Jeremy shouts, cutting off my tirade. "What the hell are you talking about?"

"The listening device you sent to the base for me. I had no idea what it was and I just left it out in the living room, you damn idiot. You should have warned-"

"Lu." His tone drops from frustrated to serious, making me pause. "I didn't send you anything to the base. No one has. We wouldn't blow your cover doing something like—"

He's still talking but I can't hear anything. Tossing the phone to the couch, I crouch on the floor and put my head in my hands as the past few weeks piece together.

Brooke was right, I knew who the mole was all along but didn't understand it until now. When the picture clears, I rise from the floor and snatch the phone from the couch and call Gabe.

This ends today.

CHAPTER THIRTY-EIGHT
GABE

My pocket won't stop vibrating but informal meeting or not, I can't answer my phone in front of CO. It's insistent. As soon as it stops it picks back up again. I crack each knuckle one by one and clasp my hands behind my back to keep from answering it.

There's no doubt it's Luce. She has to be confused as to why I left her. But the bastards were right, I had no authority in that room. It was a CIA matter, and as much as I wanted to stay and defend her, to protect her from their poison, I would've only made it worse.

So instead I came here to figure out options. A plan.

Thank the fuck CO was here when I barged into his office at 0500.

The first hour was spent briefing him on the night's events, what little I know, and how Luce doesn't believe Matt is the mole. There wasn't push back on the fucked up mission, almost like he'd already been debriefed. When he mentioned in an offhand remark that Matt was going to make it, not dead like those fuck sticks made me and Luce believe, he physically restrained me to stop me from wrapping my bare hands around their necks.

Then he dropped the next bomb of the CIA's plans for me. When he said they weren't planning to give Luce the promotion, it was a lie for them to use her to get me on board, but put me in the lead strategist position she's been vying for, he stood in the door frame—side arm drawn—to keep me from storming out.

I sink down on to a leather chair that somehow smells faintly of her peppermint shampoo and rub a hand down my face. Tonight with Luce and the Russians, dad going to the ER, and now all this new information, even for a SEAL I'm at the max.

"What can we do for her?" I ask, there's no hiding my exhaustion.

CO paces his office, which is what I'd be doing, but if I stand, there will be no holding back from leaving this room and going to her. Sitting, white knuckling the leather arms of this chair, is where I need to stay for the moment.

"We have a few bargaining chips," he says but doesn't explain. "Do you think she'd want out?"

Everything she's said the past few weeks races through my mind. "I think she liked the idea of the CIA but now that she knows what it is... What it turned her into...Being here, what I've seen from her recently...she's different."

"I agree."

"But I don't want to make the decision for her. She deserves options, not for me to dictate what she's going to do with her career, just because I think that agency is fucked up."

"But it could be her life, they seem to think she's disposable."

The leather pulls at my skin as I release the arms to crack my knuckles again. "I know and if I had it my way, I'd say do whatever you need to do to get her out. But it's her call." The last two words are hard to say aloud.

"Then let's get her in here to discuss options, Wilcox."

Fucking finally is what I want to say, but instead go with a "Yes, sir" and slide the still vibrating phone out of my front pocket.

Luce's face fills the screen when I swipe right to answer her call.

"Luce, I-"

"I know who it is," she says through rushed breaths on the other end of the line. The sound of her car roaring to life fills the background.

"What?" I push from the chair and look to CO. There's a panicked, excited tone in her voice I've never heard before.

"I figured it out after you left, which we will talk about later, and I know who it is." Okay, definitely more excited than scared, which helps my tension drop a level.

"Who is it?" I ask, making CO turn to me with an expectant look. "Who is it, Luce?"

"I'm on my way to the CO's office right now, he needs to know."

"I'm in his office right now."

The silence from her end has me looking at the screen to see if the connection was lost.

"Luce?"

"Gabe. Listen, be careful, it's his admin. Hell, I can't even think of his name right now—"

"Travis?"

"Yes! Him. It's him. I know it's him. I found—"

This time I know the connection has been lost when the phone goes silent.

Fear like I've never known settles in my gut. I hit her cell number on the screen and press the speaker button. It goes straight to the automated voicemail message.

"Fuck." I toss the phone across the room to CO. "Keep trying her." I command and stalk to the office door. The wood door cracks down the center from the force of it slamming against the wall.

I'm going to kill him. All of this. My life. Flakes' life. His men.

My breaths are labored with restrained anger as I stare at the empty desk in front of me.

I storm back into the office and rip my phone from CO's hand. "Where's your piece of shit admin?" I say through clenched teeth and try her cell again.

Voicemail.

"He said he was heading to sick bay this AM. What's going on, Wilcox?"

"It's him. She said it was him then the phone disconnected."

When he doesn't reply, I glance up from the phone. His face

flushed crimson, lips pursed together so tight they're white. "That motherfucker." He finally says through clenched teeth. "When he didn't make it through the program, he wanted this role because it meant he was still a part of the overall SEAL team."

"That's bullshit," I mumble under my breath as I try to call Lucia again.

With a smirk he reaches for the phone on his desk. "We will find him. And for the shit he's put Hackenbreg and his platoon through, I think I'll let them be the ones to do it."

Hell no.

"Sir, I-"

"Go find her, Wilcox. That is your priority right now. Find her, and then you join the hunt for the piece of shit."

A brief nod and I'm through the door, racing out of the building.

———

The flashing emergency lights halfway between her place and base have traffic backed up in every direction. Something deep down tells me it has to do with her.

Every movement is slow, like I'm walking through a dream on the verge of waking up, as I turn off the Jeep and step out to investigate the scene.

The morning sun has me shielding my eyes with my hand to see anything.

Only one car is visible.

Black sports car, t-boned but the other car involved isn't anywhere. I push past a police officer, taking a step closer to confirm what I already know, it's her Camaro with the airbags deployed and side door crunched in and there's no guessing what the red smears are from.

Fucking hell.

I try to take a deep breath in but can't.

A hand presses against my chest stopping me from getting any closer to the wreckage.

COVERT AFFAIR | 331

"Sir, you can't go any closer."

"That's my damn girlfriend's car," I yell in his face which makes him take a step back and rest a hand on his sidearm.

"Okay, man, I get that, and I'm sorry, but you can't get any closer."

"Where the hell is she?" Another look around for an ambulance but I don't see one. "Which hospital did they take her to?"

The young police officer shifts on his feet and avoids my hard stare.

"What?" I ask as I grip my hands behind my back to not shake the answer out of the kid.

"We don't know," he mumbles with a flinch.

My hands fall limp at my side.

"What do you mean you don't know?"

"A bystander called in the accident and when we got here the driver, your girlfriend, was gone. Her wallet and purse are in the car but she...isn't."

"Tell me everything," I demand and cross my arms across my chest readying to hear a nightmare played out in real life.

With each word the hope of finding her slips and the fear of what's happening to her right now grows. The bystander's account said a small SUV came out of nowhere and rammed Luce's car, then the driver of the SUV dragged her, unconscious, to his car and sped off.

Get your fucking shit together.

She needs me to get her back, focused on what to do next, not standing here focused on what could be happening to her.

She needs me now more than ever, I can do this for her.

I will get her back then kill that damn traitor. Slowly.

A black Suburban whips up to the scene. The cop and I turn to see what's going on.

"What the hell," I spit out and stride over to the two men who, up until thirty minutes ago, were on the top of my shit list. When they see me approaching they start in my direction.

"Where is she?" The younger one, Jeremy I think, says. Fucker number two in my mind.

"How the hell would I know?" I turn to look at the totaled Camaro.

"I just got here. I was on the phone with her when it happened. Why weren't you two with her?"

"Did she say who the mole is?" Fucker one asks taking a step closer.

"Why weren't you two dipshits with her?" I growl.

Fucker two stares at the pavement. "She kicked us out."

Of course she did. Damn, she's so fucking brave.

I look from the wreckage back to fucker one with my brows furrowed and ask, "How did you know to come looking for her then?"

Fucker two coughs to bring my stare to him. "Her cell phone has a tracker." I narrow my eyes further, making him take a step back. "We all have them. But the signal stopped about half an hour ago. Right here. So we came looking for her."

"Some guy took her," I say and start pacing trying to figure out how to play this without giving up the mole's identity. She had a reason to call me, to want the CO to know first, not these assholes. "Any other way to track her?"

Fucker one shoots a side glance to fucker two.

"Tell me. Now," I demand.

"Officer Wilcox, you can't—"

I reach over and grip fucker one on the shoulder, giving it a good squeeze as I push him against the showy ass SUV they showed up in. "Here's the thing. I can. And I will. And you can. And you will give me everything I need to get her back. Because if she's hurt or…" I clear my throat to not voice the worst that could be happening right now. "Because you took your sweet-ass time to get me her location. I will end you. I will feed you to the fucking sharks and love watching them chew your screaming body alive."

Fucker two steps beside us with a panicked look on his face. "We have trackers. GPS signals on all our agents."

"The cell—"

"No, Officer Wilcox. On our agents." The way he emphasizes the word *on* I know he means *in*.

"Agent Dungan, he can't—" A little extra squeeze on fucker one's shoulder, right near his neck, makes him drop to the ground in pain.

"Just find her," fucker two yells. One look at him and I know he's sincere about it. No matter what happened in that house tonight, he cares about her. Hell, everyone does once they get to know her.

Leaving fucker one on the ground massaging his shoulder I turn to the Jeremy guy. "I will get her back or die trying. Give me the information I need."

CHAPTER THIRTY-NINE
LUCIA

D ang my head hurts.
       And my arm.
And ribs.

Heck, everything feels like I've been tossed around like a rag doll.

The soreness and pain firing every time I think about moving is familiar, but this rocking, the slow up and down even when I don't move, isn't.

Shit, what happened to me?

Where am I?

Rising panic sends my pulse racing and makes it harder to breathe. I force my eyes open, no matter the searing pain it causes. But the second they open, I slam them shut again to protect them from some kind of glaring light.

"Come on, Agent Rizzo, I don't want you to miss any of the fun," says a voice I recognize.

"What the hell happened to me?" I demand, my voice raspy against my dry throat. I try to swallow but it hurts like shit, and I'm suddenly aware my mouth is so dry there's nothing to swallow. Shifting to my side, to get farther away from the man now laughing at my pain, I

slam against some kind of soft wall, and the movement makes the rocking worse. "Where am I?"

"So many questions. I figured this was the only place to keep you contained, out of your comfort zone if you would. So here we are. I think it's perfect for many reasons."

Gathering what little mental strength that's left in me, I force my eyes open and keep them that way, no matter the pain of the sun searing into them. The light makes the low pounding in my head increase to a fast thundering. On shaky arms I push up from the ground, which isn't ground at all, and take in the surroundings.

Blue.

Deep blue everywhere, every inch around us—outside of the zodiac we're in—covered in dark blue.

Arms shaking, I lower back down into the boat and close my eyes.

This can't be happening.

"I really must thank Wilcox for getting you to open up all those times you were in your house. It helped me greatly. Now—"

"What do you want from me?" I rasp. "They already know it's you. I told Gabe before…" I stop as the blips of memory play. "You hit me. In the car you hit me and brought me…."

He chuckles again like he's in on some private joke. "You, my beautiful Agent Rizzo, are my insurance policy."

Travis takes a step and his shifting weight sends the rubber boat to rock deeper on each side. My already-queasy stomach erupts. I barely get over the side before vomiting. Which helps with the stomach issue, but makes the rest of my body scream in pain. It's only when I sit back in the boat, wiping my mouth with my sleeve, that I notice dried blood coating my t-shirt and jeans.

Every move hurts, but I start to slide my sleeves up to inspect the wounds.

"Nothing that will kill you in the next few days."

"And why do you need me to survive the next few days?" I groan as my head falls into my hands and I push on my temples attempting to stop the throbbing.

"Oh, I just need you to survive the next hour or so, but my business partners, well, they will want more time with you." The satisfaction in his voice makes my stomach roll. "With the price they're paying they might want a couple weeks with you."

"Sounds like a party," I say, or think I say loud enough for him to hear. Between my pounding head like a damn train and my hearing still not 100% everything is muffled. And getting worse. "Why did you do it?" If these are my last few hours might as well make the most of it in case I survive this ordeal.

"Money, of course." When I gain enough strength to look up into the light, at him, he's sneering down from the front of the boat. "Do you know what the Navy pays someone in my position? Shit. Complete shit for someone with my intellect. They had no idea what they have in me. Their dumbass obstacles and endurance test in the program weeded me out but they were too damn stupid to see what else I could bring to the table."

"And what's that?" I ask to keep him talking. In a subtle move, I flex my right calf a few times to feel for the knife I tied to it before running out the door. Elastic pulls at my dry skin, sending a wash of relief through my veins, calming some of the panic that was on the verge of bubbling out of control. The dumbass forgot to search me after pulling me out of the wreck.

His mistake.

"Are you fucking serious? What's that?" he shouts. My hands fly to my ears. "For weeks I skirted you. You...I knew who you were from the fucking beginning. I'm fucking smarter than you and that dumbass Williams. Those meathead SEALs together couldn't see what they missed out on. So, instead of working with them I decided to work against them. I found some buyers on a back channel, and all have been willing to pay. Big. But I have to say, when I listed you as an asset I was willing to sell off..." His piercing whistle makes tears well. "Damn, am I glad that dumbass Beasley didn't run you off like I planned."

"You...you're the one who gave him my information?"

His insufferable, cocky laugh makes me want to choke him. "No, I let Hackenbreg incriminate himself on that one. He never knew the message I relayed from the CO was never actually given. Stupid piece of shit."

I have to get off this boat. If the other men come, if I get on another boat, I'll never get back.

Without drawing attention I inch up my pant leg to get my hand wrapped around the hilt of the knife.

A roaring behind us makes my hand pause. Travis leans over to look behind me and smiles.

"Looks like your ride is almost here."

Travis stands but I call out, dragging his attention back to me. "Why Tony? Why only his platoon?"

"Ah, Officer Hackenbreg, the fucking tool. You've met him. Thinks he's damn near perfect. Treats me like I'm his fucking bitch." His shoulders rise and fall in an exaggerated shrug. "So I made him pay for it. But it hasn't always been just his platoon, it's only been recently that I narrowed the information I sold. The information wasn't that much to be noticed early on, everyone assumed it was bad intel from your agency. But I upped my game for Tony. Fucking Tony. I was hoping he'd get nailed, I even offered a guy a discount if he could promise to take Tony out personally. No luck. Guess I'll just have to circle back around one of these days and do it myself."

Larger waves smack against the rubber of the boat right before a large, white fishing boat pulls along side us and cuts its engine.

Turning to get a better look is harder than expected. My teeth hurt from clenching to keep from crying out from the pain. Thankfully the boat is on the side not facing the sun, giving my burning retinas a break.

Up on the boat two men dressed in black, their faces covered along with their arms and legs, stand along the rail, each wearing machine guns strapped to their chests. A third man is up near the front, casually leaning over the railing talking to Travis.

I have to get off this boat. It's either die trying or die, slowly, by their hand.

Travis raises his voice, like he's taken off guard by something the other man suggested. The main man on the fishing boat laughs and nods to one of the armed men.

They're going to kill him.

I realize it just before Travis does giving me a half a second head start.

All my muscles and joints scream and nearly give out as I push to a standing position.

Three things happen at once.

Travis lunges for me.

I stumble into the water.

And the first of many rounds is fired off.

CHAPTER FORTY
GABE

This isn't going fast enough. We should have left sooner.

Even with the cold wind whipping off the ocean sweat beads on my brow and neck. Keeping my finger away from the damn triggers is more difficult than ever as we jet across the water towards the last place fucker two had a signal on Luce. That was almost two hours ago. A lot can happen in two hours.

I go to rub a hand down my face but the full gear and being packed in the zodiac like fucking sardines prevents me from moving.

Fuck, two hours is a long-ass time.

What the hell is he doing out there with her in the middle of the damn ocean?

This is one death I won't feel bad about, when this fucker dies, we should request a damn national fucking holiday.

Fuck, I hope she's not scared. But Luce wouldn't be, she's strong and can handle any situation. Plus she knows I'll come for her, hopefully that is enough to get her through…fuck. My stomach churns at the mental images of what could be happening, what I've seen done. What I've done before.

There's also the possibility she was hurt *before* being dragged out here. I saw the car. The blood. Even if he hasn't touched her, there's no way she escaped the wreck without injuries.

What if we're too late?

I crack my knuckles and neck.

"Get your shit together, G," Flakes yells from his side of the boat. Looking up from the gun in my hand I shoot him a glare which would make most men piss themselves, but I'm met with a similar glare from him. "Don't make me sideline your fat ass."

"I'm fucking fantastic, shithead. Just get us there faster."

"We are, G."

"Two hours ago she was fucking—"

"I know the time line you fool," he shouts. "Don't forget, I've done this before too, and as much shit as I gave her early on, I want her back too."

The boat goes silent. The smacking of the waves against the hull and wind screaming in our ears are the only sounds. They all know what's at risk. Not only for me, and apparently Flakes too, but because of what she was doing for them.

Earlier, while we geared up, we told Flakes' team everything. All about the mole, Luce and her real identity, and what she has been doing the past few weeks to get this bastard. A few of the men were pissed, others unfazed, but they all understood what she had risked to help. What she had done for all of us. This is why the boat is silent. This is why tensions are so strung tight. Getting her back, protecting who we all agreed is now a part of our team, is priority.

We all shift forward as the boat slows then stops completely.

The engine cuts.

"I've got something," says Lovall from the helm. He pulls out his scope and starts adjusting it. I'm seconds away from ripping it from his hands to do it myself when he says, "Sir. You need to see this."

His words have me swallowing back the bile rising in my throat. I will not fucking vomit in front of Flakes' men. Fuck, this can't be good.

Flakes takes the scope and holds it against his eye.

It takes less than a few seconds for him to turn. The gnawing in my gut churns again at the tight look on his face.

"It's the stolen zodiac. One body in the boat and another floating beside it. We proceed with caution, but there doesn't seem to be any other threat."

The entire boat roars to life, pushing us closer to what feels like my own death. If anything happened to her, if I can't hold her again, or hear her laugh, or her smartass mouth...nothing will ever be right again.

Flakes stands as we approach and jumps onto the other boat once we are close enough. "It's that fucker Travis. Damn." Not able to wait a second longer, I push off the side of the boat and jump over to meet him. "There has to be at least ten bullet holes in this fucker. Someone was pissed off at him." Flakes drops the body and leans over to fish the other one out of the water.

When he flips the body over for us to see his face, Flakes looks up, brows raised.

"I don't recognize this guy, do you?" he asks as he looks back to the body to inspect it again, but this time with a closer look.

"No. Grab his fingers and we'll run the prints when we get back to base." I stand in the middle of the boat and look out on to the vast, blue ocean. The sun has started to set and in the next hour it will be pitch black out here. "Where is she, Tony?" I try to keep the worry and desperation out of my tone, but fail miserably. Even I hear it. "Where the fuck is she?"

"I don't know, man, but I hope she's not out there swimming. She's smarter than that right?"

"She can't swim."

Flakes' brows shoot up in surprise then narrow once realization hits. "You mean to tell me she pushed a fucking navy SEAL into a damn training—"

My hand goes up to stop him. "I know, believe me I know. It's that damn temper of hers." Turning to the men, I scan the group. "Who has communication back with base?" The fucker Beasley stands and nods.

"Fuck. Fine. Get those CIA fuckers on the line and tell them we need new coordinates." Beasley nods and turns to do as he was told. "If they give you any shit about it, tell them I'll rip apart their damn agency from the inside out, starting with those two fuckers, if they don't give us the information we need to find her. Now."

The anger and fury that has been building all fucking day, since those two fuckers stepped into her living room—hell, before that even, when I found her getting the shit beat out of her by that fucking Russian—boils over and all control is lost. Turning to the dead body of the man who put all this in motion, I kick the shit out of his side, then his head. Again and again.

"Feel better?" Flakes asks as he peers down at where I now sit on the edge of the zodiac.

"A little, yeah, but I'll feel a whole lot better when we find her. Alive."

"We will, man. She's a fighter. Wherever she is, she's giving them hell, you can believe that. Fuck, they might even send her back with a damn bow just to get her to shut the hell up."

My head hangs between my shoulders, and I interlace my hands behind my head. "I don't know what will happen to me if I lose her now. I've just had her, I can't—"

"Stop that shit," Flakes growls and attempts to pull me up. "We will find her. She will be fine. Then you and hot shot CIA can go make superhuman fucking babies together who will annoy the shit out of me. Focus on finding her, G. Use that damn mind of yours to bring her home, not this lame-ass sad shit." He smirks and looks ever my shoulder to make sure none of the boys are listening then leans in. "And once you do get her home, don't you fucking dare let her leave San Diego. She belongs with us."

Beasley's talking stops my reply.

"We have new coordinates. Twenty miles northeast of here. Waiting on satellite images now."

Flakes nods then directs his attention back to where I'm still sitting.

"Let's bring her home, G."

Home.

Flakes was right. Home. That's what she is now. A home I've never known, but now that I've found it, now that I love it, I'll give up my life to save it.

CHAPTER FORTY-ONE
LUCIA

For the third time in less than thirty minutes I'm bent over dry heaving into the corner of the room. Tears roll down my cheeks from the pain it sends from my ribs, to the still-constant throbbing in my head, and of course my shoulder, which is clearly dislocated.

Stupid ass.

Not sure if I mean them or me.

I'm the one who didn't go willingly into the boat after they fished me out of the water. I'm the one who put full dead weight, making them pull harder than needed.

The dislocation part sucks, but the searing pain did push my temper into warp speed which resulted in having no concern for my safety, and I kicked one of the guards overboard.

That idiot Travis should have seen it coming. He was the idiot who expected honor among thieves. Or terrorists in this matter.

It wasn't a long boat ride to their ship. I made myself stay conscious the entire time to take in every exit, every weakness in the group to hopefully use to my advantage later. The ship seemed to be some kind of cargo boat and the only way in or out of the lower deck they brought me down is one set of stairs settled in the middle of the ship.

Only one way in. One way out.

If Gabe and…

No.

When Gabe and Tony come, I need to have some kind of distraction in place to give them an opportunity to get down those stairs. Something that will pull the men's attention to this shit of a room where they have me housed. If I do, I can use the knife still strapped to my leg and fight my way out. Somehow.

I'm strong, but with this and last night, I'm at my limit. There is only so much more I can take. But I have to be strong until he gets here.

Strong.

I can be strong. I can wait for him. There is no doubt he's out kicking ass and pissing everyone off trying to find me. Hopefully, Jeremy's told him about the trackers we all have by now, and Gabe's already nearby ready to save the day.

They will come for me. But when they do, if this stupid-ass plan of mine is going to work, I have to have two functioning arms.

Whimpering, I glance around the room looking for the best angle to help set my shoulder.

Fuck, this is going to hurt.

CHAPTER FORTY-TWO
GABE

Familiar anticipation calms my anxious nerves. She's there, right there. So close I can see the shithole of a boat she's held on. Within the hour she'll be with me, safe.

The tracker can't give vital signs, unfortunately, but the signal is still clear. She's there.

"Let's get this shit done." I whisper through gritted teeth as I check my magazines for the hundredth time in the past couple minutes. The metal against metal, the clicking and snapping relaxes me further sending me into a familiar trance.

"She's fine, G. Let's go over the plan again, fuck, this could be a shit show."

"The plan will work," I say and slip into the water without a sound, which isn't easy with all our gear but years of practice make it second nature. "Beasley will provide sniper cover from here. You, me, and the other five go up the side of the ship, take out the fuckers holding Luce and bring her back to the boat in one piece."

Small waves smack my shoulder as another man slides into the water beside me.

"We have no idea how many men are on board, G. We never go in with this little intel." I don't take offense to his frustration and questioning the plan; it's this damn situation, not me. This isn't ideal, but it's what we have to work with, and we need to move now. With a huff he tosses his legs over the side of the boat and slides into the water. "Your plan, you lead, G. Let's get our girl back."

"My girl."

"Yeah, whatever."

We are invisible in the water as we approach the rickety ship. Hell, hopefully the ladders on the sides don't break under our weight, by the rust coating each rung there's a strong possibility they could. Flakes is beside me as the other five swim to the other side. If the bastards on board hear anything, they'll think it's nothing more than a wave hitting the boat or something jumping in the water—they always do—fucking fools. They have no idea the hell that's about to rain down.

This part of the mission, no more planning, no more anticipation only action, is normally the part I love the most, but right now... everything I want and need is on that boat. It changes things.

There is no enjoyment, no excitement, only pent up fury and fear, which, if I'm not careful, will obliterate the small amount of restraint I have on my actions. Each rung up the ladder, my heart thunders, and the excitement of getting her in my arms again grows. She's close. So close.

Peering over the deck for a quick visual, I duck back and whisper into my communication piece.

"Two starboard side, AKs." Peeking over again, I scan the deck a second time. "One more guarding the door, looks to lead below deck. Let's get her back boys."

Opposite us a man dressed in black, face painted, slips over the side, blending into the shadows, knife in hand, and slinks across the deck towards the two men. I do the same.

The two bastards never see us coming.

The crack of the neck breaking echoes out onto the water while the other chokes as his throat is slit from ear to ear. With a quick look, I find Lovall smirking.

Flakes and our other men, now on deck, inch towards the final armed man.

Movement to my right has Lovall and I both turning, drawing our guns. But before we can get a lock, a body hits the rotting wood with a loud thump, blood seeping out of the bullet wound on his forehead.

Damn, I love snipers. Even if it is Beasley on the other end of that scope.

The rhythm of our feet prowling, the now-steady beat of my heart erases any of the earlier fear. This is where I excel. This is where we win.

Every. Damn. Time.

I'm a warrior, I will get her back. She will be safe. Fuck those bastards, thinking they could keep someone like me back. They had no idea who they were fucking with. If they thought we'd all be pussies like Travis, they were wrong. And they will pay for their mistake.

Hand on the handle, Flakes turns, eyes each of us to make sure we are set for cover fire, and pulls the door.

It doesn't even open an inch before rounds and rounds of bullets pelt the thick metal. I fire off a few rounds through the opening and jump back as the door slams shut.

"We need another way down there," he shouts, no longer caring who hears us, obviously they know we're here and who we're here to get. Hopefully, they won't be chicken shits and try to use her as leverage to get us to leave.

We spread out, checking the sides looking for windows or other hidden doors but come up empty. The stairs, the heavily guarded stairs, are our only option.

I stare at the rusted metal door and mentally start running through our options. A scream cuts through my thoughts. The hairs on my arms and back of my neck stand at attention.

Luce.

Another scream filters up the stairs and cuts off my air supply.

Pain and anger lace her screams for help.

Damning the consequences, I reach for the handle to get to her, to kill the bastards who are hurting her but Flakes shoves me aside.

"You fool, you'll get yourself killed," he yells.

I'm about to say, I don't give a fuck, when shots firing from below, but not up to the door where we are waiting, grab all our attention.

Another shot rings out again not towards us. More like they are firing on each other. Then we hear it. Confusion below, men yelling and feet pounding against the metal floor below.

This is our chance.

A miracle distraction.

Flakes opens the door an inch, then an inch more. Just as we expected, their attention is elsewhere, no longer concerned with protecting the only access point down into the hull. I prowl down the stairs first, gun raised to fire if anyone so much as breathes too loud, and the other six follow just as noiselessly.

We fan out at the bottom of the stairs, each going in a different direction in search for Luce and other hostiles.

A single bang to my right and in my ear piece, "fucker down" is spoken, but no idea by who.

Another to my left.

I clear every corner, every fucking place she could be stashed but still no Luce. Sweat rolls into my brows and falls down my cheeks. Where is she?

Something up ahead catches my attention. Two steps closer. A body, a male body dressed in all black like the ones we already took out.

Keeping the gun raised and eyes straight ahead, I kick the bastard checking to see if he's alive, but my foot is met with dead weight. Blood pools around him.

The door he's dead in front of is open an inch, but no light shines from inside. I ease in, gun first.

Every nerve ending fires as I inch into the room and near explode when my raised gun is met with another.

"Luce?" I say, bemused.

In the earpiece Flakes screams, asking what's going on, but how in the hell do I describe this scene?

The gun that's aimed at my head lowers, and I lower mine. Her back is pressed against the far wall. I start for her, but my boot hits something. Another body lays dead on the floor, blood everywhere. And a unique-looking knife, covered in red, is laying discarded on the floor beside him.

Looking back up with a shocked, proud smile, I'm surprised to see her wearing a small, weary smirk on her lips. She looks like shit. Dirty as hell, hair stuck to her face from the damn sauna-like temperatures in here.

"Luce," I whisper and take a step towards her. "Are you hurt?"

Only one of her shoulders rises in a shrug as she slides down the wall, that I now realize has been supporting her. Fuck.

"Lucia." I say and take another hesitant step, almost afraid what I'm going to find.

One arm is cradled in her lap while the the other still has a death grip on the gun in her hand.

"How bad are you?" I whisper, but Flakes hears it loud and clear, sending him into a frenzy.

"Not great, Officer Wilcox," she says, but there's no strength behind it. Stepping over the body, I crouch down, putting us eye-to-eye. "I knew you would come. I knew you would come for me." Streams of tears fall down her dirty cheeks, making them black by the time they drip off her jaw. Cupping her face, I swipe at the steady stream with both thumbs. "Gabe?"

"Yeah, sweetheart?"

"Get me off this fucking boat."

The belly laugh that erupts is more out of relief that she's making sense and in one piece than from finding her comment funny.

"Well then, sweetheart, let's get you off this fucking boat and get you home." There's no pushback or hesitation when I scoop her off the floor and cradle her against my chest.

Warmth spreads every place our bodies connect, sending waves of relief knowing she's in my arms. Safe. Alive.

"I waited for you," she whispers against my neck. "I knew you would have to come down those stairs. I waited till you were here. I knew you would come. I love that you came for me. I love that you didn't give up. I really just love you. Just you."

The heat building in my heart dies when her head rolls and hangs back.

"Luce?"

No answer.

Flakes is at the bottom of the stairs waiting to provide cover. "Is she okay?"

"I don't know, she was just talking," I yell as I charge up the stairs, careful not to jostle her too much. "Luce, sweetheart, talk to me."

Out in the fresh air, I lay her down on the deck and start searching for wounds. All I can find are superficial, nothing life-threatening. But what if I'm missing something?

"G," Flakes says, but I keep searching for other wounds. "G, we have to get off this fucking ship."

"Why did she pass out like that? What if I'm missing something? Fucking hell, Tony." Terror causes my heart and lungs to constrict at the thought of her not surviving the night.

"Gabe, get her off the damn floor and get your girl onto our damn boat. We can't do anything for her here. We need to get her back to base."

I nod. He's right, but I still can't move.

I'm a Navy fucking SEAL, trained to overcome any situation, but this...there's no training for this. My heart is lying unconscious on the deck of some terrorist ship. What the fuck is the protocol on that?

Shaking my head to clear the fog the terror has caused, I wrap her back in my arms and stand.

"You're right. Let's get her home."

CHAPTER FORTY-THREE
LUCIA

Mist and splashes of water sting my cheeks, pulling me awake. The throbbing in my head and searing pain in my shoulder have me wishing I could pass out again.

"Luce, sweetheart, you gotta wake up." The pain and agony in the voice give me the strength to pull my eyes open, despite it hurting like hell. It's pitch black wherever we are but even in the darkest of night I'd be able to lock with those blue eyes.

"You're safe. Taking you back to base now. Based on the goose egg on your temple, I'm assuming you have a concussion, but other than that I don't see anything."

"My shoulder," I croak out. "My shoulder was pulled out. I put it back in."

The hold he has on me tightens.

"You're safe now. We got you. Here drink this."

I drink and drink and drink from the water bottle he presses to my lips. "We?" I rasp and break eye contact with him for the first time since opening my eyes to look around. The corners of my vision sparkle as I roll my head.

"Hey there, sweet cheeks, glad you woke up. G, here, was having one hell of a hissy fit when you passed out on him." I can't really see him, with all the dark gear and face paint, there's concern in Tony's tone even though his words say otherwise.

"Yeah, well, setting off a grenade, getting run down by that jackass, getting taken by a bunch of asshole terrorists, then waiting around in a shitty holding cell for you water mammals to finally make your glorious appearance, I think I was allowed a quick nap, don't you?"

"Damn, woman," says a voice I recognize but can't place immediately. "I'm just glad we all know the truth. I don't feel like such a damn pussy anymore, knowing it wasn't just any ol' civilian broad who nearly drowned me. Fuck, with you surviving the past forty-eight hours, I should be glad you didn't off me that day."

"I was feeling generous," I rasp and try to move off Gabe's lap. There is some resistance at first, but with the second push against his arm, he loosens his hold. "So you know." Glancing around the dark only the whites of their eyes are visible in the moonlight. "You all know the truth."

"Yeah, we all know," says a man at the end of the boat. "And it makes a lot more sense than some guy cheating on someone like you. I knew there wasn't a fucker stupid enough to do that."

"What the hell is he talking about?" Gabe whispers into my ear sending a shiver down my spine. Taking it as me being cold he wraps me closer against his warm, hard chest, careful of the shoulder of the arm I'm cradling.

"Nothing," I say back, and look down the boat again. "Everything I said stays true. What I learned about you, what I learned about all of you—" A few heads whip my direction, I'm sure wondering what I uncovered about them. "Stays with me. Since you weren't the mole, there was no need to spill your secrets."

A wave smacks against the boat shifting me sideways, the fast movement jarring my shoulder.

"Motherfucking shitballs!" I scream into the night and hold my arm tighter against my stomach.

The entire boat erupts in laughter, except for the brooding water mammal behind me.

COVERT AFFAIR | 357

"What happened to your shoulder?" Gabe asks, restraining his anger by clenching and unclenching his fists.

"I jumped off the boat when the bullets started but the guys who took me, bought me actually, weren't about to let me get away or die trying. It popped out of socket when they hauled me up onto their boat. I wasn't as cooperative as they expected."

"Not surprising," says Tony, now sitting directly across from us.

"How'd their guy end up overboard?"

Somehow, even with all the crap in the past forty-eight hours, I smile. "I kicked him overboard for hurting me. The main guy didn't want to wait around, so he shot his guy in the chest and we took off. Brutal, but I mean he is a terrorist so..."

"And the two guys you took out before I got there?"

After taking another long drink of water, I snuggle closer against him, loving the feel of him. His strength. His warmth.

"Yeah, well, I knew you guys would come." The entire boat grumbles in agreement. "And knew there was only one way down to where they were keeping me. I was devising a plan on how to shove my shoulder back in socket when I heard something above me. On deck. And I knew you were there, so I had to think fast. I waited until they fired up those stairs, trying to keep you from getting to me, then slammed my shoulder into the wall a few times, screaming bloody murder because it fucking hurt and to draw them into the cell. It worked. They didn't know I had my knife on me, weren't prepared for my attack. The first guy never saw me lurking beside the door. I slit his throat and grabbed his gun before anyone else knew what was happening. The guard outside the door almost had me, got a couple rounds off before I was able to fire back."

My eyes grow heavy, the steady beat of Gabe's heart lulls me to sleep.

"Not so fast, sweetheart," Gabe says and tilts my chin up so I'm staring into his eyes. It hurts like hell, but it's worth it to see and feel the overwhelming emotions pouring through those blue eyes. "You shouldn't sleep with a concussion."

"But it sounds so lovely," I mumble and give up the fight of keeping my eyes open.

"Luce."

"Lucia."

"Come on, Luce, open your eyes, you gotta stay awake until we get back to base."

It sounds like a solid plan, for me to stay awake but unfortunately there is zero control I have over my eyes shutting. With his arms enveloping, protecting from the biting wind, I fall back asleep, but this time knowing I'm safe and will be until I wake up.

———

Unease is quickly erased as I take in the empty desk in front of CO Williams' office. It's cleaned out, nothing sits on top like they are expecting it to be occupied any time soon. It's only been a couple of days since my SEAL buddies pulled me from that awful boat and brought me home.

Home.

San Diego, or just back stateside, the word works for both. But for how long, only this meeting will determine that.

After being patched up by the base doctor and released, Gabe filled me in on everything CO Williams told him the day I was taken. It wasn't as shocking as it should have been, which says a lot, but there was no hiding the disappointment when those assumptions were confirmed. I'll never be enough for them, they will take and take until there's nothing left of me.

Before, there was never a possibility of moving to San Diego, giving up my growing career, but now, after what Gabe shared, things have changed. But even though my outlook on the agency has changed, do I really want to move here, give it up to be with him?

Gabe mentioned something about options but didn't have details. Which is why I'm here standing in front of CO Williams' office.

Options. When was the last time someone gave me those?

CO Williams' voice booms through the cracked, closed door in response to my light rapping. Straightening my sling and shirt as best possible, I push open the door and step in, the normal arctic blast first to greet me.

CHAPTER FORTY-FOUR
GABE

For the third time in two minutes, I rip off my gloves and check my phone.

"Damn, man, she's only been in the meeting for an hour. Give her some slack." Flakes says from across the mat, taking a drink from his water bottle. Fighting him, the hand to hand combat, is exactly what I need to take the edge off.

Fuck, what if none of the options are good or even what she wants? What will I do? There's no way in hell I can live without her, the thought alone makes things go hazy, but can I live without the SEALs to be with her?

"Let's go, man. Stop fucking thinking about it. It will work out."

Sliding my gloves back on, I say, "Such a different tune from a few weeks ago. You realize that, right?"

He shrugs and takes a step closer, arms at the ready. "Yeah, well, maybe I was jealous before." My brows shoot up in surprise at his confession. "And not just about you two." We stalk around the mat, staring each other down.

"What does that mean?"

His arms drop. "Man, I've had my eye on the CIA for a while. I wanted options after," he waves his gloved hands around the gym. "All this. When she walked in, being the one broad I couldn't get and having the fucking spot I want. Hell, man." Coming out of his daze, his arms raise again. Taking that as he was ready my right arm comes around for a swing which he ducks under and takes a step back.

"Anyway, she's different with you, maybe that pissed me off too."

This time, it's my arms that drop to my side. "What do you mean different?"

"I don't know. It's like..." he looks to the ceiling for a second. "With everyone else, she's on her game, ready to jump into action if needed. But when you're around, she's just a chick. It's like you being you makes her be her. Some shit like that."

"Some shit like that?"

"Fuck off man, I'm not Dr. Phil."

The door to the gym flies open. We both turn. One of Flakes' men jogs towards us and stops. He looks to Tony, then me.

"She's leaving," he says.

When realization sinks in, I turn, no doubt red-faced, to Flakes. "You had her fucking followed?"

He smiles and slugs my shoulder. "Yeah, well, you are my best friend, fuck stick. I figured the talk with CO would go one of two ways. Her coming here right after to share good news, or her running so she doesn't have to give you the bad. Looks like she's running. And like a good damn friend, I wanted to know so you would know."

"What, to prove your damn point again?" I yell making the entire gym go silent.

His lips press together and he looks down to his gloves. "No, you dumbass." When he looks back up there's a mischievous smirk on his face. "So you can stop her."

CHAPTER FORTY-FIVE
LUCIA

The plane is stuffy. Maybe because I'm stuffed between two large guys in this middle seat. An entire paycheck to get on this flight to DC for a middle seat, and not even direct. I won't be there until tomorrow at this point, but I have to get out of here before I lose my nerve.

I hope he gets the cryptic text I sent just before turning my phone off, and understands why I have to take off like this.

It's a new life, one I'm excited about, but still nerve-wracking because it wasn't in my plan. The one I've been going step-by-step along until today. That's scary as shit.

Who would have thought this is where I'd end up. Brooke is going to flip out when she finds out.

It takes a bit of finagling to get the seat belt out from under me without leaning on the two men beside me too much. One grunts, and the other moves to the side so my bad shoulder doesn't hit him.

A deep sigh to calm my nerves, I lean my head back. The stewardess announces the doors are closing and all cell phones should be turned off. Good thing I did that before boarding the plane, no way I'll be able to maneuver to get to my phone.

The heat snuggled between these two and the hum of the engines as the plane taxis away from the gate ease my anxiety. It doesn't take long before my eyes grow heavy and close completely.

CHAPTER FORTY-SIX
GABE

"Seriously. You threw out 'national security risk,'" I yell behind me.

"We needed to stop that plane. What else was there to do? And it is a damn national security risk if you go bat shit crazy because this hot as fuck woman dumped your ass without a goodbye and then you couldn't protect our country the way you need to. National security risk. I rest my case," Flakes jokes to my right, jogging alongside me. Lovall and Beasley, plus a few of my guys who know what the hell is going on, are right behind us.

"There it is," yells one of the guys.

We slow our approach. The plane had just started to back away from the gate when we called in the security threat. Now it waits. Waiting for someone to come "clear" the aircraft.

Oh, hell.

We are going to get our asses chewed out for this one. This is by far the stupidest stunt Flakes has done. Recently.

"What are you going to say?" Flakes asks.

What am I going to say? What am I going to say knowing she was trying to leave without even a fucking goodbye? A big part wants to let her go, but deep down I know I'll never recover if I do. She has to know I don't want this life without her. There is no life without her.

The door opens as a truck with stairs attached sidles up next to it. With a shove on my shoulder Flakes steps back and motions up the stairs, surely wondering what I'm waiting for.

To grow a fucking set, that's what.

"Don't be a fucking idiot, you idiot. Go get her. She belongs here. With us."

The other men grunt their agreement.

Fine.

Taking the stairs two by two, I nod at the flight attendant who's at the door, gaping and shaking like a leaf. Damn, I feel kind of bad making her think she's in danger all for two seconds with the woman I love.

"Agent Lucia Rizzo," I shout down the plane. I scan every row, each seat until the most radiant green eyes lock with mine. "Please come with me."

"What the hell are you doing, Officer Wilcox?" she says and stands but doesn't make a move towards the aisle.

Every set of eyes on the plane bounces from me to her and back again.

"I'm stopping you from making a big fucking..." an old lady near me gasps. "Sorry. From making a big mistake, that's what. Now get off the plane." Remembering our reason for stopping this plane in the first place I add on, "It's a matter of security, ma'am."

"Security my ass," the older lady eyes her for her language but Luce just rolls her eyes, which makes an almost-smile pull at my lips. She looks around the same time I do. All eyes are wide, staring at her like she's hiding some kind of suicide vest beneath her sling. "Seriously," a hand motions to the people around her. "Now, they think I'm the bad guy."

"You are, Agent Rizzo."

"I'm not a guy so..."

"Yes, apologies. I remember establishing that fact the first day we met. Okay you're the bad woman."

"How so?"

"You're leaving."

"Yes, I am, but Gabe—"

"You can't leave," I spit out, not able to hold back any longer. Damn, I didn't want to do this here, but she won't get off this damn plane. I run a hand down my face and say, "Before you, Luce, I was only surviving but that's not good enough anymore. Not after you. You…will you just get off the fucking damn plane?" I shout and punch the wall making the flight attendant shriek in surprise. "Sorry."

When I look back up, she's scooting around some big guy and steps out into the aisle.

"So angry for a trained water mammal, Officer Wilcox," Luce says with a smirk and starts down the stairs. "Seriously. You brought back-up?" she says over her shoulder when the other guys waiting at the bottom come into view.

"They helped me stop the plane." At the bottom of the stairs I grip her shoulders and turn her to face me, not letting my hands drop. "You can't go, Luce. Please don't go. If you don't want to live in San Diego, fine. I'll go wherever you want to after my contract's up, but don't just leave without telling me. We can make it work. With us, we can make it work, please don't fucking walk away. You're mine and I won't let you go that easy."

The roaring of jet engines fills the silence as we stare each other down.

"Guys, can you give us a second? Maybe go clear the plane you've now delayed under the 'security threat' umbrella."

"Hell fucking no. I ran all this way, hell, I was—"

"Shut the fuck up and go clear the plane," I growl, turning to my best friend.

With a few grumbles they file up the stairs into the plane.

After they disappear into the aircraft she turns, those big, green eyes shimmer with unshed tears.

"Guessing you didn't understand my text."

"You didn't send a text, sweetheart."

"I did."

"You didn't."

She groans and smacks a palm against her forehead. "Whatever. I agree. With everything you said just now. But it's not that simple, Gabe. I—"

"It is that simple if you love me and I love you…" Wait. "Are you saying you don't love me? Is that what this is all about? Fuck, Flakes was right, I got in too deep and you—"

"Holy hell. Stop acting like a damn idiot," she snaps. My jaw snaps shut to keep from interrupting. "Of course, I love you. How could I not? We just work. And when I was saying it's not that simple I meant all of this isn't that simple. My life is in DC."

I shut my eyes to hopefully keep her from reading my obvious disappointment.

Soft hands grip my face. "Gabe, look at me." Rallying courage like I've never had to before, I look to her. "I wasn't leaving."

My chest constricts making breathing difficult.

"But you were getting on that damn plane. You just said—"

To shut me up two fingers press against my lips and her gorgeous smile grows.

"My home is in DC which means I have to go back to DC to get my stuff. I worked it out with CO Williams and I have a week's leave to get my life moved from DC to San Diego, then…you're looking at the lead CIA liaison for the San Diego based SEAL teams."

The way she's bouncing from one foot to another, plus the full face grin, her excitement is palpable.

"I'll be giving insight into various missions and targets. The other agents on base will report to me. I'll be approving anything that happens between the agency and the SEALs. Do you know what that means?" she squeals. "I get you and my career too."

Unable to hold back a second longer, I wrap my arms around her neck, careful of her shoulder, and pull her close. Nuzzling her hair I take a deep breath in. My eyes flutter closed at the familiar scent and revel in the fact that she's not leaving.

"You could have led with that, you know. I was fucking dying."

"I know," she laughs against my chest. The way her giggle vibrates against my chest is nothing new but at the same time is, because we're new. No more secrets. No more lies. Just us together. "Where's the fun in that, though? Besides, remember I said we needed to fight more. It works out well for both of us."

"Luce."

"Gabe."

"I love you. I meant what I said earlier. No more only surviving, I want to live with you. Only you. Forever."

Peeling her off my chest I take her face in my hands, tracing her cheek bones with my thumbs, and pull her lips against mine. Her immediate sigh and the way she sinks against me is everything.

Forever.

Sounds like a fucking great place to start.

EPILOGUE

Six months later....

"Cheers!" I say as the three of us clink our glasses together. "So how does it feel to be a free man?"

"Fucking terrible," Tony pouts and leans back in his chair. "She's getting everything."

"Well, you were the one cheating on her so..."

"She was cheating, too," he yells and downs the entire glass in one swig.

"But you started it," I say and stick my tongue out at him, making Gabe chuckle beside me. The rumbling of his laugh vibrates in my chest, sending delicious thoughts of when he's given that same laugh with his face between my thighs.

"Stop it, you two," Gabe says and starts brushing two fingers up and down my bare forearm. He smiles at the goosebumps that appear. "It's done. Now she can be happy, and so can he."

"Fine," Tony and I grumble in unison.

It only takes a few minutes before a young, attractive waitress catches Tony's eye. With a quick goodbye he climbs onto a stool at the bar and starts chatting her up.

"He has a problem. You know that, right?"

"What problem is that?"

"That he can't keep his damn thing in his pants."

"Jealous?"

Pushing off his chest, I turn to face him. "Ugh that'd be a negative, sailor. Just making an observation."

"Well then, tell me the real observation, sweetheart."

With a smirk I settle back against his chest and watch Tony. "His ego is enormous, but you knew that. Heck, anyone who knows him can see that, but there's something else to him. It's bothered me since, well the beginning, but I could never put my finger on it. But now I know, after seeing him today and now. He's scared of commitment not because of the whole 'sleeping with one woman the rest of his life' thing, I think it's because he's scared to set himself up for heartbreak. Like he has these massive walls up that no one, not even you, will ever see behind. Because if we do, then leave him, he wouldn't recover. That's what I see."

"Nice observation, soldier. What do you see when you see me?" Gabe asks, pushing me off him a little for us to face each other again. But still one arm is dropped over my chair and the other rests on my knee. This is one of the things I used to hate, the touching—the protective almost smothering attention from a guy, but with Gabe it's different. He does it not to lay claim to me but because he honest to goodness can't keep his hands off me.

His words, not mine.

With a lazy once-over his broad shoulders, trim waist, pausing at his dark denim-clad crotch I say, "I think you're a goner, Officer Wilcox."

"How so, Agent Rizzo?" he says, returning my smirk showing those damn dimples I love.

Yes, love.

Damn, do I love him and those damn dimples.

Those stupid dimples that have gotten him out of many, many arguments. Well, the dimples and his wicked tongue.

"You're a goner for me. For us."

"And what about you, sweetheart? Are you a goner for me? For us?"

Intensity burns behind his eyes along with a flash of anxiety and worry.

"Most definitely. As hard as you've fallen for me I've fallen for you."

"Good."

"That's all you have to say?"

He thinks about it for a second and smiles. "Marry me."

No words form as my jaw hangs open.

"Wh….wha…what?"

"You. Me. Forever. What do you say sweetheart? I love you. Fuck do I love you. I want you mine for forever. And ten damn years after that. I don't want to call you my girlfriend anymore, not when my dreams are of you being my wife."

"Dreams?" I'm not sure I'm breathing.

"Yeah of the future. It's you and me, Luce, that's all I see. So what do you say?"

Who am I kidding, the answer is simple.

I love him and he loves me. We are that couple that will make it forever. We are the ones people are jealous of because we make it look so damn easy. It won't be, but if it's with him then whatever we go through, as long as we're together, it will be worth it.

"Vegas?" I say with a growing smile.

He slams his lips against mine and pulls me close, yanking me out of my chair. When we come up for air he rests his forehead against mine and smiles like he's just won the lottery.

"Vegas."

Preorder Book 2 in the SEALs and CIA series today!
Tony's story will hit kindles November 2021

Covert Vengeance

If you loved A Covert Affair check out my Protection Series with book 1, Mine to Protect.

Sign up for my newsletter to stay up to date on new releases, exclusive content, and behind the scene peeks into my writing life.

ALSO BY KENNEDY L. MITCHELL

Standalone:

Falling for the Chance

Finding Fate

Memories of Us

Protection Series: Interconnected Standalone

Mine to Protect

Mine to Save

Mine to Guard

Mine to Keep (Coming December 2021)

SEALs and CIA Series:Interconnected Standalone

Covert Affair

Covert Vengeance (Coming November 2021)

More Than a Threat Series: A Bodyguard Romantic Suspense Connected
Series

More Than a Threat

More Than a Risk

More Than a Hope

Power Play Series: A Protector Romantic Suspense Connected Series

Power Games

Power Twist

Power Switch

Power Surge

Power Term

ABOUT THE AUTHOR

Kennedy L. Mitchell lives outside Dallas with her husband, son and two very large goldendoodles. She began writing in 2016 after a fight with her husband (You can read the fight almost verbatim in Falling for the Chance) and has no plans of stopping.

She would love to hear from you via any of the platforms below or her website www.kennedylmitchell.com You can also stay up to date on future releases through her newsletter or by joining her Facebook readers group - Kennedy's Book Boyfriend Support Group.

Thank you for reading.

ACKNOWLEDGMENTS

I feel like I should always start this list out with my three main supporters. My amazing husband who supports me through this incredibly expensive hobby. Then of course comes my two besties Emily and Christine (yes if you read my first book they were the two main characters). I wouldn't have gotten this far without these three.

Second, I added new beta readers this year who helped shape the story beyond my expectations. So thank you Kristin, Reading.Cafe book blog and Nan at Chasing Away Reality book blog. You three fixed the, kind of major, issues no one else found!

As always my editor was amazing. She's patient with me, teaching me as we go, and supportive like no other.

Without all these people this book wouldn't be here. So thank you to everyone!

Oh and the person actually reading this part....thanks You reading this book means the world to me. I have hundreds of stories in my head that need to come out and this is just one of them.

Until next time – happy reading.

PLAYLIST

"Lost on You" – LP
  "Somebody Else" – The 1975
  "I need you" – Faith Hill
  "Thunder" – Imagine Dragons
  "Legends" – Kelsea Ballerini
  "See You Again" – Elle King
  "Boxes" – Goo Goo Dolls
  "Fix My Eyes" – for KING & COUNTRY
  "New Year's Day" – Taylor Swift
  "Perfect" – Ed Sherran
  "One More Light" – LINKIN PARK
  "Slow Hands" – Niall Horan
  "Let's Hurt Tonight" – OneRepublic
  "Somebody to Love" – Queen
  "The One" – The Chainsmokers
  "Ink" – Coldplay
  "Colors" – Grace Potter & The Nocturnals
  "Human" – Rag'nBone Man
  "Marry Me" – Thomas Rhett

"Greatest Love Story" – LANCO
"Breathe Me" – Sia

Made in the USA
Columbia, SC
27 October 2021